SHADOWMOOR

A Medieval Romance

Book Six of
The de Lohr Dynasty Series

By Kathryn Le Veque

Printed by Dragonblade Publishing in the United States of America

Kathryn Le Veque Novels

<u>Medieval Romance:</u>

The de Russe Legacy:
The White Lord of Wellesbourne
The Dark One: Dark Knight
Beast
Lord of War: Black Angel
The Falls of Erith

The de Lohr Dynasty:
While Angels Slept (Lords of East Anglia)
Rise of the Defender
Steelheart
Spectre of the Sword
Archangel
Unending Love
Shadowmoor
Silversword

Great Lords of le Bec:
Great Protector
To the Lady Born (House of de Royans)

Lords of Eire:
The Darkland (Master Knights of Connaught)
Black Sword
Echoes of Ancient Dreams (time travel)

De Wolfe Pack Series:
The Wolfe
Serpent
Scorpion (Saxon Lords of Hage – Also related to The Questing)
Walls of Babylon
The Lion of the North
Dark Destroyer

Ancient Kings of Anglecynn:
The Whispering Night
Netherworld

Battle Lords of de Velt:
The Dark Lord
Devil's Dominion

Reign of the House of de Winter:
Lespada
Swords and Shields (also related to The Questing, While Angels Slept)

De Reyne Domination:
Guardian of Darkness
The Fallen One (part of Dragonblade Series)

Unrelated characters or family groups:
The Gorgon (Also related to Lords of Thunder)
The Warrior Poet (St. John and de Gare)
Tender is the Knight (House of d'Vant)
Lord of Light
The Questing (related to The Dark Lord, Scorpion)
The Legend (House of Summerlin)

The Dragonblade Series: (Great Marcher Lords of de Lara)
Dragonblade
Island of Glass (House of St. Hever)
The Savage Curtain (Lords of Pembury)
The Fallen One (De Reyne Domination)
Fragments of Grace (House of St. Hever)
Lord of the Shadows
Queen of Lost Stars (House of St. Hever)

Lords of Thunder: The de Shera Brotherhood Trilogy
The Thunder Lord
The Thunder Warrior
The Thunder Knight

Time Travel Romance: (Saxon Lords of Hage)
The Crusader
Kingdom Come

Purgatory

Other Contemporary Romance:
Lady of Heaven
Darkling, I Listen

Contemporary Romance:

Kathlyn Trent/Marcus Burton Series:
Valley of the Shadow
The Eden Factor
Canyon of the Sphinx

The American Heroes Series:
Resurrection
Fires of Autumn
Evenshade
Sea of Dreams

Multi-author Collections/Anthologies:
With Dreams Only of You (USA Today bestseller)
Sirens of the Northern Seas (Viking romance)
Ever My Love (sequel to With Dreams Only Of You) July 2016

Note: All Kathryn's novels are designed to be read as stand-alones, although many have cross-over characters or cross-over family groups. Novels that are grouped together have related characters or family groups.

Series are clearly marked. All series contain the same characters or family groups except the American Heroes Series, which is an anthology with unrelated characters.

There is NO particular chronological order for any of the novels because they can all be read as stand-alones, even the series.

For more information, find it in **A Reader's Guide to the Medieval World of Le Veque**.

Table of Contents

CHAPTER ONE

March 1236 A.D.
West Yorkshire, England

THE CLOUDS ARE *rolling in….*

Gazing up at a sky the very same color of his eyes, a knight dressed in expensive protection and riding a sleek black Frisian inspected the swollen dark clouds that were rolling in from the west. The wind was blowing, wet and damp, and he could smell rain upon it. Birds scattered overhead, sensing a change in the weather.

A storm was brewing.

The knight's blond hair was blown about in the breeze as he looked at his surroundings, trying to determine the best route to stay ahead of the rain. He was surrounded by moors and hills in the stark green and brown colors that were so vibrant it was as if the hand of God had slashed the shades across the landscape in the undiluted brilliance of a heavenly touch. The sun was near mid-point in the sky, creating grand illumination for the vivid imagery but that would soon be muted when the clouds began to gather.

The town of Bradford was about an hour behind the knight, to the south, and to the north he really couldn't recall any major town that might provide him with shelter to weather the storm. An inn, a stable, or even a castle or manor house would do at this point. He didn't want to be caught out in a Yorkshire gale because it would likely blow him right over. Therefore, he decided to turn around and head back to Bradford where there was a particular inn with a particular wench he had spent the previous night with. He wasn't completely opposed to returning.

So he reined his big horse around and headed back in the direction he had come. The road was rocky, uneven, and well-traveled as the only road from Bradford and Leeds to the northwest of England and into Scotland. His horse kept kicking up rocks as it trotted along, that jaunty trot that was so indigenous to the Frisian breed, and the knight knew it was because the horse knew he would be returning to the stable he had been housed in the night before where the stable boy had fed him grains and honey out of a bucket. The horse had quite a memory and the knight slapped the big black neck affectionately.

"More gluttony, my fine friend?" he asked the animal. He laughed softly when the horse tossed his head as if to agree with the question and he patted the big neck again. "You and I are much the same, Ares. I am rather looking forward to gluttony as well. With some debauchery thrown in. We shall make a time of it, my fine lad."

The horse snorted. Grinning at his horse with the big appetite, the knight's mind wandered back to the inn he had stayed at in Bradford, The Cow and Calf, and he rather found himself looking forward to a good bed and warm fire. So many of his nights were spent sleeping beneath the stars as he traveled that a bed was always welcome. Such comforts were few and far between.

He was a wanderer, this knight. He had never been able to settle down in one spot, much to his father's disappointment. He loved his father very much and hated to disappoint the man, but it simply wasn't in his nature to settle down. He much preferred the life of a wanderer, the Prodigal Son as it were, always traveling, sometimes being paid to fight for lords who needed his highly-trained services or sometimes entering tournaments for the money the purse could provide.

Money had never been an issue with Sir Daniel de Lohr, the only son of the Earl of Canterbury and a very important member of the

House of de Lohr, inarguably one of the greatest houses in England. His uncle, Christopher, had been King Richard's champion many years ago and the man was now the Earl of Hereford and Worcester, the biggest landholder on the southern Marches.

Daniel had, therefore, fostered at the finest homes and he'd been trained by the finest men. He knew that, some day, he would be forced to settle down in Canterbury and assume the title Earl of Canterbury upon the passing of his father, which was something he didn't like to think about. In spite of his wandering ways, he was a very sensitive and emotional man, and he loved his family a great deal. He missed them. But that wandering spirit in his soul kept him traveling and seeking new adventure. Perhaps it always would.

But that was his life right now. He had freedom and no commitment, and that was exactly what he wanted. Life was good now and he loved his ability to go where he wanted to, when he wanted to, without anything holding him back. Even now, he had been on his way north to visit a friend's Northwood Castle. William de Wolfe, the great Wolf of the Border, was one of Daniel's dear friends, as were most of the de Wolfe pack knights – Paris de Norville, Kieran Hage, and Michael de Bocage. The de Lohrs and de Wolfes were intertwined, their fathers having been great friends and allies, so Daniel and William and the other knights had served together, several times, in situations where strength in numbers and knights was needed.

It was a strong association and Daniel enjoyed visiting William. The last he had seen the man at Northwood Castle, William's seat of service, had been six years ago but he'd seen him twice since then, both times in London. They'd had a great time together, as usual, but William had just gotten married to a Scots lass and wouldn't shut up about her. Daniel finally tried to strangle him just to have some peace from the love-struck knight, although it had all been in good humor and they'd both been drunk at the time. Still, Daniel had good memories of it. But more good memories at Northwood Castle would have to wait until the fickle weather held long enough for him to make it to Northumberland.

The wind was picking up as he headed back to Bradford and the clouds were beginning to fire big, fat drops at him. Not a lot of rain, but enough to be annoying. Reaching behind him, strapped onto the back of his saddle, he moved to collect an oiled cloak used against the elements. He didn't want to be soaked through by the time he reached Bradford. As he fumbled with the fastens, the wind began to howl in his ears, racing across the flat moors until it hit a windbreak, namely him, and it was quickly reaching the point where he needed protection against it. Just as he moved to untie the last leather fasten, he caught sight of movement on the rise to the east.

It was a child, running as fast as his little legs would carry him. The hill he was running upon was open for the most part, with no trees or foliage, but there were rocks and crevices, making a straight run impossible. Daniel watched curiously as the child drew closer, leaping over rocks, falling down and rolling a few feet, before leaping to his feet again and running as if his life depended on it. Indeed, it was most curious behavior and Daniel found himself wondering what had the child so inspired to run like a rabbit, recklessly and swiftly. He soon had his answer.

Over the rise, following the path of the child, came a big man on a well-fed brown rouncey. Whereas the child had found a path among the rocks, the man on horseback swung wide of the rocks, which took him off his path slightly, but made for a clearer run. It soon became apparent that the child, and the man on horseback, were coming straight at Daniel and the child, as he came closer, appeared to be a little lad. Furthermore, there was no mistaking the expression of fear upon the child's face.

Already, there was a hint of fear in the wind.

"Help me!" the child burst in a breathless, terrified voice. "Please, help me!"

Daniel frowned, looking between the child and the man who was quickly closing the gap. He didn't want to interfere with a child running from his father but, somehow, this didn't seem to be the case. The man on horseback was well dressed against the coming storm while the child was clearly in rags. Something didn't seem right. Daniel let go of the oil cloak he was unfastening from his saddle and turned in the direction of the child.

"Why are you running?" he asked, glancing to the man on horseback. "Why is that man chasing you?"

The child reached Daniel, tripping and falling at Ares' feet. The big black horse danced about nervously as the boy picked himself up and tried to move behind the horse to use it as a barrier against the approaching rider.

"Please, help me!" the child cried again. "Don't let him take me!"

Daniel tried to follow the child as he attempted to run behind the horse. Ares was dancing about, trying to kick out at the little boy. "Hold," he commanded firmly. "Stop trying to get behind my horse because he will kick your head off. Now, why does this man want you? What did you do?"

The child was in tears; blond sandy hair and a round dirty face that was streaked where he had wiped at his eyes. "Sir, I did nothing," he sobbed.

Daniel lifted his eyebrows. "Nothing?" he repeated. "That does not make sense. Why does he want you if you did nothing?"

The little lad used his dirty tunic to wipe his nose. "He wants my sister," he said. "He kept me in the vault because he wants her to marry him, but I ran away! I escaped and he wants to put me back! Please don't let him!"

Daniel scratched his head, greatly puzzled by the accusation. But one thing was clear; the child was terrified and disheveled, a dirty little creature who, upon closer examination, only had one shoe. And he wasn't very good at listening because he still kept trying to move behind the horse to hide. Like any scared creature, it was an instinct to protect himself and it occurred to Daniel that the child's swift answers to his questions bespoke of the truth. No hesitation, no struggling for words. Everything had come forth fluidly. Swiftly, Daniel reined Ares about and managed to bend over and grasp the boy by the arm. As the child wailed, Daniel lifted him up and laid the boy across his lap, holding him firm.

The wind was whipping around them now and the man on the fat rouncey was very close, slowing the pace of his steed as he came upon Daniel. Daniel looked closely at the man. He was very well dressed in an expensive cloak and well-made boots, and his horse was quite fine. It was clear the man had money. As the man drew close, he pointed to the child in Daniel's lap.

"My thanks for capturing him," he said pleasantly. "I shall take him off your hands, friend."

Daniel didn't make any move to surrender the child. "Who is he to you?"

The man lifted a gloved hand in a dismissive gesture. "A servant," he said. "A very naughty servant. I will take him from you."

"I am not a servant!" the boy cried, trying to slither off of Daniel's lap for fear that he would soon be back in the hands of the man he had been running from. "He kept me in the vault! I want to go home!"

"Shut your hole, boy," the man growled, then looked to Daniel with growing impatience. "Give him to me and you shall be on your way. We will not trouble you further."

Daniel wasn't going to hand the boy over until he got to the bottom of what was really going on. Based on everything he'd seen and been told, something told him not to reject the boy's claims so easily.

"He says he is not your servant," Daniel said, trying to remain neutral. "He also says that you kept him in the vault because of your desire for his sister. Is this true?"

Overhead, thunder rolled as if to punctuate the seriousness of the conversation now. Gone was the friendliness from the man's expression.

"That is none of your affair," he said. "Give me that boy."

The man's reply told Daniel most of what he needed to know, including the fact that the boy was more than likely not lying. The expression on the man's face was vicious, as if Daniel had stolen something from him. There was outrage and hazard there, a hint of the true darkness beneath the expensive clothing and feigned friendly manner. Daniel was a good judge of character; he'd always had the gift, and didn't doubt the child in the least now.

The man before him was not as pleasant as he wanted Daniel to think he was.

"The lad has asked for my help," Daniel said. "I would be a less than chivalrous knight if I did not determine why you are chasing a small child across the moors. Why would he tell me this story if it was not true? He does not know me and I do not know him. Why would he create an elaborate story to ask for my assistance?"

The man was starting to grow red in the face. "You will give him back to me if you know what's good for you," he growled. "You do not know who you are toying with."

Daniel would not be threatened. "Neither do you," he said.

The man's eyebrows flew up in outrage. "Just who in the hell are you?"

"You first."

Now the man was growing agitated at this big, blond stranger who evidently couldn't be bullied. "I am a nephew of Henry," he said through clenched teeth. "I would assume you know who the king of England is? I am of royal blood, you fool, so if you do not want the entire royal household down upon you, then you will give me that boy and forget you ever saw him. Is that clear?"

Daniel was struggling not to laugh at the man's conceit. He had a way of provoking men into madness, toying with them, driving them daft with frustration while he remained cool and collected. It was a game he particularly enjoyed with the arrogant and ridiculous, including the idiot before him.

"It is clear," he said evenly. "But it is also clear that you do not know it is my uncle who commands the royal military on the Marches, as the Earl of Hereford and Worcester. High Sheriff of the Marches, I believe his title is. And my father is the Earl of Canterbury, who has command of four royal garrisons in Kent and Sussex. Between my uncle and my father, they control thousands of royal troops in southeast England as well as on the Welsh Marches so, clearly, *you* do not know who you are dealing with. I am a de Lohr, heir to Canterbury, and if you have not heard the name, then you are most definitely the moronic buffoon I thought you were. Is *that* clear?"

With the reveal of the de Lohr name, the man's expression seemed to change somewhat. He was still red in the face but not nearly so aggressive. "De Lohr," he hissed. "I know the name."

"Good boy."

"I am Fitzroy. Roland Fitzroy, Lord Bramley, nephew of the king."

"Through whom?"

"My sister is Joan of Wales."

Daniel thought a moment on that bit of information. He knew that name. *Joan of Wales.* "She is King John's bastard daughter, as I recall," he said, because he knew a great many things about a great many people. He was an extremely sharp man; moreover, having grown up in the nobility of England, he knew much about his peerage. "I seem to remember my father speaking of your mother, once. A French noblewoman, isn't she?"

Fitzroy's expression grew smug. "You know of her."

He shrugged. "I have heard *of* her," he clarified. "A Lady Clementine or Clementina, I believe. But I also recall hearing that she only had one child by John."

"She did," Fitzroy said with confidence. "My sister."

Daniel cocked an eyebrow. "If that is the case, your half-sister may be the daughter of a king, but you are not related to John, or even Henry, in any fashion."

Fitzroy's smug expression turned into something of a grimace. "I am considered a nephew," he said, his jaw ticking. "The king is my uncle."

"Not by blood."

"It does not matter! It is the Fitzroy name I bear!"

"You more than likely gave it to yourself, did you not? You are not the son of a king."

"Dare you argue with me about this?"

Daniel smiled, without humor. "Your relationship to the king is only by way of an illicit relationship and nothing else," he said. "You use your sister's bloodlines to further your prestige and you gave yourself the surname of Fitzroy. Therefore, I outrank you by blood and family ties, and you will tell me the truth about this boy or I shall take the child with me and ride off. Well? I am waiting."

Fitzroy's weathered, sweaty face looked as if it were about to explode. He began to grind his jaw. "This is none of your affair, de Lohr," he said. "You have no business interfering. The boy belongs to me. I want him back."

"How does he belong to you?"

"I told you! He is a servant!"

Throughout most of the conversation, the boy lying across Daniel's thighs had remained still, but now that the focus had returned to him, he began to kick again.

"I am *not* his servant!" he shouted. "He took me away and will only let me go home if my sister marries him!"

The child was lifting his head, trying to sit up or slide off Daniel's legs again so Daniel shoved him back down again. His big hand on the lad's blond head, he looked at Fitzroy.

"If this child is a servant, what is his name?" he asked. "What does he do for you? Who are his parents and what do they do for you?"

It was too many questions, rapid-fire, and Fitzroy became flustered. "His name is Gunther," he said. "He… he is a page. He works the kitchens. His father is… it does not matter what his father does for me. Give me that boy. I will not tell you again!"

Beneath Daniel's hand, the child was still trying to lift his head. "That is *not* my name!" he said, sticking his tongue out at the man. "I do not work in your kitchen!"

Overhead, thunder rolled again and the fat drops of rain that had been sporadically pelting them now began to come down with a vengeance. Daniel looked up at the sky. "We will continue this conversation at a later time," he said to Fitzroy. "I will not stand out in this rain and risk my health. Where is your home?"

Fitzroy threw a thumb back over his shoulder. "Bramley Castle," he said. "Come and bring the boy."

Daniel shook his head. "The boy and I will find shelter elsewhere," he said. "I will question him. If I do not like his answers or it seems as if he has been lying to me, I will bring him to you."

There wasn't much to say to that unless Fitzroy wanted to fight Daniel for the child. He did, in fact, unsheathe his expensive broadsword, to which Daniel responded by unsheathing his own. But Daniel didn't cast the child aside with the hint of an oncoming battle. He held on to the boy, who continued to lift his head and stick his tongue out at Fitzroy. Daniel found himself shoving the boy's head down again and again to stop him from antagonizing Fitzroy. The final time, Daniel thumped the lad on the head, hard enough to make him yelp and lower his head, rubbing at the thumped area.

But Fitzroy wasn't paying attention to the sassy lad. He was singularly focused on Daniel at this point because the situation was no longer between him and the boy, but between him and Daniel. His hint to move to battle had been meant to force Daniel to drop the boy, not wanting to be encumbered in a fight with the child on his legs, but Daniel hadn't released the child because he perhaps sensed the ruse. He held on to the boy by the collar of his scruffy tunic, which was a thick weave of wool and torn on the edges. Daniel had a firm hold of it so the boy wouldn't slip off as his big black stud danced about nervously, preparing for the first strike.

But the first strike wouldn't come from Fitzroy. He was no fool. He could simply see by the way de Lohr handled his weapon and his horse that this man was not one to be trifled with, and Fitzroy hadn't seriously battled against a man in years. He hadn't needed to. He always had his henchmen do it, but they weren't with him at the moment. They had all split up to hunt for their escaped prisoner and Fitzroy happened to be the one to come across him. So as far as he knew, his men were still off searching.

Therefore, he was without support. He would not fight this big blond knight who handled a heavy sword as if it were a feather's weight, because he was a coward at heart who liked to stand behind his paid swordsmen. Therefore, he sheathed his sword and shook a meaty fist at Daniel.

"You will regret this, de Lohr!" he shouted. "I will track you and take the lad back by force!"

Daniel didn't say a word; he didn't have to. His battle-ready position said it all. He kept his sword unsheathed, just in case Fitzroy decided to charge him, but the man evidently decided that it would be foolish to try because he abruptly turned tail and charged back off the way he had come. The wind whipped about his cloak and hair, giving him a rather wild look as he crested the hill and disappeared from sight. When he was gone, Daniel pulled the boy up from his lap by the collar.

"Now," he said, looking the lad in the eye. "You have made a good deal of trouble for me. What am I to do with you?"

The boy pointed off to the north. "My home is not far," he said. "Take me home and my papa will reward you."

Daniel gave him a wry look. "With what?"

"What food we have," he said. "I am sure Papa will feed you."

It was a rather pathetic offering; *what food we have*. From the way the boy was dressed, it was obvious that his family had no money. But, truth be told, Daniel wasn't even sure the boy was telling the truth or that any of this story was real. Maybe he really *had* just stolen Roland Fitzroy's kitchen servant, but something told him that was not the case. Something told him the boy's predicament was real.

He supposed there was only one way to find out. As the weather worsened, the need to seek shelter was urgent. The rain was coming down now, fairly steadily, and Daniel lowered the boy to the ground.

"Go home," he said. "I will follow."

The lad took off, running with only one shoe across the wet and muddy ground, heading north. Daniel spurred Ares after the child and the horse seemed discontented that he would not be returning to his stable boy and honeyed grains. His big black tail switched angrily, catching Daniel in the legs as if to whip him. It was as close to a tantrum as the horse could come but Daniel remained stoic in the face of his spoiled horse, following the boy across the flat moor with the gradual rise to the east, crescendoing to a mountain with rocky boulders strewn across the crest.

Daniel glanced up at the great rocks on the top of the mountain, now partially shrouded by the clouds as the nasty weather settled in. The rain was growing worse and his little guide was slowing down. The little boy was becoming exhausted so after about a mile, Daniel pulled up alongside the lad and lifted him onto the saddle again. Breathing heavily, the lad pointed off to the north and Daniel spurred the horse forward, galloping across the muddy moor in the direction indicated.

The rain grew steadily and Daniel could feel the boy tucked up behind him, no-doubt soaked to the skin. He would have liked to have pulled forth his oiled cloak but the child was sitting on it. Therefore, there wasn't much he could do except bear the elements until they reached their intended destination, which he hoped would be soon given the fact that lightning was starting to fill the sky. He had never liked lightning, especially when he was out in the open, so he spurred the horse faster, traveling the road that was quickly becoming muddied.

They traveled for quite some time as the road paralleled the great crag to the east. The lightning was sporadic, fortunately, but Daniel still felt a great sense of urgency to reach shelter. The little boy behind him was wet and shivering; he could feel it. Up the road, over a hill, across a section of moor that had the road turning to the west before looping around and heading north again, they pounded through the rain. Ares was running at a good pace, snorting and throwing foam, and Daniel knew he'd have to ease the horse back shortly. He didn't want the steed to become overworked. Just as they neared another rise in the road with wet, cloudy moors to the north as far as the eye could see, the lad tugged on Daniel's sleeve and pointed to the east.

"That a-way," he said. "My home is that a-way."

Daniel noticed there was a fork in the road ahead, with a rather large road running east, up into the hills. Wiping the rain from his eyes, he directed Ares up that stretch of road where the rain was beginning to carve channels into the bare earth of the roadbed. Ares was wet, and very unhappy that he was wet, because the horse didn't like water very much. He kept switching that big black tail around and, more than once, Daniel heard the boy yelp because he'd been struck by wet hair. It could sting like a bee. Up the road they went, plunging deeper into the remote wilderness of the moors, when the road took an upturn, at a fairly steep angle, and Daniel glanced up to see something at the top of the crest.

It was shrouded in mist but he was quite sure he could see a structure of some kind. As he drew closer, he realized that he was looking at a fortress built from the same gray limestone rocks that littered the top of the crag. In fact, the castle itself seemed to be built upon the massive boulders that lined the top of the mountain, blending into the rock and into the hill as if the fortress and rock and hill were all of one body.

It was quite fascinating, actually, and the closer they drew to the mighty fortress, the more impressed with the sheer size Daniel became. Indeed, it was a vast bastion that crouched impressively upon the crest of the mountain. Daniel was rather surprised at the sheer size of it, considering he never even knew there was a castle in this location and he thought he knew most of the areas of England to that regard. But this one was tucked away, sitting like the gods atop Mount Olympus.

But there was more to the structure than just the fortress. As Daniel moved up the road, he could see that there was a village built up all around it, homes built from the same craggy rock with sod roofs and sod sides. There were fenced-off sections he assumed were gardens and corralled areas for farm animals, and even the animals were well-sheltered in their rock homes against the storm.

The road ended at the gates to the giant fortress. The gates were made from iron, with no wood at all and, considering how barren the moors were of trees, it wasn't surprising. But the gates were an enormous web of layered iron, forged and secured with great iron rivets. There were also men on the other side of the gate, peering back at Daniel as he reined Ares to a halt. The lad, seeing that they had arrived, flew off the back of the horse, slipped in the mud, and then ran for the gate.

"I have come back!" he shouted. "Where is Papa?"

The men at the gate, seeing the child, scrambled to open the panels and soon, men were heaving at a giant iron chain that slowed cranked open the gates. But the gates had a safety feature: another chain was strung across them so they could only open so far, admitting only one man at a time and certainly not a man on horseback, so the boy bolted in through the open gates and shouted at the men to open it further so that Daniel could enter. Men, dressed in little more than rags themselves and furs collected from the hunt, unstrung the rusted iron chain across the gates so that Daniel and Ares could enter.

The lightning resumed in chorus and lit up the sky overhead as Daniel entered the gates, which were quickly shut behind him. The little boy ran off as Daniel paused a moment, drinking in the sight before him; the enormous perimeter walls concealed something of a mixed settlement inside. There was a stone keep, literally a block-shaped tower at least three stories tall, which was situated near the center of the fortress with its own moat surrounding it, and then there were several other buildings made from stone with steeply angled roofs covered in either sod or some kind of thatching.

It was a curious sight. The settlement didn't look like a Norman castle, or even some of the ancient Celt ruins that Daniel had seen, but rather an odd mixture of the two. There were people inside the walls, men as well as women, and smaller hovels that looked to be homes constructed in the same style as the homes he had seen outside of the walls, except these structures didn't depend on sod so much for the walls. Everything was simply made of stone with the exception of the roofs.

But there was one thing that everyone, and everything, in the bailey had in common – everything was wet and muddy, and the people milling about in the rain seemed to be going about chores or duties, those things that needed to be done in spite of the weather. It was actually quite busy but Daniel was coming to notice, it also seemed to be a rather bare place – the people were poorly dressed against the elements and even their homes seemed rather pathetic. A couple of the structures had smoke coming from their roofs from cooking fires inside, but that was all he saw as far as comfort. It all seemed rather gloomy and barren. As he began looking around for someplace to stable his horse, the young boy suddenly returned with an older man running after him.

"Him, Papa!" the lad was shouting above the rain, pointing at Daniel. "It was him! He saved me!"

The man following the young boy was heavy-set, dressed in little more than rags himself, but he went straight to Daniel and extended his hands to him.

"Sir!" he cried. "Is it true? Did you bring my son back to me?"

Daniel could see the abundance of gratitude on the man's wet face and he dismounted Ares, wiping water from his eyes. "I found the lad running from someone named Fitzroy," he said.

The heavy-set man threw his arms around the boy, holding him tightly. "I thank God for sending you in our hour of need," he said, quite emotional. "There is no knowing what that vile lord would have done to him. You have my undying gratitude, my lord. How can I thank you?"

Daniel glanced up with lightning streaking across the sky again. "You may thank me by showing me a dry place for my horse and someone to tend him. He requires food and rest."

The man let go of the boy long enough to indicate for Daniel to follow him across the muddy yard and to a long, slender stone building that was nestled against the outer wall. The man waved him on, eagerly, and Daniel followed the man inside, into a low-ceilinged stable that was surprisingly warm and dry. Abruptly out of the elements in the long building that smelled heavily of urine and animals, Daniel immediately began removing the tack on the sopping horse.

"I need something to dry him with," he instructed, setting the saddle aside and separating his saddlebags from the saddle. "A coverlet or towel of some kind. Anything will do."

The man and the young boy scurried away in an attempt to fulfill Daniel's request, the young lad returning shortly with an iron scraper used to scrape sweat or moisture off of a horse's coat. Daniel pulled off the heavy saddle and set it aside, using the scraper to remove the obvious moisture on Ares, who was sniffing around the young lad perhaps looking for something to eat. The last young lad he had been around had fed him that wonderful honeyed mixture. One young lad was as good as another as far as the horse was concerned, but when the boy didn't produce anything right away, Ares began nibbling at his clothing.

"Oy!" the boy yanked away from the horse, fearful. "He is trying to eat me!"

Daniel was still scraping water off of his horse. "He is not trying to eat you," he said. "But he might find interest in your skinny arm if you do not bring him something to eat."

Worried, the boy rushed off, returning with an armful of dried grasses and brush, which he deposited in front of Ares. The horse sniffed at it curiously and, deeming it sufficient for his needs, began crunching on it. Daniel eyed what his horse was eating because it didn't look like hay.

"What is that?" he asked the boy.

"It is dried scrub grass from the moor," the man answered, coming up behind Daniel with a dirty blanket in his arms. "It is what we feed our animals in the winter – that, and whatever else that is left over from the harvest. Now, here is a blanket for your horse, my lord – this is all I could find. It should warm him at least."

Daniel took the blanket and shook it out before tossing it over Ares' back and rubbing the horse with it. After a few moments of rubbing and drying, he realized the young boy and man were still standing behind him, perhaps somewhat hesitantly. They were all strangers to one another, after all, even if Daniel was something of a savior. They were naturally curious about him, perhaps even fearful of him. Daniel looked at the pair as he continued to dry his horse.

"Now," he said, mostly looking at the boy. "Let us start with formalities since I risked my neck to save you. What is your name, lad?"

The child looked at him with those big blue eyes and cold-pinched nose. "Gunnar," he said. "Gunnar l'Audacieux. This is my papa."

Daniel looked at the big man beside him. "Does Papa have a name?"

"I am Etzel, my lord," the man replied, putting an arm around the child's shoulders. "You have returned my heart to me. I do not know how I can ever repay you for your kindness."

Daniel looked between the two of them quite seriously. "There is no need to repay me, at least not beyond what you are already doing," he said. "But who is Roland Fitzroy and why did he abduct the boy? Your son tells me that the man did it because he wants his sister. Is this true?"

Etzel nodded hesitantly, still holding tight to his son as if afraid to let him go. He looked at the boy. "It is true," Etzel said. "But the situation is more difficult than even that. I knew that Fitzroy had my Gunnar but I do not have the men needed to get my son back. I do not even have the money. Fitzroy wanted Leese, and Shadowmoor, in exchange for my son. He would take nothing else."

Daniel cocked his head. "Leese and Shadowmoor?" he repeated. "What are those?"

Etzel smiled weakly, revealing stained teeth. "Liselotte is my daughter," he said. "We call her Leese. Shadowmoor is the fortress you see around you. This castle, as it is, has been the home of my family for two hundred years."

Shadowmoor. It was a desolate-sounding name. In fact, it was a desolate-looking place and the name was therefore very fitting. Daniel stopped rubbing his horse, finding himself more interested in the conversation.

"Impossible," he said. "There were no stone fortresses two hundred years ago. Everything was built from wood."

Etzel shook his head. "Not on this moor," he said quietly. "Wood is difficult to come by and when we have it, we burn it. Rock is plentiful. There has been a rock fortress here since the Romans came. But that is a story for a warm fire and a cup of ale. Will you accept my hospitality for saving my son?"

Daniel nodded as the thunder rolled overhead. "I will," he said. "I do not plan to travel in this weather."

Etzel nodded, releasing Gunnar long enough to mutter something to the boy and send him running off. Daniel watched the boy flee the stable, eyeing the father's anxious expression a moment before returning to the horse. He moved to dry off the still-dripping mane.

"It is difficult for you to let the boy out of your sight," he commented.

Etzel looked at him, agreement replacing the anxiety in his expression. "I still cannot believe he has been returned to me," he said, his voice tight with emotion. "I did not think I would ever see my son again. It is a miracle."

Daniel rubbed at the wet black mane, like ink. "I would suggest, for the future, that you do not let him out of your sight at all if you know that Fitzroy is hunting him," he said, looking at the man. "Although I do not involve myself in the affairs of others unless I am well paid for it, it would seem that I cannot avoid being involved in this unsavory business. Your son ran to me for help and Fitzroy was in pursuit of him. Based upon what your son told me, I chased Fitzroy away so now, it seems, I am involved whether or not I want to be."

Etzel nodded, remorseful. "I am sorry for that, my lord."

Daniel could see the man was truly regretful. He turned back to his horse. "It is not something I can change now," he said. "Let me finish drying my horse and then you can explain to me what, exactly, I have gotten myself in to. I think I deserve that much."

Etzel nodded, seemingly resigned and even embarrassed at the difficulty this stranger was now facing on his behalf. "You deserve an explanation, my lord," he agreed. "As I said, it is a story best told by a warm fire. When you are finished with the horse, the hall is across the ward. I will wait for you there."

Daniel simply nodded and Etzel quickly left, heading out into the driving rain beyond the stable. Daniel stood there a moment, thinking on the situation, before pursing his lips wryly and turning back to the horse. What he'd gotten himself into, indeed. He'd gotten himself into trouble that had literally run right into him. He was coming to think that he probably should have turned the other direction when he'd seen the young boy coming at him. But, *no*… he had to be a hero and help the lad out. Now he'd made an enemy out of a smarmy lord who seemed to have a penchant for abducting children.

Brilliant, Daniel, he scolded himself. *What have you done now?*

He would soon find out.

CHAPTER TWO

THE SOUND OF the bubbling pot made for not only a pleasant sound to combat the rain, but those steamy little bubbles gave forth the most delicious smell.

A tall young woman with skin the color of cream and cascading hair that looked like molten bronze stood over the very large iron pot and stirred it gently with a wooden spoon. Since the kitchens of Shadowmoor were mostly outside and currently being swamped by the storm, the young woman and a few others had moved the kitchen into the hall so they could utilize the enormous fire pit in the center of the room to prepare the evening meal. Although the bread ovens were still outside and being rained upon even as the bread baked on the inside, creating steam that hissed off of the stone oven as the rain fell upon it, but the majority of the meal had been moved inside to keep it out of the elements.

This meant that a massive iron pot sat upon hot stones at the edge of the fire, and the stewed contents bubbled away quite happily. The young woman stopped stirring the contents and watched it boil for a few moments, pleased that she and her family would have a tasty stew to eat for the next several days.

It was a pea stew, made from dried field peas that she and some of the other women of Shadowmoor had collected over the summer and fall, when the peas were ripened and growing hard. The peas had all been shelled and carefully stored in big barrels because they would feed the inhabitants of Shadowmoor through the winter and wet spring.

There wasn't a great deal of agriculture in the stark western moors where they lived, but there was plenty of what little there was. Peas, barley, carrots, some beets, and sheep kept their bellies full enough and the woman with the bronze hair kept busy with making sure the inhabitants of the castle had enough to eat. Although she was the daughter of the lord, this wasn't a rich house. They worked very hard to keep themselves together and even harder as of late. Bad fortune seemed to have visited them quite often over the past several months. But the young woman, and her mother and father and brother, worked hard to be grateful for what they had. But at times, it was difficult.

Lady Liselotte l'Audacieux moved away from the fire now that the stew was bubbling, moving to complete a few other chores before sup. Tall, she wasn't terribly slender but rather the right mix of narrow waist and round hips that looked most pleasing through the simple clothing she wore. She had long legs and long arms, with long tapered fingers that her mother told her were angel's fingers, and her facial features were something just this side of heaven as well.

Dark lashes, dark brows, and hazel eyes against her pale skin made Liselotte's beauty quite legendary, something that had unfortunately not gone unnoticed by a neighbor to the south. Lord Bramley had been demanding her hand for the past four years, ever since he saw her on the street in Bradford as she passed through the town with her father. She had been nearly fifteen at the time and Lord Bramley had demanded marriage at that very moment, to which her father had staunchly refused. And that refusal had been the beginning of a four-year-long nightmare.

A nightmare with seemingly no end. As the other women were moving about the hall, preparing for the coming meal, Liselotte sat at one of the three big feasting tables in the room to cut small green apples that her mother was so fond of. As she chopped, her mind wandered to the continuation of the nightmare and the depressing state of Shadowmoor with her brother's abduction and Lord Bramley demands of both marriage and Shadowmoor.

Of course, Liselotte's father had refused to turn over his daughter and his fortress, but that left poor little Gunnar in a terrible position. Liselotte adored her younger brother, ten years younger than she, and his predicament was a heartbreaking one. More than once, she had tried to leave Shadowmoor to go to Bramley Castle so she could exchange herself for the boy, but her father had confronted her every time and prevented her from leaving. He told her that he was praying very hard for divine intervention and he was certain that God would hear their prayers and send help for young Gunnar.

As long as Lord Bramley thought he could get something for the boy, he wouldn't harm him, so Etzel had been convinced his son was safe for a time. But that time would run out. Meanwhile, life went on at Shadowmoor as Etzel prayed and Liselotte conspired to make another attempt to reach Bramley Castle without her father stopping her. Unlike her father, she wasn't convinced that divine intervention was possible. The only thing Bramley would understand was an army bigger than his was, but Shadowmoor could provide no such army. The situation, therefore, was precarious.

As Liselotte sat and cut up the small apples that would soon be boiled with spices for a tasty compote, her father entered the hall and headed in her direction. As Liselotte looked up, her father seemed to be waving his arms all over the place.

"Leese!" he cried. "Have you heard? Gunnar has returned!"

Startled, Liselotte nearly dropped her knife. "He *has*?" she exclaimed, a hand flying to her mouth in shock. "But – but how? When?"

Etzel patted her on the shoulder, his round face alive with excitement. "Only now," he said. "He escaped Bramley and a knight happened to rescue him and bring him home. We must offer prayers to God for His great mercy!"

Liselotte was looking up at her father, still stunned with the news. "A knight *found* him?" she asked. "Who is this knight?"

Etzel continued to pat her on the shoulder. "A very big and important knight," he said. "I do not know his name. He saved Gunnar and that is all I need know. He is in the stable with his horse but will be here soon for the meal. What is on the menu this night?"

Liselotte set her knife down. She didn't feel much like cooking any longer, more than eager to see her brother and see for herself that the lad was in good health. In fact, her heart was nearly bursting with eagerness to see the little lad she was so very fond of. It was difficult to keep the tears from her eyes, tears of pure joy.

"Pea stew," she said, wiping at the tears that threatened to escape, "and the last of the boiled mutton. There is also cabbage boiled with vinegar and cinnamon."

Etzel made a face. "More peas," he said unhappily. "Is there nothing else?"

Liselotte shook her head patiently. "Papa, there is not anything else and you know it," she said. "The peas and mutton will fill bellies and that is all we need to be concerned with. Now, where is Gunnar? I must see him."

Etzel was looking over at the bubbling pea stew as he spoke. "I sent him to your mother," he said. "He is in the keep so that she may see him. I have also told him to make sure his chamber is prepared, as the knight can sleep in his chamber and Gunnar can sleep with me. I've not seen my son in twenty-three days and I do not want him out of my sight."

Liselotte understood. Gunnar's abduction had been very hard on her father. He adored the boy, who was smart and funny and sweet, in great contrast to Etzel's eldest son who had turned out to be massive disappointment. There were three l'Audacieux siblings but only two were close to Etzel's heart.

The eldest was not discussed and for good reason.

Brynner l'Audacieux had gone the path of proper education to become a knight and had, in fact, been knighted at Okehampton Castle in Devon six years ago. He had, by all accounts, been one of the finest swordsmen in England, at least according to his trainers, but he was also very emotional and volatile, and after meeting, and losing, a certain young lady almost three years ago, Brynner had turned into a drunk who had no interest in his sword any longer or the knighthood.

This included anything to do with Lord Bramley; he had never lifted a finger to help his family against the man. These days, Brynner sat in his chamber and drank, or he wandered the moors aimlessly before returning to Shadowmoor to drink some more. Etzel had tried to help him; they had all tried to help him. But Brynner didn't want any help. He was still stuck as his life had been three years ago when Lady Maud had decided to marry his closest friend.

Resigned to his eldest son's fate, Etzel simply didn't speak to the man any longer and barely acknowledged him even when he saw him. Disappointment and sorrow had separated him from Brynner, and he didn't like for anyone in the family to speak the man's name. It was simply too painful.

Which is why Etzel was so attached to Gunnar. Liselotte knew this, which was why she was so glad, for her father's sake, that Gunnar had returned. He was the only thing that kept the old man going. She patted her father's hand as she stood up from the table.

"I would see to my little brother now," she said. "I must see him with my own eyes."

Etzel watched her go. "He is well, daughter," he said, happiness in his voice that Liselotte hadn't heard in weeks. "I promise you that he is."

"I believe you, but I must still see him."

Etzel smiled sadly at the daughter he knew harbored much guilt about her brother's abduction. It wasn't her fault but she had taken the lion's share of the blame for it. Four years of Lord Bramley's antics against her, against everyone at Shadowmoor, had been a heavy burden for the stoic young woman to bear.

But the immediate crisis was thankfully over with and there was much reason to rejoice for the moment. As Etzel went off to find a full jug of ale from the vault that ran beneath the hall, Liselotte continued to walk across the hard-packed earth of the hall, heading for the great door that would spill her out into the rainy yard beyond. She was most determined to see Gunnar and hug the boy before yanking his ear and making him scream. The thought made her smile. She loved to tease the lad because he put up such a fuss, but it was all done in good humor. There was never any malice between the two.

It was a silly joy she never thought she would know again considering Bramley had taken Gunnar and the man's terms of release were non-negotiable. She never thought she would again pull at his little ears. At least, that had been her sad thoughts mere moments before. But Gunnar had come home.

A knight had brought him home. Liselotte wasn't nearly so curious about the knight as she was simply eager to see her brother, so she didn't linger on thoughts of the heroic stranger. Just as she reached the entry to the hall, the big door heaved back and caught her as she put her hands up to open it. Caught off balance, she stumbled back as a big hand shot out to steady her.

Sky-blue eyes were gazing back at her.

The biggest man she had ever seen had hold of her. Liselotte's eyes widened at the sight. With saddlebags and sword slung over one shoulder, he was dressed in layers of wool and mail, with enormous gloves on his hands. He was very tall, with very broad shoulders, and his chin-length wet hair had a hint of the blond color beneath the damp. With his square jaw and long nose, he looked like a Viking god she'd once heard of in a myth. And those eyes… those starry eyes of brilliant blue… looked back at her with some curiosity.

Dare she say it… *even with interest?*

It was a moment Liselotte would remember for the rest of her life, as if the gloom had been pulled away and suddenly, glory was filling her vision. There was no other way to describe it.

"Forgive me, my lady," the man said in a deep, rather booming voice. "I should not have been so clumsy in opening the door. In my haste to get out of the rain, I fear I may have injured you."

Liselotte was actually dumbstruck. All of Shadowmoor was cursed with colorless, plain men and now, in their midst, came a shining star unlike anything she had ever seen. Was she actually dreaming this encounter? Had she gone mad? She seriously wondered.

"You did not," she said, noticing that his big gloved hand was still holding her steady. "I… I am Liselotte, Etzel's daughter. My father is Lord of Shadowmoor. Who are you?"

The man smiled, big dimples carving into his cheeks when he did so. "Sir Daniel de Lohr at your service, Lady Liselotte," he said. Then, his gaze turned appraising. "So you're the one."

"The one *what?*"

"The one who would drive men to do bold and reckless things. Now, I understand."

Her cheeks flushed a deep red, knowing he meant it as flattery and wholly unpracticed in accepting such honors.

"Understand?" she repeated. She thought she sounded rather silly, as if she were stammering. "What do you mean, my lord?"

Daniel let go of her arm and stepped into the hall, closing the heavy door behind him. He faced her, his eyes glimmering in the weak light. "I understand that you are the fairest maiden in all of Yorkshire," he said. "No wonder that fool Bramley would go to such lengths to demand your hand. Now, I understand his motivation completely. You are exquisite."

Liselotte seriously thought her face might burst into flame. She was utterly off guard with his kind words and she lowered her gaze, having no idea what to say to the man. As she cleared her throat softly and scratched her head nervously, Daniel spoke.

"I have said too much," he said quietly, a hint of a smile on his lips. "Forgive me. I did not mean to offend. But when I entered this hall, I did not expect to see someone of your beauty. It is, indeed, a privilege, my lady."

Liselotte couldn't help the silly grin that was slowly taking over her

expression. "You did not offend me," she said. "I
been a very long time since I have heard such prai

Daniel's eyebrows lifted. "Why?" he asked. "A
blind men?"

She laughed, giddy, and he followed suit. I
unexpectedly enchanting moment. Having no id
man's flagrant charms, Liselotte simply turned away from him, indicating the hall with its three scrubbed feasting tables.

"Will you please sit, my lord?" she asked. "My father says you are to be our guest of honor tonight. I am not sure that providing you with a meal is entirely suitable for the man who saved my brother, but rest assured that we will provide you with the best that we can. You honor us."

Daniel gladly followed her as she crossed the floor towards the tables. He never took his eyes from her. "The honor is mine," he said smoothly. Then, he shrugged. "Truthfully, it all happened so fast. One moment, I was seeking shelter from the storm and in the next, your brother was throwing himself at me. It all happened quite by chance."

Liselotte was listening closely. "God must have had a hand in it," she said seriously. "My father has been praying constantly for a miracle since Gunnar's abduction. It would seem that God sent you to our aid."

Daniel wasn't a big believer in God, or the hand of the heavenly host for that matter, but he didn't say anything to that regard. He simply smiled.

"Then I am happy to be of service," he said.

Liselotte returned his smile, a gesture that didn't come easy to her. She had never been the giddy or smiling sort, but Daniel seemed to bring it out in her. In just the few short seconds they had known one another, she had smiled more than she probably had in months. Daniel seemed to have that easiness and that joy about him, a manner that was infectious.

"And we are very grateful," she said, indicating for him to take a seat by the fire and dry off. "Will you sit and warm yourself? The quite horrendous."

…iel looked at the fire, feeling the warmth of it pulling at him. …te," he agreed. "Thank you for your hospitality, my lady."

As he moved towards the fire, Liselotte moved in front of him, quickly pulling forth a stool for him to sit and he smiled his thanks. She smiled in return, her gaze moving from his face to the sheer size of the man as he set his saddlebags and sword to the floor. More than that, he was dressed quite finely. She'd never seen such finery, on any man, indicating he was someone with some means. Her curiosity grew.

"You are welcome," she said. "May… may I ask where you were going on your travels? I do hope your kindness towards my brother has not interrupted your plans too much."

Daniel shook his head as he pulled off his heavy gloves and began untying the neck of his sopping cloak. "Nothing was interrupted, I assure you," he said, removing the cloak and laying it across the stool to dry. "I was traveling north to visit friends, but they can wait. Saving a child is more important."

Liselotte liked his answer. She also noticed that he was now fumbling with his tunic belt, or girdle, a wide leather strip that encircled his narrow waist. It seemed he was having trouble with the buckles due to his cold fingers and she indicated the girdle.

"May I help you with that?" she asked.

He nodded and lifted his arms when she rushed at him, deftly pulling at the buckle on the belt. "Thank you, my lady," he said. "I fear my fingers are the least bit frozen. Navigating the buckle is difficult."

Liselotte could see that. In fact, in her haste to help him, she was quite close to him and her heart began to do strange things in her chest. Flutter… *thump*… and giddiness swamped her. It was an unfamiliar feeling, one that left her quite breathless, and she was actually coming to think that something might be wrong with her. Was she becoming ill?

Or was she simply too close to a man who set her heart to racing?

With quivering hands, she pulled the girdle off of him and set it aside, standing back to see if there was anything else she could help him with. She was eager to be of service, eager to be close to him, and having no idea why the man should make her feel as if she couldn't catch her breath. But she really didn't care.

She rather liked it.

The tunic that the girdle had belted was loose now, and quite wet, and Daniel bent over and tried to pull it off but because it was wet, it was sticking to him, and he had it halfway off when it became stuck. Liselotte rushed to his rescue yet again, pulling off the tunic and finding a place on the stones to put it near the fire so that it would dry. Beneath the tunic, however, Daniel had a heavy mail coat on and it was as wet as everything else, making it more than heavy and quite cumbersome. He tried to shake it out a bit, water droplets falling on the floor.

"I see you are quite adept at removing clothing," he told her, a glimmer of jest in his eye. "But I assure you the mail coat will not go easily. It will fight you all the way as you try to remove it and then laugh at your failure. Are you prepared for the battle, my lady?"

Liselotte sensed his humor. It was very endearing. "I am, my lord," she said, pretending to be serious. "I shall prevail."

"Are you certain?"

"I am, my lord."

"Then let us commence."

With a grin, he bent over and began to shake the mail, which was beginning to seize up in spots, a prelude to rusting. Liselotte had never removed a mail coat in her life but it seemed logical to take it by the arms and she did, tugging as Daniel twisted his body in a way that suggested he had done this many times before. Liselotte was able to get one arm of the mail coat off of him when a booming voice echoed across the hall.

"God's Bones, Leese!" Etzel had just come up from the underground vault to see his daughter wrestling with the knight. "Get away from that, girl! That is a man's task!"

Liselotte stepped back as her father jumped in and began to tug and pull, managing to yank the mail off. It was a very heavy coat and Etzel immediately called for servants, producing two men who had been bringing in wood for the fire. Etzel instructed the pair to dry off the mail and scrub it down so it would not rust, which brought words of appreciation from Daniel.

"You speak like a man who has known a coat of mail or two," he said as the servants took his mail away. "Thank you for your assistance."

Etzel indicated for Daniel to sit near the fire now that he was stripped down to his sweaty, dirty under-tunic, and leather breeches. "In days long past, I was a knight myself," he said. "I suppose I still am, but that was a long time ago."

Daniel took the offered seat, acutely aware that Liselotte was moving to sit across the table from him. He was pleased, as it would make it easier to look at the woman. And he intended to do a lot of looking.

"I cannot believe it was too long ago," Daniel said. "You are not that old."

Etzel smiled weakly. "You are kind, my lord," he said. "I am old enough. Old enough to remember the days of prosperity at Shadowmoor. Old enough to… well, it does not matter. Let us speak on you; I do not even know your name."

Daniel glanced at Liselotte as he answered. He simply wanted to look upon her again, as if he couldn't keep his eyes off her. When their eyes met, she smiled and his heart jumped, just a little.

An interesting reaction from a man who thought he was immune to such things.

"As I told your daughter, my name is Sir Daniel de Lohr," he said. "I was traveling north to visit friends when I happened across your son. Now, you will tell me who this Lord Bramley is and why he is so intent to marry your daughter that he would abduct your son to gain his way."

The warm expression on Etzel's face faded. "It has been the situation with us for such a long time that it is difficult to remember the times before this crisis," he said. "I suppose I should start from the beginning. The House of l'Audacieux is a direct descendant from the last great ruler of the kingdom of Elmet, a man by the name of Ceretic. Ceretic was a great king and many generations of great rulers descended from him including my great-grandfather several times over, a man by the name of Rombald, who was the last of the great line before the Normans invaded. The Normans rather liked Rombald, it seemed, and gave him the name Rombald l'Audacieux – or, Rombald the Bold. All of the land from Cross Hills to the north, Bradford to the south, and Ilkley to the east was granted to Rombald by the Normans because Rombald knew the land and was very capable of keeping peace for the Normans. Under his guidance, his people were obedient to the Normans and Rombald was able to keep most of his lands intact because of it."

Daniel was listening with interest. "I see," he said. "And these lands still belong to you?"

Etzel nodded. "Indeed, they do," he said, his expression hardening. "And there was prosperity for all until the advent of Lord Bramley."

Daniel shook his head in disgust. "I knew he figured into this somehow," he said. "What is the issue with the man?"

Etzel reached over to collect the cups that had been left out on the table, moving to open the earthenware jug of ale he had brought up from the vault. He uncorked the top, with its mud seal, and began to pour.

"*Everything* is the issue, my lord," he said. "Bramley is a nephew of the king and he was given a small plot of land and a small castle to the southwest, Bramley Castle, about four years ago. Immediately, he started harassing my villages and sending his men to steal from the peasants. Because Shadowmoor had lived in peace for so long, our army was long gone and only citizens, remnants of the kingdom of Elmet, still live here. We have not had need for armed men for decades because the Normans always provided what we needed. But that ended some time ago and there was no hardship about it until Lord Bramley came. The truth is that he wants Shadowmoor and my lands for himself and he wants to marry my daughter to claim them. He is trying everything he can to drive us to starvation so he can claim the fortress."

Daniel rubbed his chin unhappily. "Have you written to the king about this?" he asked. "Surely Henry can do something."

Etzel sighed heavily. "I have tried to send men with a missive," he said. "But Bramley watches all of the roads from Shadowmoor. He has intercepted everything I have tried to send. He has many men at his disposal while I have few. Shadowmoor is supposed to collect tariffs from the roads leading south, as is our hereditary right, but Bramley now takes those for his own. He killed one of my men who tried to stop him. He even burns any crops we can manage to plant during the planting months or he otherwise destroys them. He has made living quite difficult but that is his intention. He is trying to drive us out."

Daniel frowned. He wasn't keen on tyrants in any form and since he'd had his own run-in with Lord Bramley, he could easily see what Etzel was explaining. Roland Fitzroy, Lord Bramley, definitely seemed the type.

"But why does he want it so badly?" Daniel asked. "No offense, my lord, but this place does not look like much worth having."

Etzel wasn't hard pressed to agree. "It is nothing regal, I admit," he said. "But there is a forest to the north that is part of my lands and it is rich in hunting. There are also water rights that supply villages south of us, including Leeds, plus six villages whose taxes I used to glean as income. The truth is that these were once-great lands but Lord Bramley has managed to ruin them. My people starve and we scrape by a meager existence."

Daniel shook his head. "What about the taxes you mentioned?" he asked "Surely you can purchase food or men with them?"

Etzel looked embarrassed. "Lord Bramley steals everything he can get his hands on and the villagers are so frightened of him that they give him all they have and more besides."

Daniel was starting to get a very unpleasant picture of what had been going on at Shadowmoor for the past four years. The abducted child was only the latest in a string of offenses. He sat forward, his elbows on the table as he considered the situation. He knew he shouldn't involve himself in any way, but the truth was that he was already involved. He became involved when Gunnar ran to him for help. Still, he'd done his duty and saved the boy, but that didn't solve the problem. He had saved the child only to have Bramley abduct him again, or worse. He was starting to feel a great deal of sympathy for Etzel and his lovely daughter and struggling not to. It wasn't his problem.

But that didn't seem to matter much because Daniel had an innate sense of right and wrong, and of wanting to help those in need. These people were definitely in need. Perhaps it was the knight in him that wanted to be chivalrous, or perhaps it was the de Lohr who had, for generations, fought for right and good. In any case, in just these few short minutes he had spent with these people, he knew it would be difficult to walk away from what they were facing on a daily basis.

He wondered if he could do any good for them.

"Well," he began, drawing in a deep breath. "The facts are these – Roland Fitzroy says he is a nephew of the king but the truth is that he is not. His sister, and his sister only, is the bastard daughter of King John, which makes Roland a non-blood relation, if at all. Truth be told, I wonder if he is even who he says he is. He could simply have told you that to lean on you and steal your lands. He could be just a greedy man who has confiscated Bramley Castle, taken the name, and concocted a story about him being a relation to Henry. Nothing has been proven with regard to his relation to the king."

Etzel nodded. "That is true," he said, "but, as I said, I have been unable to send a missive to Henry to discover the truth of it. And how would you know so much about Lord Bramley?"

Daniel scratched at his chin again, pensively. "He told me," he said. "When I would not return your son to him, he told me who he was and threatened me. I threatened him right back."

Etzel's eyebrows lifted in surprise. "You did?" he said, both appalled and thrilled. "What did you say to him?"

Daniel's gaze drifted to Liselotte, sitting politely silent as the conversation went between her father and their guest. When Daniel looked at her, however, she smiled rather shyly and averted her gaze. Daniel's attention lingered on her.

"My family name is de Lohr," he said to Etzel. "Have you heard of it?"

Etzel's brow furrowed in thought. "I am not sure," he said. "I think I may have. Something to do with King Richard?"

Daniel nodded. "My uncle, Christopher, was King Richard's champion," he said. "My uncle is also the Earl of Hereford and Worcester and High Sheriff of the Marches. My father is the Earl of Canterbury and controls several garrisons in Sussex and Kent. Between my father and my uncle, they have tens of thousands of men at their disposal, enough to overrun Bramley and wipe him from this earth. Bramley didn't seem to like my promise that I would do just that."

Etzel stared at him, stunned. "Tens of thousands of men?" he repeated. "Is your family so powerful?"

Daniel nodded, a modest gesture. "All that and more," he said quietly. "They are champions for justice and, in this case, it seems as if a great injustice has been perpetrated upon you by a fool. I will send word to my uncle, whose seat is much closer to Shadowmoor than my father's is, and ask him what he knows of Roland Fitzroy. I will further ask him to send men for protection for Shadowmoor until this situation with Lord Bramley can be settled."

Etzel had no idea what to say. He looked at his daughter, who was equally astonished, before returning his attention to Daniel and shaking his head.

"But…," he started, stopped, and started again. "My lord, your offer is most gracious. Incredibly gracious. But we are not your responsibility in any way. I could never repay your father and uncle for any services they provided us and we certainly cannot provide for any army to be stationed here. We can barely provide for ourselves."

Daniel could see that it was an embarrassing admission for the man, refusing such generous help. But Daniel waved him off.

"My uncle's army travels with their own provisions and a quartermaster," he said. "You would not be expected to provide for them with the exception of shelter. And, certainly, no repayment is expected. I offered, did I not? That means this will cost you nothing."

Etzel was still looking quite stunned. Sickened, too, as if overwhelmed by everything Daniel was telling him. The man was genuinely speechless for a few moments as he tried to process everything.

"But why?" he finally asked. "Why would you do this for people you do not know?"

Daniel glanced at Liselotte, whose astonished expression was much like her father's. "Your circumstances of cruelty from Lord Bramley leave you shocked to realize there is still some good in the world," he said. "What I offer, I do because it needs to be done. I do it because it is the right thing to do and I expect nothing in return. Clearly, this is none of my affair and I could just as easily leave tomorrow and you would never see me again. That is more than likely what I should do because what is happening at Shadowmoor is none of my affair. But the fact remains that I saved your son from a man who is systematically attempting to destroy your family and your life. I did not save him to let him fall back into Fitzroy's hands at a later time, so in a sense, I have made your problems my own. I did it the moment I told Fitzroy that I would not turn Gunnar back over to him. So, you see, your problems have, in a small way, become my own because now Fitzroy, or Lord Bramley, or whatever he calls himself now sees my refusal to return Gunnar to him as an insult. I am now his enemy as well. Does this make sense to you?"

Both Etzel and Liselotte nodded. "It does," Etzel said. "It makes a good deal of sense and I must apologize that you find yourself involved. It is not your war to fight."

"It is now," Daniel said, cocking at eyebrow at the man to emphasize his point. "Therefore, I will send a missive to my uncle regarding the situation and ask for aid. I will also have my uncle send word to

Henry to relay Fitzroy's activities against Shadowmoor. In addition to my uncle, I will also send a missive to the Earl of Wrexham for aid because he is just a few days to the north and aid will arrive faster. My family is allied with the earls of Wrexham, the House of de Wolfe, so they will send what I ask for. Soon enough, this place will be overrun with soldiers and knights, and that idiot Fitzroy will be too fearful to strike against you any longer. We shall take Shadowmoor back for you, l'Audacieux. Have no doubt."

Etzel could only sit there and stare at the man. Then, as Daniel watched, he broke down in tears. "It is the answer to my prayers," he sniffed, embarrassed at his display of emotion as he struggled to regain his composure. "Since Lord Bramley came, I have prayed for divine intervention to help us with the man. And now God sends it in the form of a single knight. I can hardly believe it."

Liselotte quickly went to her father to comfort him, putting her hands on the man's shoulders as Etzel struggled. She was close to tears herself as she looked to Daniel.

"My lord," she said softly. "What my father says… we have indeed prayed for help. We did not know how or where it would come from, but we believed that it would come someday. Yet, what my father has not told you is the toll it has taken on our family and our people. Starvation and little hope have made Shadowmoor a dismal place. My own mother took to her bed last year and has not risen; she remains an invalid, praying for death because she is so miserable. When my younger brother was abducted, we did not tell her for days for fear of what it would do to her and when we finally told her… she has not been the same. It is my hope that Gunnar's return can bring some life back into her, and now with your magnanimous offer of aid… you are truly an answer to prayer. We are forever in your debt."

Etzel regained control of his composure enough to nod, wiping sloppily at his wet face. "What she says is true," he said. "We are in your debt, always willing to be of service to you and your family. Although I have nothing to pay you with, no money to speak of, I would gladly give you my daughter's hand in marriage. It is the only thing I have of value. Liselotte is a good girl with many skills. She is not rich, of course, but she would make a fine and dutiful wife."

Liselotte's eyes widened to the point of bursting from her skull while Daniel, equally as shocked by the unexpected offer, was left scrambling for a reply that didn't sound like an insult. What shocked him more, however, was the fact that he very nearly agreed to the proposal right on the spot. Liselotte was an unearthly beauty and he felt drawn to her as he had never felt drawn to a woman in his life, not ever, but the fact remained that he had only known her for a few minutes at best. Perhaps the only thing he felt for her was a great appreciation for her beauty and nothing more. In any case, he had to bite off an immediate reply, fearful that he would get himself into trouble. He did so want to agree based purely on superficial reasons.

But he couldn't.

"That is a very generous offer, my lord," he said, sounding a bit rattled. "Of course, if I was in the market for a wife, I would accept your offer without question, but alas, I am not. I do not intend to marry, at least not any time soon. But I would be more than happy to find your daughter a husband if you are in the market for one – mayhap a knight who could bring his army with him and provide protection to Shadowmoor. I know many fine knights who would fill this role, in fact."

Liselotte, who had thus far remained silent and polite throughout the conversation, could no longer remain so.

"I do *not* need for you to find me a husband, my lord," she said, sounding righteously insulted. Then she looked at her father. "And you should not have made him such an offer, Papa. See how uncomfortable you made him? What a terrible thing to do to us both. You made it seem as if you are desperate to make me his burden and that is not fair."

Etzel seemed genuinely surprised by her reaction. "I did not mean it so," he insisted, looking between Daniel and his daughter. "I simply meant that you are the only thing of value I have. You are very valuable to me, Leese. You know that."

Liselotte shook her head at her father in frustration and turned away, moving away from the table and back over to the fire pit where Daniel's clothes were drying. She pretended to tend to them when what she was really doing was making sure Daniel couldn't see the flush to her cheeks, a flush of great embarrassment and humiliation. So he didn't want to marry her; she did not blame him. She wasn't worth marrying but at least he had the tact not to say so. No man in his right mind would think a penniless maiden was worth marrying. Still, she was quite mortified by her father's suggestion, hoping Daniel wouldn't rescind his offer for assistance because of it.

But rescinding his offer was the furthest thing from Daniel's mind, in fact. He watched Liselotte move away from the table to tend to his drying clothing, trying not to make it obvious that he was staring at her, concerned for her reaction to her father's tactless proposal. She was offended, he could see that, but he clearly hadn't meant to offend her. He wanted to make amends.

"She is more than likely the most valuable thing in all of Yorkshire and, I would suspect, the most beautiful maiden in all of Northern England," Daniel said, loud enough for her to hear him. "If I was the marrying kind, I would accept your offer with great glee. In fact, I have never had a finer offer in my life. But the truth is that I do not even have a home. I travel constantly and that would be no life for a wife. Women want a home and children, and I could not provide that. It is a sorrowful thing to admit."

Etzel sighed with relief, happy he'd not offended the man with his offer of marriage. "You understand that I had to offer," he said. "She is the only thing I have of value."

Daniel's eyes drifted to Liselotte as she knelt next to the fire. He could see her profile with her upturned nose against the firelight. "She is the most valuable thing in all of England," he said, quietly now. "But I am wholly unworthy of her."

"You will tell me if you change your mind."

"I will."

They fell silent after that, drinking the cheap ale in their crude wooden cups, each man pondering the unexpected course the future had taken. Daniel, for certain, was feeling a bit of excitement at the future because he now had a purpose. He was a man who thrived on purpose, and on a challenge, and he considered the immediate future both of those things. Moreover, he was a man who loved to deal out justice, which Lord Bramley was sorely in need of. Once the man realized that the House of de Lohr had taken over Shadowmoor, he would think twice before continuing with his harassment. But, it seemed, the trick would be getting a missive past Lord Bramley's men, who evidently watched the roads. Indeed, that would be the key.

As Daniel engaged Etzel in a conversation about all of the roads leading south, Liselotte was closely listening. She could hear just enough conversation to make sense out of it and it was clear that her father and Daniel were plotting to get a message through Lord Bramley's net. It was something her father had not dared in years but now with Daniel's arrival, there was renewed hope. Perhaps something could really be done. But she was distracted when a couple of serving women brought in the freshly baked loaves of bread from the outside oven, so Liselotte turned from eavesdropping on the men's conversation to serving up the evening meal.

Mealtime at Shadowmoor was a bit different because one of the key components, the flat stale bread used for a plate or trencher, was noticeably absent. Trenchers were made from precious bread and since food was relatively scarce, Liselotte had a stack of reusable clay plates at her disposal. She had made them herself out of heavy gray clay found on the banks of the River Aire, not far to the west, that had been shaped into flat rounds and baked in the bread ovens until they were very hard. An old woman whose family lived at Shadowmoor, on the outskirts of the walls, had shown her how to fashion the plates. She was an old lady who had seen much hardship in her life and knew how to deal with it.

In fact, the entire populace of Shadowmoor had pulled together over the past four years, all three hundred and sixty-eight of them, to help each other through this difficult time. No one ever blamed Liselotte for Lord Bramley's harassment. In fact, those who lived at Shadowmoor were quite protective of their young lady. But Liselotte felt guilty for their suffering nonetheless, just one more thing to feel remorse over in a long line of such things. It was difficult at times not to give in to the weight of self-pity.

As Etzel and Daniel weighed their options for sending missives, Liselotte collected the first clay plate and spooned a goodly portion of the thick pea stew onto it. Onto the stew she put the best piece of boiled mutton she could find. On a separate plate, she spooned a large portion of the boiled cabbage and, with a small loaf of freshly baked bread, brought the feast to Daniel and placed it in front of him. When he looked up at her with gratitude, she smiled timidly.

"We do not have much to share but you are welcome to what we have, my lord," she said. "I hope it satisfies your hunger."

Daniel looked down at the food before him. "It looks delicious," he said. Then, he focused on her face again. "I have never seen such a fine feast."

Liselotte's smile turned modest and grateful, and she moved back to the fire to prepare her father's meal as Daniel dug in to his with gusto. The pea stew was tasty and salty, and the bread was surprisingly good, as was the cabbage. The mutton tasted old but he simply shoved it into his mouth as if it were the most marvelous thing in the world. He would never let his hostess think otherwise.

Soon, Etzel had his meal and the two men were devouring everything before them. Young Gunnar entered the hall just as they were beginning to eat and, sitting on his father's lap, ate from his father's meal until Liselotte brought him his own food. But it was clear that Etzel didn't mind his boy stealing his food. He hugged the child and encouraged him to eat from his plate even when they boy had his own food in front of him. When Liselotte finally sat down next to her father with her own plate of food, she too fed Gunnar off of her plate.

Daniel watched the interaction between the three and he could see how much family love and devotion there was. It was quite clear how glad Etzel and Liselotte were to have Gunnar returned to them, and that knowledge touched Daniel. Being quite close to his own family, he understood those bonds. That love that only a family can have for each other. It also underscored to him the tragedy of the trouble the family had faced against Lord Bramley.

"Tell me, young Gunnar," Daniel said as he slurped up the pea stew with his bread. "Have you seen an education, lad?"

Gunnar, mouth full of bread, nodded his head. "Papa would take me to Ilkley to the priests," he said. "They taught me something of reading from the Bible but I have not been back to see them in a long time."

Daniel was curious. "Why not?"

Etzel spoke. "Because of Lord Bramley," he said. "He watched the roads, as I told you, and has chased us off when we try to reach the town. We simply stopped trying."

Daniel swallowed the food in his mouth, eyeing Gunnar. "We shall remedy that," he said, "because you will have to learn to read and do arithmetic when you become the Lord of Shadowmoor. A good lord must be educated."

Gunnar had an odd look on his face. "I will not be the Lord of Shadowmoor."

Daniel's brow furrowed as he took another bite. "Why not?"

Gunnar collected his cup of watered ale and drank. "Because my brother will be the lord."

Now, Daniel looked surprised at the introduction of another family member. "You have a brother?"

Etzel simply nodded, lowering his head and shoveling food in his mouth. When he didn't seem inclined to answer, Daniel looked at Liselotte, who seemed hesitant to speak on the subject.

"Aye, my lord," she said, eyeing her father. "Gunnar and I have an older brother."

Daniel wasn't quite sure why the three of them seemed so subdued with the mention of another brother. "Where does he live?" he asked.

"Here, at Shadowmoor," Liselotte said. "He is… ill. Sickly."

Daniel nodded in understanding. "I see," he said. "A pity. A strong older brother with a good sword might have helped you fend of Lord Bramley."

Etzel set his cup down on the tabletop, rather heavily. It was a mask for a gesture of frustration. "He used to be a fine sword," he said. "He used to be the finest in the land. But his sword hand, and his honor, was consumed by drink and that is the way he wants it. When we salvage Shadowmoor, it will be to turn it over to a drunkard who cares little for anything other than himself."

It was a statement wrought with anger and sorrow. Daniel quickly surmised that the subject of the older brother was not a pleasant one.

"Forgive me for bringing up a painful subject," he said. "I was not aware."

Etzel seemed to calm, realizing how harsh he must have sounded. "I know," he said. "I apologize if I was abrupt. Brynner does not associate with the family and we do not associate with him. He wishes it that way. You can expect no help from him because, as you can see, he has left us to fend for ourselves as if he wants no part of us. It is shameful but true."

Daniel suspected this was not the time for any further questions about the son Etzel identified as Brynner. It was a puzzling and seemingly sad situation, but he knew it really wasn't any of his affair. He had already imposed himself on the family enough so he respected the information he was given as all he needed to know. It was evident they didn't wish to speak of the brother so he changed the subject.

"My lady, your father and I were discussing all of the roads that lead south from Shadowmoor, roads or paths that Lord Bramley might not be watching," he said, looking to Liselotte as he pulled apart the last of his bread. "He tells me that there are two roads, a main road and a smaller one, and then two smaller paths that lead over the hill towards Hawksworth and Guiseley. Can you think of any other roads that might be worth attempting when I try to send a message south?"

Successfully diverted off the painful subject of Brynner, Liselotte's brow furrowed thoughtfully. "I do not," she said. "Do you intend to take the message yourself?"

Daniel shook his head. "I intend to hire a messenger."

Liselotte seemed hesitant when she spoke. "I see," she said. "If that is the case, then I have been thinking… mind you, we've not had the money to hire a messenger but if we did, what if we were to go north to the villages of Cross Hills or Eastburn and find someone to take the message south? Lord Bramley doesn't necessarily watch the roads leading north too much, only the ones that converge south towards Bradford. He more than likely would not think much of a lone messenger providing the man had money to pay Bramley's road tariff. We have never tried to slip a message past him that way."

Etzel looked at his daughter with some curiosity, as if he wasn't certain her idea was a sound one, but Daniel smiled broadly at her. He didn't seem to have the same reservation. "A brilliant idea, my lady," he said. "Why didn't I think of that?"

Liselotte grinned, blushing to the roots of her hair. "We have never had a reason to try something such as that," she admitted. "We do not have the means."

Daniel cocked his head. "But you have men here at Shadowmoor who could take a message and mayhap not be recognized or harassed," he said. "Men who could take it straight to Henry."

Etzel answered. "It takes money to travel," he said. "We have none."

"None to spare?"

"None at all."

Daniel didn't doubt that in the least. Shadowmoor was clearly poor but he thought they might have some small stash of coinage tucked away because certain items did need to be purchased. Therefore, he was surprised to hear there was absolutely nothing.

"Then where do you get money for flour and ale?" he asked. "You must purchase such things from a mill or a brewer wife."

Liselotte drank the last of her ale. "We spent all summer and into the fall collecting wild grains," she said. "It is what we use for the ale and flour, but even that store grows low. We will conserve until the early summer when the grains began to reach a state where they can be harvested early."

Daniel looked at his clay plate, the meal he had just finished off. "Is everything you collect wild? You purchase nothing?"

Liselotte shook her head. "Nothing, my lord."

Which meant they shared their precious stores with him when he could have just as easily purchased a meal in town. He'd never seen such a level of poverty with people who had been forced into such circumstances.

"Well," he said thoughtfully. "If I am to remain here to help you with Lord Bramley, I will pay for my lodgings and I will start tomorrow when we go north into the town to seek a messenger. I will purchase whatever supplies I can find there and bring them back. Is there anything specific that you need?"

Liselotte was dumbfounded. She looked at her father, fearfully, before replying. "Need?" she repeated. "I do not understand."

Daniel could see he'd confused her with his question. Perhaps it was a question she had never heard in her life. "If I am going to eat and sleep here, then I must pay for that privilege," he explained again. "I intend to pay for it by purchasing supplies. Do you have a cow for milk and cheese?"

Liselotte stared at him, her features pale with surprise. "We… nay, we do not," she said. "We ate the cow."

Daniel nodded decisively. "Then I shall purchase a cow or two," he said. "If I am going to stay here, I must have cheese. I cannot do without it."

His statement left no room for debate. Liselotte had no idea what to say, looking to her father to see what his reaction was, but Etzel seemed just as speechless as his daughter. He understood that their guest, their savior, had the right and expectation to eat what he wanted to eat, but

Etzel also knew that Daniel was preparing to supply them with things they could not possibly pay him for.

"My lord," he said. "Forgive us our inability to provide sufficiently for you, but we cannot reimburse you for that which you intend to purchase."

Daniel looked at the man. "I do not expect you to," he said. "Do you understand that I am paying for my keep by purchasing supplies? It is not usual for the host to reimburse a guest the cost of his upkeep. I will purchase the items I need for myself, but I will purchase enough to repay you for housing me. I am not sure how much plainer I can be to this regard."

Etzel and Liselotte looked at each other, unwilling to protest for two reasons – they didn't want to offend their guest and, truly, it had been a very long time since they had been supplied with enough to eat. Perhaps it was their hungry bellies willing to overlook their pride. In any case, they didn't protest or argue purely out of surprise for what Daniel intended to do. He seemed quite determined to do it and he was quite clear that there would be no need for monetary compensation.

It was a wonderful thought, and one that brought about great relief, but there was still the matter of pride. Etzel wasn't used to taking charity and it was difficult to accept that this knight wished to provide them with sustenance. As he wrestled with that pride, Gunnar climbed off his father's lap and went to Daniel.

"Are you so rich, then?" he asked. "You can buy a cow?"

Daniel grinned at the wide-eyed boy, who was really an adorable lad. "I can," he said. "I can buy most anything I want. I am fortunate that I have the means."

"But if you travel all of the time, as you say, how do you make your money?" Liselotte asked. "Shouldn't you serve a lord or, at the very least, have a trade?"

Daniel's gaze turned to her, that angelic face. "I am actually not a true vagabond," he admitted. "I am titled and I hold lands within the Canterbury earldom. Lord Thorndon is my title, in fact. I have property that generates income for me and men to staff my holdings."

Gunnar was interested. "What holdings?" he asked. "Do you have a big castle and lots of men with swords?"

Daniel grinned. "I have two small castles, in fact," he said. "And my father's men staff them as outposts."

"But you said you had no home," Liselotte pointed out. She couldn't help it. "Yet you have two castles?"

Daniel nodded. "I do," he said. "But I have never lived at them. Mayhap someday I will, but for now, the floor of my home is the land and the roof of my home is the sky. All of England is my home and I like it that way."

Liselotte simply nodded, perhaps not entirely happy to hear that answer, as Gunnar continued with his questions. "Have you seen lots of battles, then?" he asked. "Have you killed a lot of men?"

"Gunnar," Etzel admonished softly. He smiled weakly at Daniel. "He is young, my lord. Blood and battles excite him."

Daniel put a big hand on Gunnar's blond head. "When I was young, they excited me as well," he said. "But that is a story for another time. It would seem to me that you and I have had an extraordinary day and I, for one, am looking forward to sleep. What say you, young Gunnar?"

Gunnar shrugged. He wasn't quite ready to go to bed. "You are sleeping in my chamber," he said. "Shall I show you where it is?"

Daniel nodded, rising wearily to his feet. His saddlebags were over near the hearth along with his tunic and cloak, which were now virtually dry from the intense heat of the fire. Gunnar ran alongside him and then darted in front of him, trying to help him with his things. Daniel nearly tripped over the skinny agile boy.

"I will show you where to sleep," Gunnar said. "Come follow me!"

Daniel slung his saddlebags over his shoulder and collected his broadsword, still packed carefully in its sheath and propped against the saddlebags. By this time, Liselotte and Etzel were up because their guest was about to retire for the night.

"Are you sure you have had enough to eat, my lord?" Liselotte asked. "My brother seems to be rushing you away. Surely you would stay and enjoy the remainder of the ale?"

Daniel shook his head. "Nay, my lady, although your offer is gracious," he said. "I will retire for the night for tomorrow, we will take a trip into the nearest northern town to find both a messenger and some supplies. It will be a big day for us all. In fact, my lady, I would consider it an honor if you would accompany me. I may have need of your guidance and expertise. I am a stranger to his area and you are not. Your knowledge will be invaluable."

Liselotte was thrilled at the prospect of accompanying the man into town. But she looked at her father for permission first and, when the man gave her a brief nod, it was all she could do not to gush like an excited fool.

"If you think I would be of help, my lord," she said. "I am happy to go with you. Only…."

"Only what?"

"I do not leave the fortress too often," she said honestly. "My father is afraid that Lord Bramley's men will capture me and take me back to him."

Daniel shook his head firmly. "That will not happen with me as your protector," he said. "Therefore, you will be ready at dawn to depart. We have a good deal to do tomorrow and I do not want to delay."

"Can I go?" Gunnar begged, jumping up and down. "Please? Can I go?"

Etzel put his hand on the boy's head. "You have been away from home for weeks yet you want to leave us again so quickly?"

Gunnar was still jumping up and down. "To town, Papa, to *town*!"

Etzel could never refuse the boy. There was so little in his life to be excited about and especially as of late. He could hardly deny that hopeful face. He grunted reluctantly.

"Very well," he said. "But you will not be a burden and you do everything your sister and Sir Daniel tell you to do. Do you understand?"

Gunnar was nodding eagerly, now running for the hall entry where the rain and thunder still pounded outside.

"Come on!" he stopped at the door and turned to yell for Daniel. "Come with me!"

Daniel wriggled his eyebrows at the eager lad and, begging his leave of Etzel and Liselotte, followed the happy boy to the door, soon disappearing out into the rain. Etzel and Liselotte stood there long after Daniel had disappeared, both of them looking at the open entry door, both of them pondering the drastic course their future had taken. It was a lot to absorb.

"Do you think he means what he says, Papa?" Liselotte asked with concern. She turned to her father. "It seems too good to be true. Do you really think he means to help us with Bramley?"

Etzel shrugged in a gesture that suggested he really didn't have an answer. "I would like to think so," he said, turning back to the table where the ale was. "He has made a lot of promises. It would be good if he kept them, for your sake."

"What about yours?"

Etzel shook his head. "I have lived my life, Leese," he said. "But you are young and beautiful. You still have your life ahead of you. It would be good if Sir Daniel really was the answer to our prayers."

Liselotte sighed. "We have been so long without hope," she said quietly. "Mayhap God has been testing us. Mayhap He has sent Daniel to finally give us hope."

"Do you recall the story of Daniel in the Bible, taught by the priests?"

Liselotte nodded. "He was saved by God from the lions."

Etzel expression softened, his gaze turning distant. "Mayhap God has sent Daniel to save *us*."

"Do you think Daniel de Lohr is a messenger from God?"

Etzel collected his half-empty cup. "I like to believe in divine assistance," he said. "Whether or not de Lohr is divine, he has nonetheless been sent to help us. He is an answer to our prayers. That is what I choose to believe."

"Then we are to trust him?"

"We have no alternative but to go on faith. What is left for us if we do not trust him?"

He seemed rather firm about it. As Etzel finished what was left in his cup, Liselotte went to see to what was left over from the meal so she could prepare for tomorrow's feeding. All the while, however, her thoughts lingered on Daniel de Lohr and his timely appearance. Was he really sent from God? Her father seemed to think so. But Liselotte was a bit more pragmatic.

Time would tell the tale if Daniel de Lohr really meant what he said.

She very much hoped that he did.

CHAPTER THREE

The next morning

GOD... THAT CHEAP, horrible ale was the stuff of nightmares.

It always gave him the most terrible headaches the next day following a binge, an ache that traveled all the way down his neck and into his chest. His stomach, ruined from years of drinking anything he could get his hands on, was shriveled with sharp pains this morning.

Sharp pains like the ones that filled his very soul.

Brynner l'Audacieux had managed to stumble out of bed well before dawn, just as the rains from the previous night were trickling off. With a throbbing head, he had staggered out of the vault where he slept, the sub-level room beneath the keep that he kept only for himself, and stumbled out into the ward. His first trip had been to the kitchens to see if there was any drink to be had, as his father tended to move it around, hiding it from a son who kept hunting for it, and the best he was able to come up with was half a jug from the night before. It had been enough. Taking it with him, he grabbed most of the bread left from the previous evening and ate it, using the cheap ale in the jug to wash it down.

The guards at the gate, huddled around a fire for warmth, had seen him coming and knew the routine. It was usual with him. They already had the gate open enough to allow him to pass by the time he arrived and he slipped through the gate and out into the moors beyond before the sun even rose. It was dark and wet and near freezing, but Brynner didn't care much. The cold seemed to be the only relief for his head on days such as this.

The storm from the previous night had cleared out, leaving wet and soggy land in its wake. The ground was heavy with scrub, muddied down and mashed, and the cold wind that blew up from the east had icy fingers that dug into a man's chest, causing him pain every time he drew in a breath. Brynner was dressed in what he was usually dressed in; a heavy tunic, breeches made from leather, and a cloak that had once been fine and expensive. All three of those items were heavily worn and extremely dirty because Brynner never took them off. He slept in them, and drank in them, and at times had vomited in them, so they were beyond the normal filth of man.

In fact, he'd worn the same clothing for the past three years, ever since he'd gone to meet his lover and she'd told him of her plans to marry another. He'd never been able to change out of them, wearing them like a weighty suit of armor to remind him of that day his heart had been ripped from his chest. He needed those dirty clothes in a way he couldn't describe, not only as a reminder of that terrible day but also as penitence.

With every step of the boots that had holes in them or every whiff of that horrific smell of his tunic, he was reminded of Maud. Only in moments like this, when he wasn't drunk, did the pain and the smells weigh heavily on him, so heavily he could scarcely move. It was the drink that allowed him to forget. Drink had become a weapon against those memories and the punishment those dirty torn clothes brought about.

That was Brynner's life these days. He wasn't particularly tall but he was still strongly built, his battered body still holding some semblance of its former shape in spite of the fact that he was slowly trying to kill himself. He had the same bronze-colored hair that his sister had and his features were quite handsome still, although drawn and shaded from the self-abuse.

In moments of lucidity, however, he inevitably thought of his lovely Maud and her reasons for leaving him. Her father had insisted she marry another man, one of his choosing; a man who brought great wealth and an alliance to her family. Maud hadn't wanted to marry him but she had been duty-bound, leaving Brynner, her love, a burned-out shell.

Her duty, his curse.

Brynner alternated between hating her and forgiving her. Sometimes he did both; he hated her sense of duty, the one that had cost him everything. He hadn't been strong enough to pull himself out of his funk and move on with his life. All he could do was try to hide from the pain and pray that, some morning, he simply never woke up.

But that hadn't happened yet, so on this dreary and cold morning he was forced to face that pain once again. He stumbled away from the gates of Shadowmoor, out into the darkened moor beyond, his thoughts turning from Maud to where he would get his next drink. His father kept ale around the castle, and sometimes even wine, but he tried to hide it from his son who seemed to have an uncanny ability to sniff it out. Brynner wasn't beyond stealing ale or wine from local farmsteads, either, which he had done numerous times. That was why he always carried a dagger with him, in case he needed to threaten a farmer into turning over what alcohol he had.

Stumbling down the muddy path that led to the northeast, Brynner could see the landscape below the moor as the sun began to rise, all soft green patches and rolling hills. Fingers of gentle colors began to tint the horizon, creating stark contrast against the clouds that were moving their way east after the storm that had blown through overnight. He turned to look behind him somewhat, towards the southeast, where the horizon seemed to go on forever, and noticed figures on the road just below the moor.

They looked like specks with legs from where he was, men on horseback, but he could see them making the turn to the small road that led up to Shadowmoor. There were four of them that he could see, thundering up the road that was still muddy and slick from the rains.

Since the moors of Rombald weren't well-traveled, only men with particular business for what was upon the moor would be traveling up the narrow road, and especially so early in the morning. Curious, and somewhat concerned, Brynner turned to glance at Shadowmoor, which was perhaps a mile or so behind him. He'd wandered far this morning as he'd thought of Maud and days gone by. He was fairly certain he couldn't make it back to Shadowmoor's protective walls before the men on horseback reached him, so he returned his attention to his original direction, northeast, and began to walk quickly through the muddy path. There was a collection of boulders not far away where he knew he could find shelter of sorts, a hiding place to conceal himself from the riders. Clearly, he did not know their purpose, but the knight in him, the highly-trained warrior he liked to keep well-buried, told him to make himself scarce until the riders passed.

It was also true that he wasn't oblivious to what had gone on at Shadowmoor over the past four years. A local lord by the name of Bramley wanted Brynner's sister as well as Shadowmoor. Brynner had been away at Okehampton Castle when it all started and his father had never mentioned anything about it until Brynner had returned home and by then, Brynner didn't care about anything other than himself. Bramley's oppression hadn't mattered in his world and he'd promptly hid himself in the vault while Shadowmoor, and his family, suffered.

But Brynner stayed clear of all of that, only concerning himself with getting enough drink, but in moments like this, when he was lucid, and alone, he was concerned with four riders heading for Shadowmoor because they could quite possibly be Bramley's men. He knew they patrolled the area around Shadowmoor but he'd always managed to stay clear of them. This would, again, be one of those times. He planned to hide.

So he took off as fast as he could, heading towards the boulders that would shield him from the riders. Everything was so wet that it was difficult for him to gain traction in the mud and in his worn and ragged boots, it was even more difficult. He was sliding everywhere, trying to run, falling on the thick and wet heather that covered the moor and then picking himself up to continue on his path.

Before drink had swamped him, Brynner had been very fast indeed but the advent of alcohol every day for the past three years had dulled his senses. He wasn't as quick as he used to be. Struggling and slipping, he continued towards the boulders.

Unfortunately, his antics had attracted the attention he was trying to avoid. As the sun rose against the stark moor, it wasn't difficult to see something moving along the hillside, scrambling across the wetness left from the rains. The four men who had been heading up the side of the hill had seen him from afar and had closed in on him easily. Brynner had no idea they were upon him until he heard the thunder of hooves and, by that time, it was too late.

Panicked, Brynner tried to scramble up part of the hill that was too steep for the horses to go but he couldn't get his footing and ended up tumbling down. He rolled down the hill, ending up in the center of the four horsemen.

Covered in mud, with a throbbing head and now with fear in his heart, Brynner sat up, his baleful expression on those surrounding him.

"What do you want?" he demanded. "Why do you bother me?"

The man in the lead was big and well equipped. He rode a stunning roan warmblood and he was dressed as a knight but he wasn't wearing a helm. None of the men were, which was strange considering the amount of weaponry they had with them. They looked as if they were ready for battle. The man on the roan peered down at Brynner, on his arse in the mud.

"Why are you running?" he asked in a heavy French accent. "What are you doing up here, far away from civilization?"

Brynner scowled. "That is not your affair."

The Frenchman sat back in his saddle, pondering the reply, before looking around, back over his left shoulder to see Shadowmoor up in the distance as it perched upon the crag like a great beast of prey. He scratched his head.

"That old castle is the only thing up here," he said. "Did you come from it?"

"If I did?"

"It was simply a question, *mon seigneur.*"

They asked about Shadowmoor, which tipped Brynner off that these men may be exactly who he feared they were. *Bramley.* He was feeling vastly threatened and trying not to let it show. He had been a knight, once, and a very good one, and that training began to kick in. It had been a long time since he'd needed it. He forced himself to calm and collect himself because panic would only get him killed. Slowly, he stood up, trying to brush the mud off of his breeches.

"That castle means nothing to me and I mean nothing to it," he said evenly. "I will be on my way now."

He started to move, pushing his way out from between the horses. But the Frenchman wouldn't let him go so easily.

"Wait," he said. "Please do not go, not yet. What is your name? Can we at least be civil to one another?"

Brynner paused to look at him. "Why?" he asked. "You mean nothing to me, either."

The Frenchman smiled at the answer. The dirty, disheveled man on foot was so bitter that it was rather amusing. "And you mean nothing to me," he said. "But I would like to know if you know anything about that castle up there. Have you been out here walking the moors for very long?"

Brynner shook his head. "Not very long."

"Have you seen anyone come to, or leave, the castle?"

Brynner's expression turned impatient. "No one comes or goes from that place," he said. "It is dead, like these moors. People live there, but they are dead, too. The whole place is dead."

"You speak as if you know this for certain."

Brynner thought, at that point, that he had probably given too much of himself away. He had tried not to but his head hurt and he wasn't thinking clearly. But, then again, he rarely thought clearly these days, so it was inevitable that he falter. Now it was a matter of trying to cover for his foolish tongue.

"I have grown up on these lands," Brynner said. He was being deliberately vague and, in a smart move, turned the conversation away from him and on to them. "Where did you come from? These roads are not well traveled. You must have been heading for the castle if you are on this moor. What business do you have at that place?"

The Frenchman's dark blue eyes settled appraisingly on Brynner before speaking. The wind, whipping around them, lifted his shaggy blond hair.

"As you said, that is not your affair," he replied. "You will not tell me yours and I will not tell you mine. We are at an impasse."

Brynner shrugged and turned away. "Good," he said firmly. "Then there is no more to say to one another. I will wish you fair winds and Godspeed, then, and be on my way."

One of the men moved his horse so that Brynner couldn't push past the animal. Boxed in and frustrated, Brynner turned to the Frenchman with a scowl.

"Now what?" he demanded. "I have nothing more to tell you. My aching head and I would be grateful if you could allow us to pass."

The Frenchman leaned forward on his saddle, noticing a jug that had fallen to the side when the man had slid down the hill. It now lay half-buried in the wet heather. He dipped his head in the direction of the jug.

"The root of your evils, *mon seigneur*?" he asked.

Brynner turned to see what he was referring to, embarrassed that the evidence was there for all to see. He may have been a drunkard but it was a private affair as far as he was concerned. He didn't like to go announcing it all over the place. In a huff, he stomped over to pick up the jug. Embarrassed or not, he wasn't going to leave it behind.

"It is the root of many evils," he said, bending down to collect it. "May I go now?"

The Frenchman's gaze lingered on Brynner and, for a moment, he didn't say anything. Behind those dark blue eyes, there was a good deal going on. *Calculating.* Now, he had an idea as to finding out what this man knew. Where he came from. Perhaps he could find out even more than he'd hoped for.

As many times as he had come up to the moor, named for an ancient Saxon king, he'd never run into anyone like the man standing before him. All he'd come across were frightened peasants who could barely speak, people scraping the land, trying to scratch out an existence. But not this man; he was well spoken and seemingly intelligent. But he was also in a very bad state and the Frenchman could smell the alcohol on him, even at a distance. It was a weakness that the Frenchman wanted to exploit.

Something told him he had a prime opportunity right in front of him.

"What are you drinking?" he asked Brynner. "Whatever it is, I know where there is better drink. And large quantities of it."

Something flashed in Brynner's eyes, something that foretold of great interest in the Frenchman's words, but that flash of interest was quickly gone. What replaced it was something that could only be described as humiliation.

Sorrow.

"I have what I need," he said, lifting the jug. "Move your men and I will be on my way."

"I will pay for your drink," the Frenchman said quickly, not wanting to lose this opportunity. "You need not pay for any of it. I travel about with these three fools for companionship and it is rare to speak with a stranger. Come and drink with me. Your companionship is payment enough."

The thought of flowing wine was enough to cause Brynner to swallow any pride or fear he may have felt. He knew it was wrong; God help him, he knew it. He knew he could be placing himself in a horrible situation. But lured by the thought of endless alcohol, he couldn't help the interest. Like a siren's song, it called to him and he could not resist.

It was stronger than he was.

"Where?" he finally asked. "Where will we go?"

The Frenchman pointed to the east, in the direction of the village of Ilkley. Nestled against the base of the soggy hills, it was a fairly bustling town with commerce.

"There is an inn called The Bridge and Arms in town," he said. "I have supped there before. Good food and drink. Come and join me. It looks as if you could use a meal."

Brynner didn't care about the meal. He only cared about the drink. Everything in his body was screaming for it. Yet, he was still thinking cautiously in spite of his need. He presumed that the men wouldn't try to kill or harm him if they were in a public place with witnesses and even people who might give him protection. More than that, he was fairly certain he didn't have a choice in this situation. They weren't going to allow him to leave. But he wanted the drink so badly that he was willing to dance with the devil to get it.

"I know the place," Brynner replied. "I've not been there in years."

"Then come with me."

Brynner didn't say a word. He simply started heading in the direction the four men had come from, to the road that would take them back down the hill to the road that ran north and south along the edges of the moor.

To the drink that await him.

As the sun crested the horizon and cast rays of light over the wet land, Brynner and his four new companions made their way down the moor to the road below, heading towards The Bridge and Arms. They slipped and slid in the mud all the way down the hill.

All the while, however, Brynner kept wondering what these men wanted of him, but he was fairly certain he already knew. He was certain they were the same men who had been harassing Shadowmoor for years. Bramley and his men wanted Shadowmoor and wanted Liselotte, and they'd already abducted one l'Audacieux son. Brynner didn't know that Gunnar had been returned the night before, however, and assumed that he was now the second abducted l'Audacieux male. In his own stupidity, they'd managed to corner him.

But he was a different case altogether. He wasn't a young boy, but a man and heir to the property Bramley sought. Once they found that out, and Brynner was more than likely sure they would once alcohol loosened his tongue, he wouldn't be surprised if there wasn't some kind of negotiation involved with him to try and gain the place.

With enough alcohol, Brynner knew he'd agree to anything.

And that concerned him.

As for the Frenchman, he wasn't quite sure what he had in the slovenly man but something told him that his fortune had been good this morning. At least, that was what he thought, but it wasn't to be the case – he would miss the opportunity he should have been looking for less than an hour later when the object of his lord's greed, a lovely woman with pale skin and bronze hair, left the gates of the destitute fortress and headed north. By that time, however, the Frenchman and his guest, a man whom he soon confirmed to be the brother of the sought-after woman, were well on their way to being drunk and making plans. The Frenchman discovered very quickly that his guest craved alcohol more than money, so it wasn't a matter of a bribe.

It was the matter of a promise.

The situation was about to become quite interesting.

☙

THE STORMY WEATHER had cleared up and there was hardly a cloud in the sky. It was breezy as the sun rose, reaching fingers of gold and pink across the landscape, stretching out as far as the eye could see.

It was a bucolic vision just after dawn and would have been quite perfect had it not been for the fact that man, beast, and land were a sopping, muddy mess. Everything was wet and the oversaturated ground was littered with massive puddles of water. As Daniel emerged out into the ward from the keep, he made sure to avoid those watery traps as he crossed the bailey and headed towards the stables.

It was cold outside, too, a far cry from the warm room he had spent the night in. The very tiny room had been surprisingly clean and the bed had been mostly comfortable, so he really had nothing to complain over and he'd slept very well. He didn't much equate comfort with this destitute fortress, but he'd been pleasantly surprised by Gunnar l'Audacieux's small bed.

Therefore, after a heavy sleep through the storming night, he'd awoken refreshed and proceeded to dress. Donning a heavy linen tunic that smelled like a dead body beneath his mail coat, because he'd not washed it in weeks, and then donning a heavy leather coat with fur trim around the neck and sleeves, he'd headed out into the coming dawn.

Shadowmoor's box-shaped keep was surrounded by its own moat, a ditch dug around the structure while the structure itself was slightly elevated. It was cold; the eastern horizon turned pastel shades and breath hung in the air in foggy puffs. Daniel looked at his surroundings as he headed for the stables, finding some interest in Shadowmoor in general. People were about at this early morning hour, scrounging for firewood for cooking fires, and the smell of smoke was already heavy in the air. He looked at the faces as he passed them; everyone looked tired and hungry, wrapped in their meager rags against the freezing temperatures. The inability to create work for themselves or trade with neighboring villages, all of these things prevented by Bramley, had taken their toll. Daniel thought that everyone looked very much like the walking dead.

Hopeless.

But there was more to it than even that. As he neared the stables, it occurred to him that there were, literally, no animals at all at Shadowmoor – no dogs, no chickens, and he realized when he'd been in the stable the day before that he'd only seen two other horses. No animals because they had all been eaten by starving people. Although he'd had mutton the night before, he recalled that it tasted old and he thought it was perhaps because Lady Liselotte had been trying to stretch the meat.

Perhaps because that was all they had left.

It was a rather pathetic thought but it underscored the desperation of the people of Shadowmoor, desperation that idiot Bramley had forced them into. After a good night's sleep, Daniel was feeling more compelled than ever to help these people although, even after his explanation on his reasons to Etzel the previous night, there really wasn't any true factor why he should. He hadn't particularly made an enemy out of Bramley, or at least he didn't think he did in the long run, but he'd used it as an excuse to stay and help. Something was pulling him towards this destitute, hopeless place… or perhaps *someone* was pulling him towards it.

That was more than likely the answer.

Liselotte.

A woman with pale skin and bronze-colored hair. There was something sorrowful about her due to her circumstances but beneath that sorrow, he could see the fight and determination. She may have been persecuted but she hadn't given up. He hadn't spoken to her a tremendous amount yesterday but in the brief conversations they'd had, he'd sensed a good deal of strength in her. She wanted to fight, and she wanted to win, even though her circumstances had prevented much of that. Still, she didn't surrender, but there had been something in her manner that suggested she was very happy to have help in her fight, help in the form of Daniel.

Perhaps he simply liked the idea of being her savior, of coming to the aid of people who had nowhere else to turn. Or perhaps he liked the idea of being her savior alone; he wasn't sure. It was a matter of pride, too – he had found a purpose he could be proud of. Or perhaps the simple fact of the matter was that he wanted a beautiful girl to be indebted to him, to admire him and to show her gratitude.

Perhaps this entire endeavor was ego and nothing more.

But he would have to figure it out later because he had tasks to complete on this day. Just as he entered the stables, he nearly ran headlong into Etzel and Liselotte and Gunnar. Ares was saddled, as were the two other horses in the stable, and it looked to Daniel as if everyone was waiting for him. The horses were ready, and so were Liselotte and Gunnar. They were both heavily wrapped in wool clothing and Liselotte wore an old faded cloak, lined with fox fur, that must have been very beautiful, once. Daniel came to a halt when he saw the crowd and his eyebrows lifted.

"So I am the lazy one today?" he asked. "You are all eager to go to town and I am the one who could not drag my carcass out of bed? I am ashamed."

Gunnar laughed; even Liselotte and Etzel grinned. "We wanted to be ready to depart when you were, my lord," Liselotte said. "We have not been waiting long."

Daniel's gaze lingered on Liselotte in the early morning light. She was dressed in faded clothing, but on her, they were the garments of a queen. She held herself regally, with pride, and her hair was pulled into a braid that draped elegantly over one shoulder. Truthfully, Daniel could have stared at her all day.

"Forgive me for making you wait at all," he said, "but I found that I slept so solidly that before I realized it, morning had come."

"Here!" Gunnar was suddenly in front of him, thrusting something in his face. "To break your fast!"

Daniel had to step back in order to see what Gunnar was so excited to show him. He could see that it was a piece of bread from last night, now hard and crumbly. It was a rather large piece and he hesitated before accepting it.

"This is quite kind of you," he said, looking at the boy. "Have you broken your fast this morning?"

The enthusiastic smile faded from Gunnar's face and he suddenly appeared uncertain. "I… I did not," he said, glancing to his father and sister over his shoulder. "But I am not hungry. This is for you."

Daniel smiled faintly at the boy, putting his hand on the blond head. "You are more than generous, but I, too, am not hungry," he said, suspecting that the family had gone without food that morning so they could give it all to their guest. "If you do not eat this, it will go to waste."

Gunnar was quite uncertain now, lowering the chunk of bread in his hand and looking to his father and sister for guidance. Daniel could see the indecision and he patted the boy on the head before removing his hand and turning to his horse.

"Hurry and eat it, young Gunnar," he said. "Otherwise, my horse, who is a glutton, will smell it and he will want to eat it. I would rather see you have it than him. Were the horses fed, by the way?"

Etzel nodded. "They were fed dried grasses, my lord," he said. "I am sorry that I do not have grain to offer your horse. He is a very fine animal."

Daniel nodded, slapping the beast on his shiny black neck before mounting. "Aye, he is," he said. "His name is Ares and he is like a brother to me. We have seen much together, he and I. It looks as if he has been brushed."

Etzel nodded, moving to help Liselotte mount her horse. "He has been," he said. "My stable master loves horses. He sleeps with them, in fact, so they are never alone. I am sure he took great pleasure in grooming your steed."

Daniel slipped his boots into the stirrups and gathered his reins. "And I am equally sure that Ares took pleasure in being groomed," he said. "He loves attention and if he does not get enough of it, he will kick and snort until someone pets him. And if he is not petted the correct way, he will bite. He is very spoiled."

The horse threw his head as if to agree and Daniel grinned, directing the horse out of the stable yard. Liselotte was on a small mare that had seen better days, an old animal with a sunken back. Etzel picked up Gunnar, with the piece of bread still in his hand, and put him on the animal behind his sister. As Gunnar held fast to his sister's slender waist, the horse followed Daniel out of the stable yard at a leisurely pace. Etzel followed.

"I have thought much on our conversation last night, my lord," Etzel said to Daniel, "about heading north to find a messenger, and I do believe the village of Siglesdene would be the best place for you to go. When you leave Shadowmoor, go west to the main road and then north. That road will take you right into Siglesdene."

Daniel was listening, closing tight his gloves against the cold temperatures. "How far?"

"It will take you about three hours, less if you move swiftly."

"If Bramley's men are watching the roads, then I want to move swiftly."

Etzel understood. "They usually watched Shadowmoor but since they abducted Gunnar, they stopped watching," he said. He was hesitant to say anything more but knew that he must. "Now that my boy is returned, it is quite possible they will be watching Shadowmoor again, knowing you have brought him home. Be vigilant, my lord – they will want what you have."

Daniel looked at him. "What is that?"

Etzel glanced at Liselotte. "My daughter," he replied. "That is all they want."

Daniel turned to look at the woman, riding silent and lovely atop the old mare. He considered what Etzel said before pulling Ares to a halt. "Then get her off that mare and put her on with me," he said. "I am sure the mare will run much faster with just Gunnar's weight on it and Ares is very strong. He can easily carry two people swiftly."

Etzel was already on the move, shifting the horseback passengers until Liselotte was seated behind Daniel and Gunnar had the old mare all to himself. The young boy was quite thrilled, actually, for now he could pretend to be a knight on his mighty steed, just as Sir Daniel was. Once Liselotte was situated and Daniel could feel her soft hands holding on to his torso for support, he spurred Ares forward again.

"How many men does Bramley usually have out and about," he asked Etzel as they approached the iron-web main gate. "Do they travel in patrols?"

Etzel nodded to the question. "They travel in patrols of two or three men," he said. "I have seen as many as four patrols out at one time but as of late, there have been less. However, as I said, that may have changed since Gunnar was returned to us yesterday."

"You think that Bramley will have his men sitting on Shadowmoor again?"

Etzel nodded. "It is possible."

Daniel thought very seriously about that. It wouldn't do any good for him to purchase supplies in town and hire a wagon to bring them back to Shadowmoor only to have to fight off Bramley's men, who could quite possibly be lying in wait for them. Nay, he didn't like those odds at all. He had to have men to protect the supplies as well as the l'Audacieux offspring. *Liselotte.* God's Bones, he would feel horrible if his lack of foresight caused her to fall into Bramley's hands. And with that, he began to cook up a plan.

It was necessary.

"When we leave, you will lock these gates and remain inside, no matter what," Daniel told Etzel. "I will return as soon as I can, but you will lock up Shadowmoor and stay here until I return. Is that clear?"

Etzel nodded. "That is a normal way of life for us, my lord. You need not stress the obvious."

Daniel nodded, satisfied. "Good," he said, watching as the big iron gates began to slowly crank open. "If we do not return tonight, do not be afraid. I am not sure how long it is going to take us to conduct business so do not be concerned if we do not return right away. I have missives to send and other business to conduct. It will take time."

Etzel nodded, wondering if he was doing the right thing by allowing two of his children to leave with a man he'd only met the day before. Was he being foolish? Was it possible that Bramley had even hired this man who called himself de Lohr, a man who had pushed his way into Shadowmoor and demanded the trust of the occupants? Etzel's determination that Daniel should be the answer to prayer began to waver a bit, but he fought it. He was fairly certain that Bramley hadn't sent him, especially based on what Gunnar had told him. Still, it was difficult for him to watch his children go with a man he'd only just met, one who promised to help him. What was it he had said to his daughter the previous night?

We have no alternative but to go on faith.

That was a true statement. Still, it was very hard to watch his children ride out with the knight. Even after the gates closed behind them, Etzel climbed to the battlements and watched the big black horse and the little brown mare travel down through the green and brown moors until they were out of sight.

Then, the real worrying began.

CHAPTER FOUR

THE TOWN.

Liselotte wasn't used to seeing so many people. So many well-fed, busy people. It was something of a shock as they entered the outskirts of Siglesdene a little over three hours after leaving Shadowmoor. The sun was up and, on this day in mid-March, it seemed as if every farmer in a twenty-mile radius had turned up with produce and animals to sell. Liselotte had never seen so much merchandise – from cabbage to fruit to bees – and she was shocked.

Shocked… and disheartened.

Was it true that life went on like this, lively and busy and full, while she and her family were trapped in their bastion on the hill by a greedy lord? Was it really true that life went on around them and people were actually happy? She couldn't honestly remember the last time she had ventured into a town because Bramley had kept her so bottled in. It was safer not to try. But riding with Daniel on his fat black horse, she felt safe as she had never felt safe in her life. It was difficult to describe but she knew that she liked it. She was both thrilled and relieved and, truth be told, rather giddy about it. But it didn't take her long to realize that the true source of her giddiness wasn't just the town.

It was the knight.

He was a very big man with big arms and hands, and she rather liked riding behind him, politely holding on to him so she wouldn't fall off with the horse's bouncy, prancing gait, but it was a fact that she had never been this close to a man who wasn't a relative. Even before the event of Bramley, Etzel had kept her fairly sequestered from men, so this situation was quite new to her. The fact that she was here bespoke of Etzel's utter trust in Daniel de Lohr, as if the man's rescue of Gunnar gave Etzel complete faith to trust him, alone, with his precious daughter. Etzel had spent four years protecting her from Lord Bramley but de Lohr had managed to dissolve that inherent protectiveness, from father to daughter, in one heroic move.

And Liselotte wasn't the least bit upset about it.

Truthfully, she was glad her father had permitted her to go to town with Sir Daniel, even if he *had* allowed Gunnar to come along as a kind of juvenile chaperone. Surely Daniel wouldn't do anything unseemly with a child about. But the mere fact that Gunnar was along so soon after returning home after his abduction told Liselotte that Etzel was truly insane with trust over Daniel. There was no other explanation.

We have no alternative but to go on faith.

That was what her father had told her the previous night and it was clear he had meant what he'd said. So Liselotte held tight to Daniel as they entered the outskirts of the town, bustling with activity. Peasants were moving stock in and out of the town and there were innumerable vegetable carts. Children ran about with dogs chasing after them, barking, and as the three of them pushed towards the heart of the town, they entered the merchant's part of the village. Near the center of town, and the well that provided water for a goodly portion of the village, the merchants of Siglesdene were deep in the heat of their business for the day.

Liselotte looked at all of the bustle around her, of the amounts of food, and she felt rather sick. It was so very clear that life outside of Shadowmoor was prosperous. She was sick on behalf of her family, who had to scrape by on wild grains and the occasional animal that was caught and killed, while others in Yorkshire didn't seem to have that same level of hardship. Of course, it was March, and the produce wasn't as fresh or plentiful as it would become in the summer months, but the vegetables and other foodstuffs she was seeing were those that had been stored away. Farmers still had to make their living and people still had to eat, even when crops weren't abundantly producing. As she looked on, Daniel startled her from her thoughts.

"May I make a suggestion, my lady, on where to start?" he asked. "If I may be so bold, it seems to me that we should find the grain merchant first and purchase what we can from him. Grain is the most precious of commodities in this season. We should get it before others do."

Liselotte could only see his profile as he turned his head to talk to her. It was such a handsome profile and she almost lost sight of his initial question as she studied it.

"Aye," she said quickly, trying not to sound as if she were day-dreaming about the man's comely looks. "Grains will be a popular purchase. Uh… Sir Daniel?"

His head was still turned, looking at her from the corner of his eye. "My lady, I would be honored if you would simply call me Daniel," he said. "No one calls me 'Sir'."

"Why not?"

He shrugged. "It is too formal," he said. "I do not like to hear it from people I am familiar or friendly with. It is a barrier of formality that I do not like. Therefore, I would ask that you simply call me Daniel."

Liselotte was surprised at the lack of propriety coming from a knight of his caliber. But the man had been friendly and congenial since the beginning of their association, so she supposed she really shouldn't have been all that astonished with it. He had so far conveyed a friendly, sometimes humorous personality, unlike anything she'd ever seen before.

"Very well," she said. "If that is your wish."

"It is," Daniel said, looking to Gunnar on the horse beside them. "But you must call me 'O Great One'. Is that clear?"

Gunnar could sense the humor and he grinned. "Why can't I call you Daniel, too?"

Daniel pretended to be imperious. "Because I demand respect from those I have saved," he said with mock severity. "Mayhap tomorrow I will permit you to call me Daniel, but not today. Today, you will call me 'O Great One' at all times. Is that clear?"

Gunnar giggled. "It is."

"It is *what*?"

"O Great One!"

Gunnar was snorting as he said it and Liselotte grinned as well, watching the interaction between her brother and Daniel. God's Blood, it was good to have her brother back and smiling again. She'd missed him so terribly.

"I will tell you a secret," she said to Daniel, eyeing Gunnar as she spoke. "He is very ticklish and he hates to have his ears pulled. If he disobeys you, such punishment would torment him."

Daniel grinned broadly at the boy. "Is that true?" he asked. "Are you really ticklish?"

Gunnar's eyes flew open wide. "You will never know!"

"You will never know *what*?"

"O Great One!"

Daniel fought off laughter as he turned away from the boy, who was kicking furiously at the old mare, trying to coerce it into moving forward. Daniel made a noise with his tongue, like clucking, and that was enough of a noise to move Ares forward without any kick at all. As the big black horse moved forward, the lazy mare followed.

Peering around Daniel's big frame, Liselotte could see that they were heading to an area that looked like a livery; there were horses in a small corral, a few sheep, goats, and a barn-like structure. There were people moving in and out of the structure with sacks of grain over their shoulders. It was a busy place.

"Daniel," Liselotte said quietly. "How much grain do you intend to purchase?"

Christ, he loved hearing his name come out of her mouth, spoken in her sweet and sultry voice. He could have listened to that all day and well into forever. But there wasn't time for sweetness like that, at least not at the moment. Eyes on the barn-like structure ahead, he spoke.

"I am not entirely sure," he said. "I would see what the price is first and then we will proceed."

"You will not buy too much, will you?"

"That is for me to decide."

It was a rather short reply, as if it weren't any of her business, so Liselotte didn't ask any more questions after that because he didn't seem willing to discuss it. As they reached the livery with its goats and sheep and horses, Gunnar immediately jumped off the mare and ran to see the goats. There were several young kids and he was quite excited about them.

Daniel watched the boy pet and play with the goats, a smile on his face, as he helped Liselotte off of the horse. When her feet hit the ground, he dismounted after her, his gaze seeking out the man in charge. As he hunted for the man, Liselotte spoke.

"Gunnar had a pet goat but we were forced to eat it."

Her voice was soft and sorrowful. Daniel looked to her, curiously, before turning to see Gunnar sitting on the ground, hugging one of the young kids as if it were the most precious thing in the world. Daniel tried not to let his mood darken as he watched the boy kiss the little goat. A young boy's pet had been a victim of their poverty, a sorrowful thing, indeed.

"You did what you had to do in order to survive," he said quietly. "You mustn't feel guilty over it."

Liselotte watched her little brother, grief on her features. "He loved that goat," she said. "He had raised it since it was a kid and it followed him everywhere. He even slept with it. But when it became apparent we would have to eat it, as there was virtually nothing left, he cried for days. I felt so terrible for him but we had no choice."

Daniel's gaze lingered on Gunnar as the boy giggled when the little goat began nibbling at his hair. "You did what you had to do," he repeated. "But you needn't worry. I will replace the goat."

Liselotte looked at him sharply. "I did not tell you that so that you would buy him another goat," she said. "I simply told you that to explain why he ran straight for the goats and why he, even now, wallows in the mud with them."

Daniel nodded, turning away from her to once again seek out the man in charge. "I know," he said evenly. "But he seems quite happy with his little friend and after the trials the lad has been forced to endure, mayhap a goat will be just what he needs to regain his humor."

Liselotte didn't know what to say to that. She watched as Daniel headed over to a man he thought might be in charge. In truth, she really wasn't sure what to say any longer to Daniel and his determined ideals. He seemed convinced that he was going to buy them the world and she wasn't convinced she could discourage him. She'd tried, Etzel had tried, but Daniel was resolute to do what he wanted to do. He was stubborn, that one. Gallant, but stubborn. She had never in her life met anyone like him.

And she rather liked him and his determination.

It was hard to keep the smile off her face now as Daniel and the man in charge of the livery entered intense negotiations about what Daniel needed and just how much he was willing to pay. She pretended to be watching Gunnar but her senses were attuned to Daniel. He had a very congenial manner about him and rather than be firm and stern with the man who owned the livery, he engaged the man in pleasant talk about the weather, the local harvests, and eventually having the man talk about himself to the point where he knew a good deal about the man and it was as if they were friends already. Liselotte could hear them laughing.

Unable to deny her attention any longer, her gaze moved to Daniel and she watched him in animated conversation. There was something very magnetic about him, an attraction she found very hard to resist. But there was no point in dreaming about a man who would never settle down or take a wife. Even if he could, she wasn't in his class. She had seen his reaction last night to Etzel's proposal offer and she'd seen the man's revulsion. At least, that's what she thought it was and she didn't blame him. She was sure that Daniel, from the great and powerful de Lohr family and a future earl himself, could have any lady in the entire world. A young woman living in poverty, with no fine clothing or fine education, was of no interest to him.

The smile faded from her face. She couldn't hold out hope for what could never be. Lowering her gaze, she turned away from Daniel and the livery owner and wandered over to the edge of the livery property overlooking the avenue. While Daniel and the livery owner chatted and Gunnar still played with the goats, Liselotte watched the people on the avenue go by. The sun was higher in the sky now and the day was bright, wind still whipping about, blowing leaves down the street as everyone went about their business. It was actually a lovely day, with everything fresh and clean after the storm, and she felt much as if she'd been asleep for the past year, hidden away from the busy world. So much of the scene before her was new and exciting.

The livery was situated near the center of the commerce district and there were businesses grouped together – spices, wine, and food items were across the street, down to the left, while directly across the street were furs and cloth. Additionally, next to a very large cloth merchant was a seamstress who had all manner of loosely stitched dresses hanging from the top of her stall and in the doorway. It looked to be a thriving business with a good deal of merchandise.

It immediately had her interest. Liselotte could see the surcoats, blouses, and aprons hanging up on display and she was enthralled with the colors and fabrics as they waved about in the breeze. She'd never seen such beautiful things and her feminine heart, the one that loved all things beautiful as most women did, was drawn to the sight. She couldn't resist. As Daniel conversed and Gunnar played, Liselotte slipped across the street to the beckoning garments.

The very first one in her line of sight was a form-fitting garment with tin buttons down the front, made from a heavy fabric that had been dyed a shade of lavender. The sleeves were long, the neckline high, and it was absolutely magnificent.

Awed, Liselotte reached out to gently touch the fabric. It was soft, like angel's wings. But then she looked at her own garment, something very old and worn that had belonged to her mother, and she was suddenly very embarrassed at her appearance. She wished she had such a fine gown as the lavender one to wear. But her embarrassment didn't last long because her attention fell on a very long, billowy, woolen gown dyed an exquisite shade of deep blue. Curiosity and awe took over again. She went to look at the blue garment, inspecting the craftsmanship on it, when she heard a voice behind her.

"You have good taste," someone said. "I had my eye on that dress, too."

Startled, Liselotte turned to see a young woman, about her age, standing a few feet away. The young woman was petite, with dark blond hair and blue eyes, and she was very finely dressed. Overwhelmingly self-conscious in the face of such a well-dressed woman, Liselotte let go of the blue dress and stepped away, giving the young woman a wide birth.

"Forgive me," she said. "I did not mean to… I am sorry that I was in your way."

The young woman shook her head. "You are not in my way," she said. "In fact, my father would be glad if you stood between me and that garment. He does not want to buy me anymore dresses but, of course, he cannot deny me."

She was grinning as she said it but Liselotte was feeling uncertain and awkward. She wasn't very socially adept outside of Shadowmoor, mostly because she was never really around people that she didn't know. Shadowmoor was an isolated world, so to speak to those outside of that world was not something that happened very frequently. Liselotte was out of practice.

"It… it will look lovely on you, I am sure," Liselotte said.

She started to turn away, to make haste back to the livery, but the young woman stopped her. "I have not seen you around here before," she said. "I come here weekly and know most everyone on the street of merchants, but I've not seen you. Do you live nearby?"

Liselotte paused in her flight, turning to the young woman and feeling very nervous. "I… I do not live too far away," she said. "I… that is to say, I do not come into town very much. I have not been here in a long time."

The young woman was appraising Liselotte as she spoke, and that meant her clothing. Old, out of date, and repeatedly mended, they were hardly the garments of a well-brought up lady, but the young woman didn't show any particular reaction to the terrible clothing. In fact, she showed no real reaction at all.

"Then you live locally?" she asked.

"I do."

The young woman smiled. "My name is Glennie," she said. "Glennie de Royans. My father is Baron Cononley. We live a few miles away at Netherghyll Castle. What is your name?"

Liselotte dipped into a polite curtsey. "I am Liselotte l'Audacieux," she said. "I am from Shadowmoor."

Glennie cocked her head curiously. "Shadowmoor?" she repeated. "Is that not the Saxon settlement?"

Liselotte nodded. "It is," she said. "You have heard of it?"

Glennie nodded. "I have, indeed," she said. "I was born at Netherghyll and recently returned home from court, so I know this area well. Shadowmoor always had an eerie, ghostly feel to me. The name evokes images of phantoms and lost loves and moonlit moors. It is very romantic!"

She was giggling as she said it and, in spite of her discomfort, Liselotte couldn't help but grin. A pleasant conversation with another young woman, seemingly friendly, was difficult to resist.

"It was originally called *Beschattet Erde* a very long time ago," she said. "That means shadowed earth, or shadowed land. I am not sure when it became Shadowmoor but it has been called that since my father's grandfather. A long time, indeed."

Glennie was listening with interest. "Shadowed land," she murmured as if seeing the romance in such a title. Then, she eyed Liselotte a moment before pushing past her and towards the blue dress Liselotte had been inspecting. "I am happy to know you, Liselotte. Since returning home, I have no friends here at all. If you live at Shadowmoor, then you are not very far from Netherghyll. Mayhap you will come to my home on my invitation and stay for a visit. I should like the companionship. With only my brother and father and nurse as company, I am ready to climb the walls and throw myself from the battlements out of sheer boredom."

Come to my home. Liselotte had never had such an invitation; not even a hint of one. She could hardly believe what she was hearing and, truthfully, had no idea how to respond. Was it even possible that this friendly young woman should actually want her company? Dressed as a pauper as she was, she was astounded at the possibility and, that being the case, she was naturally suspicious of the woman's motives. She tried to remain neutral and noncommittal.

"That is very kind of you, my lady," she said. "I… I do not have any friends, either. I never leave my home. Today is a rare day because…."

"My lady!" came a shout. "Lady Liselotte!"

A voice came from across the avenue and both Liselotte and Glennie turned to see Daniel heading in their direction with Gunnar trailing after him. Gunnar was skipping and hoping, sliding in the mud, but it was obvious that the lad wasn't happy. He had no goat in his arms, frowning at Daniel as Daniel focused on Liselotte with great concern.

"My lady," he said again as he drew close. "What happened? Why did you run off?"

Liselotte could see the concern in his expression and she could hear it in his voice. Her heart leapt at the realization, so very flattered that he might actually feel concern for her safety. Even if nothing could ever come of that concern, she was still touched. But she didn't want him to be angry with her for walking away while his back was turned and she hastened to soothe his manner.

"My apologies, Sir Daniel," she said quickly. "You were engaged and I did not see any harm in looking at this merchandise. I was still close to the livery. It has been so long since… that is to say, I have not seen such fine… I mean… I did not mean to pull you away from your business, my lord. I am very sorry."

She suddenly bolted past Glennie, bypassing Daniel, but Daniel reached out and grasped her by the arm before she could get away. Her cheeks were red; he could see that. He hadn't meant to be harsh with her but when he'd discovered her missing, it had truly frightened him. Considering what he'd been told about the man who very much wanted to have her, Daniel was thinking that perhaps some of Bramley's men must have snatched her, at the very least, until he saw her across the avenue speaking with a well-dressed blond. Still, he'd been given quite a start which must have come across rather harshly. He hastened to ease his manner with her.

"No need to be sorry," he said steadily, preventing her from moving any further. "I thought mayhap a gaggle of trolls had carted you off. I think between Gunnar and me, we might have a chance of saving you from the Troll King, but I am very glad we do not have to put that theory to the test. So you are looking at merchandise? I think you should. I also think you should pick out a few dresses for us to take home."

He was looking at the garments hanging over his head by the time he was finished speaking and Liselotte looked at him in utter shock.

"Take… take some home?" she repeated.

Daniel let go of her arm, his gaze on the lavender outerdress with the tin buttons that had originally caught Liselotte's attention. He fingered the fabric.

"Aye," he said, nodding firmly as he pulled the dress off the peg. "I like this one. What others are there?"

"This one, my lord," Glennie said, holding up the dark blue wool so that Daniel could see it. "The lady was looking at this one, too. I think it would look splendid on her."

Daniel looked at the pretty blond, dipping his head gallantly. "And you would be correct, my lady," he said, turning to glance at Liselotte. "You two know each other, then?"

Glennie shook her head. "We have only just introduced ourselves," she said, her gaze seriously scrutinizing the very handsome Daniel. "I realize it is extremely improper for me to introduce myself, but I am willing to break protocol. I am Lady Glennie de Royans. My father is Baron Cononley. We live at Netherghyll Castle, not far from here."

De Royans.

A warning bell went off in Daniel's mind at the mention of the name. In fact, it was more like a screaming clang. It was as if cold water had just been thrown on him. The mere speaking of the name caused him to falter for a moment. But it was only a brief moment. Quickly, he regained his composure but he was still reeling with surprise. He knew that name; God help him, he knew it. And it wasn't in a good way. His heart began to pound, just a bit.

"Lady Glennie," he repeated suspiciously. "*De Royans*?"

"Aye."

He blinked, a gesture of realization. "Surely… surely you are not Adalind de Aston's Glennie?"

Glennie's face lit up. "You know Adalind?" she gasped. "She is my best and most true friend! Oh, how do you know her? Please tell me!"

Daniel felt as if he'd been struck. The composure he'd so recently recovered fractured again, stronger this time, and all of the wind left him. It was a struggle not to react to the revelation before him – Adalind's Glennie.

Sister of the man I helped kill.

"Adalind is my niece," Daniel said as evenly as he could. "Her mother is my eldest sister. My name is Daniel de Lohr. I saw Adalind, just this past year, and she spoke very often of you. She said that the two of you fostered together at Winchester Castle."

Glennie was nodding eagerly. "We did!" she confirmed. "For many years, we were the best of friends! But Adalind left me last year to return home. I could not stay at court without her because it simply wasn't the same, so I came home as well. I have not spoken to her in so long. Is she well? Please tell me any news of her, sir. I would love to hear it!"

Daniel simply looked at her, trying very hard to remain polite, because the irony of running in to this woman was unfathomable. Of every town in England, Daniel had ended up in a locale that reminded him of a very bitter and frightening episode in his life. He was struggling with his composure, with his terrible memories of the de Royans name and hoping the lady didn't notice.

Where to start with news of his niece, Adalind de Aston du Bois? Daughter of his eldest sister, Adalind had returned to Canterbury Castle from Winchester the previous year, much pursued by men from court. Although Daniel hadn't been at Canterbury at the time, he'd heard tale from Adalind's eventual husband, Sir Maddoc du Bois, that men had come to court Lady Adalind, lured by her beauty, and Maddoc had been forced to fight off many men.

Being the captain of the guard for Daniel's father, Maddoc had known Adalind for most of her life and hadn't shown any romantic interest in her until she'd returned from court. Then, and only then, had the blind man's eyes been opened to what a stunning woman Adalind had grown in to. He'd asked for her hand and Daniel's father, as head of the family, had given it. But Maddoc wasn't the only man who'd wanted to court Adalind.

Enter Brighton de Royans.

Adalind and Maddoc had met Brighton at a birthday celebration not long after Adalind had returned home and Adalind, knowing he was Glennie's brother, had been very friendly to him. But Brighton had mistaken that friendliness for something romantic and had made his want for the woman known. He'd even challenged Maddoc for her hand. When Maddoc had been badly injured in the challenge, Brighton abducted Adalind and ran away with her.

And that had been the beginning of a horrific saga for Adalind and Daniel and the entire de Lohr family. With Maddoc hovering near death, it had been up to Daniel to track his niece and Brighton and when he caught up to them, Brighton had been wounded in the ensuing fight. But Daniel had saved the death blow for Maddoc, as it was the man's right, and Maddoc had pulled himself from his death bed to avenge his beloved Adalind and slay Brighton.

It had been a brutal and gruesome battle that had seen Brighton succumb to his injuries and as Daniel stared at the lovely face of Glennie de Royans, it was clear from her question that she'd not heard about her brother's fate. Or, if she had, then she hadn't heard enough information to make her understand that the de Lohrs were related to his death. She'd not even acknowledged the de Lohr name when Daniel told her who he was.

Therefore, it was an unexpected and tense situation Daniel found himself in as he looked into Glennie's flushed face. It was difficult not to feel anger at the entire de Royans family for what Brighton had done, for the hell he'd put the de Lohrs through, but Daniel reminded himself that Glennie had nothing to do with her brother's antics. She was an innocent woman.

Still, the bitterness lingered. The wounds of Brighton's actions were still fresh.

"Adalind is quite well," Daniel finally said. "She married last year."

Glennie was astonished. "She did?" she gasped. "To whom?"

"A knight in my father's service."

Glennie was overjoyed. "I am so happy to hear this," she said. "I was afraid she would have married one of those fools who had followed her home from court. She was much pursued, you know, and the other women at Winchester were so jealous of her. My poor Adalind."

She must not know about anything that has happened since Adalind had returned home! Daniel thought to himself. It was very clear that she knew nothing beyond the day that she and Adalind separated at Winchester and Daniel actually felt some pity for the woman. She had no idea what her brother had done or that he was dead. It was a sad state of affairs all around.

He smiled politely.

"She is very happy now," he said. "When next I see her, I will give her your best wishes."

"Please do," Glennie agreed eagerly. "I would like to hear of her wedding and her new husband, Sir Daniel. Will… will you and Lady Liselotte join us for sup tonight at Netherghyll Castle? My father would be very happy to have you, as would my brother, Caston. He serves my father. My other brother serves Norfolk. Do you know of him? His name is Brighton."

Daniel nearly choked. He'd not expected that question in the least but the conversation had naturally brought it about. He had to make a split-second decision about confiding the truth on what he knew of Brighton de Royans and he decided that, at that moment, it would not be something he wished to divulge, mainly because if he said that he knew the man, it would bring up an entirely new line of questioning he was unwilling to indulge in. He wasn't a liar by nature, but in this case, he felt it was the only safe thing to do. He shook his head.

"Alas, I do not believe so," he said, quickly changing the subject. "As for the meal, your offer is most gracious, but I must discuss it with my hostess, Lady Liselotte. I am a guest of her family, after all."

Before he could say anything to Liselotte, who had overheard the conversation, Glennie was whirling on the woman.

"My lady," she said. "Would you and your guest please sup with us tonight at Netherghyll? It would be such an honor to have you both. We've had so little company and we have a new cook, all the way from Paris. She makes the most marvelous dishes!"

Glennie was trying to make it all sound greatly appealing but it ended up bringing tears to Liselotte's eyes. At Shadowmoor, they could barely keep body and soul together, eating family pets because they were desperate, and Glennie was speaking of a fine French cook and marvelous dishes.

It was all so horribly ironic. Liselotte had no idea what to say, terrified she was about to make a fool of herself, but the expression she gave Daniel was enough to prompt the man to step in. Liselotte looked as if she were about to cry and Daniel took pity on her. He thought, perhaps, that all of this – the trip to town, the chatty lady – was just too much for the normally-isolated young woman. She was overwhelmed with it all.

"Your offer is very kind, Lady Glennie," he said, "but I believe my hostess actually had plans already set for this evening. However, let me discuss it with her and I will give you a firm answer. Will you be shopping in town much longer?"

Glennie nodded, sensing that her invitation had not been all that welcome. She was coming to feel somewhat embarrassed, although she knew not why. All she knew was that Lady Liselotte seemed to be stricken by the offer somehow, as if it were something greatly offensive.

"Just a little while longer," she said, her gaze moving between Daniel and Liselotte. "If… if you come, Lady Liselotte, mayhap you will wear this beautiful new outerdress that Sir Daniel has selected for you. It will be most becoming on you."

Horrified at the thought that Daniel was about to buy her a dress, Liselotte looked at Daniel in shock and he, in turn, answered for her yet again.

"I will see if I can convince her," he forced a smile at Glennie, moving back towards Liselotte. "It was a pleasure meeting you, Lady Glennie. Now I see why my niece spoke so highly of you."

Glennie's smile brightened although she was still confused about Liselotte's behavior. She thought the young woman seemed rather sad, dressed in pauper's clothing as she was. It didn't occur to her that the woman couldn't afford anything else because she came from Shadowmoor, which everyone knew was a very old and prestigious Saxon settlement. Sir Daniel had even called Liselotte "lady", which meant she was nobility. It simply didn't occur to Glennie that she was looking at a destitute noblewoman because she had never genuinely seen such a thing. Living in the finest homes all of her life, Glennie thought all of

English nobility lived that way. It wasn't her fault. It was simply the life she had been exposed to.

With a timid wave, Glennie turned away and headed back to her guard, who had been standing on the avenue, watching their mistress dutifully. Daniel watched the woman as she walked away before turning to Liselotte.

Her head was down, her fingers to her nose as if pinching off any attempts to cry. He spoke softly to her.

"Why are you upset?" he asked. "Did she say terrible things to you?"

Liselotte shook her head, sniffling and struggling to regain her composure. "Not in the least," she said. "She was very kind and friendly. But I… I have no use for friends."

"Why not?"

She looked at him sharply. "I am not of her world, Daniel," she said. "Surely you can see that."

Daniel's gaze was intense. "What do you mean?"

"You *know* what I mean."

"I do not. Explain."

Liselotte sighed heavily. "Must I?" she said with frustration. "I do not dress as she does. I do not travel in the same circles. She comes from wealth and I do not. I have never fostered. I have nothing in common with her."

Daniel's heart was being twisted, just a little, because Liselotte was actually verbalizing her plight. He sensed that she was a proud woman and it, therefore, must have been quite difficult for her to admit her shortcomings. He turned to look at the garments hanging up all around them.

"It seems to me that in addition to the food stores I will buy, I will also purchase some of these dresses for you because I like to see a woman well-dressed," he said. "I have no one to buy fine clothing for; my mother has my father and I would never buy clothing for my sisters because they are too selective and demanding, so it would truly give me great pleasure to purchase something fine for a lady. Would you allow me to do this for you?"

Liselotte shook her head. "Nay," she said flatly, taking Gunnar by the hand. He had been standing impatiently next to her. "Let us go and make your store purchases so that we may return home."

She was starting to walk away. "Liselotte," Daniel called after her, his voice low and firm. "*Stop*."

She did, although it was haltingly, as if she weren't sure she wanted to listen to him. She didn't turn to look at him but rather stood there, holding on to Gunnar as the boy fidgeted. Daniel made his way over to them, pulling Gunnar out of her grip.

"Go to the livery and pick out the goat you want," he told the boy. "We will join you shortly."

With glee, Gunnar raced back to the livery yard as Daniel watched. He swore the boy was jumping into the air, thrilled at the prospect of another pet goat. As Gunnar disappeared from view, Daniel turned to Liselotte.

"Now," he said in a low voice, "I realize you have spent the past few years living in fear and poverty and isolation. I am very well aware of that. But that is soon to change and you cannot behave like a frightened child every time you come in contact with someone like Glennie. Was she deliberately rude to you?"

Liselotte shook her head reluctantly. "Nay."

"Precisely," Daniel said, moving so he could look her in the face. She had her head lowered and still wouldn't meet his eye. "She was *not* unkind to you. In fact, she invited you to her home for sup. It would be very rude of you to decline. Moreover, we can ask her father to send a messenger to my uncle's home on the Marches. It saves me from having to find someone myself. Furthermore, it is quite possible we can make an ally out of de Royans in your fight against Bramley. Do you understand what I am saying?"

So there was a practical reason for Daniel wanting to accept Lady Glennie's invitation. Liselotte understood that now, daring to look up at him.

"I understand," she said. "But... but I have nothing fine to wear. And I do not say this so that you will purchase something for me. I say it because it is the truth and I would be ashamed sitting at her table looking like a pauper."

Daniel nodded patiently. "I know," he said. He still had the lavender dress in his hand and he held it up. "I like this one. Let us go inside the seamstress' stall and you can try it on. She can fit it to you so that you may have something lovely to wear tonight."

Liselotte looked longingly at the garment; it was stunning, more beautiful than anything she had ever seen. She sighed faintly. "But I cannot pay for it," she spoke the obvious. "My father may not like the fact that you have purchased clothing for me. It is a very personal gift, my lord. It is unseemly. Do you not see this?"

Daniel was smiling faintly. "I do," he said. "But I told you that I have no one special to purchase such things for. You would be doing me a favor, really. Please do not deny me the pleasure."

"But...!"

"*Please*?"

Liselotte sighed heavily now, frustrated yet understandably excited about the fact that she was about to gain a new dress. God only knew, she couldn't remember when she had last been given something new. She had been wearing her mother's cast-offs for so long that old clothing was simply normal for her. Even before Bramley's persecution, she wore her mother's cast-offs but at that point in time, they didn't look so terrible because they had the money and opportunity to mend and adjust them with finer fabrics or threads.

But that was long ago. Now, Daniel was offering her something new and beautiful, and that feminine part of her, the vanity part that she had not been able to indulge, was outweighing the refusal that was on the tip of her tongue. Her father might be angry with her for allowing Daniel to purchase such a thing for her, but as her gaze fell on the lavender garment, she didn't much care. After a moment, she nodded her head.

"Very well," she said reluctantly. "If you must."

Daniel grinned broadly, that impish grin that was so dazzling. "I must."

"Do I have *any* say in the matter?"

"None whatsoever."

He grasped her by the hand and pulled her back towards the stall where the seamstress, a very old woman, came out to meet them. She had been sitting inside with her daughter, watching her customers outside of her stall, and when the big blond knight removed one of the garments she had for sale, the old woman knew she had a paying customer. Now, she was on her feet to greet them.

But she wasn't the only one who was interested in a sale. Glennie, seeing Daniel and Liselotte as they spoke to the seamstress, came away from her guard and returned to the seamstress' stall, once again lauding the beauty of the dark blue wool. Daniel agreed with her wholeheartedly and picked up the garment, handing it over to the seamstress for Liselotte to try on as well.

From that point on, it seemed to be all Glennie and Daniel as they sought to dress Liselotte in beautiful clothing. No one could stop either one of them, both of them used to having their way, both of them stubborn. Liselotte simply stood there dumbly while they rolled all over her, unable to stop the tide of goodwill that swamped her. She'd never in her life had anyone care about her, personally, so all of it was something of a new experience.

But it was an educational experience as well. Living alone and isolated, and far away from the ever-changing tides of fashion of the world, Liselotte learned much about garments on that day – the types of fabrics as well as the type of dress. The lovely lavender dress, she came to learn, was a type of garment known as a *cottehardie,* simply a one-piece garment with long sleeves, tin buttons down the front, snug bodice, and full skirt. Once she put it on, it was absolutely stunning on her long torso and full breasts. It was also a bit indecent the way it clung to her, but she was in love with it from the beginning. It was soft and warm and beautiful… *she* felt beautiful.

She'd never felt beautiful in her life.

Daniel must have thought she was beautiful, too – his expression softened into great appreciation when he saw her in the lavender and he immediately told the seamstress that he would buy it. Liselotte was flattered by his expression, perhaps even embarrassed by it, and she averted her gaze shyly because he was looking at her so intensely. She thought that the selection of the lavender dress might be the end of it, of his determination to buy her clothing, but it wasn't. Daniel and Glennie handed over several more garments for Liselotte to try on and Glennie even helped her to put them on.

The next thing Liselotte donned was the dark blue wool, a type of garment known as a *houppelande*, which meant it had a voluminous skirt, big sleeves that were wide open at the end, and buttoned up all the way to the neck. It was heavy, and meant to be worn over dresses like the *cottehardie,* and absolutely gorgeous. But the cavalcade of clothing didn't stop there; it was seemingly endless. Glennie had discovered a simple *outerdress*, a lesser version of the *cottehardie*, in a dark shade of yellow that she loved, and forced Liselotte to put it on which at this point was not a difficult thing to do. Liselotte was beyond protesting any longer as she, too, was caught up in the frenzy of fashion.

The dark yellow wool was stunning, and it was also warm and durable, which made it an excellent dress for every day. Charging through the shop with the grace of a rutting bull, Glennie also found a fur-lined cloak made from undyed wool that was very heavy and warm, and quite elegant. When Liselotte put it on over the dark yellow, it was a striking combination.

But even more than outerwear, innerwear needed attention, too. Having seen what Liselotte was wearing under her worn clothing, Glennie discreetly collected several shifts and some warm hose, handing them to Daniel without even telling Liselotte that she had given them to him. In fact, she didn't even mention to Daniel why she had selected the under things but when he saw what they were, he seemed to know why. Liselotte had absolutely nothing and Glennie was simply seeing to her needs.

It was a kind gesture, Daniel thought, which was starting to sway him away from any bitterness he might have felt toward Glennie because of her brother's actions the previous year. She seemed to be genuinely kind, a very compassionate woman, as Daniel's niece had once told him. In truth, Glennie only wanted to help and Liselotte seemed to need help, so it was a natural action on Glennie's part.

As Daniel watched the two women interact, he thought that Glennie seemed somewhat lonely, and very enthusiastic for a new friend, which was touching. Daniel was coming to wonder if Glennie, the pampered and wealthy lady, was just as lonely as Liselotte was in her poor isolation. Perhaps both ladies were so lonely that this trip to town, for the both of them, had been quite fortuitous. Daniel found himself hoping so, for Liselotte's sake.

But Glennie wasn't so discreet about her loneliness as Liselotte was. She was obvious about wanting to make a friend while Liselotte really had no idea what that even entailed – what being a friend really meant – because she had never had one. As Daniel began bartering a price with the seamstress for the lot of dresses, Liselotte tried on two more gowns, both forced upon her by Glennie. One was a woolen *outerdress*, red in color, which was lined with linen, and another was a big *houppelande* that was a medium shade of blue with gold embroidery around the cuffs of the sleeves. It was very lovely and very well made.

At that point, Liselotte was overwhelmed with what was going on, overcome by her first shopping excursion. She'd stopped being hesitant about it long ago and, now, it all seemed a bit surreal to her. The garments were beautiful, warm, and well-made, and she felt like a princess as she tried on fine gown after fine gown, looking at her image in a big polished bronze mirror that the seamstress had leaning against the wall.

Liselotte had never seen her reflection before other than in a pool of water. Therefore, the image of her in the bronze mirror was quite astonishing. She could see the shape of her face clearly and even the shape of her eyes and nose, even if she couldn't see the color of her eyes. But that didn't matter; for the first time, she was getting a good look at herself and scrutinizing her features even more than she was scrutinizing the clothing. Was it truly possible that she was attractive, a comely sort, when she was in proper clothing?

She thought that Daniel seemed to think so because he couldn't seem to take his eyes off of her. Liselotte could feel his gaze, weighty and full of interest, and when she would turn around to look at him, he would simply smile. One time, he even winked. She thought it was quite bold of him and turned away, quickly, before he could see her smile.

She was most definitely smiling.

It was a game they played as she tried on dress after dress. As Daniel and Liselotte subtly flirted, Glennie continued her mission through the seamstress' stall and came across combs and pins, part of the seamstress' inventory because she was a provider of all things for a fine lady's dress. Therefore, after Liselotte put on the exquisite red *outer-dress* that complemented the bronze color of her hair, Glennie pulled her new friend's hair out of the existing braid and proceeded to comb Liselotte's hair, dividing it into three sections. She then braided each section and pinned it up at the nape of the neck in a rather big elaborate bun.

There was a lot of brushing, pulling, and poking going at the back of her head, but Liselotte kept her mouth shut. Truth was, she had never been fussed over before and was curious to see the outcome. By the time Glennie was finished, Liselotte's hair was magnificently dressed, pinned to her scalp with iron pins and a big tin butterfly comb as adornment. It was quite stunning and Liselotte caught sight of herself in the bronze mirror again, this time as a properly dressed young lady. She didn't look anything like the woman she knew with the old much-mended clothing. She looked like a beautiful refined woman, most deserved of her long and royal Saxon heritage.

She looked like a queen.

The tears started to come.

Daniel, still in intense negotiations with the seamstress, caught sight of Liselotte in the red wool, with her hair so exquisitely braided. The sight literally took his breath away; she was so regal and beautiful with her long neck and long limbs. He simply stared at her for a moment, his heart doing strange things in his chest. He'd never felt so entranced in his life over a woman, like he couldn't take his eyes from her. It was an odd sensation but not an unpleasant one.

At that moment, something changed for him.

It was a definitive moment as he realized he wasn't going to easily leave this woman once he'd saved her from Bramley. That was the first thing that popped into his mind – leaving her after he'd subdued the lord who had been persecuting her. Somehow, someway, he was feeling more than he should have for that lovely, poverty-stricken woman and that both frightened and intrigued him. He wasn't sure how it was possible that he was feeling something odd, something… *warm*. Aye, it was definitely warm.

The bachelor's soul, that hard and stalwart thing, began to show cracks.

But before he could ponder that event, he noticed that Liselotte was weeping. He left the seamstress mulling over his last offer and went to her as she stood in front of the mirror, wiping her eyes. He even looked at Glennie, who was standing behind Liselotte with a smile on her face. When he gave her an expression that silently asked why Liselotte was weeping, Glennie merely shrugged. It was clear Glennie had no grasp on the moods of the woman she was trying very hard to be friends with.

"Liselotte?" he asked softly. "What's the matter?"

Liselotte was looking at herself in the mirror, the tears falling faster than she could wipe them away.

"There is nothing wrong," she said hoarsely. "I… I have simply never seen myself like this before."

Daniel smiled, standing next to her and looking at their reflection in the big bronze mirror. As tall as Liselotte was, and she was tall for a woman, Daniel was a head taller than she was, filling up the mirror with his soaring height and enormous shoulders. As he watched her struggle with her first glimpse of just how beautiful she was, he spoke softly.

"When I was young, I remember hearing a tale of a Saxon princess who was the fairest woman in all the land," he said quietly. "It was said that men would come across the sea, lured by her beauty, to bring her something precious, hoping to win her heart. Men would bring gold, or silver, or diamonds and rubies, all of it meant to show the princess just how rich they were and hoping to lure her interest. But then one man came and he was not rich. He brought her a simple box and when she opened it, there was a lock of his hair inside. It was the only thing of value he had to give. It was enough because she immediately fell in love with him and they lived happily forever after."

By this time, Liselotte's tears were mostly gone and she turned to Daniel. "I have not heard that tale," she said. "What was the princess' name?"

He looked at her. They were standing very close to one another and it was difficult for him to focus on her question. There was something innate within him that simply wanted to kiss her sweet lush lips. Normally, he would have given in to that impulse, but for some reason he didn't. It seemed to him that if he did, it might forever damage the relationship building between them.

For the first time in his life, he didn't want to ruin anything that had to do with a woman.

With Liselotte.

"Ostara," he said softly. "And the simple man she fell in love with was Wuldor who, as it turned out, was really a great warrior in disguise. He commanded a powerful army."

Liselotte smiled faintly. "That is a sweet story," she said. "But why tell me of it?"

Daniel looked back in the mirror, now seeing the profile of her face as she looked up at him. Even her profile was exquisite. It was a struggle to resist the urge to pull her into his arms.

"Because you are the princess," he admitted. "It matters not what you wear, my lady. What matters is what lies beneath. You are the locket of hair in that plain box; what lies inside the plain clothing is the most valuable thing in the world. Someday you will present yourself, just as you are, to the right man and he will be yours forever."

With that, he walked away, leaving Liselotte standing there in awe, mulling over the kindest words anyone had ever spoken to her. More and more she was becoming enamored with Daniel and for very good reason; he could make her feel as if she were the most beautiful and important person in the world.

She'd never known anyone like him.

"He is enchanted by you," Glennie whispered over her shoulder. "Can you not tell?"

Liselotte turned to Glennie in shock. "Nay, he is not," she insisted, feeling embarrassed. "I… I do not even really know him. I have only just met him. He was of service to our family and continues to be so. It is nothing more than that."

It was the truth, although she didn't elaborate on how, exactly, they had met. Something like that was far too shameful to divulge to someone she did not know. But Glennie didn't seem to care for the details. Her gaze lingered on Daniel as the man stood over the seamstress yet again.

"He is quite handsome," she said, appraising him. "And he is a de Lohr. Do you know much about the House of de Lohr?"

Liselotte shook her head. "I admit that I do not."

Glennie began to fuss with the red dress, speaking as she did so. "They are one of the greatest houses in all of England," she said. "If I understand Daniel's position in the family correctly, his father is David de Lohr, whose brother is Christopher de Lohr. Christopher de Lohr was the greatest knight in England during the reign of Richard the Lionheart. Daniel is a very important man. And you say you have only just met him?"

Liselotte nodded. "As I said, he has been of service to us."

Glennie's gaze moved to Daniel once again. "My father should like to meet him," she said, sounding rather seductive. "Is he married?"

"Nay."

Glennie grinned. "Good."

Liselotte wasn't sure what Glennie meant by that but she knew, instinctively, that she didn't like it. She'd never experienced jealousy in her life and had no idea it was *that* particular emotion currently filling her veins. All she knew was that she wanted to throttle Glennie for looking at Daniel so… so *hungrily*. She wasn't happy about it in the least.

As Glennie bent over to see how much the bottom of the dress needed to be hemmed, Liselotte focused on keeping her irritation with the woman in check. Glennie was trying so hard to be kind that it wouldn't do for Liselotte to try to gouge the woman's eyes out in punishment for the way she was looking at Daniel. Not that Liselotte blamed her, of course; he was certainly something spectacular to see.

Coyly, she thought she might take another look at him, too. As she turned to glance at him as he stood over near the entryway to the stall, she caught sight of men and horses on the avenue beyond the window.

Familiar horses and familiar men immediately had her attention, and it took Liselotte a split-second to realize whom, exactly, she was seeing. Panic gripped her and she rushed away from the bronze mirror towards Daniel, her heart in her throat.

"Daniel," she gasped, grabbing hold of him and pointing to the street. "Those are some of Bramley's men. They must not see Gunnar!"

Daniel whirled about, seeing what had Liselotte in a panic, and the mood of their happy shopping day abruptly plummeted. It wasn't unexpected to see Bramley's men in town, considering what Daniel had been told about how the man covered the roads, but Daniel cursed himself for letting Gunnar out of his sight. That was his fault. Immediately, he sought to make amends.

His knightly training kicked in, as did the cool and collected de Lohr manner. The entire family of men was bred for battle, unafraid to take up arms, unafraid of a fight, and as cool as a snow-frosted night when it came to facing danger. Men like Daniel and his father, uncles, and cousins had all been trained to understand that calm heads prevailed over all, and that strategy usually triumphed over brute strength.

Strategy, of course, was what Daniel did best. He was a hellion in a fight, one of the best swordsmen that England had ever seen, but he was also able to get by on his wits where most men would have been stumped. Now, he was about to put that brilliance to the test.

"Stay here," he commanded quietly, firmly. "Stay back in this stall so they do not see you. I will go and get Gunnar and bring him back here."

Liselotte had terror in her eyes, utter terror when she looked at him. He could see that inherent fear that years of Bramley's aggression had provoked. Gently, he touched her cheek in a comforting gesture before pushing her back to the bronze mirror where Glennie was still standing. It was back in the shadows, away from the entry. Holding up a hand as a silent gesture for her to remain, he bolted from the stall.

It was busier now that the morning had advanced and there were many people on the avenue conducting business. Daniel kept his gaze on the two big knights and three or four men-at-arms that Liselotte had pointed out as Bramley's men as he crossed the muddy street and rushed onto the livery property. Fortunately, those men were moving away from him, into the center of town, so he was able to move about with relative freedom. But he knew that could change in an instant.

When Daniel finally entered the livery yard, he found Gunnar tucked back towards the barn, with two little goats in his arms. Daniel quickly made his way to the boy.

"Gunnar," he hissed, grabbing the lad around the waist and heaving him up. "We must go. We will come back for the goats, but right now, we must go."

Gunnar wasn't at all happy about being taken away from his new best friends. "Why?" he asked. "Why must we go? You said I could have a goat!"

Daniel was already moving out of the livery yard, heading for the avenue. "You can," he said, swinging Gunnar up over his shoulder like a sack of grain. "Now, lie still. Hang over my shoulder and do not move. Is that clear?"

Gunnar had no idea what Daniel meant. He tried to get up, to push himself off of Daniel's shoulder, but Daniel slapped him on the behind with a trencher-sized hand. Gunnar howled.

"Go limp, I say!" Daniel hissed, louder.

Frightened, Gunnar did as he was told, his entire body hanging limp over Daniel's shoulder. He couldn't have known that it was Daniel's plan so the boy wouldn't be recognized, his upside-down face planted into Daniel's back. Daniel moved swiftly across the avenue, dodging wagons and people, before finally reaching the seamstress' stall. Just as he moved for the entry, Glennie was coming out, heading for her guard.

Daniel wasn't concerned with Glennie in the least and therefore didn't say a word to the woman as she passed him. He was more concerned with taking Gunnar to safety. He blew into the seamstress' shop and took Gunnar from his shoulder, setting the boy down next to his apprehensive sister. Liselotte put her arms around the child, greatly relieved.

"Thank God," she breathed as she hugged Gunnar. Then, she looked at Daniel. "Did the men see you?"

Daniel shook his head. "They did not," he replied. "Even if they had looked at me, they would not have known me, for I have never seen any of them. It was a simple thing to rescue young Gunnar – again. What were you meant to call me today?"

The question was directed at the boy, who still wasn't entirely pleased that he'd been pulled away from the goats. He sighed. "O Great One."

"You say that without enthusiasm."

"O Great One!"

He shouted and Liselotte grinned, hugging her brother. "You have our thanks," she said to Daniel. "Two of those men, the knights, are Bramley's close companions. I am rather surprised to see them here without their liege."

Daniel pondered that particular bit of information. If what she said was true, then he wondered where, in fact, Bramley was.

"Do they always travel together?" he asked.

She nodded. "When I have seen them, they have been together."

Daniel glanced over his shoulder at the street beyond, half-expecting Bramley to make an appearance. "Who are those men?" he asked. "Do you know them by name?"

Liselotte nodded. "The blond man is Jules la Londe," she said. "He is Bramley's most trusted knight. The other knight, with the darker hair, is Oliver de Witt."

"And how do you know this?"

"Because they have come to Shadowmoor on more than one occasion, trying to negotiate for me," she said. "At least, that is what they tried to do in the beginning. They were very polite. We came to know them by name. But when they did not get their way, we saw them for what they truly were. La Londe killed an entire herd of cattle we had. Killed them just because he could. He killed the men tending the herd, too."

Daniel's gaze lingered on her as he digested the information. Knights like that were ruthless, indeed, so he made a mental note of what he was up against when it came to Bramley's stable. He had a feeling he would be seeing them again at some point.

"I have heard the name of la Londe," he said. "I seem to recall my father telling a story about a la Londe he knew, long ago, but I cannot recall what it was. In any case, we are out of his sight for now. You remain here with Gunnar and I will go and see what those men are up to. We still have business to conduct in town and I do not want to be looking over my shoulder every minute."

Liselotte agreed, nodding her head firmly. "Be careful," she said, reaching out to touch his arm. "Those men are not to be crossed."

Daniel grinned smugly, patting her hand. "Neither am I."

In spite of her fear, Liselotte returned his smile. She couldn't help it; he had an infectious smile that invited her humor as well as her trust. It was difficult not to look into that face, that expression, and not believe everything he said. Daniel de Lohr had confidence that bordered on arrogance, but in his case, it was well justified. He meant what he said and he had the skill, and the intelligence, to support it. She was very glad he was on their side.

She was very glad he was on *her* side.

But that adoring moment was cut short when they heard raised voices in the avenue beyond the seamstress' stall. Both Daniel and Liselotte turned towards the sound to see that not only had Bramley's men returned, but now they were engaging Glennie in a conversation that had her escort intervening. Simply by the tone of the conversation, the tension was obvious. Something bad was happening.

When the blond knight, still on horseback, made a swipe to get at Glennie by pushing one of her escorts aside, Daniel was on the move.

The situation was about to get interesting.

CHAPTER FIVE

Bramley Castle

16 miles south of Shadowmoor

"IT IS NOT as if you *need* your property," Roland was saying. "You have no army to defend it. You have nothing at all by which to hold it. All that Shadowmoor represents to you is a derelict legacy. Why would you hold on to such a thing?"

Brynner was well into his fourth big cup of wine, a very good wine that his host, introduced as Roland Fitzroy, Lord Bramley, had provided. Spanish wine, he'd been told. It was smooth and sweet, and he'd gulped it down. Now, his head was seriously buzzing and the familiar lethargy of drink filled his veins. But knowing who his host was, and what he wanted, Brynner was trying to stay on an even keel. He was deep in the heart of the enemy and trying to keep his head above water. The Spanish wine, however, was making it difficult.

"Because it will be mine," Brynner said with as much force as he could muster. "It is mine, left to me by my forefathers. Shadowmoor was not always so weak; it used to be the mightiest fortress in all of western Yorkshire. Back in the days after the Conquest, when the Normans came, Shadowmoor even had Norman troops stationed there. My ancestors knew how to keep their lands, even from the invaders, and I will not be the one to lose what they fought so hard to keep."

Roland was listening carefully. Seated in his solar, the one that smelled of the expensive furnishings he surrounded himself with, he'd spent the past three hours trying to reason away Shadowmoor from the drunken heir. He'd never met the man before but based upon where his men had found him, and based upon the man's admission as Brynner l'Audacieux, eldest son and heir of Etzel, Roland couldn't have been more pleased. It was everything he wanted – well, nearly everything – dropped right into his lap. The sting of losing the youngest son, the little blond-haired lad, the day before was far lessened with the event of the eldest, who had been captured wandering drunkenly on the moors.

It was an answer to his prayers.

So Roland sat across the table from Brynner, plying him with as much fine wine as the man could drink, poured into a big golden cup, and attempting to seriously break him down. These l'Audacieuxs were a foolish bunch, he'd come to the conclusion, and now with the eldest, who was clearly besotted with drink, Roland was certain that he could gain what he wanted from the man. No more useless attempts to control Shadowmoor and gain the lord's daughter; no more small game in the abduction of the youngest son in an attempt to extract what he wanted. No more games, no more attempts, at all.

Now, he had what he wanted.

But it wasn't as easy as all of that. Roland, coming to see that the heir to Shadowmoor was sharp even with drink filling his mind, was quite certain that he had to promise the man something equal in exchange for that broken-down fortress. He'd been thinking that for the past hour; l'Audacieux wasn't simply going to hand over his legacy and trying to convince the man that he had no more use for Shadowmoor didn't seem to work, either. Roland, seeing the weakness for alcohol, was coming to think he knew what would. It didn't take a scholar to figure it out.

Therefore, the tactics were changing. If he couldn't get it one way, he'd get it another.

"When you inherit Shadowmoor, what then?" he asked. "It will still be broken-down. Do you intend to live in squalor the rest of your life?"

Brynner's red-rimmed eyes gazed steadily at the man. "Why do *you* want it so badly?" he countered. "It will still be just as derelict if I turn it over to you. Why is it so important to you?"

Roland tried to sound very logical. "Because it adjoins my lands," he said. "When I acquire Shadowmoor, I will be the largest landholder in this area. The towns will be mine and so will their tariffs. The roads will be mine to tax as I see fit. Why else *should* I want it?"

Brynner snorted. "For those very reasons, I suppose," he said. "Greed is a bold and aggressive thing, you know. You have been showing such greed for my property for four years. I may not associate much with my family, but by virtue of the fact that I live at Shadowmoor, I know what is going on. I have heard that you want my sister and the castle, and will do anything to get them both. I have seen how you have cut off Shadowmoor from the rest of the world, trying to starve us out. It has not worked in four years. Now you have run out of options so you have your men capture me to negotiate for my legacy? You must want it badly, indeed."

Roland smiled thinly. "Mayhap I do," he said. "I have the money and the resources to restore Shadowmoor. You and your foolish people scratch by an existence up on that rocky hill, bereft members of a once-great society. Do you think I want to live in this tiny castle for the rest of my life? Of course not. I want the big fortress on the mountain. All things must evolve, l'Audacieux. It is time for Shadowmoor to evolve. It is time for you to let someone else make it great again."

All Brynner could hear was the arrogance of a man who believed he could do anything he pleased. There was no humility or goodwill in his statement; only the greed that Brynner had spoken of. He may be a drunkard, but Brynner knew people. He knew men like Roland only understood the material things of life and would stop at nothing to get them.

"It takes more than money and resources to make something great," he said. "It takes a love of the land, a connection to it."

"Do you have that connection to it, other than your heritage?"

Brynner didn't reply at first. He turned to his drink, slurping at it, contemplating the question. The answer was obvious. "Nay," he finally said, bitterness in his tone before he could stop it. "It was where I was to raise my own family but that will not happen. Shadowmoor will die out when I do."

Roland capitalized on the man showing some weakness. "Then why wait so long?" he demanded. "Why not let me have it and you can go and spend money and travel to your heart's content? Do you not understand, man? I am offering you money if you will only do me one small favor. Give me Shadowmoor. Let me have this thing you care nothing about."

Brynner looked at him. "I did not say I did not care for it," he said. "It is still my legacy."

"But it is a dead legacy."

"It is all that I have."

"I will pay you so that you can buy another one!"

Brynner shook his head. "Money cannot buy what I want."

Roland would not give up. He was a bargainer by nature, and a bad one most of the time, but it was still his inclination. He wanted something very badly and he wasn't going to give up. He looked to the wine in his cup, swirling it, putting together the pieces of his final proposal. His mind was working quickly.

"My father's family is from France," he said casually. "I inherited a small chateau from my father in Lire, in the Loire Valley. That is wine country, my friend. The chateau produces a good deal of fine wine every year. Wouldn't that be worth more to you than a broken fortress on a desolate moor?"

Brynner was interested. God help him, he really was and was trying not to show it. It was quite possible that Lord Bramley was lying but it was equally possible that he wasn't. Still, Brynner had some semblance of restraint. Not much, but a little.

"You said your father is King John," he said. "If you are truly his son, then why did he leave you only a small chateau? The son of a king should inherit an earldom, at least."

For the first time since Brynner appeared in Roland's lavish solar, Roland's confidence took a bit of a hit. He shrugged, smiling coyly.

"I said that my sister, Joan, is John Lackland's bastard daughter," he said. "Joan and I have different fathers, but we are siblings. It is through her that I am related to the kings of England. My real father, my mother's husband, died years ago. 'Tis his chateau I have inherited. I will give it all to you if you will do something for me."

Brynner could see that Roland had stretched the truth a bit when they first met because, clearly, he'd said that he was the son of a king. That's what Roland had told him. Now, that fact had changed slightly. It made Brynner distrustful of the man all the more but the fact that Roland had an excellent wine cellar kept him from taking his leave of Bramley Castle altogether. He hadn't had wine like this in years. More than that, he suspected he *couldn't* leave – the four men that had brought him to Bramley Castle were still here, lingering in the shadows, and watching everything.

Men with swords.

It occurred to Brynner that his host wasn't going to let him leave at all, at least not until he had what he wanted. A promise, a bargain, a vow to turn over Shadowmoor. That's what this was all about and Brynner supposed he had known that from the start. But the lure of wine was stronger than concern for his life and property, so he'd allowed himself to become a captive guest of Lord Bramley. If he wanted to leave, which he did eventually, then he would have to play Roland's silly game. There was little choice.

Truth be told, however, Bramley's offer intrigued him and he couldn't even hate himself for being weak.

The chateau produces a good deal of fine wine every year....

"Then you are offering me this chateau?" Brynner asked.

Roland nodded, a gleam in his eye. "I am," he said. "It produces great quantities of excellent wine every year, wine you could just as easily keep for yourself or sell if you had a mind to do so. It would be yours to do with as you please."

My own wine. Brynner had to admit that it was very appealing. The suspicion that the man was lying was overshadowed by the thought of copious amounts of wine at his disposal, forever. Even on the remote possibility that it was true, Brynner thought that it was worth the risk. He could listen to the man's entire proposal at the very least. Perhaps he was, indeed, a fool clinging to a derelict fortress with no real meaning to him other than it was his legacy.

His tomb.

Perhaps it really *was* time for Shadowmoor to evolve.

"Very well," Brynner said, draining the last of the wine in his cup. "I am listening."

Roland sat forward, so swiftly that he nearly knocked over the nearly-empty pitcher of wine. "You will accept my offer, then?"

"I said that I was listening. I am waiting to hear your terms. Whether or not I agree is another matter."

Roland didn't take this opportunity lightly. This was the closest he'd come in four years of bargaining, wheedling, and dirty tricks in his quest to acquire Shadowmoor. He was so eager that sweat began to pop out on his brow. He didn't want to destroy this chance, this one chance to obtain what he very much wanted.

"Since you are clearly concerned with giving up your legacy, I will provide you with a new one," he said. "My chateau in France, the wine it produces, fifty gold crowns, and fifty men shall be yours. Does this appeal to you so far?"

Brynner nodded. "It does."

Roland's expression turned somewhat hard at that point as he pushed the wine pitcher aside and leaned on the tabletop. His dark eyes were riveted to Brynner.

"I do not want to wait for Shadowmoor," he said. "In order to gain the lands in France, you must do two things for me. Convince your father to abandon Shadowmoor before the year is out. If he refuses, you will kill him and turn the fortress over to me. That is my first condition."

Brynner tried to conceal his shock at being asked to commit patricide. "And your second?"

"Convince your father to award your sister to me as my bride or simply turn her over to me once your father is dead. I will need a wife and your beauteous sister is the lady I will have."

He laid out his conditions without any emotion. It was all very businesslike, as if they were simply conducting business which, in Roland's mind, they were. There was nothing emotional attached to this, nothing of sentiment. It was simply a business proposal, but a very concise one. Brynner gazed back at him, losing the battle against concealing his shock.

"So you want Liselotte, after all," he said. "Although I do not have much use for my sister, she has always tried to be kind to me. You will not abuse her, will you?"

Roland shook his head. "Of course not," he replied. "I simply want her as my wife. She is quite a prize. You do not think I would damage a prize, do you?"

Brynner shrugged. "You have asked me to kill my father," he said. "How am I to know what you intend to do with my sister?"

Roland waved him off. "I will put her in a lavish bower and fill her full of my sons," he said. "What else is a wife good for?"

At those callous words, a flash of the love that Brynner had lost came to mind, the gentle smile and soft skin of Lady Maud. *What else is a wife good for?* Brynner had no idea because he would never have one. The one he wanted was the wife of another, more than likely being filled with the man's sons. The skin that was meant for Brynner, the body he'd so cherished, was now the privilege of another man to touch. Sickened, Brynner reached for the nearly-empty pitcher of wine and poured what was left of it into his cup.

"Liselotte is a good girl," he said, his voice muffled as he drank. "You'll not harm her."

"I thought you said you had no use for your family?"

Brynner swallowed the sweet wine. "I do not," he said. "But I could just as easily marry her off to someone who would pay me well for her and not abuse her."

"I told you I would not abuse her."

"So you've said. But what of my younger brother? Do you want him, too?"

Roland shook his head. "I have no use for the child."

"Nor do I."

Roland's eyebrows lifted. "You really are indifferent to your family, aren't you?" he asked. Then, he sighed heavily. "I suppose I can take the boy. He can work in the kitchens or the stables. I will find a place for him because I presume it would please your sister, after all. I want my wife happy."

He seemed rather jovial at this point, congenial even, and Brynner knew it was because he thought he'd struck the great and final bargain for Shadowmoor. Truthfully, Brynner couldn't think of any real reason to refuse. A wine-producing chateau in France was much more appealing than a derelict old fortress upon the cold, windy moors of Yorkshire. That was, of course, providing the chateau really existed.

Brynner mulled the proposal over again, thinking on the terms… killing his father, turning his sister over to a man who would view her simply as a prize… and he could feel a twinge of remorse. Nay, more than that – of conscience. He had no real use for his family but it wasn't their fault. It was his choice, his fault, and he knew it. Still, his life was ruined, by his own choice, and Roland's offer was appealing. To spend the rest of his life drowning his sorrows in his own wine was more than he could have ever hoped for.

It was better than a derelict old fortress that he didn't want, anyway.

"Very well," he said. "I will accept your terms. I must return to Shadowmoor and see if I can convince my father to abandon the fortress. I will send word to you on the matter when I have had a chance to speak with him but, meanwhile, I want assurances that you will hold up your end of the bargain."

Roland was so thrilled to hear of Brynner's agreement that he was willing to do most anything. "Of course," he said eagerly. "What would you have me do?"

Brynner cocked an eyebrow to emphasize his point. "Send the fifty men you intend to give me with the fifty gold crowns, to the Cock and Comb Tavern in Ilkley. Do you know where it is?"

Roland nodded. "I have been there."

"You send those men and the money to the inn," he said. "They are to wait there for me. I will send one of those men back with word for you as to my discussion with my father. Those men, and that money, belong to me regardless of what happens with my father. Is that clear?"

Roland frowned. "You cannot only accept half of the terms of a bargain once it has been struck," he said. "It is all or nothing."

"This is the closest you have come to acquiring Shadowmoor since you set out to do so," he said. "Are you going to quibble over a few men and coins?"

Roland's frown deepened. "You said you would turn it over to me one way or the other."

Brynner nodded. "And I will," he said. "But you are promising me a chateau, the existence of which cannot be proven. I have accepted your terms on faith. You, too, must go on a little faith. I will uphold my end of the bargain to the best of my ability and abandon Shadowmoor, but on the chance that chateau does not exist, I still want men and money from you. Is that clear?"

Roland hadn't given Brynner nearly enough credit. He thought the man was a drunkard, and he was, but in spite of that, his mind was still very sharp. It appeared that the drink couldn't dull what seemed to be a very keen intellect and reasoning. Roland grinned.

"You are no fool, l'Audacieux," he said. "Forgive me for thinking so."

Brynner couldn't help but notice that there was no straight answer about the chateau. "Does my wine empire, in fact, exist?"

Roland picked up his cup, averting his gaze. "You will have to take some things on faith."

"And you are willing to lose fifty men and fifty marks of gold on that?"

"Either way, I get Shadowmoor. And you get enough money to keep you supplied in wine for years to come."

It was an ambiguous answer at best. This game they had played since the beginning of their encounter had finally come to a head; the stage was set and the terms agreed to, but Brynner wasn't sure who was getting the better part of the bargain. He was coming to think that he'd made a deal with the devil.

And hell was opening up wide for them both.

CHAPTER SIX

"YOU WOULD BE wise to leave the lady alone."

The four men that comprised Glennie's escort heard the deep threatening voice from behind and turned to see a very big blond knight standing a few feet away. It was the same knight who had been in the seamstress' stall, the one making purchases for the lady that Glennie had befriended. But the knight wasn't looking at the de Royans soldiers as they tried to usher Glennie back to her carriage; the knight was looking at the men who had all but tried to assault Glennie.

It had been a bold and terrible move on Glennie, who was quite frightened by it. The man who had made the swipe for her, a big knight with shaggy blond hair, leaned forward on his saddle, his gaze apprais-ing the knight who had challenged him.

"This is none of your affair, my gallant friend," he said. "The lady is unharmed. No need for heroics."

Daniel didn't like the feel he was getting from the man; arrogance mixed with feigned-friendliness. Daniel knew the type; they would pretend to be friendly, congenial even, but they would turn on a man in an instant and plant a sword in his chest. Therefore, Daniel knew he had to take a somewhat proactive stance in order that Glennie and her escort should be allowed to leave without further trouble. Daniel intended to hold the knight's attention at least that long.

"Actually, this *is* my business," he said, turning to Glennie and her escort. "Take her home and stay there. I will come later tonight."

Glennie was already loaded up in her carriage, looking at Daniel fearfully, but she nodded, snapping to the escort that was standing around looking rather confused at Daniel's words. But the soldiers began to move quickly as Glennie hissed at them and Daniel, seeing that she was on her way to departing, returned his attention to the shaggy blond knight. He knew his next move had to be bold and strategic, so he proceeded carefully.

The game was on.

"La Londe, is it?" he said "You serve Lord Bramley."

That statement wiped the smile from la Londe's face. "How in the hell do you know that?"

Daniel smiled, without humor; he could see that, already, he had the man off guard, which was his plan. He wanted the man's full attention so Glennie and her escort could get away. In fact, he even took a few steps to his left, which would take Glennie out of la Londe's periphery entirely. At this moment, Daniel wanted to ensure that he was the only one la Londe was looking at.

"I know many things about many people," he said. "Your name sounds familiar to me. Did you or your father or grandfather serve Richard or John?"

La Londe was looking at Daniel with extreme suspicion. "*Who* are you?"

Daniel hesitated to tell him. Since the man served Bramley, he wondered if Bramley had made mention of the knight who had identified himself as a de Lohr when he'd refused to return Gunnar l'Audacieux. La Londe had four men with him and Daniel had none. If it turned into a fight, he didn't want to leave Liselotte and Gunnar alone as he tried to battle men out to do him harm. Therefore, he was evasive in his reply.

This time, he was more to the point.

"Someone who can cause you more trouble than you will know how to adequately handle," he said, his voice low. "You will leave this town now and I will forget that you molested the lady. Linger and I will be forced to act. Is that clear?"

La Londe studied him, as if trying to determine if the man was lying or not. "Act how?" he said, looking around. "You are alone."

"Do you truly want to test that theory?"

La Londe cocked his head. "If you are not alone, where are your men?"

Daniel sighed faintly. "You only have four men with you," he said. "Do you truly wish to stir up such trouble? I will wipe you from this earth if you move against me and no one will miss you. This I vow. Therefore, leave now while you still can. I will not tell you again."

It was a clear threat. La Londe's gaze lingered on him, undoubtedly trying to figure out if the knight meant what he said. Something in the man, in the deadly gleam of his eye, conveyed that he was being truthful. This was no knight to be trifled with. La Londe then glanced to Glennie who, so far, hadn't left as she was supposed to. She and her escort had moved, but not very far, and the escort now had their hands on their weapons. It was clear that they were ready to jump in and assist Daniel.

Although la Londe wasn't entirely certain that the big knight meant what he said, he wasn't willing to take the chance that he did. He'd come to town to steal some food and harass unattended women, not fight with a knight who was clearly ready for such a thing. He wasn't ready to die or to be humiliated. He was a man who enjoyed dominating the weak because he could, and when he came against someone who was stronger than he was, it was a given that he would back down without trying to make it look like he was. La Londe tended to be all posture and very little fight unless he had to.

It was safer for him that way.

With men around him ready to fight, la Londe broke out into a grin. The, he laughed, turning his horse away from Daniel. He pointed to Daniel as if it were all a big joke.

"I will remember you," he said, somewhat lightly. "I never forget a face. If I see you again, I will kill you."

Daniel smiled in return, as if he, too, were in on the joke. "I will look forward to that day," he said, casually bending down to pick up a stone that was near his foot. He tossed it in his hand casually. "But I can promise you that I will not be the one to lose my life."

La Londe snorted. "Is that so?" he said. "You are confident, my friend. Confident, indeed."

Daniel's smile faded. "Confident for good reason," he said. Then, he suddenly tossed the rock, aiming it right for the big buttocks of la Londe's horse. The rock pinged the animal and the steed bolted, nearly dumping la Londe. "I never lose!"

He shouted the last words as la Londe clung to the horse, which was now racing wildly out of the town. La Londe's men charged after him, all of them creating quite a ruckus as they followed their leader. Daniel stood there a moment, watching them leave, before giving a sigh of relief. He hadn't particularly wanted to create trouble in town on this day but it was possible that he had. It was possible that la Londe would return with reinforcements, looking for him. Therefore, he was coming to think that it was best if they left as soon as they could to avoid any further problems. He turned to Glennie and her escort.

"Go home to Netherghyll," he told her firmly. "I will bring Lady Liselotte and join you there shortly."

Glennie was looking at him with big eyes, having witnessed the entire confrontation with la Londe. "I am sorry I did not leave right away," she said. "I told my men you might need help if that terrible knight started a fight."

Daniel shook his head. "I appreciate your concern, but it was not necessary," he said. "Go home now."

Glennie wasn't listening to him. She clasped her hands together in front of her chest, nothing short of adoration on her face. "I cannot thank you enough for your intervention, Sir Daniel," she said, her tone soft with gratitude. "You are my champion!"

Daniel wasn't particularly comfortable with the gleam in Glennie's eyes. She was looking at him rather… hungrily. He'd seen predatory women in his time and if he didn't know better, he'd swear that lovely Lady Glennie had the look of a man-hunter.

"No need to thank me, my lady," he said evenly. "Go, now. We will be along shortly."

Glennie heard him this time, his final plea, and nodded eagerly as her escort scurried to collect their mounts. Two soldiers drove Glennie's carriage while the other two rode escort on their well-fed horses. Glennie waved to Daniel as the carriage headed out of town, off to the north, and he simply lifted a hand to acknowledge her and nothing more. He wasn't about to wave back. As Glennie and her escort passed from his view, he turned and headed back into the seamstress' stall.

Liselotte and Gunnar were still where he had left them, tucked back in the shop and out of view. Daniel entered the shop, his gaze falling on Liselotte as she looked back at him anxiously. He smiled.

"I chased them away," he said. "But it would be prudent for us to leave before they return with more men in their ranks."

Liselotte nodded. "Agreed," she said. "We have never been able to figure out just how many men Bramley has because Bramley Castle is such a small fortress, but we think that he has at least a hundred armed men at his disposal. Certainly enough to cover the roads around Shadowmoor."

Daniel considered that information. "Then we must be gone," he said, looking at her as she stood there in the red dress that emphasized her lovely figure and her hair attractively arranged. She looked like a goddess. "You will wear that dress to Lady Glennie's supper tonight. And we will take the lavender dress, the yellow dress, and that big blue outer-coat with the embroidery that you tried on. The only thing they do not have for you are slippers, but I can purchase those somewhere else. Madam!"

He was shouting for the seamstress, who hustled over with the excitement of her very large sale. And what a sale it was; three dresses, an outer-coat, three shifts, three pairs of warm hose, and a few other things that Glennie had collected including hair pins, combs, a small bar of lumpy soap that smelled of rosemary, and a phial of beeswax and marjoram to ease cracked skin and lips. In all, it was quite a collection and the seamstress threw in a small wooden chest to carry everything in. The seamstress' daughter packed all of the booty into the chest as Daniel paid the woman with several silver coins from a leather purse he kept tucked into the heavy belt around his waist.

Daniel was just finished paying the seamstress her silver coins when it occurred to him how poorly dressed Gunnar was. The thought hadn't entered his mind that the boy might need to be better dressed, considering they had been invited to a fine house for supper, so he discussed the boy's state of dress with the seamstress to see if she had anything that might be suitable for the lad. Much to Gunnar's distress, she did, and Gunnar soon became the focus of the seamstress' particular brand of expertise.

As Daniel and Liselotte stood back and watched, Daniel with a grin and Liselotte with concern, the seamstress and her daughter took charge of Gunnar. As the boy howled, they stripped him down to nearly nothing and, seeing how dirty the skinny boy was, asked permission to bathe him. Laughing, Daniel gave permission and the pair sponged the dirt from Gunnar's body while the boy yelled and danced around unhappily. Eventually, he started to fight back but Daniel quickly put a stop to that. He explained to Gunnar that he could no longer run around, looking like a dirty little pizzle, and that all young men should be properly dressed.

So poor Gunnar, unable to resist what was happening to him, stood there and wailed as the women finished cleaning the dirt off of his body and put him in a pair of wool chausses that were really undergarments for girls. There were two legs and a tie around the waist, which was perfect for the skinny lad, and on top of that they put a linen shift, cut off at the knees, and then a brown woolen tunic that was too big for the boy so they cinched it up the waist with a strip of leather.

Since Gunnar had lost his meager shoes when he'd run from Bramley, the seamstress sent her daughter to the leathersmith down the street to see if he had anything for the boy's feet. As the old seamstress cut Gunnar's shaggy hair with a sharp knife in an attempt to clean the boy up a bit, the daughter returned with two small leather slippers that the leathersmith had made for a young boy who had died before his parents could pay for the shoes. They were a bit too small but at least they were something, and Daniel paid handsomely for young Gunnar's first decent pair of shoes in his entire life.

In fact, he paid handsomely for the entire set of clothing and Gunnar, who was still unhappy about the entire event, wasn't hard pressed to admit that his new clothing was quite warm and free of vermin. He had bites all over his skin from the bugs that had infested his clothing and found it rather surprising that his new clothing wasn't chewing up his skinny body. With his clean skin, new clothes, and cut hair, he looked like an entirely different boy.

Daniel may have entered the seamstress' shop with two siblings who looked as if they had just crawled out of a gutter, but he left with a beautifully dressed young woman and her cleaned-up younger brother. With Liselotte's small wooden chest slung over a broad shoulder, Daniel couldn't help but grin at the pair as they inspected each other as clean, well-groomed individuals. They had lived so long in squalor that something clean and new was almost something beyond their comprehension. Liselotte seemed a bit more awed by it than Gunnar, who ran at the first mud puddle he saw with the intention of jumping in it until Daniel called him off. Momentarily confused, the child realized his new clothing would not look so new if he covered it in mud. With a grin, he avoided the puddles.

The bustle at the livery had calmed down a bit but based upon the initial discussion with the livery owner when Daniel had first arrived, the man had held aside several sacks of barley, two precious sacks of wheat, five sacks of oats, and one sack of rye grain. Daniel negotiated with the man for the use of one of his wagons to cart away the sacks and promised to return it. As the men were loading sacks onto the borrowed wagon and a groom began to hitch up a team of horses, Daniel proceeded to purchase four goats from the livery owner – two kids for Gunnar and a male adult and female adult. He also purchased a cow and her calf, and seventeen chickens at a very good price.

Since they were going to Netherghyll that evening, Daniel told the livery owner he would come back for the animals and the wagon in the morning, and the livery owner agreed to store everything inside the livery under guard. Pleased with what he had been able to acquire in town, Daniel finished paying for everything and had the groom collect Ares from the barn, where the horse had been gorging himself on oats. The horse was unhappy that he was taken away from his feeding to be saddled and Gunnar was unhappy that he had been separated from his two goats. In fact, the boy was in tears. As Daniel helped the groom saddle Ares, Liselotte went to her sorrowful brother.

"Gunnar," she said softly, trying to be sympathetic. "You shall see your new friends on the morrow. We will sup tonight in a grand house with more food than you have ever seen. That should make you happy, shouldn't it?"

Gunnar was trying not to dirty his new clothes as he squatted in the dirt, playing with his new friends. He pulled one of them into his arms, hugging it, as the second kid nibbled his hair.

"I want to bring them with me," he said, sniffling.

Liselotte bent over, her hand on his newly-cut hair. "Let them remain here tonight where they will be safe and fed," she said. "Tomorrow, we shall take them home and they can sleep in your chamber with you, I promise."

Gunnar wiped at his nose. "It is Sir Daniel's chamber now."

Liselotte smiled. "You slept in Mother's chamber last night," she said. "I am sure she would not mind if you slept there with your goats."

He frowned. "I do not like sleeping with Mother," he said. "She wants me to sleep next to her, all bunched up!"

Liselotte laughed softly. "You mean that she hugs you?"

He nodded fiercely. "I do not like it."

Liselotte stroked his pale hair. "Tonight we will sup at a great house and mayhap they will have a bed, just for you," she said. "If not, you may sleep with me and I promise not to hug you."

He was somewhat hesitant about that. "Do not pull my ears, either."

"I will not, I promise."

"Can't I bring the goats?"

Liselotte shook her head. "They will be happier here, just for tonight," she said. "They are yours. No one can take them away."

He wasn't crying any longer but he was still dubious, so very sad to leave his new pets. "We… we will not eat them, will we?" he asked timidly. "If we are going to eat them someday, I… I do not want to take them back to Shadowmoor."

Liselotte's smile fled. "We will not eat them, ever," she said. "I promise you that. I will not let you feel such sorrow again, Gunnar. I will turn the goats loose and chase them away before I would put them in a stew. I am sorry we had to do that, but you know that we were starving. We had nothing else."

Gunnar looked up at her with his big blue eyes. "What happens if we have nothing else again?"

Liselotte's gaze moved to Daniel, who was now moving in their direction. Her features took on an odd expression, something between hope and adoration. She couldn't help it when she looked at him, this man who was different from any man she had ever met. He was so full of joy in life, and of giving. She'd never known anyone so generous and even though she knew there was no hope of anything between them, still, it wasn't difficult for her to give him her heart.

Even if it would only ever be her secret.

"Somehow," she said softly, "I do not think we will ever have to worry about that again."

ଓ

Netherghyll Castle
5 miles northwest of Siglesdene

DANIEL WAS GENUINELY concerned about meeting the entire de Royans family.

Beneath skies that had been clear most of the day but were now starting to gather clouds as the late afternoon approached, he could see a dark and expansive structure on a distant rise and he wondered what kind of place bred a man such as Brighton de Royans. Glennie had seemed normal enough but that didn't mean much; she was a female and it was in her breeding to be docile and silly. But her brother had been aggressive, intelligent, and determined, determined enough to try and kill Daniel's best friend and force Daniel's niece to marry him.

It was a bold and reckless man who gave such little regard for others. Therefore, Daniel was understandably curious, and concerned, about meeting the rest of the family.

He had no idea what he was in for.

But he pushed those thoughts aside as Netherghyll Castle was sighted. He wanted something from de Royans and he was willing to have contact with the family of his dead enemy in order to get it. Focusing on the castle, he could see dark walls that encircled the top of the entire hill like the embrace of a great iron chain.

Intimidating and enormous, it made quite a sight from a distance and even more intimidating the closer he came. The narrow road that they were traveling upon cut through the green hillside, ending in a massive fanged portcullis lodged into the wall itself.

As Daniel, Liselotte, and Gunnar drew even closer, they could see just how big the walls of Netherghyll really were – at least twenty feet in some spots, an impenetrable fortress of stone and might. The walls were dark, built with a dark gray granite that was prevalent to the area, and they were pocked in places from both age and perhaps a siege or two. From the looks of the place, Daniel could guess it had been there for a couple of hundred years or more, maybe even before the Normans came. It was sturdily built, sunk deep into the mountaintop.

"I have seen many castles in my time, but this place is impressive," Daniel said. "I am surprised I've not heard of such a big place this far north. Curious."

Liselotte, holding on to Daniel as she sat behind him, gazed up at the tall walls. "See how the gray stone blends into the sky," she murmured. "It looks as if it is part of the gray clouds above."

Daniel grunted softly. "The walls are tall enough to touch the sky, that is for certain," he said. "This place cannot be more than ten or twelve miles from Shadowmoor. Do you know much about it?"

Liselotte shook her head. "I have heard the name of the castle but I do not know anything about it," she said. "If I have been told, I have forgotten. Truthfully, even before Bramley came, Shadowmoor mostly kept to itself. We were not known to be hugely allied with our neighbors."

Daniel turned his head enough to catch a glimpse of her. "Why not?"

She shrugged. "It has always been that way," she said. "I seem to remember my father saying, once, that when our ancestors struck a deal with the Normans to allow them to keep the castle, it alienated them from other Saxon households in West Yorkshire. I suppose we were looked upon as traitors. I think the old prejudices still hold, which is why no one has helped us with our problem with Bramley. We have not asked for assistance and no one has offered."

They were coming up to the enormous portcullis and Daniel could see soldiers through the grate. "Then mayhap that will change after tonight," he said. "As I said before, the invitation for sup tonight is fortuitous. Mayhap more fortuitous than you know."

She looked at him, only really seeing the back of his head. "How?"

"Mayhap it is time to establish new relationships with your neighbors."

Before she could question him, Daniel announced himself to the sentries at Netherghyll's big gate and the portcullis began to immediately crank open. The chains strained, creaking, and when the portcullis was about halfway up, Daniel proceeded in, followed by Gunnar on the little mare.

The bailey of Netherghyll was fairly vast and oddly garden-like; there were actually patches of grass that seemed to be well manicured, but the complex that comprised Netherghyll's keep was truly of interest. There didn't seem to be one keep but three buildings pieced together around what looked to be a central courtyard, all of them positioned right in the middle of the bailey. The building farthest to the west had the pitched roof and single story of a great hall, while the building attached to it on the east side was tall, about three stories, and built square and block-like. The third building, attached to the south side of the eastern building, was two stories tall and rather long, like barracks. There were small windows cut out at regular intervals.

In all, it was a very big and a very odd complex, far more than Daniel had imagined it would be. More than that, it was evident that the de Royans had wealth. De Royans men were well-dressed and their horses were fat. Daniel again thought of Brighton, and how well-trained and well-equipped the man had been, and it was all starting to make some sense now. Netherghyll Castle clearly had the means. From its fellow castle not far to the south, Shadowmoor, the difference between the two fortresses was like the difference between night and day.

As they came to a halt near the strangely built keep complex, Gunnar leapt off his little mare as Daniel lowered Liselotte to the ground. In her lovely red dress, he was impressed anew every time he saw her. He dismounted Ares, his eyes still on her, as several grooms rushed up to take the animals, most of them focused on the big black war horse with the impressive build.

Ares, an attention seeker, began frisking the grooms for any signs of treats in their pockets and the young grooms seemed quite amused with the horse's antics. Daniel assured them that it was all right to feed the horse a treat or two. Like a proud father, he was not opposed to having his precious horse spoiled by others, and as he held out his elbow to Liselotte, a shout from the direction of the keep caught their attention.

"Greetings!"

Daniel and Liselotte turned in time to see Glennie approaching on the arm of an older man, both of them coming from the building that was presumably the one-storied hall. Glennie was trying to tug the man along but he wouldn't run with her so she stopped pulling on him and scurried on ahead to greet their guests.

"I am so happy that you have come!" she said excitedly, looking at Liselotte, still in the red gown from the last time she saw her. She rushed the woman. "You are beautiful, my lady. I am so glad that you purchased that dress. The red color is exquisite on you."

Liselotte smiled timidly as Glennie grasped her hand. "Thank you, my lady," she said. "You have excellent taste in selecting it for me."

Glennie simply grinned, broadly, and pulled Liselotte along with her as she approached the older man. "Papa," she said. "This is Lady Liselotte l'Audacieux. Her father is lord of Shadowmoor. My lady, this is my father, Sir Easton de Royans."

Liselotte curtsied politely. "My lord," she said. "My deepest gratitude for your invitation to sup tonight. Allow me to introduce my brother, Gunnar l'Audacieux, and our noble escort is Sir Daniel de Lohr."

"It was Sir Daniel who saved me from those terrible men in town, Papa," Glennie said before her father could respond to the introduction. "He was positively heroic."

Daniel forced a smile at Glennie's enthusiasm as the woman's father looked him over. Easton was a handsome man with cropped blond hair and a bald spot right on the top of his head. He was big and had been muscular once, but in his middle age, much of that had gone to fat.

Still, he wasn't unattractive in the least, and as Daniel looked at the man, he could definitely see the resemblance between Easton and Brighton. *So this is Brighton's father*, he thought. *He is a man with some joy on his face because he does not yet know his eldest son is dead.* It was a sobering thought, but one that had Daniel on his guard. He would be supping with, and asking help from, a man whose son he had helped kill. But that didn't matter; he wanted something from de Royans and he would have it. As Daniel wrestled with the familiar bitterness that the de Royans name provoked, Easton smiled at his guests and extended his hand to Daniel.

"Sir Daniel," he said, shaking Daniel's hand when the man reached out. "You cannot know the depths of my gratitude. Glennie told me what happened in town today and you have my undying thanks for saving her. I am in your debt, sir."

Daniel shook his head as he released the man's hand. "It was no trouble, I assure you," he said. "It was my pleasure. Having us in your home for sup is certainly thanks enough."

Easton was still smiling, still inspecting Daniel. "You are a de Lohr," he said with admiration in his tone. "It seems as if I have heard that name my entire life. When I was a very young man, I served as a squire in The Holy Land with Richard, and the name de Lohr was often spoken with appreciation. Are you related to Christopher or David?"

Daniel nodded. "David is my father," he replied. "Thank you for remembering him so kindly."

Easton nodded. "Indeed," he said, his pale blue eyes glimmering. "To have a de Lohr save my daughter is quite an honor. It will give me something to boast about."

Daniel laughed softly. "I am flattered, but it was truly no trouble."

Easton simply nodded, his gaze then moving to Liselotte. Something in his expression changed then; it went from stark admiration of the de Lohr name to something a bit more curious. Interested, even. He studied Liselotte a moment before speaking.

"And to have the daughter of the Lord of Shadowmoor in my home is a great honor, indeed," he said sincerely. "I am sorry that your father and I have never met. It seems as if I am always running about, conducting business, and never giving time to my neighbors. It is something I hope to rectify in the future."

Liselotte smiled politely. "And it seems as if we simply keep to ourselves and never leave the fortress much," she said, wondering if the man was expecting an invitation to visit and not wanting to give him one. She sought to change the subject. "Thank you for your gracious invitation to sup, my lord. Netherghyll is quite a large place. I would imagine it has a very prestigious history."

Easton nodded. "It does, in fact," he said. Then, he held out his elbow to her. "May I accompany you inside, my lady? We can speak in the warmth of the hall. It looks as if the weather is about to turn on us again."

Liselotte took the man's elbow, glancing at Daniel as she did so. He smiled encouragingly at her, having seen how awkward she was in social situations, and he was proud that she had handled herself quite well so far. Liselotte must have sensed his approval because a faint smile flashed across her lips before Easton lead her away.

Daniel watched her go, unable to take his eyes from her in her gorgeous red dress. She looked like an angel and his heart began doing strange things in his chest. It was fluttering and jumping, making him feel breathless, and it was all directly related to his vision of Liselotte as she walked away. Something about her was causing these strange symptoms. If he hadn't known better, he would have thought that he was smitten with her. But that was impossible.

... wasn't it?

"Sir Daniel?"

Broken from his train of thought, Daniel turned to see Glennie standing next to him, smiling prettily. She held up her hand, very close to his arm.

"Will you please escort me inside?" she asked sweetly. "I am so glad you and Lady Liselotte have come. I am looking forward to this so very much."

Daniel forced a smile at the woman because she was looking hungrily at him again and he felt much like *he* was about to be on the menu this evening. Figuratively, of course, but he knew he would have to be on his guard. He didn't like that lustful gleam in Glennie's bright eyes....

"Of course, my lady," he said gallantly, extending his elbow to her. "It would be my honor."

Glennie snatched his elbow and nearly sent him off balance with the force of her grab. Daniel was thinking that it felt very much as if she'd latched on to him forever. He wondered if her fingers were going to burrow into his arm like tree roots so that they would never be separated, and he would be forced to drag the woman around for the rest of his life as she hung off of his elbow like a giant growth. If Lady Glennie had anything to say about it, he was sure he'd never make it out of Netherghyll at all.

As he'd suspected all along, he knew a hunter when he saw one.

Daniel waved Gunnar along with them as they headed for the long building with the steeply pitched roof and, in spite of Glennie's nonstop chatter, Daniel still found himself watching the sway of Liselotte's hips in front of him. It was seductive, alluring to the point of distraction. But he continued to smile periodically at Glennie as she talked, simply to acknowledge that he was listening to her. She didn't have his complete attention but it wouldn't do to insult her since he wanted something from her father this night. Offending Glennie would not aid those plans. Therefore, he tolerated her attempts to flirt with him. He did not, however, flirt back.

The doors to the hall were open as they approached; great wooden panels with plates of iron bolted to them that had the de Royans coat of arms. It was a three-point shield with an ax emblazoned upon it and very impressive. Following Liselotte and Easton into the rather big room, Daniel was hit in the face with the stale warmth from the blazing hearth. It smelled heavily of rushes and of freshly baked bread, and he looked up as they entered and he could see the enormous crossbeams that stabilized the roof and the slats of thatching across the beams. The big room was well built.

To his right, a hearth as tall as he was burned furiously, spitting smoke into the room, which gathered up by the thatched ceiling. There were several dogs grouped near the hearth and Gunnar ran straight for them, falling to his knees as many happy dog tongues came out to lick him. As Daniel watched, one very big black dog that weighed more than Gunnar did decided to lie across the boy's lap and Gunnar crowed with laughter. Daniel couldn't help but grin at the happy boy, surrounded by equally happy dogs. He was in heaven.

"Remind me to check the dog pack before we leave to make sure I have not left a boy behind," he said to Glennie. "I do believe he will be happy there for the evening."

Glennie laughed softly at Gunnar, who was now lying on the ground as a dozen dogs licked him and tried to play with him. "They are quite friendly," she said. "My father and brothers adore dogs, so they are always well-fed and very happy."

Brothers, Daniel thought. *Like Brighton.*

The return of Brighton threatened to sink his mood again but he fought it, reminding himself that he was here at Netherghyll for a reason. He wanted something. Therefore, he forced himself away from thoughts of Brighton yet again as Glennie pulled him away from the dogs and over to the long scrubbed feasting table where Easton was politely seating Liselotte.

Daniel immediately noticed that there was already food on the table; several loaves of bread, dried fruits, and two bowls of something that turned out to be pickled onions. Instead of trenchers, there were actual plates of pewter set out as a display of the de Royans' wealth, meant to impress visitors, and Easton was already helping Liselotte spoon onions onto her plate. Bread, butter, and some kind of stewed fruit were near the bread as well as a silver salt cellar in the shape of an apple.

It was quite a display of prosperity and Daniel took his seat after courteously helping Glennie into hers. But he came to notice that all of the food was coming at Liselotte first, and rather quickly, and he watched her carefully, wondering how she was going to handle the situation. She'd probably never seen so much food in her entire life.

Knowing that her family had been facing starvation, Daniel was concerned that Liselotte might be overwhelmed by it all, but so far, she was handling it with grace. Much better than he was handling Glennie, who was now sitting conspicuously close to him. He would scoot over an inch or two, and she would do the same. He was scooting his way right off the bench so, after three or four scoots, he finally came to a halt and began to help himself to the food. There was no use in trying to move away from her, as she wouldn't be discouraged.

"You were going to tell us some of the history of Netherghyll, my lord," Daniel said as he ripped apart a hunk of bread, deliberately not helping Glennie with her meal because he was becoming irritated with her. "I have traveled a good deal in Yorkshire but have never heard of the place. You are somewhat remote."

Easton was being quite solicitous to Liselotte, who seemed unsure of the man's attention. She kept trying to serve herself but he was doing it for her, making for an awkward situation, but Easton seemed undeterred. He continued to help her whether or not she liked it.

"Somewhat remote, aye," he said as he waved over a servant who had just entered the hall carrying a heavy iron pot with a boiled beef knuckle in it. "But we sit near the road to Carlisle, the only such road in the west of England, so we are not too terribly remote. The location of Netherghyll was chosen for that very reason – near the road to Carlisle. The Cononley barony stretches from Eastburn all the way north to Skipton. It borders Shadowmoor's lands to the south."

Daniel was listening with some interest, settling down to his food as Glennie served herself. "Yet you are not allies with Shadowmoor?"

Easton paused in his attempts to assist Liselotte. "I think that Lady Liselotte can confirm that the Lords of Shadowmoor have always kept to themselves," he said. "When Glennie told me she had met Lady Liselotte in town and had invited her to sup, you can imagine how surprised I was. I should like very much to know my neighbors to the south, but historically, Netherghyll has never much associated with Shadowmoor."

Liselotte could see that the man was attempting to be tactful. "My lord, you need not stand on politeness," she said. "Shadowmoor has, indeed, always kept to themselves, and has for many years. It has always been thus. I was trying to explain the reasons to Sir Daniel today – my ancestors sided with the Normans when they came and, therefore, became outcasts amongst their neighbors. It is still that way. It has never changed."

Easton nodded, relieved that the lady understood the situation. "I always thought the Lords of Shadowmoor simply did not wish to associate with the rest of us."

Liselotte looked up at him. "That may have been true in the past, but it is no longer the case," she said. "Although we have nothing to offer by way of strength in an alliance, I am sure my father would like to come to know his neighbors."

Easton smiled at her in such a way that provoked Daniel's displeasure. Much as he didn't like the way Glennie was looking at him, he clearly didn't like the way Easton was looking at Liselotte. He was coming to think he'd come into an entire nest of hungry people, men seeking women and women seeking men. He struggled not to let his expression show it.

"It is unfortunate that you did not know your neighbors before now," he said, distracting Easton from Liselotte. "I am sure that Lord l'Audacieux could have used your help four years ago when the persecution of Shadowmoor began."

Easton's brow furrowed curiously. "What persecution is that?"

Daniel nodded to the servant with the pot of beef, and the man began to slap meat onto Daniel's plate. "The men who tried to assault your daughter in town today are sworn to a lord who has been making life miserable for Lady Liselotte and her family," he said. "Have you heard of Lord Bramley?"

Easton was thoughtful, scratching his forehead. "Is he that man who took possession of Bramley Castle a few years ago?" he asked, watching Daniel nod. "I do believe I heard about him when he first took possession of the lands near Bradford. A traveling merchant, who stayed here one night, mentioned that he had sought shelter at Bramley the night before. He mentioned that the man was a nephew to the king, but other than that, I've not seen nor heard of Bramley since that time."

Daniel pursed his lips ironically. "That is because he has spent all of his time harassing Shadowmoor," he said. "They do not have the means to defend themselves against him and he wants their lands, so much so that he has nearly starved them out. And you say you've never met the man?"

Easton was concerned about what he was hearing. "I have not," he said. "He has stayed away from me."

"That is fortunate. How big is your army, my lord?"

"I carry nearly nine hundred men."

Daniel slapped the table as if to emphasize his point. "That is why," he said, looking at Liselotte. "It is my suspicion that he is going after Shadowmoor because you do not have the standing army that Netherghyll has. But once he has your property, however, he will have a great deal of land that borders Netherghyll. It is quite possible, at that point, he will begin a campaign of harassment against Netherghyll to confiscate her lands as well."

Easton's concern doubled. "Do you think that is true?" he asked, aghast. "Who is this man? If he is the nephew to the king, then he will summon Henry's troops to aid him, will he not? And what does that say for me? I am loyal to Henry – would he really send troops to purge me from my own home?"

Daniel held up a hand because he could see that Easton was growing quite upset. "I do not know, my lord," he said, "but I intend to find out. I met Bramley on my journey north, in fact. He was chasing young Gunnar across the moors."

Both Easton and Glennie turned to look at the boy, who was still happily seated on the floor with the dogs surrounding him. "*That* child?" Easton was appalled. "Why would he chase him?"

Daniel cocked an eyebrow. "Part of his campaign of harassment," he said. "He had abducted the boy and was trying to use him to coerce

Lady Liselotte's father into turning over both the lady and Shadowmoor to him. He wants to marry Lady Liselotte and he wants the fortress quite badly, but the boy escaped his custody and, fortunately, I found him before Bramley did."

Now Easton and Glennie were looking at Liselotte. "That is terrible," Glennie gasped. "Is this really true? Lord Bramley wants to marry you?"

Liselotte was uncomfortable that the conversation had suddenly turned to her but she fought that discomfort. "Aye," she said. "He saw me in Bradford four years ago with my father and immediately made an offer of marriage. My father refused, of course, and since then, we've known nothing but aggression from Bramley. At first, he tried to woo me, and my father, but when we refused, he turned to starving us out, burning out our villiens and making our lives miserable."

Daniel could see that Easton and Glennie were appalled by what they were hearing and he thought that it was perhaps the right time to press his agenda. Now that he had their sympathy for Shadowmoor, he intended to take advantage of it. It was the entire reason he had come to Netherghyll.

"When I found Gunnar and refused to return him to Bramley, the man tried to bully me, but, of course, his tactics did not work," he said. "He then proceeded to tell me that he was the nephew of Henry but when I interrogated him, I discovered that it is his sister who is actually John's bastard, meaning that Lord Bramley, whose gave his real name as Roland Fitzroy, is not related to the king at all by blood. In any case, Bramley wants Shadowmoor and it is my intention to send a message to my Uncle Christopher, who is a mere few days' ride away, and ask for reinforcements for Shadowmoor. I will also ask my uncle to send word to Henry about Bramley, or Fitzroy, or whatever he calls himself, and inform him of the man's actions against Shadowmoor. I was hoping you could supply me with a messenger who can ride swiftly to the Welsh Marches for this purpose. I hope you can see that by doing this, I may be saving Netherghyll from Bramley's wicked intentions as well."

Easton was nodding before Daniel even finished speaking, obviously in full agreement. "Of course I will," he said. "Write your missive tonight and I will send the man at dawn for the Marches. This is outrageous. I will send men to reinforce Shadowmoor at once until the de Lohr army arrives."

Daniel shook his head. "Nay, my lord," he cautioned. "That would only turn Bramley's attention on you. Stay out of the fight for now and protect your property, and that means keeping close watch on your daughter. If Bramley discovers she is from Netherghyll, and if it is really his intention to lay siege to Netherghyll after he has conquered Shadowmoor, then you must protect her. He will try to use her as he has tried to use Lady Liselotte and her siblings."

The happy, friendly mood of the meal had now become one of great concern and apprehension, but Daniel was pleased by it. It was exactly what he wanted – to have de Royans as concerned about Bramley's movements as he was. Easton, his brow furrowed, shook his head with disgust.

"She will not leave Netherghyll again until this situation is resolved," he said. "Thank you for bringing this to my attention, Sir Daniel. It would seem that we owe you a great deal of gratitude, for many reasons. That you should be concerned for people you do not know speaks of your character and chivalry, my lord. It will not be forgotten."

Daniel looked at the man, the father of an enemy he had helped to kill, and something within him began to waver. He had wondered what kind of people would have raised a son like Brighton, and he had been apprehensive of this meal all along, but now that he had spent some time with Easton, he couldn't honestly see any aggression or recklessness in the man. Easton conveyed nothing but gratitude and politeness, and had since the beginning of their association. Daniel wondered if it was merely good behavior for a guest, but he didn't think so. He didn't get the impression that this was all an act for their benefit.

Perhaps the de Royans weren't such a bad family, after all.

"I am happy to be of service, my lord," he said. "I would do the same for any respectable lord."

"You *will* stay the night, won't you?" Glennie asked, interrupting their repartee. "We so rarely have guests and we would love to have your company."

Daniel was actually glad for such an invitation because it meant he didn't have to wander back out in the night and find shelter for him and Liselotte and Gunnar. Now, they could stay under a good roof with good food and a warm fire. He felt comfortable enough with Easton and Glennie to accept the invitation.

More than that, it would be an opportunity for Liselotte to sleep in a good bed and have all the food she could eat. He was quite certain it had been years since she'd had enough food at her disposal and it was perhaps that reason, more than anything, to accept their hospitality. The poor woman had known enough hardship in her life and his gaze moved to her, lingering on her.

Liselotte's head was down as she continued to stuff herself with bread, clearly trying to store up for the days to come when she would be hungry again. It hurt his heart to see that. Daniel wanted her to know prosperity at least once in her life, knowing her next meal would be as plentiful as the last. More than once, if he had anything to say about it. But for tonight, he wanted her to know something wonderful.

"We are grateful for your hospitality," he said to Glennie. Then, he turned to Easton. "I will write that missive to my uncle tonight before I retire."

Easton nodded. "Excellent," he said, holding up his pewter chalice so that the nearby servant would fill it with good wine. "Now that the matter is settled, let us speak on something more pleasant for the sake of the women. Surely they do not wish to hear of wicked lords and threats of sieges. Will you tell me where you are from, Sir Daniel? Where does your father now make his home?"

Now that his purpose at Netherghyll had been satisfied and a messenger would soon be sent south to the Welsh Marches, Daniel relaxed a little. Perhaps it was the wine, or perhaps it really was the company, but he nonetheless felt himself easing. He delved into his succulent beef.

"My father is the Earl of Canterbury," he said, taking a bite. "It is a title he inherited from my mother's father because the man had no male heirs. It is title I will inherit upon his death."

That seemed to impress Easton a great deal. "And your uncle is the Earl of Hereford and Worcester," he said. "I remember that title from long ago."

Daniel nodded as he chewed. "He received that title right before King Richard's death," he said. "My uncle has many sons, however, so there is an entire succession of de Lohr offspring in line for that title. My cousins Curtis, Richard, Myles, Douglas, and Henry."

"And you are your father's only son?"

"I am the only male, and the youngest, with three older sisters."

"Papa, remember that I told you my friend Adalind is Daniel's niece?" Glennie said to her father. "Lady Adalind de Aston is the daughter of Daniel's sister."

Daniel glanced at the woman as he chewed. "My oldest sister, in fact," he said. "But her name is no longer Adalind de Aston. It is now Lady du Bois."

Glennie was enthusiastic for that married title. "Tell me of her husband," she said. "You said that she married a knight in your father's service. Do you know him, then?"

Daniel nodded as he took another bite of beef. "He is my closest and dearest friend in the world," he said. "He is a man of great honor and skill and I adore the big clod. Adalind could have done far worse, I assure you. They are quite happy together. Did she never tell you about Maddoc du Bois, Lady Glennie? You and Adalind were such close friends that I am surprised she never told you."

Glennie's eyes widened. "*Maddoc*?" she repeated in surprise. "She married her Maddoc?"

Daniel grinned. "So she did tell you of him."

Glennie nodded wildly. "She did!" she said. "Her beloved Maddoc! I am sure she mentioned his surname but I did not recall it. I only knew him as Maddoc. He was all she ever spoke of. So she truly married him?"

"She did."

Glennie crowed with delight. "I cannot tell you how thrilled I am to hear this," she said. Then, she grasped her cup of wine and held it aloft. "I must toast their marriage. A toast to my dear friend Adalind and her handsome Maddoc. I wish them great joy and happiness, always."

Daniel, Easton, and Liselotte raised their cups in salute, drinking to the toast. Daniel, in fact, drained his cup and a nearby servant quickly filled it. He continued shoving beef into his mouth.

"When I see her next, I will tell her of your good wishes," he said. "She will be very happy to know that I finally met her Glennie. She is quite fond of you, you know."

Glennie was watching Daniel eat, her expression soft. "And I am very fond of her," she said. "I hope to be able to…."

Glennie was cut off when the great entry doors to the hall were pushed open and a figured appeared from the wet bailey outside. Moving in shadows it came, a figure of a man that blended with the dark of the hall. As it came closer into the light, dripping armor was illuminated, glistening in the firelight.

The man was moderately tall with a head of wet hair which, as he came closer into the light of the hall, turned out to be blond. He was broad shouldered, and quite obviously a knight from the way he was dressed and the weaponry he wore, but the moment his features came into focus, Daniel felt as if he had been hit in the belly. He could hardly believe the vision that faced him.

Ghosts do exist, he thought. *Dear God… they truly do.*

CHAPTER SEVEN

BRIGHTON DE ROYANS had returned from the dead.

It was a phantom, come to haunt him. Daniel was convinced. But he blinked his eyes and took a deep breath, steadying himself before realizing that the man facing him in the wet armor wasn't *exactly* Brighton. Thank God, it wasn't. But it was a man who looked very much like him and Daniel was sure that this was the brother Glennie had spoken of, a man by the name of Caston. *God's Bones*, Daniel thought, shaken by the vision. *Was it really possible for brothers to look so much alike?*

Servants closed the heavy door behind the knight as he approached the table. He glanced at his father and his sister, but looked curiously at Daniel. When Liselotte came into full view, he looked even more curiously at her. Much as his father's expression had shown, there was interest there. A twinkle came to his eye.

"We have guests?" the man asked in a voice very similar to what Brighton's voice had also sounded like. "I had no idea. Forgive me for being late to sup."

Easton stood up, indicating Daniel first. "You have been gone all day and could not have known of our guests," he said. "I will introduce you to Sir Daniel de Lohr, son of David, Earl of Canterbury. He is from the famous House of de Lohr, Caston, so behave yourself. His charming companion is Lady Liselotte l'Audacieux, daughter of the Lord of

Shadowmoor. My lord, my lady… meet my son, Sir Caston de Royans."

Daniel stood up politely to greet the man, still somewhat rattled by the appearance of a dead man. "My lord," he greeted evenly. "Your sister and father have been kind enough to have us for supper this evening."

Caston grinned, throwing Daniel off his guard even more because he even smiled like Brighton. It was all Daniel could do to try and conceal that shock as he resumed his seat. Caston sat at the end of the table, accepting the cup of wine that a servant handed to him.

"Welcome to Netherghyll," he said to Daniel although he kept eyeing Liselotte. "Not as grand as the de Lohr properties, I am sure, but we like it here. What brings you up into Yorkshire? You are far from Canterbury."

Daniel nodded, taking another big gulp of wine because he found he needed it; was this God's cruel joke that he should spend the evening with a man who looked a good deal like his dead enemy? The evening was beginning to get interesting.

"I am, indeed," he said to Caston. "I was heading north to visit friends and my path took me by way of the road to Carlisle."

"It is fortuitous, Caston," Easton said seriously. "He has come to save Shadowmoor and Netherghyll. Have you heard of Lord Bramley, the man who assumed possession of Bramley Castle a few years ago? It seems that the man has launched terrible aggression against Shadowmoor in an attempt to force the Lord of Shadowmoor from his home. Bramley claims to be a nephew to the king but it seems that he lies about that. Sir Daniel fears that if Bramley is able to confiscate Shadowmoor, then he might want Netherghyll next."

Caston listened to his father, brow furrowed. He didn't seem too concerned about the situation. "I have heard of Bramley but I've not met the man," he said, looking to Daniel. "What makes you think he will try to acquire Netherghyll?"

Daniel sounded much less sensational than Easton had. He was factual. "Because the man has been trying to obtain Shadowmoor for four years in a constant campaign of harassment," he said. "He watches the roads, steals the tariffs due to Shadowmoor, burns out their villiens, and has starved out the castle. They cannot make a move without Bramley's men descending on them."

Caston shrugged. "But that does not guarantee he is after Netherghyll."

Daniel nodded. "That is true," he said, appreciating that Caston didn't seem quick to frighten. "But think on it this way; Bramley's lands adjoin Shadowmoor from the south. Netherghyll adjoins Shadowmoor's lands from the north. If Bramley is an ambitious man, and all indications are that he is, would it not be logical for him to join his lands to Shadowmoor's, and then move to take Netherghyll's next? That would make him an enormous land holder. He would have everything from Bradford all the way up to Skipton."

Caston could see the man's point now and a bit of concern entered his manner. "That would make sense," he said, his gaze lingering on Liselotte, who had thus far remained completely silent throughout the conversation. "My lady, is it as bad as all that? Has this Lord Bramley truly harassed Shadowmoor so terribly? I must apologize that this is the first time I have heard about any harassment of our neighbors."

Now that the focus of the conversation was on Liselotte, she looked at bit startled by it. From the moment Easton had begun spooning dishes onto her trencher, she had shoved the food into her mouth as discreetly as possibly, but she'd been shoving as much in as she could without choking on it. She was starving. She hadn't eaten beef in well over two years and here, a massive knuckle was staring her in the face. That, plus the creamy-white bread and butter, the pickled onions, and a sauced fish dish, had all made it onto her plate in big quantities and into her mouth. She was gorging herself to the point of becoming ill and now that everyone was looking at her, she began to feel nauseous and embarrassed. But she looked Caston in the eye as she answered his question.

"My father and I first met Lord Bramley in the village of Menston," she said. "Do you know where that is, my lord?"

Caston nodded; he rather liked the way she spoke, with a very faint lisp he thought charming. "I do," he said. "It is southeast of us, on the other side of Rombald's Moor."

Liselotte nodded. "That is correct, sir," she said. "It is a small town and one that is part of my father's estate. We were in town collecting tariffs and Bramley saw me. He immediately went in pursuit, and I do mean very heavy pursuit. He would not leave me alone; he never left my side and had his men bring me all manner of gifts that, we found out later, he had stolen from the merchants in town. When one man protested, Bramley's men beat him quite badly. That was only the beginning. When I refused his suit, he took to terrorizing the villages on my father's estate, stealing from peasants, killing them if they resisted. My father had men to collect taxes and dispense justice in the towns, but Bramley's men harassed and beat them so badly that they were afraid to do their job. He killed most of our cow and sheep herds just because he could. Even now, his men watch the roads from Shadowmoor, looking for more people to harass or beat. Therefore, in answer to your question, it is as bad as all that and more, my lord. It has been hell."

By the time she finished, the entire table was somber and Caston in particular. His expression was one of concern and outrage. "Then I am sorry you have had to deal with that," he said. "But why did you not send for help from Netherghyll? Undoubtedly, we would have helped."

Easton interrupted. "We have already been through that," he said, waving his son off. "Suffice it to say that we are keeping our eye on Shadowmoor but, at the suggestion of Sir Daniel, we will not send help. Sir Daniel is afraid that will turn Bramley's venom on us. Therefore, Sir Daniel is sending a missive to his uncle, Christopher de Lohr, at dawn. He will ask for reinforcements against Bramley in the hopes of defeating the man once and for all so he will leave Shadowmoor alone."

Caston listened carefully to his father before looking to Daniel. "And you believe your uncle will help?"

Daniel nodded confidently. "When I explain the situation, I have no doubt he will," he replied. "The one thing I am not certain of is how many men Bramley has sworn to him. Lady Liselotte has only seen patrols of men. My lady, can you elaborate?"

Liselotte nodded. "That is normally what Lord Bramley sends out," she said. "Groups of men. I have never seen more than six or seven together. He has never sent an army against Shadowmoor, not ever."

Daniel cocked an eyebrow. "I am wondering if he even has one now," he said. "It would be an impressive feat to starve out an entire fortress with only six or seven men at any given time."

Liselotte shook her head, thinking there was an insult against her father in that statement. "Not such a feat when you consider he is an aggressor and we have been living in peace, with no standing army, for decades," she said, trying not to sound defensive. "The people who live in and around Shadowmoor are farmers or craftsmen, not soldiers. And I believe Lord Bramley has more men than just a few because while six or seven are harassing the fortress, we have reports that more of his men are in the towns, frightening the villagers. Therefore, he has more men – we just do not know how many, exactly."

Daniel thought she sounded much as if she were defending Shadowmoor, and even her father, against some kind of implied cowardice when it came to Bramley. He hastened to ease her.

"I understand," he said. "I did not mean to insinuate your people were afraid to do anything against just a few men. I simply meant that Bramley is quite bold to do what it does with only a few men at a time. But given what you've explained, it would make sense that he has more men at his disposal."

"From what I know of Bramley Castle, it is not very large," Caston said, interrupting the exchange. "I cannot say that in my travels, I have passed by it or have even thought of it in many a year, but the last I recall, it was a small enclosure with a small keep. Hardly more than that."

Daniel listened closely. "Then it would be safe to say that if Bramley has an army, it is not a very big one?"

Caston shook his head. "He would have nowhere to house it if he did."

"One hundred men at most?"

"At the very most."

Daniel nodded, thoughtfully. "So Bramley has less than one hundred men to harass Shadowmoor," he said. "It is enough to cause havoc because Shadowmoor has no army to combat it. Netherghyll, on the other hand, has a very large army, so it makes sense that Bramley would stay clear of them. However, if he is able to obtain Shadowmoor, he would be able to house a much larger army which would be a threat to Netherghyll. If I was an ambitious man, that would be my plan."

Caston lifted his eyebrows in agreement. "There is no disputing your logic," he said. "Again, I am embarrassed to say that I have not heard about Bramley's harassment, or anything else about the man for that matter. But now that we know, we will keep an eye on the situation."

"You are not to blame, Caston," Easton said, well into his third cup of wine. He looked at Daniel as he spoke. "Caston conducts business for me outside of the castle. I cannot ride long distances these days so Caston is my emissary, usually to allies to the north. I will admit we do not travel much south of Keighley, which is the town just south of us. We do most of our business in Skipton, and for our larger needs, we will go to Blackburn or Preston to the west. I do not like Leeds, nor have I ever, so we do not travel south very often."

"Leeds is a dirty city," Caston agreed, taking a healthy drink from his cup. "So is Bradford and Wakefield, all full of dirty people. In fact, only my brother, Brighton, seems to take a liking to the south of England. He serves Norfolk and is stationed at Arundel Castle, which is not far from Canterbury Castle, I believe."

Daniel had mercifully forgotten about Brighton for a few brief minutes so to hear Caston speak of the man was like a sudden jolt, reminding him, yet again, of the fact that he'd help to kill Easton's son and Caston's brother. But he wasn't about to give away his thoughts, not now that the evening was pleasant and he had what he wanted. Well, at least they had promised him what he had wanted, a messenger come the morning, so he kept his thoughts, and feelings, well-concealed. He didn't want to do, or say, anything to jeopardize the alliance he was trying to build.

"The south of England is vast," he said neutrally. "I believe Arundel is about three days from Canterbury. My father, as far as I know, does not have any direct contact with Norfolk."

Caston grinned. "You would know my brother if you met him," he said. "He looks just like me."

"Is that so?"

"He was born fifteen minutes before I was."

A great deal was made clear to Daniel in that statement. Truth be told, he was very curious about the resemblance and was relieved to know he wasn't going mad. Perhaps the dead did come back to life at times, but in this situation, it was thankfully not the case. He breathed somewhat easier.

"Ah," he said, relief in his tone. "He is your twin."

Caston nodded, holding up his cup so a servant could fill it. "He is," he replied. "We fostered together and have done nearly everything together over the years, but he found favor with Norfolk some years back and has served him ever since. I think he likes living away from Netherghyll and yearns for the excitement that serving a warlord brings. The last we saw of him was two years ago."

"Two years ago come Christmas," Easton confirmed softly.

Daniel looked at the older de Royans and he could see a longing in his expression for his missing son. It was like a dagger to Daniel's heart, suddenly feeling so terribly bad for the man. He began to feel very torn about the situation now, wondering if he should do the honorable thing and tell them what he knew. It was only fair. But then he realized that he had imbibed three big cups of wine and knew it was the alcohol that was making him feel so soft and foolish. Telling Easton what he knew would not be a good thing, for any of them. Let them go on the assumption that Brighton was still alive and well. It would be more comforting than the alternative. Daniel finally pushed his cup away, unwilling to drink anymore, fearful of what he would say if he did.

"I have not been home for Christmas in four years," he told Easton in an attempt to comfort the man about a son he would never see again. "In fact, since I received my spurs, I have traveled this country, into Scotland, and over to France and the Danish countries. I like to travel so it is not unusual for me to miss many holidays with my family. There have been times when I have gone years without seeing them."

Caston regarded him over the rim of his cup. "You do not serve your father?"

Daniel nodded. "Technically, I do," he said. "But he does not force me to remain at Canterbury. 'Tis a good thing, too. I drive the man mad at times. Whenever he looks at me, the veins in his head start to throb."

He was grinning as he said it, causing Liselotte, who had been listening attentively, to giggle. Daniel winked at her.

"You think I am jesting?" he asked her. "It is quite true. When I was a lad, since I was the only son, the youngest child, and quite spoilt, I could do anything I wanted in my father's home and get away with it. My Aunt Elyse, who never married, is a mastery of trickery. She and I used to play all manner of jokes on my father, which would enrage him terribly. One time, he was sleeping before the fire and my aunt and I very carefully lifted soot from the hearth and sprinkled it on the palm of his right hand. Then we ticked his face and when he put his hand up to slap what he thought was an insect, he got black soot all over his face. He chased us through the house and but I was the one to get caught. He hung me upside-down by my ankles and used a switch on my buttocks. It did not really hurt but the message was obvious. It was my mother who had to save me and cut me down."

By this time, the table was laughing at him. "You were a naughty lad, my lord," Liselotte said. "Dastardly!"

Easton held up a finger as if to submit his point. "Not true," he said.

"'Tis a very clever lad. And lively. I am sure Sir David was very proud of his son, even if he *was* the butt of the child's joke."

Liselotte grinned and shook her head reproachfully, to which Daniel merely smiled. "It is still that way today, my lady," he said. "My father has come to expect all manner of jokes from me, but to tell you the truth, I am too old for such things. I suppose I must grow up sometime."

Liselotte held his gaze, a smile still on her lips, and Daniel couldn't take his eyes from her. There was something suggesting in that statement, perhaps a hint to a better future for them both. Even across the table from each other, it was the first time that either one of them had allowed any warmth to brew between them. There was some kind of magic in the air, pulling at them, creating a lure that hadn't been there before. But the truth was that some kind of attraction, in some form, had been there since the beginning. Now, with the food and wine, and with coming to know one another, that attraction was becoming too difficult to deny.

Liselotte could feel it. God's Bones, she could feel it and she'd never known anything like it. Warm and fluid, a viscous sensation like the flow of honey, filled every part of her body as she gazed at the man. It made her tremble and feel flushed at the same time. She had admired Daniel secretly since their introduction and now, as the moments ticked away, she was becoming less and less apt to hide her esteem for him. She knew there could never be anything between them but it didn't seem to matter any longer. How could she help but admire him? He was handsome and chivalrous and a joy to be around. He was all things heavenly that she never knew to exist.

She knew he would break her heart but she almost didn't care.

"Sir Daniel," Glennie said, breaking into the warm moment and shattering it with her voice. "If you travel so much, how do you have the means to do so? You have a lovely horse and big weapons, and that takes a good deal of money."

Before Daniel could answer, Easton scolded his daughter softly.

"Glennie," he said. "You do not ask a man about his money. That is impolite."

Daniel laughed quietly, lifting a hand to show he was not offended. "It is a reasonable question, my lord," he said to Easton. Then, he looked at Glennie. "I have a considerable fortune of my own but I also aid lords or friends if they require a skilled sword. I have been known to fight other men's battles from time to time. With the de Lohr name and my excellent training, I can command an excellent price. And I have also been known to enter tournaments with big purses. That is fairly easy money and I have won my share."

Glennie smiled dreamily at the thought of Daniel competing in a gallant tournament, but her amorous thoughts were interrupted as her brother spoke.

"Ironic you should mention a tournament," Caston said. "I saw postings in Skipton today that there is to be a tournament next month to mark some kind of spring celebration. I was thinking on entering."

Daniel was quite interested. "Is that so?" he asked. "Who is the sponsor?"

"The city merchants," Caston replied. "You know how that is; they pool their money for a sizable purse, which attracts decent competition as well as spectators, and then they make their money back and more besides when they sell food or other items on the day of the tournament."

"There is no lord sponsoring the event?"

Caston shook his head. "Not that I am aware of, although the Lords of Skipton Castle may have a hand in it," he said. "They usually do. De Romille is very active in his town."

"Do you know him?"

Easton replied. "I do," he said. "He is a good man."

"Will you consider entering, Sir Daniel?" Glennie asked hopefully. "If Caston enters and you enter, it will be quite exciting."

Daniel lifted his eyebrows, suggesting indecisiveness when he really was quite interested. "I am not sure," he said. "Your brother might defeat me. Then I would be ashamed. I would be forced to end my own miserable life."

It was a jest and Glennie giggled, turning to Liselotte. "Help me to convince him to compete," she said. "What fun we will have! Have you ever been to a tournament, my lady?"

Liselotte shook her head, embarrassed. There was so much of life that she had not had the opportunity to experience and she was shameful of the fact. "I have not," she said hesitantly. "I have heard they can be most exciting."

Glennie nodded eagerly, returning her attention to Daniel. "You see?" she said. "Lady Liselotte has never seen a tournament. Surely you must compete so that she has the opportunity to see it!"

"Then I must consider it, mustn't I?"

"You must!"

Daniel's attention moved to Caston. "Will you be competing, my lord?

Caston grinned. "If you are, then I will," he said. "Surely I cannot turn down an opportunity to best a de Lohr in competition."

"We will see."

"Aye, we will."

Daniel laughed, as did Caston, and the men raised their cups to one another as if to toast each other's chances were they face off in a contest. But Daniel didn't say anymore after that, quiet and thoughtful, as he nursed his wine. As Easton and Caston tossed around the reality of Caston competing in the tournament, Daniel was considering it very seriously, but not merely to impress Liselotte or win the purse for his own personal gain. He was thinking more on how far the money in that purse would go for the inhabitants of Shadowmoor if he were to win it.

Truth be told, they needed it much more than he ever could. It would be a great opportunity to provide them with coinage, as a gift, because he knew for a fact that pride would keep them from taking any of his personal fortune that he should offer them. He saw that the night before when he suggested that he should buy stores for the fortress since he was to be a guest there. They were ashamed that a guest should have to provide for his own meals. Even in town on this day, purchasing clothing for Liselotte had been a strained situation. She had resisted his attempts before Glennie managed to break her down. Therefore, Daniel knew Liselotte and Etzel wouldn't take money from him. They were too proud, and rightfully so. But winning a purse at a tournament and presenting them with that gift was quite different.

Different, indeed.

Without saying any more about it to his hosts, it was an idea he took with him when he was shown his chamber for the night by Glennie and her father. The bower was large and comfortable, and as he stood in the doorway, servants were hastily building a fire in the cold hearth that hadn't been used in a while.

As the servants coaxed forth a blaze, Easton and Daniel discussed the missive Daniel would be writing that night, the one that would summon de Lohr military might. Daniel had vellum in his saddlebags and promised to have a message to Easton within the hour, but it was difficult to keep his concentration as Glennie stood next to her father and batted her eyelashes at him. She was doing everything but stand on her head to get his attention, but he soundly ignored her.

As this foolery was going on, a servant showed Liselotte to a chamber on the floor above, and when Glennie stopped her flirtatious overtures in Daniel's direction, she suggested that Gunnar, who was still with the dogs, should like to sleep with Daniel. Daniel agreed and promised to return to the hall for the boy before he went to sleep to make sure the lad didn't spend the night sleeping in a dog pack.

Glennie seemed to think it was quite humorous, a young boy who was much happier with dogs than with humans, but she stopped giggling long enough to throw Daniel another seductive look when Easton forced her to bid Daniel a good sleep. She sauntered off after her father, deliberately switching her hips back and forth, but Daniel shut the door on her before she could turn around to see if he was still looking at her. Realizing that Daniel wasn't watching her, Glennie stormed off, pouting, after her father.

Daniel stood just inside his closed door, in his borrowed room, and silently laughed at the woman's antics.

The evening, for all concerned, had been both entertaining and enlightening.

☙

THE FIRST THING Daniel did when alone in his borrowed chamber was empty out his saddlebags to find the sturdy wooden box that contained his writing implements. He had a few sheets of vellum, a clump of uncolored sealing wax that was nearly gone, his signet stamp, sand, two quills, and about a half of a glass phial of precious ink that was wrapped up in dried grass to keep it from breaking.

All of these things he pulled forth and put carefully on a small table in the room, positioned next to the hearth. He took the next hour to scribe out a missive to his Uncle Christopher, explaining the situation at Shadowmoor and asking for both the man's military help and for his uncle to draft a missive for Henry asking him about Bramley. He knew his Uncle Christopher would take his request quite seriously because he wasn't one to make requests of his family, ever. In this case, however, he would make an exception.

Missive sanded and sealed, Daniel left his chamber and went in search of Easton to deliver the missive. He almost didn't make it – he was housed in the long, barrack-like building attached to the keep complex and it was all a bit of a labyrinth. He entered one corridor, thinking it led to the hall when it really led to a big bolted door that led out into a garden of some kind.

Backtracking, he found the correct corridor and ended up in a type of foyer with the hall beyond. A very old servant who had been sweeping the dirt floor of the hall saw him standing there and, at Daniel's request, scurried off to find Easton.

When the servant fled, Daniel delved deeper into the hall and immediately spied not one l'Audacieux but two near the hearth. Gunnar was now sleeping on the ground with the dogs all piled up around him, and on him, and Liselotte was sitting near her brother, and near the fire, with a plate of food in front of her.

She was still eating. Daniel had been smiling as he approached the table but when he saw that she was eating still, still very hungry, his smile faded. Sympathy tugged at his heart at the sight of Liselotte eating yet again, perhaps fearful she wouldn't eat again for some time to come. She was gorging herself while she could.

A sad state, indeed.

"Why are you still up?" Daniel asked softly as he sat across from her. "It is very late."

Liselotte appeared embarrassed and contrite that he had caught her eating again. She swallowed the food in her mouth.

"I… I came to see to my brother," she said quietly, just above a whisper because the boy was sleeping nearby. "I found him like this. I did not have the heart to wake him."

Daniel looked over at the boy, who was using one dog as a pillow while two other dogs were using him as a pillow. He chuckled softly.

"He certainly likes the dogs," he said. "I am not entirely sure I have the heart to wake him, either, but he cannot sleep here."

"Why not?"

Daniel looked at Liselotte. "Because he is not a servant or an animal himself," he said patiently. "All fine lads must sleep in a bed, in this case, in my chamber. There are two beds in it. I have one and he will have the other. Don't you want him to sleep in a good bed?"

Liselotte's gaze moved to her brother once more. "I suppose," she said. "But… but not yet, if you please. Let him stay just a little longer. He loves animals and was very attached to the dogs at Shadowmoor."

"I did not see any dogs at Shadowmoor."

Liselotte looked at him, sharply, before lowering her gaze back to her food. "We were forced to eat them."

Daniel should have guessed that. He felt rather bad that he had commented on the lack of dogs, now once again bringing light to their dire situation. On the heels of the natural sympathy he had for their plight, that he'd always had for their plight, he realized that he also felt quite protective over them. He really didn't know why; at first, his determination to help those at Shadowmoor had been nothing more than a mission, a self-imposed purpose, but now there was more to it. It had something to do with the beauty across the table from him, something in her eyes that showed such hope and trust in him. He'd never seen such trust, not from anyone. He didn't take it lightly.

But there was more to it than that and he knew it.

Something warm was growing in his heart for Liselotte, something he could no longer control.

"No more," he said, his voice low. "You will not worry over anything like that anymore. Eating dogs, or the lack of food… it will not happen again. I vow it upon my oath as a knight."

Liselotte still had a big piece of cheese in her hand, preparing to take a bite, but his declaration had her lowering the cheese back to the table. "May… may I ask you something, Daniel?"

"You always have permission to ask me whatever you wish."

Liselotte's brow furrowed as she thought carefully on her words. "My father told you last night that we are not your responsibility," she said. "But you continue to behave as if we are. The trip to town today, these beautiful clothes, and everything you told Sir Easton tonight… you behave as if we belong to you, as if we are your obligation. I am very puzzled as to why you should think so. You do not know us and we do not mean anything to you, yet you have taken us on as if to champion us. Please do not misunderstand; we are very grateful. My father believes that God has sent you, but I already told you that. Still… I am very afraid that somehow, someway, we will be indebted to you and there is no way we can ever repay you."

Daniel watched her from across the table, her beautiful face highlighted in the firelight. "The terrible behavior of others against you makes you surprised when someone is kind to you," he said quietly. "You want to trust that I am a man of my word but you cannot, not yet.

You are waiting for my true motives to be revealed, are you not?"

Liselotte averted her gaze, nodding her head after a moment. "Mayhap that is true."

Daniel smiled faintly. "You needn't worry that there is an ulterior motive," he said. "I… well, I suppose I am different than most men. It seems to me these days that knights in particular are cynical. They have seen so many years of war and fighting amongst the nobles of this country. Even my friends are weary of the battles, of their lords switching sides, and of the lies told on behalf of truth and justice. As for me, I see what has happened around us. I know that the king has not helmed our country as strongly or as honorably as we would have hoped. But in spite of the turmoil and ignoble lords, I choose to uphold my knightly vows of helping the less fortunate and championing the defeated. You, my lady, fall under both categories. When I see you, I see an opportunity to do something good and noble so that when I stand before God, I can tell Him I did all I could to help someone's life for the better. Mayhap that will balance out all of the sins I have committed."

Liselotte was listening to his words, understanding just a bit more of the man in that careful speech. "Then you see us as your salvation?"

"In a way, mayhap."

"Helping us is your penitence before God to right your wrongs?"

Daniel's smile grew. "It is possible," he said. Then, he reached across the table and put his hand on Liselotte's slender, warm fingers. He squeezed tightly. "When I say that my intention is to see Shadowmoor restored, I mean it. When I say that I will rid you of Bramley's suit, I mean that as well. You are too fine and noble a creature for the likes of him. You deserve a much better husband."

Liselotte was gazing into the man's eyes, her heart beating so forcefully that she was sure it was about to burst from her ribs. His hand on her fingers was just this side of heaven, bringing about a giddiness she had never known. She could hardly catch her breath because of it.

"I am not sure any man will want a woman with no dowry," she said, her voice trembling. "You know that I have nothing to offer and in spite of what you said earlier today, when you said that it does not matter what I wear because the right man will see what is beneath the clothing, I find that difficult to believe. You are the only man who has ever stopped long enough to notice our plight or help us. There are not many men like you in this world, Sir Daniel."

Daniel's eyes glittered. "I would agree," he said. "But there are exceptions. I know a few. Mayhap I will find a husband for you."

For some reason, that offer was a blow to Liselotte's heart. She didn't want him to find her a husband. She realized, as she looked at him, that she wanted *him* to be her husband. In truth, she'd wanted it all along, trying to tell herself that it could never be, but the reality was that she wanted him very badly.

Now, his offer to find her a husband made her feel like weeping. She had known all along he was going to break her heart and she hadn't cared; still, she wondered if she would be brave enough to accept the fact that he truly did not want her.

"That is kind of you," she said, pulling her hand away from him and lowering her gaze, "but I would prefer that you did not."

Daniel could sense a change in her mood. "Why not?"

She shook her head, popping a piece of white cheese into her mouth. "It would be very awkward for a man not related to my family to choose a husband for me," she said. "In fact, men will wonder why you are doing it. They will wonder what is wrong with me. You are an eligible bachelor and I am an eligible maiden. They will wonder why you do not marry me yourself."

Daniel couldn't help but think she was trying to find out, for herself, why he did not want to marry her. He thought he'd been clear about it and he should have been offended by her attempts to probe him but he found that he wasn't because she made a good deal of sense. In fact, the more he thought on someone else marrying her, the more he didn't like it. Nay, he didn't like it at all. He didn't want to be tied down to one place, to one woman, but he also didn't want that one woman to be tied down to anyone else. It was a dilemma, indeed.

The bachelor's soul began to show even more cracks now, big and gaping ones.

God, what is happening to me?

"You do not want me, Liselotte," he said quietly. "I have told you that I wander. You would not want to be married to a man who travels for months on end, sometimes years, and then returns to you when it is convenient. That is no life for you."

Liselotte still had her head down, realizing she was verging on tears. Unused to emotions of any kind, she found her defenses crumbling.

"You need not make this something that would be unsavory to me," she said. "You may admit that I am not someone you would consider marrying. You may, indeed, admit that you have no attraction to a woman with nothing to offer except a legacy of poverty. A de Lohr should marry well and I am not of your class, so you needn't make it sound as if I am the one who would not want you. Quite the contrary, my lord; I would take you as you are and I would not expect you to change, nor would I want you to. It would make you miserable to try. So do not tell me that I would not be happy as your wife for you do not know what is in my heart."

It was a startling and unexpected speech. As Daniel sat there, somewhat stunned, Liselotte suddenly bolted up from the table. Embarrassed, and verging on an emotional outburst, she tried to flee the room but Daniel stopped her. He was up, running after her, grabbing her by the arm before she could get away. Liselotte refused to look at him, trying to pull from his grip, but Daniel held her fast.

"Stop," he begged softly. "Please… stop. Do not leave."

Liselotte was trying very hard to stave off tears. "Please let me go, my lord," she said. "I… I should not have said those things. It would be better if I…."

"Quiet," he commanded. "Stop talking. Let me speak."

She shook her head but kept silent and Daniel pulled her back into the room as she tried to resist him. He knew she was terribly embarrassed but he didn't care. Something in her confession prompted something within him to speak, to confess just as she was. All of the interest and confusion he'd felt over Liselotte was whirling in his chest, demanding to be explored. All of this because she had spoken of her interest in him.

She was braver than he was in that respect.

Perhaps there was some part of him that could see being her husband, being by her side every day, exploring this woman who was so strong that nothing could break her. She was a rock, fighting and struggling for her family all of these years. He'd never seen a stronger woman, strong in both conviction and character.

She wasn't of his class? Daniel was coming to think it was the other way around.

"You are misunderstanding the entire situation, lady," he said as she struggled against his grasp. "Did it ever occur to you that the reason I feel strongly about helping Shadowmoor is because I found Lord Etzel's daughter to be quite attractive and alluring? Did it ever occur to you that the reason I purchased fine dresses for you in town today is because I wanted to see your glorious beauty clothed in something that is worthy of you? Liselotte, you are the bravest and strongest woman I have ever known, all of it wrapped up in a magnificent beauty that I have never seen anywhere in my travels. Had I run in to Gunnar and taken him back to Shadowmoor, with only your father there and not you, I might have stayed to help. I am not even certain of that. But upon meeting the glorious l'Audacieux sister and hearing of her struggles against Bramley… suffice it to say that you are the reason I am doing all of this, Liselotte. It is you and you alone."

By this time, Liselotte had stopped resisting him. She was looking up at Daniel with a mixture of shock and hope, of delight and disbelief. It was nearly everything she wanted to hear from the man… but not quite. She had opened the subject, the subject of marriage, and there was nothing left to do but forge on until she had her answer.

To push until she could push no more.

"But why would you do this for a woman you have no intention of marrying?" she asked. "What you are doing… it will be a waste of your time."

Daniel gazed into her sweet face. He wanted to kiss her very badly but he had a feeling it might not be well-received, at least not at the moment. "I never said I did not wish to marry you," he murmured. "You never heard those words come out of my mouth. I said I was a traveling man and would never marry, but I never said that I did not wish to marry *you*. We have only just met and to speak of marriage between us would be premature at best. Would you agree with this statement?"

Liselotte shrugged weakly. "I have not thought on it," she said. "But I suppose you are correct; it is foolish of me to say such things given the fact that we have only just met. Forgive me for being so ridiculous. It will not happen again."

His gaze drifted over her bronze hair, such a luscious color. He wondered what it would feel like to run his fingers through it. "If it does happen again, I will not be troubled by it," he said. "But for now, I will say this – I have never before met a woman who has intrigued me so. I am not sure what is in my heart, for it is uncharted territory. All I know is that I have never wanted to do anything for someone more than I have wanted to do it for you. You are a strong, beautiful woman and you deserve more than life has seen fit to give you. Mayhap your father was right in a sense – mayhap God did bring me to you. But you must also consider the fact that He may have brought you to *me*."

Liselotte wasn't feeling quite so embarrassed any longer, mostly because Daniel's manner was calming. He had that way about him, the great communicator that he was. He was being logical and kind, reasonable to a fault. He wasn't making her feel as if she should be embarrassed about her feelings. In truth, he seemed to have some feelings of his own.

"Why would God do that?" she asked. "I have nothing to give you."

His smile returned. "Nothing," he said. "Or, mayhap, everything. I have been wandering all of these years, happy in my freedom, but mayhap I wander because I am searching for something. My father always suggested that, you know. He felt that I was searching for something, or someone, to complete my happiness and that is why I never liked to stay in one place for long."

Liselotte felt such hope in her heart that it was close to exploding. She felt certain that he was speaking of a woman. *A wife*. "Searching for what?" she asked. "A person? Wealth? Glory?"

Daniel's eyes twinkled in the dim light of the hall. "My father suspected I would know it when I found it," he said. "Who is not to say it is a strong maiden from a broken-down fortress with an ancient royal legacy?"

Liselotte dared to return his smile. "Me?"

He lifted his eyebrows, rather haughtily. "Did I mention you by name?"

"Nay."

"Then cease your assumptions."

"*Are* they assumptions? I am the only maiden I know with a broken-down fortress. Or do you know more of us?"

His eyes narrowed. "Cheeky wench."

He said it with exaggeration and she knew he was jesting with her. The mood was much better now where even moments before, it had been full of uncertainty. Even if Daniel was unable to truly give her hope, for anything, he'd said enough. Liselotte was satisfied with as much as he was able to say. She was satisfied with his kindness towards her, for not making her feel foolish, and for his gentleness. For a man who was sworn to bachelorhood, he was strangely open and honest about things with her. It was an admirable quality.

"Then I will assume no longer," she said, a timid smile on her lips.

He nodded faintly, his gaze drifting over every portion of her face as he did. It was as if he were eating her alive, probing every feature, digesting her as only he could. Perhaps he was determining if she really was what he had been looking for all of his years. His expression suggested that he was looking for answers, but his tone, when he spoke, was neutral enough.

"I will tell you when your assumptions are warranted," he said. "In fact, when the time comes, I will tell you plainly so there will be no need for assumptions at all."

She smiled, somewhat coyly, and gently pulled her arm from his grip, turning back for the table where the remains of her meal were. It seemed as if they had said all that needed to be said but the silence between them now was comfortable enough. Almost as if they had an understanding between them. Gunnar was still sleeping like the dead in his dog pack as Liselotte headed back for the table, having no idea that, behind her, Daniel was now having something of a crisis.

Assumptions. Perhaps they had said all that needed to be said at the moment, but he was still in the throes of the conversation. He wasn't lying when he said that he would tell her plainly if, and when, he could figure out exactly what he was feeling, but the truth was that he was completely uncertain about any of it. He was uncertain of these odd sensations he felt when it came to Liselotte and he was uncertain if he would truly feel comfortable being pledged to a woman. *Having a wife.*

The mere mention of it seemed alien to him.

Daniel wasn't one to stay away from women in general. In fact, he always selected women who were very willing to let him do as he pleased and he had been in trouble because of it on more than one occasion. Fathers of compromised daughters tended not to view his actions too favorably and his own father had even been forced to pay off a few outraged fathers so they would not try to burn Daniel at the stake. But looking at Liselotte, the thought of toying with her affections, as he'd done so many times in the past, never entered his mind. There was something about the woman that commanded his respect and admiration. He would never toy with her.

But he wasn't beyond pretending with her. Perhaps it would help him understand his feelings better if he did.

The very idea intrigued him.

"Are we still friends then, my lady?" he asked as he trailed her back to the table.

Liselotte nodded. "Of course we are."

"Then as one friend to another, there is something you can help me with if you are willing."

She reached the table, turning to look at him. "Of course I am willing," she said. "How may I be of service?"

Daniel twisted his lips wryly. "I do believe we may have fallen into a nest of hunters," he said, lowering his voice. "Lady Glennie, although very kind, looks at me as if she wants to eat me and her father has that same expression when he looks at you. Do you understand my meaning?"

Liselotte had no idea what he was talking about. "I fear that I do not," she said. "What are you saying?"

Daniel wriggled his eyebrows, somewhat comically. "I mean that Lady Glennie seems on the hunt for a husband," he said. "I do not like the way she looks at me. You will be doing me a great favor if you would allow me to pretend that I am courting you. That would not only deter her from me but it would deter her father from you. It would be safe for us both to pretend such a thing. Are you willing to do that?"

So he has noticed the way Glennie has been looking at him! Liselotte pretended to be cool in considering the matter but, truth be told, she wasn't hard pressed to agree. Being naïve in the ways of romance as she was, all she could envision was the dream of pretending she and Daniel were a couple. She didn't go so far as to imagine her shattered heart once the pretending was over. If she and Daniel pretended to be a pair, then Glennie would leave him alone and she wouldn't be forced to strangle the woman. She didn't even care about Easton and whatever interest Daniel imagined from the man; all she cared about was pretending that she and Daniel were together. Perhaps something inside of her would be satisfied if she did.

A dream that may never become a reality.

"I am willing," she said. "But are you certain about this? About Lady Glennie and Lord de Royans, I mean. Are they really hunters?"

Daniel nodded seriously. "They are, indeed," he said. "Therefore, I will make it clear that you are spoken for – and so am I – and mayhap this alliance we are attempting to establish may not be ruined, after all. But I should at least like to get a message off to my uncle before Glennie's heart is crushed and Easton challenges me for your hand."

He said it somewhat humorously and Liselotte couldn't help but giggle. "God's Bones," she exclaimed. "What if he does challenge you? What will you do?"

Daniel grinned, without humor. "Run like a rabbit and leave you to his lascivious intentions."

She laughed louder. "You would not fight for me?"

"To pretend with you is one thing but to die for you is entirely another."

"Then I am shocked and scandalized. You had better amend your thoughts or I will tell Lady Glennie that you secretly lust for her."

Daniel's eyes widened. "You threaten me to tears, lady," he said. Then, he sighed with great exaggeration. "Very well. I will fight Easton if I must but know it gives me no pleasure. And if he kills me, I will haunt you from the grave."

Liselotte snickered into her hand. "I believe you."

Daniel moved closer to her, enchanted by her laughter. He realized it was the first time he'd really seen her laugh freely. She had a beautiful smile and enchanting laughter. Reaching out, he took the hand that was covering her mouth and brought it to lips, kissing it in the same place that touched her own lips. When he saw the look of astonishment on her face, he kissed it again for good measure.

"There," he said, his voice low. "That is what betrothed people do. Now, I will see you to your chamber and then return for your brother. You will sleep well this night, Lady Liselotte. You have a warm bed and my protection. Sleep without fear."

In the wake of Daniel's kiss, the humor was gone from Liselotte's manner. She was left trembling from his kiss, unable to reply when their banter had been so recently lively. Daniel must have caught her quivering lips because he took them as an invitation; quivering and sweet, he was on her in an instant, kissing her with a warm and swift mouth, suckling her lips as she collapsed in his arms. He kissed her until she could hardly breathe and even when he removed his mouth from hers, he simply stood there and held her, feeling her soft slender body pressed against his. It was the most magnificent thing he could have ever experienced.

The bachelor's soul began to shatter completely.

"Come, now," he whispered, releasing her from his embrace and holding on to her arm when she couldn't seem to catch her balance. "Take your food with you. I will return you to your chamber now."

Stunned by his kiss, Liselotte did as she was told, grasping her half-finished plate of fruit and cheese and bread as she allowed Daniel to lead her back to her borrowed chamber. He was very proper about it, opening the door for her and ensuring that she entered, and then bolted the door, before he left. As she stood just inside the door, trying to catch her breath and listening as his boot falls faded away, she could have never known that as Daniel headed back down to the hall to collect Gunnar, his heart was beating just as fast as hers was.

He felt the magic, too.

But he calmed himself, trying to pretend it really didn't matter. He'd had literally hundreds of kisses so this one was no different… at least, that's what he tried to tell himself. But he knew it was a foolish attempt. This kiss had been very, very different, more than he could put into words.

But thoughts of the kiss were pushed aside as he entered the hall. Easton was there, waiting for him, and Daniel turned the missive over to the man that was to be sent with the messenger. After that, he sat up a good portion of the night with Easton, drinking good wine and speaking on a great many things.

All thoughts of Liselotte's sweet lips faded for the moment as Daniel came to know the father of his hated enemy as a man of humor, of gentleness, and of great wisdom, and more and more he began to feel pity for the family who had lost a son and didn't yet know it. It was the drink causing him to feel such things, that was true, but it was also human decency. Brighton's foolish actions were to have a lasting effect.

Daniel began to feel anger towards Brighton, different than the anger he'd felt before. Brighton had been intelligent and skilled without a doubt, but he'd forced his hand as a stubborn and spoiled man, and now his family would feel the terrible grief at his death. A death that didn't have to happen.

The more Daniel spoke with Easton, the more he was fairly certain he could never tell the man what he knew. All risks aside, and in making an enemy out of the House of de Royans in general, he wasn't sure he could bring such pain on a man who was seemingly quite generous and normal. When, and if, Easton was ever told of Brighton's death, it would not be from Daniel's lips. He couldn't bring himself to do it, for a variety of reasons.

Deep into the night, the wine finally caught up to Easton and the man excused himself to sleep as Daniel did the same. Pulling Gunnar from the pack of dogs, he carried the boy back to their shared chamber and put him to bed. Stripping down and climbing into his bed, thoughts of Liselotte returned. He couldn't seem to shake them.

When he finally dreamt, it was with visions of women with bronze-colored hair.

CHAPTER EIGHT

"DANIEL!" GUNNAR WAS yelling. "Look! Look at me!"

It was early morning on the day following their arrival at Netherghyll and Daniel, having finished yet another conference with Easton and Caston as the men broke their fast in the great hall, was heading out to the stables to check on Ares. He was just inside the stable yard when he spied Gunnar in the midst of several goats that were quite happily frisking him for food. Gunnar giggled and twitched, pushing the goats away, but it was clear that he was as happy as a lark. Daniel shook his head reproachfully at the boy although he was grinning.

"Are those your new clothes that those goats are eating?" he called out. "You are nothing more than a goat yourself, Gunnar l'Audacieux."

Gunnar laughed happily. "They like me," he announced. Then, he pushed through the crowd of goats and ran at Daniel. "Can we go back to town today so I can have my goats from the livery? Can we take them home with us?"

Daniel reached out, putting a big hand on Gunnar's blond head. "You would like that, wouldn't you?"

Gunnar nodded enthusiastically and Daniel chuckled at the lad. This morning, in his new clothes and having slept on a full stomach, he was happy and rosy-cheeked. He looked like an entirely different boy from the one he had rescued from Bramley only a couple of days before. He nearly looked normal, without the weight of starvation hanging down upon him. It made him sad to think on the suffering the young boy had endured. Daniel's smile faded and he removed his hand from Gunnar's head.

"We will, indeed, return to town this morning," he said. "We left the stores I purchased there and we must return for them. In fact, after I have checked on my horse, I will rouse your sister and we will return to town and then on to Shadowmoor."

Gunnar simply turned around and ran back for the goats as if to get in all the time he could with them before Daniel dragged him away. His four-legged friends greeted him happily and Daniel could hear the boy giggling as he continued on into the stable. Immediately upon entering, he could see at least three stable boys crowded around the last stall that housed a big black horse. Daniel fought off a grin as he approached.

"Well," he said, watching the boys jump at the sound of his voice. "What are you doing to my horse?"

Ares nickered softly at the sound of Daniel's voice and when the stable boys turned around, Daniel could see they had various food items in their hands. One lad seemed to have a bucket of half-eaten grain while another had carrots. The third lad had bread crusts. All three looked startled and, upon closer inspection, rather guilty.

"We are feeding him his morning meal, my lord," the lad with the grain said. "He seems to be very hungry this morning."

Daniel grinned as he pushed past the boys and into the stall, slapping his big horse on the neck affectionately. "He is always hungry," he said flatly. "Look at the size of him. He eats an enormous amount."

The boys nodded in unison and the boy with the grain went back to feeding Ares, who stuck his nose into the bucket, crunching and snorting. Daniel, meanwhile, ran a practiced eye over his animal and, seeing that all was well, gave the horse one last pat and left the stall.

"See that he is fed and then saddled," he said. "I will return within the hour."

The boys nodded eagerly and returned their attention to the horse as Daniel headed out of the stable. He was just to the entry when a body appeared in his way, blocking his exit. Daniel had to step aside quickly or risk crashing into Caston, who jumped back when he realized that he had nearly run headlong into Daniel.

"Forgive me, my lord," Caston said. "I nearly bowled you over."

Daniel snorted. "It was not as easy as all that," he said, jesting. Then, he threw a thumb over his shoulder, back in the direction of Ares. "I came to check on my horse. I will be departing back to Siglesdene as soon as Lady Liselotte is ready to depart. I believe I mentioned to you this morning that we left a great many stores meant for Shadowmoor back in town. I must return them to the fortress today."

Caston nodded; he'd shared the morning meal with Daniel a short while earlier and had come to know a little about the knight from the great and mighty de Lohr family. Daniel was quite congenial, very bright, and quick of wit. He seemed to have a joke for everything. They had discussed a few things that morning, including the tournament in Skipton, and Caston was coming to think that Daniel had decided to compete although the man had given him no real confirmation. It was just a feeling Caston had.

In all, he was coming to like the wandering de Lohr son just a bit and his father was already enamored with the man, so much so that Caston was now on a mission for his father. When Daniel spoke of returning to Shadowmoor on this day, Caston held up a hand as if to beg the man to reconsider.

"I know," he said. "In fact, that is why I am here. My father and I were talking after you left the hall and my father thinks that you should leave the lady and her brother here. Since Lord Bramley seems so apt to harass Shadowmoor, it might be safer for the lady and her brother to remain here where Bramley cannot find them. Even if he discovered she was here, we have the army to protect her. Do you think the Lord of Shadowmoor would consider this?"

Daniel gazed at the man that he, too, was coming to like. Caston was a good deal like Brighton, or at least what Daniel had seen of Brighton, but he didn't seem to have that aggressive streak in him that his brother had possessed. Caston seemed more thoughtful, less antagonistic, but, of course, Daniel had only known the man a day or so. Time would tell if he was really less belligerent than his brother.

"That is a very kind offer," he said. "In fact, I am in agreement with you. It would be safer for them both to remain her. Caston… I cannot tell you the poverty that Shadowmoor has faced because of Bramley. Have you noticed how attached the lady's young brother seems to be to the dogs and the goats?"

Caston nodded. He had passed the young l'Audacieux lad on his way to the stables. "Indeed I have."

Daniel cocked a serious eyebrow. "That is because those at Shadowmoor have been forced to kill and eat all of the animals in order to survive, dogs and goats included," he said. "Bramley has contained them so much that they live on what wild grains they can gather and have eaten all of the livestock. I have no idea when they last had cheese or meat. I am sure the Lord of Shadowmoor will be very grateful that his children will, once again, be enjoying a steady diet in the safety of Netherghyll."

Caston was frowning at the thought of so much poverty. "I am ashamed that we did not know any of this, truly," he said. "They are our neighbors and we knew nothing, but as my father said, Shadowmoor has always kept to themselves. I am not sure there was any way we *could* know what was going on with them."

Daniel conceded the point. "Now, you know," he said, "and I am sure your assistance will be greatly appreciated until my uncle arrives. Your father said that the missive went out this morning."

"It did."

"Then I would expect to see my uncle and his men here before the month is out. Meanwhile, we must try to keep Shadowmoor alive and hold off Bramley until they arrive."

Caston was thoughtful. "I did not want to ask this in front of my father because he is far too peaceful in his old age," he said, "but I was thinking last night… what is to prevent you from going to Bramley and telling him that if he does not leave Shadowmoor alone, then you will bring the de Lohr army and destroy him? Mayhap the threat alone would be enough to cease his harassment."

Daniel scratched his head. "Mostly because I do not want to go alone to Bramley Castle," he said. "He could easily subdue me and throw me in the vault. I do not want to put myself in that position."

Caston could see his point. "Then what if you and I went with two hundred Netherghyll troops?" he asked. "A show of force? If he has as few men as we think he has, then he will be stupid to move against us."

Daniel grinned at the man. "Looking for a little action, are you?"

Caston laughed. "I will admit that it is somewhat boring around here," he said. "We have very little opportunity to dole out beatings to worthy foes."

Daniel laughed along with him. "I admire your attitude, but this isn't your fight."

"It isn't yours, either, from what I gather."

Daniel guffawed. "So we shall champion Shadowmoor together, my friend? We are quite noble and brave."

Caston continued laughing because Daniel was. "Or foolish."

"I would agree with that, too."

Caston slapped Daniel on the arm. "Then it is settled," he said. "I will arm two hundred men and we shall ride to Bramley Castle to tell that miscreant Bramley to leave Shadowmoor alone. It will be fun."

Daniel was enjoying Caston's humor. "Fun, he says," he grunted. "It has been a long time since I have had fun such as that."

"Me, too."

"If my father finds out, he will think I have lured you into this adventure. He will think that I have swayed you into danger."

"I will tell him that it was my idea."

Now it was Daniel's turn to slap Caston on the arm. "Excellent!" he said. "I like you already, de Royans, for volunteering to take the blame for this action."

Caston grinned as Daniel pulled him along as he headed for the keep. "It *was* my idea."

"If we are successful, it will become *my* idea."

Caston snorted softly, shaking his head. "Now I think I know how the House of de Lohr has gained its reputation for great and noble acts," he said. "Taking credit for other's work, have you?"

Daniel shook his head. "Not unless it is warranted," he teased. "All jesting aside, I appreciate your willingness to take an active role in assisting Shadowmoor. In fact, I was thinking…."

"God's Bones, I'm not sure I want to know what you are thinking."

Daniel laughed. "I was thinking that mayhap we should both compete in the tournament in Skipton," he said, "and if we win the purse, then we should donate it to Shadowmoor. I do not need the money and, clearly, Netherghyll does not need the money, so if both of us were compete, that would double the chances of Shadowmoor winning the purse."

Caston's expression indicated that he wasn't opposed to the suggestion. "I would be agreeable to that," he said. "It has been a long time since I have championed a lady."

Daniel came to a halt and looked at him. "Not a lady," he said. "Shadowmoor. The only one championing Lady Liselotte is me. You may as well know that her father has offered me her hand."

It wasn't a lie; Etzel had offered him Liselotte in marriage. But Daniel stopped short of saying he'd accepted, instead, waiting for Caston's reaction first to see how much further he would speak on the subject. It wasn't long in coming.

"I thought there might be something between you and the lady," he said. "Call it a hunch. I saw the way you looked at her last night."

Daniel wasn't sure he liked the sound of that. Was his infatuation with Liselotte so obvious? He thought he'd been rather clever about concealing it, hoping to keep his feelings only to himself. But it looked as if those attempts had failed. He simply lifted his eyebrows and turned away, resuming his walk for the keep and unwilling to confirm Caston's observations.

"Then you understand when I say that I will be her champion," he said. "But I would consider it a personal favor if you would compete and, if you win, donate the purse to Shadowmoor. They need it far more than we ever could."

Caston nodded. "I will," he said, following Daniel. "But when I do, I want you to do something for me."

"It would be my pleasure."

They had reached the great doors of the hall and Caston came to a halt, reaching to stop Daniel from entering. The men faced each other in the shadow of the hall as the morning sun rose overhead.

"Although I love my father and Netherghyll is my home," he said, "I do not want to remain here forever. My brother, Brighton, will inherit Netherghyll upon my father's death, so there is no reason for me to remain here. I have stayed these years while Brighton has gone about on his adventure, but I, too, want to live my life. I want you to speak to your uncle or your father to see if they would accept my fealty. I would like to find adventure and mayhap even fortune through the House of de Lohr. If I remain at Netherghyll, that will never happen."

Daniel's good mood fled. He couldn't tell Caston that Brighton would never inherit Netherghyll, meaning it would belong to Caston upon Easton's passing. Nay, he couldn't tell him that in the least. He was becoming increasingly despondent over the secret he bore of Brighton's death, and why he died, something he was convinced he could never share with Easton and Caston. Still, he understood Caston's need to leave his father's home and seek his fame and fortune. Daniel had been doing that for the past ten years. Aye, he understood Caston's request very well.

"Based on the conversation at supper last night, it seemed to me that you were happy at Netherghyll," he said. "Was that a conversation for the benefit of your father?"

Caston nodded, lowering his gaze. "It was," he said. "Brighton has left him and he cannot stomach the thought of me leaving his as well."

"But you want to."

"I do."

Daniel's gaze lingered on the man. "Then have no worry," he said. "When the time comes, I will insist that my father or uncle accept your fealty. My uncle has quite a large stable of knights, so one more would be welcome, I am sure. We will discuss this more when the time comes. You have my vow."

Caston was visibly relieved. "You have my thanks, then," he said. "You said that coming to Shadowmoor was fortuitous for the House of l'Audacieux. Mayhap it was fortuitous for me as well. To serve the House of de Lohr, to serve your father, would be my greatest honor."

Daniel wondered how his father was going to react when asked if he would accept fealty from a man who looked exactly like the man who had nearly killed Maddoc du Bois and abducted David's granddaughter. He had a feeling his father would not agree to it, no matter if Caston was markedly different from his wicked brother. He forced a smile.

"As I said, my uncle's service would be better for you," he said. "Much more to see and do under my uncle's command. My father is rather boring; you would find yourself in much the situation you find yourself in here."

Caston shrugged. "I admit that action would be more attractive."

"Then I will speak to my uncle when the time is right."

"Again, you have my thanks."

Daniel simply nodded, slapping the man again on the shoulder, before heading into the hall in search of Liselotte. He hoped she was agreeable to remaining at Netherghyll and couldn't imagine why she wouldn't be. She would be safe, with more food than she could possibly eat. He couldn't see why she would refuse.

He was wrong.

ଓ

"I WANT TO go home."

Daniel was standing just inside the door of Liselotte's borrowed chamber, facing a surprisingly stubborn response to what, he thought, had been a very generous offer. But Liselotte didn't want any part of it.

"You will be safe if you say here," Daniel explained patiently. "You will be warm and you will be fed. You will even have Lady Glennie for companionship. Does that not appeal to you?"

Liselotte wasn't sure she could make Daniel understand her reasons for wanting to return to Shadowmoor, but it was something she felt very passionate about. She went to him, putting her hand on his wrist as he stood in her doorway, big arms folded across his chest.

"Of course it does," she said. "But I cannot, in good conscience, remain here while my people suffer. All of the people of Shadowmoor are suffering because of me. It is me that Bramley wants and I am the reason he has kept up his harassment all of these years. I would be a terrible person to flee Shadowmoor, to live in comfort, while my family and my people live in poverty because of me. I cannot do it, Daniel. I pray that you understand my reasons."

He did. He'd never seen anyone more selfless than Lady Liselotte l'Audacieux. She would not cast aside suffering she had caused, even for her own safety. If her people were suffering, as she put it, it was her place to suffer right along with them. He sighed, putting a hand over the hand against his wrist.

"I do," he said quietly. "I understand and admire you greatly for it. But there are times when you must think of yourself, Leese. De Royans is offering you safety and shelter and food whenever you want it, hot baths, a comfortable bed, and companionship. I realize that you do not want to abandon Shadowmoor, but I am sure no one would blame you if you did. And if Bramley were to be told you had left Shadowmoor, he might lose some of his zest for harassing it. Your people might return to a normal life."

He had called her by her pet name, the name that Etzel always used. *Leese.* It sounded so sweet coming from Daniel's lips. But Liselotte didn't take the time to acknowledge it; she was focused on the serious conversation at hand.

"Bramley wants Shadowmoor more than he wants me," she said. "It would not stop his harassment. My being at Shadowmoor was simply more of an excuse for him to do what he was already inclined to do."

Daniel gazed down at the woman. Her wisdom, as always, was astonishing. He'd never met a woman like her, so wise and true, so beautiful and strong. Whatever was brewing in his heart for her was growing by leaps and bounds, and his bachelor's soul, that terribly stubborn thing, was all but crumbled in her wake. She'd smashed through it as easily as an ax through fragile glass. He had always thought his bachelorhood was stronger than that. In truth, *she* was stronger than he was.

He knew that without a doubt.

She had changed gowns this morning and wore the dark yellow wool that was incredibly striking against her coloring, her luscious bronze hair having been brushed and rebraided, pinned up in a style that had the braid circling her head from the nap to the crown. It was a stunning style on her, emphasizing her great beauty. Daniel collected the hand on his wrist, bringing it to his lips for a gentle kiss.

"I am sure you are correct," he said. "But when I look at you now, glorious and groomed and well fed and happy, this is how I wish to always see you. This is what you deserve. Returning you to Shadowmoor will only return you to despair and hunger, and I am vastly opposed to doing that. Can you not understand?"

Liselotte watched him as he kissed her hand, feeling bolts of lightning race through her body as he nibbled on her flesh. "I do understand," she answered. "And you are wonderful and gracious to be so concerned for me. But I cannot stay here and enjoy life while my people are suffering. I would hate myself for it."

He understood that. Unhappy, he sighed heavily and kissed her hand again, but that wasn't enough for him, so he pulled her into his arms and kissed her softly on the mouth, gently suckling her lips. He could feel her collapse against him, completely turning herself over in every way possible. It was instantaneous with her; no resistance whatsoever, and nothing had ever felt so right or natural to him, not ever. Having Liselotte in his embrace was an action that filled something inside of him that he never knew needed filling.

Perhaps it was that thing his father always thought he had been searching for.

More and more, he was coming to believe it.

"You taste like honey," he murmured against her lips.

Dazed from his kiss, Liselotte nonetheless giggled. "It was on the porridge I ate earlier."

He swooped in for another deep kiss, this time licking her lips, probing into her mouth gently, feeling her tremble in his arms.

"Nay," he whispered. "It is you. You taste like honey."

It was a seductive statement and Liselotte groaned softly as his tongue delved into her mouth, fully now, tasting all of her sweetness and then some. Her arms, usually just gripping him because she didn't know what else to do, snaked their way around his neck, pulling him closer. To Daniel, it was like an aphrodisiac – a response from her was all he needed to take control. Taking two steps into her room, he kicked the door shut, hearing the bolt fall simply from the momentum of the movement.

Now, he had her in a locked room and his male instincts were taking over. He'd done this many times before, with many women, so he knew what to do. He knew how to make her tremble and gasp. He knew how to find his pleasure. But with Liselotte, it was different; he reminded himself that he didn't want to use his usual tactics against her. She was to be handled differently because he didn't want to ruin what was growing between them. For the first time in his life, he truly didn't want to ruin anything. But he couldn't help the feelings that were overwhelming him.

The bed was in his line of sight but he didn't move for it. But he did let a hand drift down her slender torso, feeling her warmth beneath him, before moving up to cup a full breast. That pleasure, he would not deny himself. It was selfish and he knew it, but he wanted to touch her, to feel that fleshly fullness in his hand.

Liselotte flinched when he squeezed gently but she didn't pull away. She didn't even pull away when he carefully pulled her dress off her shoulder, pulling it down her arm, loosening the stays in the back just enough to be able to pull the dress and shift off of her breast, exposing it to the warm room. She didn't stop him at all.

His bare palm went to her naked breast and he fondled her gently, feeling her quiver at his touch, so much so that her knees actually went weak and he found himself supporting her. He kissed her passionately as he fondled her, her hard nipple against his palm, but he could stand it no longer and his mouth left hers, moving to the taut nipple and suckling firmly against it.

In his arms, Liselotte bucked and groaned, but she didn't push him away. Her hands were in his hair, holding him to her breast, as he suckled the nipple and then lapped his tongue over the breast, beneath and on top of it, moving to suckle the soft skin of her shoulder, before moving back to the nipple. He wanted more.

He had to *have* more.

The dress came off of both shoulders and now he had both breasts to suckle from. His mouth moved between them as he held her with one arm and began lifting her skirts with the other. He was intoxicated with her as he'd never been intoxicated with a woman before, not ever. Whatever he was feeling for Liselotte was blinding his senses and curbing his reason, and all those thoughts of not wanting to ruin anything between them fell by the wayside. He was wrapped up in desire such as he had never known.

He was wrapped up in *her*.

Somehow, they ended up on the bed in spite of his resolve not to. Her breasts were naked and he was feasting on them, and his right hand had made it under her skirts to her silken legs, and he was fondling the flesh of her thighs, acquainting her with his touch, before moving to the damp curls between her legs. Her virginal body was reacting to his touch, instinctively, and he gently stroked the thick lips, wet with moisture, and it was nearly too much for him to take. Her body was prepared for his entry and he knew it. His manhood was stiff and throbbing, straining against his breeches. It would have been so simple to take her at this moment.

So very simple....

But he couldn't bring himself to do it. Above his instinctive need, something held him back. Frustrated at his control, torn by his emotions, he couldn't hold back completely from her and inserted a finger into her virginal core, feeling the tight wet heat around his digit. But it was mistake; Liselotte, in the throes of her first sexual experience, groaned as his finger entered her, arching her back and bringing up her knees in an innate response to his probing.

Daniel groaned alongside her, now utterly numb to his restraint. He reached down and unfastened his breeches, allowing his heated rod to spring free. As he inserted a second finger into Liselotte's virginal body, feeling her barrier of virginity against his flesh, he lowered himself down on top of her and rubbed his manhood against the skin of her inner thigh. But with his last ounce of reason, he wouldn't do anymore, stroking his manroot against her as his fingers began to move in and out of her, mimicking the sexual act he so badly wanted to complete with her.

It was made worse by the fact that Liselotte's body was responding to what he was doing, a natural rhythm as her hips moved against his hand. His mouth was on her breasts, sucking her, as his fingers moved and his hips moved, grinding himself against her leg as his entire body strained. He even shifted his hips so that the tip of his phallus rubbed against her wet heat, jealous of what his fingers were doing. Jealous of the fact that his hand was claiming a part of her body meant only for his manhood.

Daniel was going to climax; he knew he was but he didn't care. He continued to rub himself against her, feeling her wetness on the tip of his phallus, hating himself for employing such control for once in his life. He wanted the woman so badly he could taste it. Feeling his climax coming on, he withdrew his fingers from her body, using them instead to manipulate the bud of pleasure between her legs.

Liselotte's reaction was instantaneous; her body began to convulse with the thrill of her first release and Daniel couldn't hold himself back any longer. He rubbed his phallus against her convulsing core, releasing himself onto her belly just above her dark curls. It wasn't exactly as he wanted it but it was for the best; he couldn't enter her. *Wouldn't* enter her. And he certainly wouldn't plant his seed in her and ruin her. But perhaps everything between them was already ruined, destroyed by his lack of restraint.

Destroyed by an attraction to her that he could not control.

Breathing heavily, and feeling Liselotte panting beneath him, he lifted his head to say something to her. She was lying on her back, eyes closed, and Daniel simply couldn't think of anything to say. Carefully, he lifted himself up and kissed her, gently, watching her eyes as they opened and focused on him. He smiled weakly.

"Forgive me," he whispered. "I do not know what came over me. I should not have forced myself upon you like this and I can only pray you will forgive me. Leese… you are coming to mean something to me and I suppose this was my way of demonstrating that. I find that I cannot control myself around you. But I should have. I should have…."

He trailed off, shaking his head and averting his gaze. Liselotte stared at him, trying to digest everything that had happened and everything he was trying to tell her. It all happened so fast, and so very easily. The truth was that she wasn't distressed by it, not one bit. Daniel's touch had been like magic, making her body feel things she had no idea it was capable of feeling. She hadn't been afraid of his touch to intimate places. In fact, it was as if her body had a mind of its own, welcoming what he was doing to her.

She thought back to what he'd done, the fire he'd created in her loins, and she wasn't sorry she had let him. But she was coming to wonder if he was.

"I have no regrets," she said softly. "It seemed the most natural of things."

He nodded, rather ironically. "I would agree with that completely."

"As if we are meant to be with one another."

His head came up, looking at her. It seemed that he wanted to agree but something was holding him back. Confusion, perhaps. Or even regret.

"It was very natural," he concurred quietly.

Liselotte studied his handsome face, seemingly lined with worry now. "And you regret this natural action?"

He shook his head before the words were even out of her mouth. "I do not," he said. "But what we did… ladies of breeding, fine ladies such as yourself, should not let a man do such things to you. You should have slapped me when I started."

"Would you have stopped?"

"Immediately."

"Then I am glad I did not slap you."

He started to chastise her for not being the stronger of the two of them but he ended up breaking down into soft laughter. He was trying to apologize and she wouldn't let him. Pushing himself off of her, he looked around for something to wipe his seed from her belly and spied a linen cloth near a basin of water against the wall. He collected the cloth and wiped the remnants of his bad behavior off of her flesh. Then, he carefully pulled her skirts down and reached out a hand to her. When she took it, he pulled her up into a sitting position and helped her pull her bodice back up over her breasts.

In silence, he helped her, finally tightening up the stays on her back when the dress was properly settled. But before she could rise from the bed, he sat down beside her and put his big hands on her shoulders, looking her in the eye.

"I do not regret touching you," he said, softly but firmly. "But you must understand that this is more than physical attraction. Something draws me to you, Leese. I told you that last night. Today, the feeling is stronger. I am not exactly sure what I feel but know that it is not fleeting. It is not trite or foolish. When I am ready to speak of it, I will. Remember that."

Liselotte gazed back at the man. She felt so much for him, such overwhelming things, that she was certain she was in love with him. She'd never been in love before but she could not imagine such strong feelings to be anything else. Still, she would not speak of her feelings, not until he did. She would not make a fool of herself again as she did last night. Until Daniel was ready to speak of what was in his heart, she would keep hers to herself.

She hoped it didn't kill her to do so.

"I have no expectations," she said, hoping it would ease whatever turmoil he was feeling. "Even if you walk from my life tomorrow, I still consider it extremely fortunate to have met you."

He smiled and planted a warm kiss on her mouth. "I will not walk from your life tomorrow."

She returned his smile, timidly. "I hope not."

He shook his head and gently pinched her nose, an affectionate gesture. Then, he stood up and held up a hand to help her to her feet.

"Nay, lady, you will not be rid of me so easily," he said. "But I would like for you to do something for me."

"Anything."

"Consider remaining here until this situation with Bramley is settled."

The warmth in her expression faced. "So we are back to that subject, are we?" she asked. Then, she shook her head. "I explained myself well enough, Daniel. I will return home today. Although I am deeply grateful for the offer to remain at Netherghyll, I hope you understand why I cannot."

Daniel shrugged. "I do," he said. "But I had to ask one more time."

"And so you did."

He lifted his eyebrows, accepting defeat, as he headed to the chamber door and lifted the bolt. "Then pack your things," he said. "I would like to return to Siglesdene to collect what we purchased yesterday before heading back to Shadowmoor. Be swift about it, if you will. I wish to start our travel as soon as possible."

Liselotte nodded. "It will take me only a few minutes," she said. "Shall I meet you out in the bailey?"

He shook his head. "I will make sure the horses are saddled and then I will return to escort you," he said. "We must say farewell to our gracious hosts before we go and to Lady Glennie, although I will admit that I will not miss her blatant attempts at flirtation. The woman makes me want to run and hide."

Liselotte laughed softly. "Be brave, Sir Daniel. I am sure she is not the most fearsome beast you have ever crossed."

He guffawed, loudly. "Not fearsome, but persistent," he clarified. "But I cannot blame her. I suppose I am too difficult to resist."

Liselotte rolled her eyes at his arrogance as he snorted, thinking himself rather funny. She made a sweeping motion with her hand, as if shooing him away. "Go along your way," she said. "I will be ready in a few minutes."

Daniel pulled the door open, taking one last glance back at her. "Don't you find me irresistible?"

"Be gone."

"Now I am insulted."

"I am sure it will not be the last time."

She could hear him laughing all the way down the corridor.

CHAPTER NINE

BRYNNER WASN'T SURE how he was going to explain the horse he returned to Shadowmoor on but, in truth, it really didn't matter what others thought. He didn't have to answer any questions and he wouldn't. Bramley had given him the brown steed, a bit old but still strong, to travel home on. It was far better than walking.

Usually a man who cared for nothing other than himself, and that included animals, Brynner put the horse in the stables personally and made sure it was bedded down properly. Back in the days when he had been an honorable knight, he'd had a magnificent beast that he'd eventually traded for liquor when his life went wrong. He often thought about that horse and wondered how it had fared in life, but thoughts of the horse made him think of Maud, so he tried not to think of the horse at all. It was a downward spiral if he did.

It was nearing noon on the day following his encounter with Bramley as he made his way from the stables towards Shadowmoor's keep. He'd spent the night at Bramley Castle and had probably downed a half-barrel of wine in the process, drinking most of the night and then sleeping for just a few hours before rising and departing.

Bramley had greeted him when he had awoken with more wine to take with him, making sure that Brynner knew what was expected of him from this point on. Brynner knew, very well, and departed Bramley Castle with a sense of relief for the future – relief that he would soon be swimming in drink at his own French winery – and perhaps even some remorse at what he had agreed to do in order to get it.

But not too much remorse. He was getting the better end of the bargain as far as he was concerned. Fifty men and fifty gold coins would be waiting for him at the Cock and Comb Tavern in Ilkley. He had promised Bramley he would go to the tavern after speaking with Etzel, and Brynner was rather eager to get on with what needed to be done. The sooner he convinced his father to turn over Shadowmoor, and Liselotte, the sooner he would have his wine.

If his father didn't agree, then Brynner knew what he had to do. He had tried not to think on that part of the bargain too much because he wasn't particularly eager to murder his own father but, then again, Etzel had never done much for him so in that regard, he wasn't all that sorry. At least, the part of him that needed wine badly, on a daily basis, told him he wasn't all that sorry. But the honorable son of Etzel, long buried under an avalanche of sorrow, might have shown a twinge of regret if he'd let him.

So Brynner headed to the keep, trudging through the mud of the bailey. There were people around, people who scraped by their existence at Shadowmoor and whose families had lived at Shadowmoor for generations, but they didn't acknowledge him and he didn't acknowledge them. That was usual. Brynner existed in a world of his own. No one else lived there or visited, so the people of Shadowmoor might as well have been phantoms for all he cared. At the moment, however, he was focused on finding his father and since he didn't pay attention to the man's habits, he thought to start to look for him in the keep. Just as he approached the entry, a servant dressed in little more than rags appeared. Brynner grabbed the skinny old woman by the arm.

"My father?" he demanded.

The old woman, fearful at the sight of Brynner, the drunkard and volatile son, pointed to the hall in a panic. Attention diverted, Brynner let the woman go and she scurried away as he turned for the hall. Nearly slipping in the mud as he neared the entry, he tried to scrape the mud from the soles of his worn boots as he entered the darkened hall.

There was a fire in the pit in the center of the room, but a weak one. It gave off a little heat and warmth but what it mostly gave off was the smell of urine because most everyone had used it as a urinal in the morning to relieve themselves when they had awoken. That was usual in Shadowmoor because there were no garderobes, only fire pits and holes behind the stables where a man could piss in peace. Therefore, the hall always smelled of urine to Brynner. His senses may have been dulled by the liquor but his sense of smell was quite sharp. It was a sickening smell.

He immediately spied Etzel sitting at the feasting table, carefully sharpening his two precious daggers on a very worn piece of pumice stone. Brynner kept his gaze on his father and saw when Etzel happened to glance up in the dim light, but he gave no reaction to his son's appearance and continued sharpening his dagger. Once, long ago, there had been warmth in a father's greeting but no longer. His eldest son usually ignored him so Etzel made no move to initiate conversation with the man. It was, therefore, somewhat surprising when Brynner actually spoke to him.

"Father," he greeted without emotion. "I have a need to speak with you."

Wary, Etzel stopped his sharpening. "I have no money for you if that is what you will ask," he said. "I am sorry, but I have nothing you can use for coinage, to sell or otherwise."

Brynner sat down across the table from him. The beastly old table was well-scrubbed but very worn, with one broken leg that was propped up with stones. "I have not come to ask for money," he said. "But I have a need to speak with you. It is important."

Etzel kept sharpening. "Speak, then."

Brynner noticed his father wouldn't look at him. He didn't even seem happy to see him, but that was of no great concern. In fact, it made what Brynner had to do easier.

"You have no great love for me nor do I have any great love for you," he said. "If I had even a small amount of money, I would leave this place and never think of it again. But I do not have any money. The fact remains that you leave me a bereft legacy that is of no worth to me whatsoever."

Etzel glanced up from his pumice stone. "Are you just realizing this?"

Brynner's jaw ticked at his father's lack of concern or sympathy. "Nay," he said, his tone turning unfriendly. "I have known it for years and because I have known it for years, it now comes to this – I have seen Lord Bramley. Before you fall to the floor in a panic, know this; he wants Shadowmoor and is willing to pay for it. I will not lose this opportunity because you are foolishly hanging on to a heritage that was gone two hundred years ago. The moment our ancestors brokered a deal with the Normans that allowed our kind to keep Shadowmoor was the moment we became Normans ourselves. We have been puppets of the Norman kings ever since. I care not for this land or the legacy, and Bramley is willing to pay for it."

Etzel had stopped sharpening his dagger, looking at his eldest son with some horror in his expression. "You *saw* Bramley?" he repeated, nearly choking on the words. "Why? Brynner, in God's name, why would you do such a thing? You have not spoken to me in months, yet you have taken the time to go behind my back and meet with Bramley?"

Brynner could see the fire in his father's eyes now, the fire of betrayal. He sought to play his hand. "That was not exactly how it happened, but I will not explain those facts," he said. "They do not matter, anyway. The fact of the matter is that Shadowmoor is my legacy. I do not want it. Bramley does. When you die, I am going to turn it over to him, anyway, so why continue to suffer for something that will soon come to an end? I do not want this place, Father. I want you to give it to Bramley."

Etzel set the pumice stone and the dagger onto the table, looking at his son as if the man had completely lost his mind. He shook his head, bewildered. "You want me to *give* it to him?" he said, aghast. "You have completely lost your mind, boy. Why would I do such a thing?"

Brynner sat back on the bench a little, away from the strike of the very sharp dagger that his father had put on the tabletop. "Because it is worthless to us," he said. "It has been worthless to us for generations but your foolish sense of duty and family causes you to see golden towers and cherished memories here where none exist. You were stupid to turn down Bramley's offer in the first place. He is willing to pay good money for this place. Why did you not take him upon on his offer when he first came to you? It is *your* fault that Shadowmoor has deteriorated so terribly, Father. Your selfishness has brought us to ruin."

Etzel could hardly believe what he was hearing. He'd hardly had ten word with his son over the past few years and now, he was hearing more than what he wanted to. Somehow, somewhat, Brynner was now an ally of Bramley. Etzel didn't know how it had happened, but it had. He couldn't even feel hurt or betrayal any longer; all he could feel was unadulterated astonishment.

"You *are* mad," he hissed.

Brynner's eyes narrowed. "Mayhap I am, but at least I will not be starving after you are dead," he said. "I will turn this entire place over to Bramley and welcome him. But I do not want to wait that long. If you truly adore your family as you say you do, then you will turn it over now without further delay. Bramley may still be willing to compensate you for it. Or do you take great pleasure in watching your children starve?"

Etzel had heard enough. Moving fast for an old man, he stood up and lashed out a big hand, slapping Brynner across the face. Brynner nearly toppled over with the force of the hit, managing to roll awkwardly onto his feet so that he was no longer in his father's range. He stood up, glaring at his father, as Etzel nearly climbed onto the tabletop to get at him.

"Shut your drunken mouth," Etzel growled. "You are who would spend your days and nights drowning in any kind of ale or wine you can find, crumbling under the weight of memories that you have allowed to destroy you. It is *you* who are worthless, not Shadowmoor. You were my shining star, my eldest son, and I was immensely proud of you until you turned into a spineless weakling because some woman refused to marry you. Anyone who allows himself to become a slave to a lost love has no right to accuse me of being selfish. You embody all that it means to be selfish and hopeless!"

His words hit Brynner right in the gut, right where he was most vulnerable, as he brought up the loss of the Lady Maud. Brynner's smug manner vanished.

"If I had any respect for you, those words might have hurt me," he said. "As it is, they are hollow. Father, you have no choice in the matter. Give Shadowmoor over to Bramley and he may compensate you well for it. Go live out your life in the city somewhere and spend your money. Take Gunnar and at least let the lad know what it is not to be hungry. At least try to provide for him as a father would."

Etzel was pale with rage. "Liselotte and Gunnar know…."

Brynner cut him off. "Liselotte will go with Bramley," he said. "He has made that clear. I do not understand your aversion to his marital offer. Do you think she will have a better one than that, dressing in rags and living like an animal? No decent man will want her. Bramley offers her a good life. You are a fool to have refused it for this long."

Etzel just stared at him. The disbelief, the rage, was fading as he came to understand that this situation was about to turn very, very bad. If Brynner was allied with Bramley, then Bramley had someone inside of Shadowmoor who could do a great deal of damage. It was a shame, truly. In spite of Brynner's behavior over the past several years, the fact remained that he was still Etzel's son. He remembered Brynner as a young boy, bright and happy, and he had loved that little boy. Somewhere, however, that little boy had died and Etzel had tried to love the sullen drunken man who had taken his place. But looking at Brynner now, it was like he was looking at a stranger.

An enemy.

He had to protect himself.

"Go away, Brynner," he told him. "Go back to Bramley and tell him that he cannot have Shadowmoor or Liselotte. In fact, since you are such good friends with Bramley, you can remain with him. You are not welcome at Shadowmoor. Get out of here now before I kill you."

Brynner didn't move. "You cannot banish me so easily," he said. "I am still your son, your heir. When you die, this heap of ruins becomes mine and I am not leaving it."

Etzel picked up the dagger on the tabletop. "I told you to get out."

Brynner eyed the dagger. "I will not."

Etzel was infuriated enough, and frightened enough, to be reckless. Instead of leaping over the tabletop as he'd done before, he walked around the table and approached his son, brandishing the dagger between them. The look in his eye was a distinct mixture of sorrow and fear.

"I do not know how you became what you are, Brynner," he said, his voice hoarse. "Some demon inside of you has made you careless and greedy and wicked. I will not give Bramley Shadowmoor. I do not want you to have it, either, knowing what you will do with it, and your sister, after my death. I therefore disown you. I will make Gunnar my heir. It is within my right. You and your wickedness no longer exist to me and you will leave my sight forever. I will not tell you again."

Brynner's eyes glittered, his focus moving between his father's face and the dagger in the man's hand. There was a flash of doubt in what he was doing, in the truth of his father's words, but that flash was just as quickly gone. He could see now what he had to do; his father would have to die. There was no choice now, especially if Etzel was threatening him. He knew there would never be peace between them now, not ever. From this point forward, it would always be a fight for his life.

The honorable son in him was sorry that he would never again know happiness with his father, but the drunkard who would stop at nothing to get his next drink didn't care in the least. That man was stronger. Quick as a flash, Brynner reached out and grabbed his father's hand as it clutched the dagger. From that point, the fight was on.

They struggled over the dagger for several long and painful moments, each man trying to wrest it from the other. Etzel had been strong in his youth but that had diminished with age, and Brynner's strength was sapped by the drink, so it was nearly a fair fight. But that was until Brynner lifted a fist and struck his father in the face. Etzel saw stars and stumbled back, falling over the tabletop.

Brynner had the dagger now and pounced on his father, but Etzel was able to grab the man's wrist and prevent him from plunging the dagger into his chest. Etzel lifted a knee, ramming Brynner between the legs, and Brynner grunted and faltered but maintained his hold on the knife. The two of them rolled over the tabletop and onto the floor, kicking and punching, each man trying to gain control of the weapon.

Etzel was eventually able to knock the dagger out of Brynner's hand and the blade went sliding across the floor towards the fire pit. Both of them scrambled after it but Brynner was faster. He picked it up and turned it on his father as the man ran at him.

Seeing the very sharp blade pointed right at him, Etzel tried to stop his forward momentum but he couldn't; he stumbled and fell forward onto the dagger, slicing it through his chest and into his heart. Blood gushed as he collapsed, falling head-first into the fire pit.

He was dead before hit the ground.

Stunned, and breathing heavily, Brynner turned to see his father half in the fire pit, catching fire from the waist up. He could clearly see the dagger protruding from Etzel's chest and shocked hands flew to his head in disbelief of what he had done. He hadn't really meant to kill him, only take the dagger from him, and the honorable son made a resurgence as he grabbed hold of Etzel's feet and pulled him out of the flame.

But it was too late. Etzel's torso and head were on fire and Brynner kicked dirt up over him, trying to extinguish the flames as the scent of burnt flesh mingled with that of the stench of urine. Once the flames were out sufficiently, Brynner put his hand on Etzel's neck to feel that there was no pulse. His father was dead. Then he tried to pull the dagger out of Etzel's chest but burned his fingers on the scorching metal, so he left it there.

Brynner stood up, staring down at his father and absorbing what he had done. He didn't feel the satisfaction he thought he would at his father's death. In fact, he felt some emptiness now. Perhaps it was that honorable son again attempting to feel some grief. Whatever the feeling was, it quickly vanished. Brynner refused to give it any thought. The only thing that mattered now was that Etzel was dead and Shadowmoor now belonged to him.

To Bramley.

With that thought, he went in search of his sister.

CHAPTER TEN

"YOU MUST LIKE it," Daniel said.

If Liselotte's mouth hadn't been full, she would have agreed, but it was a fact that her mouth and Gunnar's mouth were full of a sweet-cream pie that Daniel had purchased for them when they were waiting for their wagon of grain to be hitched up to a team. The smells from several bakers' stalls down the avenue from the livery had caught their attention and, whilst horses were hitched up to the borrowed wagon, Daniel had purchased several little cakes with sweet cream in the middle. Now, as they made their way home to Shadowmoor, Liselotte and Gunnar hasn't stopped eating. They were in sweet-cream heaven.

Daniel, astride Ares as Liselotte and Gunnar rode in the wagon next to a livery hand who would then return the wagon back to his master when it was off-loaded at Shadowmoor, grinned as he watched the siblings stuff themselves with treats. The old horse Gunnar had ridden to town was tied to the wagon. In truth, the cream cake hadn't been the only delight he'd purchased – there were also tarts with apples and honey and cinnamon, and little balls of dough fried in lard and rolled in cinnamon, cardamom, and honey. Daniel had purchased quite a bit of it and Gunnar was covered in sticky sweetness as he stuffed his face.

"It is quite delicious," Liselotte said, her mouth full. "Would you like one?"

Daniel shook his head. "Nay," he said. "It is for you. Besides, I do not want to lose fingers should I try to stick my hand anywhere near you or your brother. You might eat them."

Gunnar laughed and pieces of cake flew out of his mouth. Daniel burst into hearty laughter as Gunnar struggled to keep all of that food in his mouth. As the siblings continued to eat the treats, Daniel kept a lookout on the road. They were heading south on a small road that paralleled the main road to the west. It was the road that, according to Liselotte, Bramley's men patrolled regularly and demanded tariffs. Daniel didn't want to run into them so the lesser-traveled road, although slower because it wasn't as well-kept, was the better option. The last thing he wanted was trouble.

Easton had offered to send some men with him to help should the need arise, but Daniel refused for two good reasons – he didn't want to attract attention with an armed escort and he didn't want to drag Netherghyll into anything should Bramley's men attack. If Netherghyll soldiers were involved, then that would turn Bramley's displeasure against them. Daniel was trying to keep Netherghyll out of the fight as long as possible, at least until his Uncle Christopher could arrive with an army, which would hopefully be within the next few weeks.

The messenger had left Netherghyll that morning, a skinny but clever lad on a swift mount, and Daniel estimated it would take the messenger six or seven days to reach the Marches provided he covered twenty or thirty miles daily. That wasn't unreasonable on a fast horse, if the roads held, so Daniel was counting on that. Give his uncle four or five days to prepare the army, and then another eight to ten days to move the army north, swiftly, and Daniel expected to see his uncle in about three weeks. He knew his uncle would move quickly, so the trick would be to keep Bramley at bay for the next three weeks.

Daniel had his work cut out for him.

With the wheels of summoning assistance in motion, there were other things to focus on, namely the tournament in Skipton. He and Caston had agreed to enter for the chance of either of them to win the purse that would then be donated to Shadowmoor, but Daniel hadn't told Liselotte that. He would tell Etzel and let the man become accustomed to the fact that there were people willing to help him. He knew that would be a difficult concept for a man who had lived a solitary life in his solitary fortress, without any allies. Perhaps if there were some things he could bring to Shadowmoor, they would be the understanding that there were people willing to help and that allies were a very good thing. No man deserved to live a solitary life.

No woman, either.

Daniel glanced over at Liselotte as she helped Gunnar break apart one of the apple tarts. Gunnar was standing in the wagon bed, leaning up against the bench that held the driver and Liselotte. Back behind him, on the wagon bed, were the two little goats Daniel had purchased for him as pets, and once Gunnar had the tart in his hand, he rushed back to his little friends and shared his treat. That had been going on for the past hour, ever since they had left Siglesdene. It was sweet and heartwarming to watch.

Daniel's gaze then trailed to the rear of the loaded wagon where a cow and her calf were tethered, plodding along after the wagon. There was also a young ram, unhappy that he was tied up to the rear of the wagon, struggling with the rope even as he walked. Daniel had purchased a small herd of sheep and a few more goats, but he wanted to make sure there was a place to corral them before bringing them to Shadowmoor. He would have Etzel's people make a corral if there wasn't one and then he would return for the herd at that time. Until then, at least they had a cow producing milk so they could have cheese and milk, and the young ram could be slaughtered for meat.

Confident that life at Shadowmoor was about to markedly improve, Daniel turned his attention to the road again. They were nearing the turn-off to Shadowmoor, fortunately, but he wasn't any less nervous. Until they were within the walls of the fortress, he wouldn't relax. A great deal could happen between now and reaching the fortress gates. Therefore, he kept vigilant as they traveled the bleak and windy moor.

Fortunately, they were able to make it to the gates of Shadowmoor without incident. More than that, the weather held as puffy gray clouds were scattered across the blue sky by the brisk wind. At least there wasn't any rain to deal with. When the wagon entered the gates of Shadowmoor, people watched the arrival with a great deal of shock. No one had seen a cow around the place in years, so it was very definitely a surprise.

But they were hardly in the gates when a man, who had been part of the gang of men manning the front gate, ran up to Liselotte and relayed something in a panic. Daniel could see the man's agitation because he was waving his hands around. Dismounting Ares, he walked around the front of the wagon to see what the matter was as the big black horse followed him like a dog.

By the time he reached Liselotte, she had her hand over her mouth and her face was pale with shock. She was still on the wagon bench and Daniel looked at her in concern.

"My lady?" he asked. "Is something wrong?"

Liselotte looked at him, tears swimming in her eyes. "My father," she said hoarsely. "Something has happened to my father."

Daniel frowned, looking between her and the man she had been speaking with. He was an older man, dressed in rags as the rest of Shadowmoor's inhabitants were, and he looked very nervous when Daniel fixed on him.

"What has happened to Etzel?" Daniel asked. "Where is he?"

The man's nervousness grew. "Er ist in der halle."

Daniel didn't understand the language. He looked at Liselotte. "What did he say?"

Liselotte began to climb down from the wagon bench and Daniel rushed forward to help her. "He said that my father is in the hall," she said. "He says something has happened to him. I must go to him."

Daniel was concerned. "Of course you shall," he said steadily. "I will go with you. I must speak with him, anyway. Do these men all speak another language?"

Liselotte paused in her haste. "They speak the language of my ancestors," she said. "Very few speak the language of the Normans. I learned it because my mother taught it to me and to my brothers, because it was her native language, but most of these men do not know it."

Daniel understood; an isolated community would only pass down their own private customs. "Will you please ask these men to take the food stores to the kitchen and the animals to the stables?" he asked, holding on to her arm because she was already running off, trying to get to the hall to see about her father. "All of this needs to be stored and protected. After we have seen to your father, I will return to give them instructions on how it is to be distributed."

Liselotte nodded and anxiously relayed his words in that harsh, guttural language that seemed to rely a great deal on sharp sounds and odd tongue movements. Daniel thought it was all rather fascinating. When Liselotte finished speaking, the men surrounding the wagon began to move quickly, directing the wagon driver back towards the kitchens while still more men went to untie the animals. One man even went to lift the little goats out of the wagon bed for Gunnar, who stuck to his new friends closely. He wasn't going to let them out of his sight. Satisfied everything was in motion, Daniel had hold of Liselotte's elbow and he pulled her all the way over to Ares so he could collect his saddlebags before they moved swiftly for the hall.

The doors to the great hall were open as they rushed through. Daniel let go of Liselotte's arm as she charged in and began calling for her father, shouting his name. There were a few servants in the hall, startled by her appearance, and two of the women ran at her, chattering in their native language and pointing to the fire pit. Liselotte ran at it and dropped to her knees as Daniel moved closer, dropping his saddlebags on the nearest table as he came around the side of the pit to see that there was something lying beside it, covered in a woolen blanket. He didn't see until it was too late, until she tossed back the blanket, that it was Etzel, badly burned.

Liselotte screamed and Daniel rushed forward, pulling her up from the floor so she wouldn't be faced with the horrific sight. She tried to fight him for a brief moment but he held her fast, forcibly turning her head so she couldn't see Etzel's black and blistered face. A few seconds of struggle was all she could give and she burst into loud sobs, her face pressed to his chest as he held her tightly.

It was a grim discovery. As Liselotte wept over her father, Daniel's gaze drifted over the man. Only the top half of him seemed to be burned but it wasn't long before he spied the dagger sticking out of his chest. Greatly puzzled, and greatly concerned that he was evidently viewing a murder, he looked at the collection of weeping and terrified servants standing around.

"Who of you speaks my language?" he asked. "Do any of you understand what I am saying?"

One woman, hunched over, with a ragged kerchief tied around her head, nodded. "Aye, m'lord," she said in a heavily accented voice. "I understand you."

Daniel was relieved. "Good," he said. "Tell me what happened to Lord Etzel and tell me quickly."

The woman choked as she tried to answer him swiftly, coughing, as she brought forth the words. "It was Sir Brynner," she said, wringing her hands. "They argued and there was a fight. Lord Etzel fell into the fire!"

All of the servants were weeping or sniffling by this point and Liselotte yanked herself away from Daniel, throwing herself down on her father before he could stop her. She groaned pitifully.

"Papa," she sobbed. "Please… do not leave me. You cannot leave me!"

Daniel didn't try to pick her up this time; he let her cry, her head resting on the lower part of her father's body so she didn't have to look at that terrible face. She was shocked and devastated, and rightly so. This happenstance was so very unexpected and Daniel struggled to stay on an even keel. For Liselotte and Gunnar's sakes, he had to. With a heavy sigh, he returned his attention to the twitching servant.

"You are certain that is what happened?" he asked quietly. "You saw this?"

The woman nodded, turning to the other servants and speaking to them in their native language. The other servants, all four of them, began to nod their heads vigorously. Daniel didn't have to be told what they had been asked. He knew. His fury began to grow.

Brynner did it.

Daniel didn't know Brynner. He'd not yet met the man. Brynner was a member of a family that hadn't been very willing to discuss him except to explain his disconnect from them.

Now, Daniel was at a disadvantage; he knew nothing of the eldest son, the one who had evidently killed his father. There was a murderer loose at Shadowmoor and Daniel was determined to find the man and discover the truth of what had happened with Etzel. He had a difficult time believing a child would kill a parent but, then again, nothing about Shadowmoor was normal. This entire place seemed to be cursed one way or the other. He turned to the cowering servant.

"Where is Brynner?" he asked.

The female servant shook her head. "I do not know, m'lord," she said. "We heard the scuffling and saw the fight. After Sir Brynner killed his father, he left the hall. I do not know where he went."

"How long ago?"

"Not long, m'lord. Within the hour."

Daniel's mind was moving a few steps ahead at this point; he was thinking of what he would do once he found Brynner. He was quite certain the man wouldn't come with him peacefully, which meant he was going to have to force him. Having no idea of the size or skill of the man, he was determined to lay out his intentions before he acted. He needed a sword to capture him and rope to subdue him. Then he would need a place to store his prisoner while the situation was settled. But before he got too far ahead of himself, he moved to Liselotte, still weeping over her father.

"Leese," he said quietly, taking a knee next to her and putting a gentle hand on her back. "I am so very sorry for your father, but I need your help. Please, sweetheart, it is important."

Liselotte was in the throes of grief over her father's death. "He cannot leave me," she wept. "He cannot!"

Daniel felt as if he were being incredibly cruel for not allowing her time to grieve, but the truth was that he very much needed her assistance. He put his hands on her arms, pulling her up from her father.

"He is gone but I am here," he whispered. "Do you hear me? I am here, Leese. I will not leave you. But I need your help. The servants say that your brother did this and I have never seen the man. If I am to find him, and find out if he really did this, then I need your help very much."

Liselotte sniffled, wiping at her wet face as her gaze fell on her father's blackened face again. Her composure threatened to crumple.

"I cannot believe he would do such a heinous thing," she hissed, shock evident in her tone. "But if I am completely honest, I am not all that surprised to hear of this. Brynner has been so horrid and foul these past years. But something must have happened, Daniel. Somehow, my father must have said something to incite him. Brynner is mean and sullen, but he is not usually violent, at least not with his family. He usually stays away from us."

He was listening to her carefully, trying to figure out what kind of opponent he would soon be facing. "Then you are saying a mad rage must have come over him."

"Something like that."

"Do you defend him, then?"

She shook her head, her features crumpling once more. But she fought it. "Nay," she said. "I do not defend him. I am simply saying that something must have provoked him enough for him to kill."

Daniel let go of her arms, putting his hand on her face to comfort her. "I need help to find him," he said. "I do not know him on sight so you must tell me what he looks like. I would know…."

He was cut off by a collective gasp from the servants, who suddenly scattered into the shadows. Daniel whirled around to the hall entry only to be faced with a man entering from the bailey outside, the light illuminating him from behind, making him look dark and mysterious. Based on the terrified reaction of the servants, Daniel could only guess that the elusive Brynner l'Audacieux was making an appearance, and his survival instincts took over. The enemy had shown himself and Daniel mentally prepared himself for what was to come.

His own survival was the first thing he considered. His saddlebags, including his broadsword, were over on the table to his right, about a dozen feet away. He could get to his sword quickly if he needed to but he didn't want Brynner to get to it first. Therefore, he quickly moved away from the fire pit, towards his possessions. He came to a halt next to them, facing Brynner as the man came into the light.

It wasn't a monster before him, as he was coming to imagine from what he'd heard and seen, but simply a man by all appearances. Brynner l'Audacieux had his sister's bronze hair and his brother's blue eyes. He wasn't particularly tall, and he was somewhat slender. He was dressed in rags, just as the rest of Shadowmoor was, and he focused suspiciously on Daniel with dark-circled eyes. He pointed at him.

"Who are you?" he asked.

That question was rather telling because Daniel had fleetingly wondered if Brynner had heard of his arrival to Shadowmoor. He wondered if the man had heard anything at all, this man who kept himself sequestered from his family. From his question, it was probable that he'd not even heard about him. That made the element of surprise on his side to a certain extent. He was, therefore, careful in his reply.

"My name is de Lohr," he said.

Brynner was expecting more of a response and his eyes narrowed, perhaps with some irritation, when nothing more was forthcoming. His attention shifted from Daniel to Liselotte, who was standing over the body of Etzel.

"I have been looking for you," he said to his sister. "Where have you been?"

Liselotte was trembling with rage. She pointed at Etzel. "What have you done?" she demanded. "He is dead, Brynner! What did you do?"

Brynner's jaw flexed, obviously displeased at his sister's tone of voice. "He tried to kill me," he said emotionlessly. "He charged me with the knife. I assure you that I did not intend to kill him, but that is what happened. I was defending myself."

He said it so callously and Liselotte emitted gasp of disbelief. "Defending yourself from him?" she said, outraged. "He would never have tried to kill you, Brynner! You are lying!"

It was very clear that Brynner didn't like her response. His face reddened. "You will never say that to me again," he growled. "Do you understand me?"

Liselotte wouldn't back down; her grief was flooding out of her. "Then tell me why you killed him!" she shouted. "Tell me what really happened!"

Brynner didn't give her the benefit of a reply; he simply charged her and Daniel, startled at the swift movement, charged after him. He came up behind Brynner before the man could get to Liselotte and grabbed him from behind, throwing one arm across his throat and the other behind his head. As Brynner struggled, surprised and outraged by the move, Daniel growled in his ear.

"One wrong move and I shall snap your neck," he snarled. "You were going to strike her, weren't you? *Weren't you?*"

Brynner tried to wrestle against Daniel, who was substantially bigger and stronger. "This is… none… of your affair!" he grunted. "She is… my sister and… mine to do with… as I please!"

Daniel squeezed harder and Brynner started to turn red. He was in a bad way. "Wrong answer," Daniel hissed. "She is not to be touched by the likes of you. Do you understand me? Another move in her direction and I will remove your head from your shoulders. Are we clear?"

Brynner was being choked but not strongly enough to cause him to pass out; just hard enough to cause great discomfort. "Let me go!" he demanded. "I am the Lord of Shadowmoor now and you will release me!"

Liselotte looked at Daniel, started by the realization. It was true. In fact, with Etzel gone, Brynner was now the Lord of Shadowmoor. At that moment, a great deal changed. No longer was it Etzel and Liselotte and Gunnar trying to get by, living a hand-to-mouth existence like everyone else at Shadowmoor. Now, the drunkard was lord of the fortress, a man who would have sold his own mother if it meant supplying him in drink. The worst possible liege was now in charge of a fortress that was already one step above death.

God help them all.

"Daniel," she said softly. "Release him. Please."

Daniel eyed her for a long moment before complying. When he released Brynner, however, he kicked the man in the back of the knees, causing Brynner to stumble several feet away before catching his balance. That gave Daniel enough time to collect his broadsword and he held it in his left hand, an obvious message, as he moved to Liselotte's side. He faced Brynner.

"Now," he said. "My name is de Lohr, as I said, and you will be punished for causing your father's death. I do not believe that he tried to kill you first."

Brynner was several feet away, rubbing his neck. "I do not care who you are or what you believe," he said. "Shadowmoor is mine now and you will leave it immediately. You have no power here."

Daniel snorted. "That is where you are wrong, little man," he said. Usually so congenial, Daniel's manner became very deadly, very quickly. "You will answer for your father's death and I will make sure you are punished. As a prisoner, you cannot rule. It is forbidden by the laws of the land, which means the fortress passes to the next male in the family. Your younger brother is now Lord of Shadowmoor."

Brynner looked at him as if he were mad. "By what authority do you presume this?"

Daniel's eyes gleamed. "By the authority of the king of England and by the authority of my uncle, Christopher de Lohr, who is the Earl of Hereford and Worcester, and High Sheriff of the Marches. I will bring his justice to Yorkshire to rule on what you have done. Your father was a good man, without violence, and for some reason you sought to silence him. You have admitted it."

That seemed to give Brynner some pause. "De Lohr?" he repeated. "Christopher de Lohr is your uncle?"

Daniel simply nodded. Brynner, trying to gain some semblance of control over the situation now that the great Christopher de Lohr had been brought into the conversation, jabbed a finger at him.

"He has no power here," he said. "The man belongs on the Marches. That is where his jurisdiction is."

Daniel cocked an eyebrow. "His seven-thousand-man army says that he has jurisdiction anywhere he pleases," he said. "I have sent him a missive and he will be here very soon. Until that time, you will be confined to the vault. I'll not have your sister and brother threatened by a murderer running loose."

Brynner could see that Daniel was serious. He had no idea what a de Lohr was doing here, or why he was taking charge of Shadowmoor, but the man's presence seriously disrupted his plans for Shadowmoor and for his sister.

Brynner didn't like being told what to do. He had never liked taking orders, even when he had been a knight. In his mind, no man had any power over him, so Daniel's words were outraging him in the worst possible way. Feeling bullied and threatened, he made one last effort to overcome de Lohr and his demands. He wasn't going to surrender without a fight.

"You have no power here," he snarled. "I have no idea who you really are. You could be lying about your name and lying about summoning a de Lohr army. You are a usurper as well as a liar. Shadowmoor, and all within her, belongs to me and I will defend that right until the death."

Daniel flashed the sword. "I would recant that if I were you."

Brynner was growing increasingly infuriated that his words were having no impact on Daniel and with that fury, came recklessness.

"I have allies, too," he said. "Did you think you were the only man capable of summoning an army? I can summon an army in a day that will come here and cut your head off. Get out of here while you still can!"

Daniel gave him a rather droll expression. "That is fairly bold talk coming from a man who lives on the inside of a wine barrel, so I'm told," he said. "Pray tell me, who these terrible allies are so that I might laugh when you are finished."

Brynner's face was turning red again at the insult. "A nephew of King Henry," he said. "I would like to see you laugh in the face of Lord Bramley. My sister belongs to him, you know. So does Shadowmoor so, essentially, you are stealing from him. He will have something to say about it."

Lord Bramley! Daniel didn't dare look at Liselotte, but he heard her gasp. Somehow, someway, Bramley had gotten to Brynner. Is that why the man killed Etzel? Is that why the elusive Brynner was now suddenly in their midst, speaking of armies and making demands? Daniel wondered. Still, his manner remained cool. The conversation was growing interesting.

"He is not the nephew of the king, no matter what he has told you," he said calmly. "His sister is the bastard of King John. Roland Fitzroy has no relation to Henry at all, so whatever he has told you is a lie. How in the world did you fall into that man's clutches? Everything he says is a lie."

Brynner blinked, clearly stunned by Daniel's words. "How would you know about him?"

Daniel shrugged lazily. "Because he is a fool," he said in a calculated move. "Everyone knows he is a liar, but evidently, you do not. That makes you a fool, too."

Brynner's composure was slipping. His face was still red, fury bleeding out into his movements as he twitched, stumbling back to get away from Daniel and the man's big sword. Now, he was starting to falter, to lose confidence, and struggling not to look as if he was. He knew Bramley only slightly more than he knew this man, de Lohr, which was really not at all. But de Lohr seemed to know about Bramley. Brynner's composure was on a downward spiral.

"You will be sorry," he said, pointing his finger at Daniel. "You will be sorry you said such things about him."

Daniel cocked his head. "Go and tell him," he said. "You have my permission to run and tell him everything. But when you go to him, know this; he shall not have Shadowmoor and neither shall you. The two of you can climb back into whatever pigsty you crawled out of because you are not welcome here. Now, get out of here before I kill you."

Brynner's jaw flexed angrily. "I am not leaving my home."

Daniel raised the sword. "I will not tell you again."

Brynner shook his head, holding his ground, and Daniel suddenly charged after him, causing the man to bolt. He had no weapon, so to stand in the face of a man with a very big broadsword was suicide. There was no way to stand his ground. With Daniel in pursuit, and Daniel was very fast, Brynner flew out of the hall and raced across the bailey, heading for the great gates that were just starting to open because the wagon Daniel had borrowed to transport the grain was empty now, preparing to depart the bailey.

Through the mud the men ran, causing people to scatter but then stand by and watch at a safe distance as a big blond knight with a big sword chased Brynner l'Audacieux through the bailey. Brynner, who usually didn't move so fast, was running for his life, dodging people, and the wagon, before shooting through the open gates faster than he had ever moved in his life. He kept running even as Daniel came to a halt at the gates and watched him dash off down the moor.

"God's Bones!" Liselotte exclaimed, breathless, as she came up behind Daniel. "You really chased him away!"

Daniel, winded, watched the man run off. "I had no choice," he said, turning to Liselotte. "If he has had contact with Bramley as he says he has, then it would be like placing a fox in the hen house. We would have an enemy within. Therefore, he is not welcome here. Had I caught him, I would have put him in the vault and chained him to the wall."

Liselotte watched her brother as he fled down the desolate hillside. "Do you think it was Bramley who told him to kill my father?"

Daniel shrugged. "One cannot choose but to wonder," he said. "How in the world did he ever come into contact with Bramley? Your father said that he kept to himself in his chamber. I was not aware that he ever left Shadowmoor."

Liselotte shook her head, distraught from everything that had happened. "He has been known to wander the moor when the drink wears off," she said. "It is possible he ran into Bramley on one of those walks. Oh, Daniel, do you think he really will run back to Bramley? Do you think Bramley will bring his army down upon us?"

Daniel looked at her, seeing the fear and the grief. She had been dealt a terrible blow this day, on two accounts – her brother's shocking connection with Bramley and the fact that the man murdered Etzel. As if her father's death, in of itself, wasn't bad enough. Shaking his head, he put his arm around her and kissed her forehead in full view of the men manning the front gates. He didn't care who saw him.

"It is hard to say," he said. "But I will be sending a missive to Netherghyll immediately. I told Easton that I did not want him to become involved in Shadowmoor's problems, but with your father gone, I fear those problems have escalated. Can you find me a man who would swiftly ride to Netherghyll?"

Liselotte nodded, speaking to the man in charge of the gate, who, in turn, began shouting to other men. The wheels were in motion as Daniel and Liselotte headed back to the hall to absorb what had happened with Brynner, and with Etzel, and plan a course of action. With Etzel's death, much had changed. Much more than they realized.

One issue, of course, was that Daniel had just chased off the new

Lord of Shadowmoor, the man legally entitled to the fortress. That made him something of a thief. The whole situation had him needing to sit down and think things through. Much had changed. Much was *going* to change.

Daniel had a feeling it was going to get much worse before it got better. But one thing was for certain; he wasn't going to give up Liselotte, or Shadowmoor, without a fight.

CHAPTER ELEVEN

Lioncross Abbey Castle
Near Lyonshall, Welsh Marches
Seven days later

"THIS CAME FOR you, my lord. It looks as if it is from Daniel."

Christopher de Lohr was seated at the great feasting table in the enormous two-storied hall of Lioncross Abbey, his seat. He was a very old man by any standard, now in his seventy-seventh year, but he looked much younger. He acted much younger, too. His once-blond hair was now snowy white and the neatly-trimmed beard he took such pride in was darker, speckled with gray. In spite of his age, he was still sharp and still powerful, and bore the wisdom of a man who had seen much in his years on earth. He was a great man and much respected for a life well-lived.

As now, he was reaping the rewards of his life, of a big family and many sons. He had just finished a big meal and was in the process of playing with two of his grandsons, children of his younger son, Myles. The boys had toy soldiers and, being a dutiful grandfather, Christopher was prepared to wage war with them. But words from the knight who had entered the warm and fragrant hall had him distracted.

"What is it?" he asked, looking over his shoulder.

The knight who had spoken was a very big man dressed in mail and a tunic bearing the colors of the Earl of Canterbury. Sir Maddoc du Bois had a missive in his hand and extended it to Christopher. But the earl had his hands full of toy soldiers and he had to set them down in order to receive the missive. He peered at the wax seal.

"That," he said, "is the seal of Lord Thorndon, my brother's Prodigal Son. And what are you doing bringing me this missive? I thought you were returning to Canterbury."

Maddoc grinned; an exceptionally handsome man with black hair and bright blue eyes, he was the Earl of Canterbury's captain. He'd come to Lioncross on business a week ago, delivering some kind of coinage and gifts from Canterbury to his brother, and with his task finished, he was eager to return home to his new wife. But a missive from Daniel had him pausing in that determination to depart, mostly because he and Daniel were the best of friends and he was eager to know news of his friend. It didn't come often enough as far as Maddoc was concerned. He missed his friend.

"I was at the gate when the messenger arrived," he said. "All the way from West Yorkshire. The man has been riding for six and a half days, very long days I would imagine if he made it to the Marches in such good time. He said the missive was important so I thought I would bring it to you personally. I would like to hear why Daniel has sent a messenger all the way from West Yorkshire."

Christopher lifted his eyebrows. "I am interested as well," he admitted. "It is not like Daniel to send me a missive. I cannot recall when last he has done such a thing."

Maddoc scratched his neck. "There was that time that he was in trouble with a baron from Nottinghamshire," he said casually. "Something about compromising his daughter, as I recall. He did not want his father to know."

Christopher grunted as he broke the seal. "You heard about that one, did you?"

"Daniel told me. He always sends missives to you when he does not want your brother to know."

Christopher paused in unfolding the missive, looking to Maddoc. "I swear to you, if this is another missive asking for money to pay off another angry father, I will have you take this straight to my brother and let him deal with it," he declared. "Or if this is about money, asking to bail him out of a gaol because he has done something foolish, I will not pay it. I will let him rot there."

He said it rather passionately, unusual for the usually calm man, and Maddoc simply shook his head. "Nay, you will not, my lord."

"Nay, I will not!"

Maddoc broke down into soft laughter as Christopher unfolded the remainder of the missive and began to read. Truth be told, Maddoc was extremely curious as to the contents of the missive and, as he said, for the fact that Daniel was sending it to Christopher and not to his father. It had to mean there was something seriously the matter, something he didn't want his father to know. Maddoc watched Christopher's face as the man read the contents. He watched Christopher's expression tighten.

"God's Beard," Christopher finally muttered. "It seems our boy has happed upon a situation he has gotten himself involved in."

Maddoc's brow furrowed in curiosity as Christopher read the missive again and then handed it to Maddoc so he, too, could read it. As Christopher sat there and pondered the missive's contents, Maddoc read through it, equally puzzled and concerned. When he was finished, he looked at Christopher.

"Roland Fitzroy?" he repeated. "I've not heard of the man, my lord. Have you?"

Christopher shook his head. "I have not," he said. "I have, however, heard of Joan of Wales. She is John's bastard from a noble Welshwoman."

Maddoc looked at the missive again. "So this man claims he is her brother, and by that relation a nephew to the king, and he has been harassing a castle to the point of starvation because he wants the heiress?" He was looking at the missive as he spoke. "Daniel always did have the knack of finding trouble like this and championing the persecuted. So now he has found another cause and asks for your military assistance."

Christopher sighed heavily. "You are missing the point," he said quietly because his grandsons were still within earshot and he didn't want them to hear anything negative about their Uncle Daniel. "The key word in that entire missive is 'heiress'. Daniel is doing this because of a woman."

Maddoc was forced to agree. "But it sounds as if there is genuine trouble, my lord," he said. "You know Daniel would not have asked you for help unless there was a serious need. He would have simply figured it out himself without any assistance if it was at all possible."

"That is true."

Maddoc set the missive down on the table. "If you are considering not sending him the aid he asks for, look at it this way, my lord," he said. "If Daniel is sending you this request, he is not on the periphery of the situation. He is in the middle of it. If you do not send him the help he needs, there could be devastating consequences. You do not want to have to tell your brother that you did not send his only son help when he requested it and, as a result, something terrible happened."

Christopher pursed his lips irritably. "Spoken like a true advocate of Daniel and his foolishness," he said. He sighed heavily. "I will send him what he asks for. I never considered otherwise. But I am going to send him some knights as well, men in command of my army to assess the situation and see just how real the need is. If it is simply foolishness, then the knights will be under order to return my army at once. But if the need is real…."

Maddoc understood. He sighed. "My lord, you know as well as I do that Daniel is not foolish when it comes to battle or military exercises," he said. "He is the best commander I have ever seen. It is simply in his personal life where the lines blur."

Christopher thumped at the missive. "He speaks of an heiress," he said. "The lines are already blurred. But I will admit again that Daniel would not have asked for my help if he did not feel this to be a very serious situation. And I have a feeling his father would want to know this. So why ask me for help?"

Maddoc shrugged. "Because you are not as far away as Canterbury," he said simply. "You can reach him faster."

"Then the situation must be critical."

"That is my thought as well, my lord."

Christopher looked at Maddoc. "How would you like to ride to West Yorkshire and see for yourself what Daniel has gotten himself in to?" he asked. "You are his dearest friend, Maddoc. I have a feeling he might require your counsel. You seem to be the only one who has ever been able to communicate well with him. He just laughs at the rest of us, hugs us, and tells us how much he loves us. Then he goes off and does whatever he pleases."

Maddoc grinned. "I will admit I am very curious about what situation he is in," he said. "But more than that, I am anxious to see him. I suppose I could spare a few weeks to see what is happening and then report back to you and to his father. It might give Lord David comfort to know I saw the situation with my own eyes."

Christopher nodded. His gaze lingered on the missive a moment. "Maddoc," he said, "when you first arrived and I asked you how my brother's health was, you would not look me in the eye when you told me he was well. Why is that?"

It was a swift change in subject. Maddoc seemed to falter a bit. "I do not recall not looking at you, my lord."

"You did not. And you always look men in the eye." He looked up from the missive, fixing Maddoc with those great wise eyes. "His health has not improved since that illness he suffered last winter, has it?"

Maddoc took a long deep breath. "Not much, my lord."

"Is he dying?"

Maddoc shook his head. "I do not know, my lord."

Christopher continued to hold his gaze but, as Maddoc watched, tears began to fill the sky blue eyes. "I do not intend to outlive my little brother, you know. I could not stand it. If he is truly ill, Maddoc, you must tell me. I must go to him."

Maddoc was shocked to see the tears in Christopher's eyes. "He has not recovered well from the sickness in his chest, my lord," he said. "He is better, but not completely well. Lady Emilie has engaged a physic who lives at Canterbury and tends him daily. He is the same physic who tended me when I was so badly wounded last year. If anyone can nurse your brother through this, he can. I have great faith in his abilities."

Christopher's gaze lingered on him a moment longer before he sniffled loudly and hastily wiped his eyes, looking to see if his grandsons had witnessed his emotional outburst. Thankfully, they seemed oblivious.

"Then mayhap it is better that my brother did not receive this missive," he said. "Maddoc, find de Russe and send him to me. I will have you and Marc muster an army of five hundred men and march them north to West Yorkshire. A smaller army will move faster than a larger one. Go to this place, this Shadowmoor north of Bradford, and discover the truth of the situation. If it is truly serious, then send me word and I will send thousands of men northward. Meanwhile… meanwhile, I do think I should tell my brother something about this. He needs to know the whereabouts and status of his son. That is only fair."

Maddoc nodded. "Agreed, my lord."

"Get about your business, then," Christopher said as he turned back to his grandsons. "And, Maddoc?"

"Aye, my lord?"

"If Daniel really has gotten himself into a foolish mess, I hope you will punch him right in the nose."

Maddoc grinned. "Nay, my lord," he shook his head. "Daniel can fight as well as I can. I have no intention of poking the bear."

Christopher grunted. "Then I may have to poke him," he said. "He would not dare strike me back."

Maddoc laughed softly. "He would hug you, kiss you, and tell you how much he loves you," he said. "You cannot hit a man who is showing such affection."

Christopher simply shook his head and waved Maddoc off. As the knight headed out to muster an army, Christopher turned back to his grandsons. But his thoughts lingered on his nephew, his brother's only son, a man who was what all men wanted to be – strong, proud, true, honest to a fault, loving, but with a hint of the devil in him. The entire family loved Daniel dearly. Of course, Christopher was going to rush to the man's aid; there had never been any doubt.

After a long game of War with his grandsons and their toy soldiers, Christopher retired to his solar after the boys had gone to sleep to write a missive to his brother, very tactfully trying to tell the man that Daniel might be in a spot of trouble with a local lord named Bramley.

He prayed the missive didn't send his still-ill brother over the edge and onto the road north to save his only son.

CHAPTER TWELVE

Shadowmoor

IT WAS THE best time of his life.

That's what Daniel was thinking as he quit the keep, heading for the great hall under the early morning sky. The day was bright, with the rains from a few days ago having passed away, and the epic mud in the bailey that seemed to coat everything was drying up for the most part. More than that, it was evident throughout Shadowmoor that the situation, for them, had drastically changed.

That was what some food and hope could do for people – completely change their outlook and give them faith that better days were on the horizon. Those who lived at Shadowmoor, people whose families had lived there for generations, were still wearing rags, but at least their bellies were full. That gave them the strength to mend a broken roof on their one-room home, or sweep floors, or try to make their living conditions better. It gave them the will to go on.

Shadowmoor was a place where many people lived inside the fortress, with little homes built into the fortress walls, but it was also a place where some people lived outside of the fortress. Even though the gates were closed, and were always closed, people were slipping in and out, helping those outside of the fortress, everyone seemingly quite busy on this bright day.

It was good to see.

The grain that Daniel had purchased in town nearly two weeks ago now had been rationed and put to good use. Bread was baking again. And with the cow he'd bought, people had butter for that bread. There wasn't a lot of it, but it was enough. Daniel was coming to think they needed more than one cow and he was thinking on heading in to Siglesdene on this day to speak to the livery owner again, to see if he could purchase one or two more.

Shadowmoor didn't operate like most castles, that usually only functioned for the lord's family and whatever army he had inside. A castle was like a city unto itself most of the time, only providing for those who lived within, sometimes providing for a village, but more often than not only providing for itself. But Shadowmoor functioned like an entire city, and there were a couple of hundred people to feed. Therefore, more needed to be done, including more cows in the stable.

It was the idea of a purpose in life that Daniel had first considered before he had decided to aid Shadowmoor in its struggles. To help those less fortunate, to fortify those who were downtrodden. He had been a wanderer for so long, only thinking of himself, but now he was thinking of others.

Of Liselotte.

His first week at Shadowmoor had been difficult due to Etzel's unexpected death and Liselotte had grieved heavily the first day. She and Gunnar had wept together. But after that day, it was as if she realized she needed to set an example to the others, to be strong about what had happened, and he saw a change come over the woman. She was now essentially in charge of Shadowmoor and she would not let her people down. Her grief was still there; Daniel had caught her with tears in her eyes on more than one occasion, but she had quickly recovered her composure. Daniel admired her strength a great deal.

Now, almost two weeks later, she was setting a remarkable example for her people to follow and Daniel was certain that was the majority of the reason why everyone at Shadowmoor seemed to be feeling so hopeful for the future. But, of course, Daniel had given her that confidence. Through him, she could see change for the better in spite of Etzel's passing.

But it wasn't just Daniel who had inspired such confidence – things long dormant at Shadowmoor were now beginning to thrive again as the result of help from Netherghyll. Easton had sent about three hundred men to Shadowmoor when Daniel had sent him a missive about Etzel's death and Brynner's alliance with Bramley. But Easton had done even more than that; he'd gone out of his way to send supplies, including wood and peat, and food for his men so they wouldn't be a burden on Shadowmoor's meager supplies.

Caston had come along with those three hundred men and after he got over the shock of the fortress' derelict condition, he and Daniel had decided on a course of action to repair and restore the fortress. It was carefully laid out, in stages, and with the Netherghyll soldiers helping the inhabitants of Shadowmoor, the badly damaged legacy of the l'Audacieux family began to take shape again.

The phoenix began to rise from the ashes.

Walls were being repaired and more supplies were brought in. As half of the Netherghyll men stood guard in and around the fortress, the other half, along with most of Shadowmoor's residents, began fixing huts, organizing work gangs, and restoring what used to be the trade stalls. The smithy was up again, as was the tanner, and supplies from Netherghyll made it possible for these men, who had been without the tools of their trade for so long, to begin restoring tools and weapons, and repairing things like shoes and clothing. Finally, the people of Shadowmoor began to live again with help from a very generous neighbor.

A neighbor, in fact, that Daniel was coming to appreciate a great deal. Easton was vastly generous and Caston was as well, both of them rushing to help Shadowmoor as if helping a family member. The more time Daniel spent with these men, the more he appreciated them. Daniel and Caston had become surprisingly close very quickly, mostly because they had the same sense of humor and seemed to think alike.

But the more he came to know Caston, the more Daniel's guilt over Brighton's death was starting to eat at him.

He cursed the man daily for what he'd done and how he'd behaved. He'd behaved horribly and had perished as a result. Someday, Easton and Caston would learn of the man's death and it would tear them apart, for they both spoke quite fondly of Brighton, their son and brother. It was clear they loved the man and missed him. That, more than anything, was like a dagger to Daniel's heart and his resolve never to tell them what he knew began to slip. It simply wasn't fair for them not to know what Brighton had done and the result of that behavior. But, then again, perhaps it was better for them not to know and remember the man as they knew them.

It was a dilemma, indeed.

On this bright morning as Daniel crossed the bailey towards the hall, he could see men upon the steeply pitched roof of the hall repairing a section that leaked badly. Most of the men on the roof were Shadowmoor residents although a few Netherghyll soldiers were on the ground, passing up materials. The thatching supplies had come from Netherghyll as well, and Daniel made a note of just how much he was to owe Easton for the man's generosity. He was coming to think that the purse won at Skipton's tournament should simply be turned over to Easton as payment. As he pondered the monetary compensation for his generous neighbors, a shout broke his train of thought.

"You, there!"

He heard a cry over to his right, near the front gate, and turned to see Caston standing there with a grin on his face. The man had gone back to Netherghyll a couple of days ago but had evidently returned this morning. Daniel grinned as he faced him.

"Are you back again?" he said, sounding disgusted. "I thought I was well rid of you!"

Caston laughed. "In your dreams, foolish man," he said. "You cannot be rid of me. I will haunt you until the end of your days."

There was a double-meaning in that for Daniel. *If you knew what I know about your brother, that would be true.* But he kept his manner light, in the manner Caston had intended.

"Then I am a cursed man," he said drolly. "How goes it at Netherghyll?"

Caston came towards him, grinning. "Glennie wants to know if she can come to Shadowmoor and visit, but my father has denied her," he said. "She is very unhappy, so do not be surprised if she shows up one of these days in defiance of his orders. If she does, you are to spank her and send her back to Netherghyll under escort. My father told me to tell you that."

Daniel snorted. "Let Easton spank her," he said. "She is his daughter, after all."

Caston nodded. "That is true," he said. "But she is willing to risk it. She is quite fond of you, you know."

It was the first time since Netherghyll's arrival at Shadowmoor that the subject of Glennie, and her obvious interest in Daniel, had been broached. Daniel had been hoping it would never come up but it seemed as if Caston had been lulling him into a false sense of security. Now, in a sly move, it was out in the open but Daniel was prepared. He smiled faintly.

"I am sure we are all in agreement that she should not come," he said. "Based on the situation with Brynner and Bramley, and the fact that they could be planning for an attack at this very moment, she must remain at Netherghyll."

Caston nodded. "I am aware," he said. Then, he noticed a vision in yellow wool over near the end of the hall where it connected to the kitchen yard. Liselotte made an appearance with two servants trailing her; it was clear that they were in discussion. "Speaking of ladies at Shadowmoor, since Glennie is not allowed to come, mayhap it would be wise to send Liselotte to Netherghyll as well. The ladies could keep each other company. As it is, Glennie is offended that Liselotte is allowed at Shadowmoor but she is not."

Daniel caught sight of the woman, too, and his gaze tracked her.

"This is Liselotte's home," he said quietly. "She has a right to be here more than any of us do. I have tried to convince her to leave but she refuses, especially in light of Etzel's passing. She feels the need to be here for the comfort of the inhabitants of Shadowmoor."

Caston shrugged his shoulders as both of them watched Liselotte's lithe figure move through the kitchen yard and out of sight. "You do not want her to leave, anyway," he said. "You want her close to you."

It was a statement, not a question, as if Caston were confident in the subject. As if he knew. Daniel pretended to have no idea what he was talking about.

"Why on earth would you say that?" he asked. "It is for her own safety that I have asked her to leave."

Caston gave him a half-grin. "Daniel, we are friends," he said. "I am offended that you see the need to lie to me about her."

"What do you mean?"

"I see how you look at her. I have seen the touches between you two when you think no one is looking."

Daniel stared at him for a long moment before breaking down into a smile. "Is it that obvious?"

Caston laughed softly. "It is to me."

"Have you told Glennie?"

Caston shook his head. "Not until I had confirmation," he said. "It will break her heart, you know."

Daniel was still smiling because Caston was, trying not to look too embarrassed. "When you do tell her, tell her that Liselotte and I are… together. That way, she will not think this is something trite or temporary."

"Betrothed?"

"Her father offered her to me in marriage before his death."

Caston nodded. "Now, everything makes so much more sense," he said. "I have been wracking my brain, trying to figure out why you should work so hard to save this old fortress when you have no real connection to it. Now, I know."

"Indeed you do."

"I think I have known since the beginning."

Daniel slapped Caston on the arm and turned him towards the hall. "Then you are cleverer than I gave you credit for," he said, watching Caston snort. "But let us put thoughts of women aside for now. What brings you back to Shadowmoor? Or did you miss me so much that you could not stay away?"

They were nearing the open hall entry, smelling something very rare in the air. It had been a long time since the scent of freshly baked bread had filled the hall.

"I came back with fifty more men bearing tools and more nails for repairs," Caston said. "But I also came to speak with you about a few things. One subject I wish to speak with you about is the plan we had for confronting Bramley. Do you recall when we discussed that? I think we should do it sooner rather than later. Although he has been quiet since Lord Etzel's death, I am uneasy with the silence. I feel as if the man is up to something. It would be better if we take the two hundred men I suggested and ride to Bramley to tell him to stay away from Shadowmoor or he risks bringing the entire de Lohr army down upon him."

Daniel's manner sobered with the subject of Bramley. "I have been thinking on our plans to confront Bramley, also," he said. "I agree with you – I do not like the silence, either. But we made those plans before Lord Etzel was killed. Now, he is dead and the man who killed him, his own son, admitted that he is allied with Bramley. It is my suspicion that Brynner left here and ran straight to Bramley Castle, where he has been ever since. Of course, I do not know this for certain but it is a logical assumption. My point is that I expected a surge from Bramley the first few days after Etzel was killed but there has been nothing, which leads me to believe he is planning something, mayhap even something very big. I am not entirely sure that riding there with two hundred men and threatening him would scare him off at this point. It might even agitate him."

Caston pondered Daniel's point of view. "I understand what you are saying," he said. "But if Bramley is planning something, shouldn't you want to know about it?"

Daniel conceded the point. "Indeed I do," he said. "But rather than take an army with us, mayhap you and I should ride to Bramley Castle and see what we can see. Two carefully concealed knights might be able to see a great deal."

Caston rather liked that thought. "Agreed," he said. "But if we see no build-up of an army that suggests a military offensive?"

"Then we will take your two hundred men, ride to Bramley, and tell the man we'll cut his manhood off if he makes one more aggressive move against Shadowmoor or Liselotte. And that includes emasculating his newest ally and murdering friend, Brynner. In fact, I wonder what his Uncle Henry would think if he knew the man was harboring a murderer?"

Caston chuckled. "Will you tell Henry, then?"

"I think I should."

Caston was satisfied with those plans. "Excellent," he said. "Then we ride tomorrow?"

"Tomorrow it is."

With those plans out of the way, Caston moved on to the next subject. "Now," he said, "the other item I wished to discuss with you is the coming tournament. Something has occurred to me."

"You are only now realizing that I will dominate you?"

Caston laughed, without humor. "Nay," he said, quickly sobering. "It occurred to me that you do not have any equipment for the joust. Were you only planning to do the mass competition?"

Daniel nodded. "I travel most of the time and carrying a joust pole would be cumbersome," he said. "Therefore, you are correct – I was only planning on competing in the mass competition."

Caston grinned brightly. "No more, my friend," he said. "I have all of my brother's old joust poles. We have twelve of them, in fact, so you are now going to compete in the joust."

Brighton's joust poles. God, the irony of the Caston's offer was unfathomable. But he forced a smile. "You are very generous," he said. "But won't your brother mind?"

Caston shook his head. "He probably has twelve more down at Arundel Castle, where he is most of the time," he said. "You were told he serves Norfolk, correct?"

"I was."

"He is stationed at Arundel," he continued. "My brother is hell on the tournament field. He is extremely aggressive."

Daniel hadn't seen Brighton on the tournament field but he'd certainly seen him in a battle situation. He agreed with Caston's assessment completely. "And you?" he asked. "You two are twins, after all. Are you identical in that aspect as well?"

Caston shrugged. "My father says that even though we look identical, our temperaments are quite different," he said. "I will admit my brother can be aggressive to the point of obstinate at times. He wants what he wants and will stop at nothing to get it. As children, he always had to best me in everything, to be better than I was all of the time. If I was better at him in something, then he would usually punch me. That is simply his nature. My nature is a bit more calculating and subdued. I can be as aggressive as my brother, of course, but I am more clever about it."

It was the first time that Caston had really talked about his brother's personality and, suddenly, a great deal was making sense to Daniel. Even Caston was aware of Brighton's extremely aggressive nature, something that had eventually cost the man his life. But it didn't make Daniel feel any better to know any of this. In fact, it only made it worse because he liked Caston a great deal. He wouldn't have hurt the man for anything.

"Then I will have to be very careful in the coming tournament, especially if we are to joust against one another," he said. "I do not want that calculating personality turned against me."

Caston merely shrugged and turned for the hall entry where the smells of food were luring him in. “Afraid?”

Daniel grunted unhappily at the man’s assumption. “I will make sure you have a grand funeral once I am finished with you.”

Caston laughed at his arrogance as the men headed into the hall. There were people milling about inside, the same servants that had been around when Etzel had met his death, only now they were not fearful or starving. With Daniel’s appearance, all of Shadowmoor was better fed and happier in general. Therefore, they greeted Daniel and Caston respectfully and one woman was already running for food to put on the table for them. Someone was pouring wine. As the knights sat, the servants were rushing to serve them.

“So,” Daniel said as he sat down to a full cup of warmed, watered wine. “Tell me about these joust poles you intend to loan me. Are they in good condition?”

“Most are.”

“Are some of them rigged so that they will collapse the moment I come into contact with your shield?”

Caston snorted into his wine. “You should not give me such ideas,” he jested. Then, he sobered. “To be serious, I brought the poles with me in the bed of the wagon. As I said, most are in good condition but a few could use some repair. The one thing we will need is fabric for banners; all of the banners have been stripped away. Whose banners do you intend to fly?”

Daniel cocked his head thoughtfully. “De Lohr, of course,” he said. “Unless, to honor your father and his generosity, he would allow me to fly de Royans banners.”

Caston tore apart a hot loaf of bread that was placed in front of him by a hovering servant. “My father would be honored but he thought you might want to fly de Lohr colors,” he said. “Unless you have any banners with you, we will need to make a trip to town to see if we can find fabric of a suitable type and color.”

Daniel tore into his own loaf of bread. “An excellent idea,” he said. “We can go today to Siglesdene and see if the seamstress there has anything I can use. I wager that I could even pay her to sew the banners for me."

Caston nodded as he delved into his food. Daniel did the same. Their mouths were full when a small body wandered through the open entry and both knights turned to see that Gunnar was making an appearance.

The boy was dressed in the clothes that Daniel had purchased for him, but since they were the only decent set of clothing he had, he had worn them daily since Daniel had purchased them and they were becoming rather dirty and worn. Gunnar spent most of his time in the stable yard with the goats and sheep, especially with his two pet goats, and the little animals had followed him into the hall. When Caston saw it was the youngest l'Audacieux child, he glanced at Daniel.

"Has he shown any signs of livening up since I left?" he asked quietly. "Has he even come inside to sleep?"

Daniel watched the boy as he made his way to the fire pit, goats in tow. "Nay," he responded softly. "Liselotte makes him go into his own bed nightly, but he gets up after she goes to sleep and goes out to find his goats. She will not let them into the keep and Gunnar seems unwilling to sleep without them."

Caston took a long drink of warmed wine. "His father's death has hit him hard."

Daniel nodded slowly, watching the child as he sat down next to the fire and hugged his goats. "Aye," he agreed. "He goes out to the area between the stable and the outer wall where generations of l'Audacieux are buried, where we buried Etzel, and sits near his father's grave for hours. Liselotte says she has even seen him talk to the grave. He is having a very difficult time with his father's passing."

Caston went back to his food, feeling some pity for the young boy without a father and a bedridden mother. The man's death had affected the boy greatly. Only the goats had seemed to bring him out of his sad little world, which is why Daniel and Liselotte tolerated the goats in the hall from time to time. Even now, as Gunnar sat near the fire with his pets, Daniel didn't scold him for bringing barn animals into the hall. He didn't have the heart to.

"Gunnar," Daniel called out to him, friendly. "Will you come and eat with us? And bring your hairy friends."

Gunnar glanced at Daniel before returning his attention to the goats. "Nay," he said. "I do not want to eat."

"Surely your four-legged friends are hungry."

Gunnar shrugged, scratching the black-and-white goat on the head. "I have named this one Mary," he said. Then, he pointed to the all-white goat behind him. "That is Joseph. I heard a priest speak of Mary and Joseph, once."

That was as much as the lad had spoken since his father's death and Daniel looked at Caston with a mixture of surprise and pleasure. "I see," he said, wanting to keep the conversation going. "But I believe those goats are both male, Gunnar. I do not know how happy a male goat will be with a woman's name."

Gunnar lifted his skinny shoulders. He didn't have anything to say to that. Daniel didn't want the conversation to die so he kept talking.

"Sir Caston and I are going into town, Gunnar," Daniel said. "We will be passing by the same livery where we purchased your goats. Would you like to come with us? I seem to recall that there was a new litter of puppies at the livery. Mayhap the livery owner will let you have one."

Gunnar shot to his feet. "A dog?" he said excitedly. "I would like to have a dog!"

Daniel smiled at the boy's enthusiasm. "Then we shall see if we can get you one," he said. "But before we go, you must do something for me."

Gunnar nodded eagerly. "I will!"

"You do not even know what it is yet."

Gunnar ran at him, the goats trotting after him. "I will do it!"

He was close enough that Daniel could put a hand on his soft, blond head. "Eat some food now to break your fast," he said. "Then, you will go and put your little pets into the stable yard and make sure they are tended before you go and wash your face and hands. You are covered with dirt. I would have a clean young lad go with me into town. Agreed?"

Gunnar nodded happily. The lure of having a dog was too great for him to do anything else but comply. As he plopped down next to Daniel and accepted part of the man's bread loaf, Liselotte entered from the kitchen yard door.

It had been a busy morning for her. In her arms, she carried a basket that contained bowls of very fresh, soft white cheese that the cook had made from cow's milk. It was quite delicious and when Liselotte saw Daniel, she headed straight for him, thrilled to give him some cheese from the cow he had purchased. Of course, it was only right that he should have the first of the cheese that had been made about a week ago and left to harden in the coolness of the vault below the keep, the very same room where Brynner used to sleep.

But they didn't speak of Brynner any longer at Shadowmoor, as if the man had never existed, and the filthy bed he had used in the vault had been burned the day after he had fled the fortress. It had been on Liselotte's order. She wanted nothing that reminded her, or anyone else, of Brynner and his terrible deed. If she could have erased him from the earth, she would have gladly done so. But it was enough that Daniel was here, helping Shadowmoor heal in a way she had never imagined possible. He seemed to make them all forget about Brynner and his horrors. Daniel, unlike Brynner, gave them all hope.

He had given them all life again.

Liselotte's heart fluttered wildly at the sight of Daniel as he sat at the feasting table with Caston and Gunnar. His short blond hair was mussed, his face stubbled as he and Caston laughed about something. It seemed the two of them were always laughing, as if sharing a secret, and Liselotte was glad. She liked Caston, for he was polite and intelligent, and she was glad that Daniel seemed to have found a friend in the man. She hadn't been entirely sure that would ever happen because on the night they'd been invited to sup at Netherghyll, Daniel had seemed a bit standoffish when it came to Caston. It was as if he had been unsure of the man in general, but that quirk seemed to have faded. Now, they were great friends.

Liselotte found herself wishing that her father had lived long enough to see how Netherghyll had become such a good ally. She knew her father would have been deeply touched, and perhaps even a bit embarrassed, by Easton de Royans' generosity. But it would have warmed his heart and given him faith that there was some good in the world, just as Daniel had given them all faith that life was, indeed, worth living.

She sincerely wished her father had lived to see it all.

But she had more selfish reasons for her wish. She also wished her father had lived long enough to again offer her hand in marriage to Daniel. He had become such a permanent figure at Shadowmoor, as if he had been living here all along, and the only thing that could possibly make his presence any better would be if he had a reason to stay here – a wife, perchance – and Liselotte found herself more hopeful than ever in spite of what he had said, about the fact that he was a wanderer who would never take a wife.

Surely things had changed over the past two weeks. Surely he would consider marrying her and remaining by her side. He had become a part of them, so quickly, that she doubted they could survive his departure. Liselotte had long since given up trying to emotionally protect herself against him. She found herself looking forward to every single moment that she would be by his side.

A sense of self-preservation, for her, had been thrown to the wind. And she didn't care in the least.

"Greetings, gentle lords," she said as she came upon the table. "See what I have for you today – the very first of the cheese."

Both Daniel and Caston smiled pleasantly at her but it was Daniel who reached up, grasped her wrist, and yanked her down to sit. She plopped down next to him as he reached into her basket, pulling forth the soft-set white cheese.

"Ah!" he said as he set it upon the table. "A delectable feast from a beautiful maiden. What could be more appetizing?"

Liselotte giggled softly. "You had better taste the cheese before you decide."

Daniel already had his knife out, cutting into the soft cheese and handing the first piece to Caston. He cut a piece for Liselotte and then one for himself. Caston was already finished with his piece before Daniel could take a bite.

"Excellent," Caston declared. "It is quite delicious."

Liselotte chewed on the creamy mild cheese. "It is," she agreed. "The cook is making more of this but she is adding mustard and peppercorns to it. They are some of the only things we have in our stores that Daniel did not buy."

Daniel thought that sounded quite tasty. "Delightful," he said. "I can hardly wait to taste it. In fact, you and the cook have been doing an excellent job of managing the stores that we brought back from Siglesdene. You are to be commended, my lady."

Liselotte dipped her head graciously. "Thank you, my lord," she said. "The cook thinks we can make those supplies last for another few weeks at least. We are doing very well with them so far."

Daniel shook his head. "There is no need to ration them," he said. "In fact, Caston and I must go into town today, back to the seamstress where we purchased your dresses, and I will purchase more stores while we are in town. Would you like to join us? I have already promised young Gunnar that he can go and pick out a puppy. The livery owner had a litter, as I recall."

Liselotte was very interested in another venture into town. "I would like to go," she said eagerly. "But I truly do not think we need any more supplies. We can make do with what we have."

Daniel downed what was left of his warmed wine. "As I said, there is no need to ration or make do," he said as he set his cup down and stood up. "There are more supplies to be bought. Gunnar, if you are coming with us, go do as I told you – tend your goats and wash your face and hands. Join us in the bailey as quickly as you can."

Gunnar was up, mouth still full of bread, and herding his little goats from the hall. He was moving faster, happier than he had been in days. Liselotte watched him go.

"I cannot believe you were able to get him to respond to you," she said to Daniel. "He has been in such a terrible state. I do believe that is the first time I have seen him eat in days."

Daniel brushed his hands off on his breeches. "Everyone grieves differently," he said, looking at her. "You, my lady, have held yourself remarkably well. I admire your strength. But Gunnar does not have your control or your maturity. He is dealing with it as best he can."

Liselotte nodded sadly. "I suppose you are right," she said. Then, she eyed him. "Did you really promise him a dog?"

Daniel nodded. "If the livery owner will sell me a puppy."

She smiled faintly at him. "You are very good to him," she said. "You spoil him."

He returned her smile. "I like to spoil you both," he said, a twinkle in his eye. Then he gestured in the general direction of the keep. "If you are going to go with us, then go and collect your cloak. We will meet you in the bailey."

Liselotte nodded, her gaze lingering on him for a moment before leaving the hall. It was a warm expression, full of silent promises and wordless dreams. Daniel could feel what she was conveying to him, all of it, before she turned away and the spell, for the moment, was broken. He watched her go as Caston stood up behind him, draining what was left in his cup.

"Come along," he said to Daniel. "While we are waiting for your lady, you can look over the poles I brought with me. We can determine which ones may need repair and have the smithy do it while we are in town."

As Daniel followed him from the hall, his mind should have been on joust poles but, try as he might, tournaments and glory couldn't compete with lovely Liselotte. There was no doubt about it now – he was officially smitten.

… or was it something more?

He wondered. And the thought that it could be something more, for the first time in his life, didn't distress him in the least.

CHAPTER THIRTEEN

IT WAS A bright day with virtually no clouds against the brilliant expanse of sky, but to Brynner, it was hell. His head ached, his mouth was dry, and he was feeling generally ill from a serious drinking binge that had lasted most of the last two weeks, ever since he had fled Shadowmoor and arrived back on Bramley's doorstep. He'd had the unhappy duty of informing Bramley that Etzel was dead but that a usurper who called himself de Lohr had taken over Shadowmoor. Brynner had no way of ousting the man or even returning to his own fortress. The situation, as he saw it, was grim.

Understandably, Bramley had been angered by the news and of Brynner's failure to complete the task he'd been charged with. Although moderately pleased to hear of Etzel's death, the usurper was an unanticipated problem but upon the mention of the name, Bramley knew immediately who the man was – the same man who had rescued Gunnar when the boy had run away from him. The big blond knight who claimed to be part of the House of de Lohr, the one who had leveled threats and insults at him, was now holding Shadowmoor. It was a most unexpected happening.

De Lohr was a man who now stood in his way.

So Bramley didn't waste any time brooding over the situation; he acted immediately. He sent a missive to the king the very night Brynner had shown up at Bramley Castle spouting stories of being driven from his own home. Surely Henry needed to know that a member of the famed House of de Lohr was a thief and had stolen property that did not belong to him. Not only that, but he had stolen the contents of Shadowmoor and that included Bramley's bride. Well, the woman he was determined to marry, at any rate. Henry needed to know that as well. Bramley was quite certain that Henry would send help and the arrogant de Lohr knight would feel the king's wrath.

He was counting on it.

But the reply wouldn't be instant, and that infuriated Bramley. The missive had been sent almost two weeks ago and sitting around waiting for a reply from Henry had grown tiresome. Bramley had hoped for an instant response even though he knew full well that it would take at least two weeks for his messenger to even reach the king.

Still, he was impatient as well as spoiled, and decided to take matters into his own hands. He decided to solicit assistance from local lords against the man who now held Shadowmoor. Surely he could unite his neighbors with tales of the imprisonment of Lady Liselotte and the exile of a brother who only wanted to protect his sister. He could make a very sad case for Brynner l'Audacieux. At least, that was Bramley's scheme, and he intended to head to one of the great fortresses in the area and use his royal connections to elicit their assistance.

But they had to plan carefully, to find the most powerful lords in the area. Brynner, who had lived in the region his entire life, named two major castles in the area that might be of help - Netherghyll Castle, which was the closest, and Skipton Castle, which was further to the north. Bramley knew of Netherghyll and he was, frankly, more interested in that one because it bordered Shadowmoor's lands.

When he assumed Shadowmoor as one of his properties, he would have to come to know his neighbor to the north. Netherghyll was bigger than Shadowmoor and held the Cononley baronetcy, a title that Bramley rather coveted. It was old and distinguished, and someone told him that the Lords of de Royans were also the High Sheriffs of West Yorkshire. He rather coveted that title, too. But he had refrained from contacting Netherghyll since his assumption of Bramley Castle, mostly because his focus had been on Shadowmoor, but now he reasoned that it was time to expand his horizons and come to know those who would be his neighbor, eventually. Or perhaps, someday, the castle would even be his.

One could never tell these things.

So, two weeks after sending the missive to Henry, Bramley was on the road north, heading toward Netherghyll with a small contingent of men, including Brynner. He wanted to show Brynner to the Lord of Netherghyll so the man could see how worn and pitiful Brynner was with the hope that it would inspire sympathy. It was his anticipation that the Lord of Netherghyll would become enraged at the treatment of the legal Lord of Shadowmoor and offer his army to chase de Lohr away.

Bramley was determined to make a good case of it. As they neared the large village of Siglesdene this morning, he glanced over his shoulder to Brynner, the very man who would gain him a fortress and even new allies, who was riding an old mare off to his right. The man looked as if he'd seen better days.

"Do not look so glum," Bramley said to him. "This is a fine morning and I have a great deal of confidence that an alliance will be exactly what we need to salvage this situation. And you've said that you have never met the Lord of Netherghyll, Baron Cononley? I find that surprising considering the man is your neighbor."

Brynner's head was pounding with every fall from the horse's hoof. He could feel the vibrations up through him, like bolts of lightning shooting into his brain every time the horse took a step. The pain was excruciating.

"We have always kept to ourselves," he said, his voice sounding dull. "We do not know any of our neighbors and they do not know us, which worked well in your favor when you tried to starve us out. We had no one to ask for assistance."

Bramley turned to look at him, eyes narrowing. "Do not blame me for your failings," he said. "You were bereft long before I first saw your beauteous sister. I do hope de Lohr hasn't compromised her, though. I do not want another man's leavings."

Brynner didn't say anything. He didn't want to talk about his sister because he honestly wasn't sure how he felt about the fact that she was the captive of an unknown knight. He'd tried to pretend he hadn't cared for so long but the truth was that something buried deep did care. It was that emotion that was numbed every time he drank, but he wasn't drunk now. He could feel everything.

"It is possible that Baron Cononley will not even see us," he said, changing the subject. "Since I do not know the man, it is possible he will not give a thought to our situation."

Bramley wasn't deterred. "I believe I can persuade him," he said. "But if not, then there is always Skipton Castle. They are a garrison for the crown and will surely aid me considering who my uncle is. They will have no choice. Once I have them help me rid Shadowmoor of the de Lohr parasite, then I will turn them on Netherghyll to punish them for not lending assistance. Have no doubt that this will all work well in our favor."

Brynner didn't say anything more. Bramley was so full of arrogance that he swore if he poked the man with a needle, the only thing that would escape would be hot air. He'd never met a more prideful and unrealistic man. They were entering the outskirts of the town of Siglesdene now, passing farmers with carts or women taking their wares to town. Dogs and children scattered as they passed by.

Siglesdene had been around since well before William of Normandy claimed England for his own, a prosperous town that was surprisingly full of commerce. From the ports at Blackpool along the Irish Sea, the road west lead directly into West Yorkshire, so Siglesdene, and several of the other surrounding villages, were well-supplied with goods from Ireland and other countries. There was also a surprising amount of commerce from the surrounding area that went out on the road and back to the ports. In all, it was a rather continental village that had nearly everything one could want, and more besides.

Bramley knew the town because there was a tavern here that had some fairly decent whores. At least they had teeth and were relatively disease-free. He'd spent some time at the tavern but he'd spent more time at the brothel in Bradford. Still, he was somewhat familiar with Siglesdene and was thinking on stopping for a midday meal as they entered the town. A rumbling stomach made his decision for him.

"La Londe!" he called out behind him. "De Witt!"

Bramley's henchmen were riding several feet behind him. When they heard their names shouted, they spurred their big-boned horses forward. Jules la Londe, his blond hair shaggy and dirty, was the first to respond.

"My lord?" he asked politely.

Bramley pointed up ahead, into the city. "See if you can find a place for us to break our fast," he said. "As I recall, there are several bakers on the end of the Avenue of the Merchants. See if someone has enough to feed all of us."

Jules nodded, glancing back over the group. Bramley had brought along a total of twenty-three men for his trip to Netherghyll on this day and he counted heads once more, mentioning the number to de Witt, who spurred his horse on ahead. La Londe followed close behind. Once the mercenary knights were moving into the city, Bramley turned to Brynner.

"See if you can force some food down your gullet so you do not appear as if you are going to die at any moment," he said, eyeing the man. "We want the Lord of Netherghyll to feel pity for you but I need for you to actually make it to the castle and not die along the way. We will stop here and eat something before continuing on."

Brynner grunted. "'Tis not food I need but a drink," he said. "Any tavern will do."

Bramley eyed him with some disgust. "If you must."

"I must."

Bramley shook his head and turned around, facing the road ahead.

"You are a truly pathetic creature."

Brynner didn't say anything to the man. He simply eyed him balefully before looking away. They had an odd relationship, the two of them, each one wanting something from the other. That didn't mean they had to like each other, and Brynner certainly wasn't willing to give up the prospect of that winery in France or the fifty men and the sack of fifty gold crowns. Therefore, he kept his mouth shut for the sake of peace. He'd come this far, after all.

The road they were traveling on was the road that ran north-south along the east side of Rombald's Moor where Shadowmoor was situated. The road came up from Leeds, through Bramley's lands, and paralleled the mountainous moor before curving to the west once the moor became flat ground again. The road then continued on and carved a path right through Siglesdene.

From the curve of the road, however, they actually ended up entering the town from the northeast. There were people about, conducting business, and the entire road and town were generally busy. There were literally hundreds of people about on this day, hurrying to conduct their business in between rain storms. Therefore, Bramley and his party couldn't have known that entering the town from the southwest at that very moment was Daniel and the party from Shadowmoor.

The best-laid plans of men were often interrupted by forces beyond their control. The two parties were moving closer and closer to one another, neither one of them would be aware of the other until it was too late.

☙

"I WANT THE black one!"

Gunnar was referring to the puppy that was madly licking his face. In fact, he was on the ground of the livery stable, in the dirt, as six wriggly puppies all tried to jump on him and lick his face. Once again, the boy was in doggy heaven.

Daniel, Liselotte, and Caston stood by, watching the canine madness. In the busy livery, they'd managed to find the big black dog that had six equally black puppies. There was also a second litter that Daniel had been unaware of, only seen when they'd entered the stable to see the black litter. The livery owner was more than happy to sell Daniel puppies because he had an abundance of them, so Daniel crouched down beside Gunnar as the boy hugged the squirming dogs.

"They are *all* black from what I can see," he said to the boy. "And did you see the second litter over in the next stall that the livery owner pointed to?"

Gunnar shook his head. "I like these dogs."

Daniel laughed softly. "And they like you," he said. "But let us follow this course, Gunnar; since there are no longer any dogs at Shadowmoor, mayhap we should make it so that there are many. Pick out four puppies; two males from this litter and two females from the other litter, and we shall return them to Shadowmoor and hope they populate it with many more dogs."

Gunnar was thrilled. "I will!" he exclaimed. "I will name them, too!"

"What will you name them?"

"Matthew, Mark, Luke, and John!"

Behind him, Daniel could hear Liselotte and Caston laugh. The boy was once again reciting names he'd learned from the priests, names from the Bible. "But those are all male names," he pointed out. "Remember what I told you about the goats? I doubt a male goat would like to be called Mary. I also doubt that a female dog would like to be called John."

Gunnar simply grinned and Daniel shook his head at the lad, patting his head before he stood up and faced Liselotte and Caston.

"We can leave him here to pick out his dogs while we cross the street to the seamstress' stall," he said, motioning to the livery owner and pointing to the boy to indicate he was leaving him with the puppies. When the livery owner nodded, Daniel and Liselotte and Caston continued out into the stable yard. "Let us get on with our business for the day."

They moved out towards the street, noting the bustle, and noting the seamstress across the avenue, just beyond the big yew tree that grew in the middle of the street. As they headed out of the stable yard, Caston motioned to several of the twenty Netherghyll men they'd brought with them from Shadowmoor. Since Daniel was set to purchase many items, they'd not only brought the men but a Netherghyll wagon as well. Therefore, while half the men waited in the livery yard with the wagon, the other half followed Caston and Daniel and Liselotte across the street.

Daniel saw the mob behind him and rolled his eyes; the big escort had been Caston's idea since the man never traveled without one, and especially when a lady was involved. But he didn't say anything about it; if it made Caston happy, then it didn't matter much to him. They traipsed along the street with their escort of armed men, looking like the king had just arrived for all of the men that were following them.

"I fear that Lady Glennie will be very unhappy that we have come to town without her," Daniel said to Liselotte as he held out his elbow for her. "Mayhap you would like to visit her soon, my lady?"

Liselotte took his elbow gladly, holding it with both hands. "I would," she agreed. "But I do not know when I can, to be truthful. So much at Shadowmoor requires my attention these days. I do not want to leave, even for a day or two."

"Things are running very smoothly," he assured her. "I am sure a day visit to Netherghyll will not matter overly. And it would make Glennie happy, don't you think?"

Liselotte nodded. "I do," she said. "Mayhap… mayhap someday when Shadowmoor is looking fine, I will have her to visit. I cannot do that now."

Daniel looked at her, feeling proud with her on his arm. "Why not?"

She looked up at him, an expression of embarrassment on her face. "Must you truly ask that question, Daniel?" she scolded softly. "The fortress looks terrible and I have no place to entertain a fine lady. I would be ashamed."

Daniel smiled faintly, patting her hand gently. "We will change that," he said. "There is the room that your father used as his solar. We can put fine furnishings in there, much finer than anything at Nether-ghyll, and you can use that room to entertain your friend."

Liselotte grinned at his grand plans. "Somehow it does not seem right to have a grand room in the keep when the rest of the fortress still looks as if it is only half-repaired," she said. "But someday I would like to have a fine lady's solar. I used to like to paint, long ago, but I have not done that in years. Mayhap someday I will resume that passion. It would be nice to have a room for it."

They were nearing the seamstress and Daniel couldn't help but eye the new dresses the old seamstress had hanging from nails outside of the shop, blowing in the breeze like banners. He could imagine Liselotte in one of them.

"Then you shall have it," he said decisively. "Now, I have business to conduct with the seamstress. While I am speaking with her, I want you to look at the new garments she has hanging and see if there are any you like."

Liselotte looked at him, shocked. "More dresses?"

"A fine lady can never have too many, so I am told."

She snorted. "Who told you such things?"

He was evasive, grinning at her as he spoke. "Women," he said. "Or did you think that you were the only woman I have ever known in my life?"

She shook her head firmly. "With your charm, I would wager you have known more than your fair share," she said. "In fact, I would not be surprised if you have known even more than that."

His eyebrows flew up in mock outrage. "Insolent wench," he said. "I would demand you clarify that remark, but I must see the seamstress first. Stay with Caston and I will return."

With that, he took the hand off of his elbow and kissed it before letting it go. As he disappeared inside the stall, Liselotte's gaze lingered on him. Her expression was soft and dreamy, utterly smitten with the man.

"Someday, I hope a woman looks at me the way you look at Daniel."

Caston spoke softly next to her and Liselotte turned to him, grinning and embarrassed. "Is it that obvious?" she asked.

Caston laughed softly. "I think it is quite nice," he said. "I have not had the luck with women that Daniel has, but I will say this – had I known you were at Shadowmoor, not very far from Netherghyll, I would have swooped in and claimed you before de Lohr got to you. What a fool I have been."

Liselotte laughed, flattered by his words. "You are too kind, my lord," she said. "But I would not have made a good match for you. The House of de Royans requires a much finer bride. Have you no prospects, then?"

He lifted his eyebrows. "What of the House of de Lohr?" he asked. "They require the finest brides in all the land. If you are good enough for Daniel, you are certainly good enough for me."

Liselotte giggled. "Again, you are far too kind to say so," she said. "But you have not answered me. Do you have any prospects?"

Caston shook his head. Then, he shrugged. "There *is* a lady in Keighley," he admitted. "She is the daughter of one of the town elders, a merchant who trades and brokers metals. He is quite wealthy. They have property and standing."

Liselotte smiled. "That sounds like a good match," she said. "But what of the lady? What is she like?"

Caston was reluctant to speak of her, embarrassed even. In his mind, women talked of him – he did not talk of women. There was something prideful there.

"She has red hair," he said, pretending to be disinterested. "Her name is Anne. She is pretty and she can speak three languages. She also has a pet sheep that follows her around. She received it as a gift when it was a lamb and now that it is grown, it still follows her everywhere."

Liselotte like the tale of the lady with the sheep. "How charming," she said. "Mayhap one day I shall bc fortunate enough to meet her and her sheep."

He simply shrugged, evasive. "Mayhap."

Liselotte could see the subject was embarrassing for him, more than likely because it meant something to him. She liked Caston and hoped he would find happiness, even with a lady who was followed around by a sheep. But she didn't push him on the subject; she simply smiled and turned away.

As she turned to look at the blue dress that was waving in the wind a few feet away, she caught sight of something out in the street that had her heart leaping into her throat. Her reaction was instantaneous, one of fear and revulsion. Shocked, she grabbed Caston by the arm and pulled him back, back behind the dresses that were fluttering and into the shadows near the stall's entry. When he looked at her, concerned, she pointed to the avenue.

"God help us," she hissed. "That is my brother. And Bramley! There are here!"

The light mood of the shopping day was dashed in an instant at her terrible announcement. Caston's head snapped in the direction she was pointing and he could see several soldiers on horseback. There was also a man dressed in very fine robes among the soldiers, astride an expensive warmblood. Caston's sharp senses focused on the man in the robe.

"Is Bramley the man in the silks?" he asked. "Mounted on the big red horse?"

Liselotte was clinging to him fearfully. "Aye," she said. "That is Bramley. And my brother is the man without weapons, mounted on the gray horse beside him. See him? He is wearing ragged clothing."

Caston had both Bramley and Brynner in his sight. "Go inside and tell Daniel," he commanded softly. "He will want to know."

Liselotte disappeared into the seamstress shop. Caston kept an eye on Bramley and his party, who seemed to be lingering near a baker's stall. His men were eating, milling around, and he was surprised that, given the fact they were so close, Liselotte hadn't recognized them until now. But he was glad she had noticed them before they noticed her; that gave Caston and Daniel the element of surprise.

The intensity of the situation deepened.

As Caston watched Bramley dismount his horse and lose himself in a crowd of his men, Gunnar unexpectedly emerged from the livery yard. The little boy stood on the edge of the yard, where it met with the avenue, and it was clear that he was looking for his sister and Daniel. He just stood there, looking up and down the avenue, before beginning his trek across the road.

Upon seeing the child, Caston bolted in his direction. Given what he'd been told about Brynner l'Audacieux, and he'd briefly lost sight of the man, he didn't want Brynner seeing his younger brother in town. There was no telling what he would do.

Caston practically ran across the street, straight for Gunnar. Brynner and Bramley wouldn't recognize him so Caston hoped they wouldn't pay attention to a running man in mail as he headed straight for the child, swooping down upon him and lifting him into his arms. Then he made a break for the stable yard, never missing a step, praying that he could make it into the shielding confines of the stable before he was noticed.

But it wasn't to be. It was his unhappy misfortune that he hadn't been fast enough. Someone from Bramley's party began shouting at him.

"You!" Brynner yelled, dismounting his horse and waving an arm at Caston. "Who are you? That is my brother! What are you doing with him?"

Caston heard the shouting but rather than continue on into the stable yard where ten of his men were waiting, where Brynner and Bramley would no-doubt follow and create a scene, he came to a halt. His men in the yard saw him, however, and he motioned the men to him with a jerk of his head. If he was going to confront Bramley and the brother he'd heard so much horror about, he wanted to have reinforcements and he wanted to do it in the open area of the avenue. He found himself praying that Daniel would at least keep Liselotte out of sight. This was about her, after all.

All of it.

Gunnar, seeing his brother, became terrified. He turned to Caston, grabbing on to the man.

"Let us go," he said. "We must get away from him!"

Caston set the boy down, calmly, and handed him off to his nearest soldier. "Get the boy out of here," he said. "Hide him. Go!"

The soldier fled, pulling Gunnar behind him. Meanwhile, Brynner was heading in his direction, wondering why an unfamiliar soldier was running off with his little brother. He pointed at Caston and then at the soldier running off with Gunnar.

"Who are you?" he demanded again. "Bring my brother back here!"

Caston shook his head. "Alas, I cannot," he said. "You are Brynner l'Audacieux."

Brynner came to a halt, his eyes narrowing suspiciously. "How do you know that?" he asked. "Tell me who you are this instant."

Caston regarded the man a moment. He looked like someone had just dredged him from a great swampy hole. He was worn, dirty, disheveled, and reeked of urine and alcohol. He was a horrific example of a man, worse than Caston had imagined he would look.

"You do not need to know who I am," Caston said. "Suffice it to say that it looks as if everything I have been told about you is true."

Brynner's features twisted in outrage. "Who *are* you, you bastard?" he hissed. "What have you done with my little brother? I have men at my disposal to go and find him, so you had better give him to me unless you want a battle on your hands."

"What battle would that be?"

Daniel strolled up behind Caston, calm and cool. His gaze was riveted to Brynner, who was, by now, attracting the attention of Bramley's men, including Bramley himself. For the moment, however,

Daniel was only fixed on Brynner.

Animosity filled the air.

"The last time I saw you, you had just murdered your father," Daniel said because Brynner seemed somewhat speechless to see him. "I was hoping you had run off and died somewhere."

Brynner looked at Daniel in shock. De Lohr was the last person he had expected to see on this day. "*You!*" he gasped. "You… you thieving canker! I want my fortress back!"

Daniel was amused by the man's outrage. "We cannot always have what we want, dear boy," he said condescendingly. "You had best forget about Shadowmoor. It is no longer your concern."

"Why should he forget it?" Bramley came up behind Brynner. The man already had a sword in his hand, ready to launch an offensive at the sight of a man he very much wanted vengeance upon. "Shadowmoor is his fortress and you, de Lohr, are a thief. I have already sent word to Henry about what you have done. We shall see what he has to say about it."

Daniel smiled thinly. "Lord Bramley," he greeted steadily. "Or Roland Fitzroy, whatever you are calling yourself these days. I see that the Slime of the Earth has allied himself with the King of the Drunkards. How fitting."

Bramley's face turned red. "I will cut your tongue out one of these days," he growled. "Your insults will be at an end, de Lohr. I will take great delight in killing you myself!"

Daniel only grew more amused. "Delusional men are always so entertaining," he said, glancing at Caston, who was smirking at the comment. "Lord Bramley, mayhap I should tell you that I have sent word to my uncle, Christopher de Lohr, who commands the entire Welsh Marches. I already told you who my uncle is, but I will repeat myself and refresh your memory. My uncle knows about you and what you have done to starve out Shadowmoor, and he also knows that your drunken ally, Sir Brynner, killed his own father. He is much closer to West Yorkshire than Henry is so I would expect we will see my uncle very shortly. Then, it will be I who will take great delight in tearing down your castle and cutting *your* tongue out. You and men like you are an affront to decent people and must be eradicated. Your reign of cruelty is at an end."

Bramley stepped forward, in front of Brynner, even though la Londe and de Witt, who were standing with him, tried to stop him. Bramley wouldn't listen to anyone. He pointed his sword at Daniel.

"I am rousing the countryside against you," he declared. "You will not be laughing when I join forces with Netherghyll and even Skipton and run you out of Shadowmoor. If I were you, I would swiftly leave because if you remain, it will only mean your death. I am giving you fair warning."

Daniel lifted his eyebrows. "Netherghyll?" he repeated slowly.

Bramley nodded firmly. "That is what I said," he snapped. "I am going there now to seek the Lord of Netherghyll's assistance against you and your unlawful holding of Shadowmoor. We will chase you out of West Yorkshire altogether!"

Daniel was greatly amused by Bramley's plan. "*Netherghyll,* you say?"

Bramley snapped. "Are you deaf?"

Daniel scratched his chin casually. "I may be deaf, but you are certainly dumb," he said, looking at Caston. "The man said Netherghyll."

Caston shook his head with disgust, focusing on Bramley. "You wanted to know who I was," he said to the man. "I am Sir Caston de Royans of Netherghyll Castle. My father is Baron Cononley and we are allies of Shadowmoor and Daniel de Lohr. If you set one foot on my father's property, he will send his entire army after you and I promise you that you will not survive. Then we'll bury your body and the bodies of all your men and erase any trace of you from this earth. If Henry asks, we will say we have never seen you. Is this in any way unclear?"

Bramley was taken aback. He was also quite embarrassed. He looked at Brynner accusingly. "You did not know who this man was?"

Brynner was looking at Caston with horror. "I have never seen him before," he said. "I told you that I did not know those at Netherghyll."

"You should have known!"

"I told you that I did not!"

Now they were starting to argue between then, a shameful thing, indeed, but Bramley was unable to control his embarrassment. He began to shout, and shove, and the sword he had in his hand was waving about wildly. Threatened, Caston and Daniel unsheathed their broadswords, as did Caston's men. They were waiting for the charge.

With the Netherghyll soldiers all assembled, those who had accompanied Daniel and those who had remained in the livery, the odds against Bramley's men were even. As people in the street began to scatter, sensing a very big fight coming, Bramley marched in Daniel's direction and swung his sword near the man's head. Infuriated, Daniel grabbed the man by the collar and hit him right in the face with the hilt of his sword.

After that, the battle was on.

People screamed and ran as the two sides came together in a great clash. With Bramley on the ground, he was getting trampled but the problem was that Daniel wouldn't let anyone get to him to help him stand. He stood over, and on, Bramley as la Londe and de Witt charged him, trying to get to their liege, but Daniel refused to move.

Caston was at his side and between the two of them, they very effectively contained la Londe and de Witt. But then the daggers came out when the broadswords proved ineffective and when Daniel wasn't standing on Bramley, he was using his feet and fists to dislodge the dagger that la Londe held. Caston disarmed de Witt and hit the man in the head hard enough to knock him unconscious. With de Witt down, Caston turned his attention to la Londe.

The shaggy Bramley knight was overwhelmed by Daniel and Caston, who went at him with a vengeance. At one point, Bramley tried to get to his feet when Daniel was distracted with la Londe, but when Daniel saw Bramley trying to rise, he kneed the man in the head and sent him back to the dirt, dazed. With Bramley and de Witt down,

Caston subdued la Londe and Daniel went after Brynner.

Brynner was not armed but he was fighting a fairly good fistfight against a Netherghyll soldier. Daniel came up behind him and threw him in a headlock, dragging him to the outskirts of the battle. Squeezing the man with his big arm, he rumbled into his ear.

"You evidently did not hear me the first time when I told you that if I saw you again, I would kill you," he said. Then, he released Brynner by throwing the man to the ground. As Brynner struggled to stand up, Daniel snatched a sword from the nearest soldier and tossed it to Brynner. "Now you are armed so this is a fair fight. Let us get on with this because you are hardly worthy of my skills or my time."

Brynner stood there, looking at Daniel with more contempt than Daniel had ever seen. But behind that contempt was a great deal of sorrow and shame, a maelstrom of emotions that weren't necessarily directed at Daniel. It was simply the turmoil that was being battered about, like flotsam, in Brynner's soul.

"There was a time when I was unbeatable with a broadsword," he told Daniel. "I should have probably told you that before you gave me a weapon."

Daniel lifted his sword offensively. "It does not matter," he said. "I will make short work of you no matter how great you think you are."

Brynner snorted, with some irony. He looked at the sword, a short-blade sword usually used by men-at-arms. It had been the first time he'd held a sword since he'd given his up those years ago. Since he'd sold it, just like his horse, to pay for his drink. Now that he held it in his hand, he felt somewhat different. Memories swamped him.

"I know you believe I am a drunken fool and you are not far wrong," he said, "but there was a time when I served Okehampton with my sword. That was years ago, but I was quite good."

Daniel was about to charge the man but something in his tone made him pause. "You served at Okehampton?" he asked, unable to conceal his doubt. "Hugh de Courtnay?"

Brynner nodded. "I did, indeed," he said, holding up the sword to inspect it. "I am a knight, like you. I was one of de Courtnay's captains. I had prestige and money. I had a great deal. I was even part of the contingent that de Courtnay sent to support Richard Marshal against Hubert de Burgh a few years ago when de Burgh was accused of squandering royal money, so you see, de Lohr, that I have not always been as you see. I was great, once."

Daniel had to admit that his opinion of Brynner changed slightly after that speech. The House of de Courtnay, rulers of Okehampton Castle, were a very fine family and known for their military acumen and the conflict he had spoken of, against Hubert de Burgh, was something his uncle had mediated in. If Brynner had been part of that situation, then that gave him some credibility. Of course, he could have been lying, but Daniel didn't think so. There was something in the man's eyes that suggested he was being honest, perhaps for the first time in a very long while. Daniel frowned.

"Then what happened to you?" he asked. "What happened that you should drown yourself in drink and ally yourself with the likes of Bramley?"

Brynner features were full of irony. "It does not matter any longer."

"It might make a difference in whether or not I ram my broadsword through your belly. Tell me what happened to you."

Brynner eyed him a moment before shrugging. He was fairly certain he couldn't hold off Daniel if the man was truly intent on killing him and, to tell the truth, he wasn't all that afraid to die. But something in holding a sword again, any sword, brought back memories he thought he'd long buried.

"A woman," he said after a moment. "She was to marry me but chose another on the eve of our marriage. Life was not worth living after that. Now that you know, call me pathetic and do whatever it is you plan to do. But know that, once, I was a good knight. I could have given you a good fight under the proper circumstances."

Daniel lowered his sword completely. The look on his face straddled the line between irritation and disbelief. "A woman?" he repeated.

"You let yourself fall apart over a woman?"

"Aye."

At least he was honest about it. As the battle went on around them, Daniel found himself in the midst of a very odd conversation with a man he had sworn to kill, for Liselotte's sake. The man had murdered his own father. But the conversation with Brynner had opened Daniel's eyes to a great many things.

In fact, for the first time in his life, he understood the pain behind Brynner's statement – not being able to have the woman he loved. Daniel thought of Liselotte and what he would do if he was unable to have her. It was then that he began to realize that whatever he was feeling for her, the strength of what was in his heart, surely must have been love.

It could be nothing else.

From the wanderer who swore there was no woman on earth that he would ever fall in love with, it was a shocking realization. Confusion began to swamp him.

"Then you must have loved her a great deal," he finally said.

Brynner nodded, still looking at the sword. "I did."

Daniel wasn't sure what to do now. The man had confessed his demons to him, or at least the root of the issue, and Daniel was torn about the situation. He was also swept up in his own personal turmoil. Perhaps Brynner had reasons for being the way he was and, to Daniel, there was always something redeemable about a man. Especially a knight. Perhaps in loving the man's sister, Daniel could understand what had driven Brynner to this point in his life. Surely there was no greater sorrow than a love unreturned. But his indecision to deal with Brynner at the end of a sword changed when Brynner suddenly charged him.

For a drunkard, he was very fast, and Daniel barely had time to raise his weapon before Brynner was on him. In that split second, Daniel ducked down so that Brynner passed over the top of him and, in the same movement, brought his sword up into Brynner's soft belly. He felt it when his sword penetrated Brynner's torso, cutting through the man, cutting deep. Brynner collapsed, mostly on Daniel, and the two of them tumbled over.

Daniel immediately withdrew his sword as Brynner lay in the dirt and the rich red blood began to flow. It trickled in a steady river from Brynner's body, mingling with the moist dirt of the street. Shocked with the rapid turn of events, Daniel knelt over Brynner as the man gazed up at the sky, his eyes wide and staring.

There wasn't much Daniel could say to the dying man but he found that he was angry at him for having charged. "Why did you do that?" he demanded. "It did not have to be this way."

Brynner swallowed, labored, and looked at him. "You were going to kill me, anyway."

Daniel sighed sharply. "I do not know," he said. "Mayhap I was. But mayhap I was not. We were talking… you made me feel pity for you and your plight. A man can always change, l'Audacieux. Why did you not give yourself that chance?"

Brynner swallowed again. "My… my father's death," he mumbled, fading. "It really… it was an accident. He tried to charge me and I grabbed his dirk. I did not… intentionally kill him. You will tell my sister that."

Daniel exhaled slowly, with regret. "Why did he charge you?"

"Because I… I wanted him to give Shadowmoor to Bramley."

"But why?"

Brynner's eyes moved to the sky again, as if seeing things that Daniel could not. A man with a perpetual scowl on his face for the past few years, ever since Maud left him, now his expression held an element of calm.

"Because I wanted a winery in France," he said, breathless now that his life was ebbing away. "I was promised that, you know. Shadowmoor for the winery. But mayhap… mayhap finally having some peace will be the better bargain. You did me a… a favor…."

With that, he exhaled one last time and his eyes closed. Daniel stood over the man, feeling sorrow and regret that he did not expect to feel. But something Brynner said stuck with him… *I was promised a winery….*

Clearly, the man was made an outlandish promise by someone who wanted something from him, badly enough that he would prey upon the man's weakness to get what he wanted. The same man who couldn't beg, borrow, or buy Shadowmoor, the same one who had starved them to the point of hopeless poverty. Everything had happened because of Bramley's greed.

Infuriated, Daniel stood up, his sights set on Bramley. He was going to beat the man senseless once and for all, giving him a beating he would never forget. Men like Bramley understood two things – their own wants and violence. That was literally all they understood. But Daniel understood a good deal more than that. He pushed through the men who were still wrestling, still fighting, and finally spied Bramley over near the edge of the skirmish.

Bramley was dirtier than usual, covered with mud from the road he had fallen upon, and there was a trickle of blood coming out of his nose. Daniel threw men out of the way to get at him and by the time Bramley saw him, it was nearly too late. Bramley screamed and de Witt was there, having recovered from being knocked out, and the man charged at Daniel. Daniel dropped low, missing de Witt's first strike, and came beneath the man with a crushing blow to his chin. De Witt, already dazed from having been knocked senseless, fell over and was trampled by men who were still fighting. Daniel reached out for Bramley and grabbed the man by the hair.

The punches began to fly. Daniel was so angry that his emotions were fueling his fists, and he beat Bramley down to the ground with his heavy blows. Bramley tried to protect his face but the more Daniel pounded him, the more dazed he became until he could no longer protect himself. Blood spurted from a broken nose and cut lips, but still, Daniel kicked and pummeled him. He finally picked the man up and tossed him over the side of the livery fence, coming around to find his victim barely stirring in the horse dung. As Bramley flirted with unconsciousness, Daniel stood over him.

"Now," he said, his lips white with rage. "This is your final warning. You will forget about Shadowmoor, and Netherghyll, and anything else you have your eye on in this region. You will go back to Bramley Castle and you will stay there. If I see you again, make no mistake – I will kill you. That is a promise. For the chaos you have caused because of your greed and selfishness, you deserve nothing less. When my uncle arrives, I am going to send him to Bramley Castle and let him deal with you. You will be lucky if you survive him. Is this in any way unclear?"

Bramley was on his belly, trying to rise to his hands and knees. "I… I will kill you, you bastard," he breathed, spitting out two teeth. "I will tell Henry what you have done."

It was the wrong thing to say. Daniel kicked the man, as hard as he could, in the belly and Bramley went down, rolled up into a ball and suffering a world of pain. But Daniel didn't care and he didn't look back. He picked him up and tossed him over the other side of the livery fence so he was back in the street again so his men could get to him. Daniel marched out of the livery yard, his gaze finding Caston.

The Netherghyll knight had a bloodied lip but he was smiling, thinking this all to be a good deal of fun. But his smile vanished when he saw Daniel.

"Gather your men," Daniel told him. "We will finish our business here and return to Shadowmoor. If any of Bramley's men continue to fight, kill them. I am finished with this bastard and all he stands for."

He sounded furious and Caston's brow furrowed. "What happened?" he asked, looking around. "Where is Bramley?"

Daniel simply nodded his head in the direction he had come from. "He is in a world of hurt right now," he said. "I will tell you about it later. But if I could impose upon you to have your men collect Brynner l'Audacieux's body for transport back to Shadowmoor, I would be grateful."

Caston's eyebrows lifted in surprise. "He is dead?"

Daniel nodded. “He charged me,” he said. “I had no choice. I was defending myself. But it was a reckless move, something I am coming to think was not an accident.”

Caston nodded in understanding, wondering what the full story was behind it. He would find out later. For now, Daniel didn’t seem to be in a talking mood and he didn’t blame him. He began to shout to his men to stand down, to withdraw from the skirmish, and as he and his men settled down the fighting, Daniel headed back to the seamstress’ stall where he had left Liselotte.

He didn’t relish telling her that her older brother was dead, at his hand no less, but it had to be done. Even if she had no use for the man, he was still her brother. Surely there were still some familial feelings involved at his passing. But when he finally found Liselotte, cowering at the rear of the seamstress’ stall, he couldn’t have been more wrong about her reaction.

He would swear, until the day he died, that the relief on her face was a palpable thing.

CHAPTER FOURTEEN

Canterbury Castle, Kent
One week later

THE WIND WAS blowing off of the sea to the north, creating great and blustery conditions around the castle and town of Canterbury. It was cold and damp, as a squall had passed through only minutes before. Everything was sopping, struggling to dry out as the clouds cleared and the sun appeared. In the bailey of Canterbury Castle, a man dressed in heavy robes and a woolen scarf around his neck emerged from the big square keep and headed for the gatehouse.

He looked like he was running, sloshing through the mud and glancing over his shoulder every so often as if looking to see who was following him. He'd escaped the keep, really, before his wife grew wise to the fact that he was out in the elements, because he'd heard tale from a servant that there was a messenger at the gatehouse, a royal messenger, and he wanted to get to the messenger before his wife discovered he was outside.

He loved his dear wife and he knew that she was only concerned for his health, but sometimes her constant attention annoyed him terribly. She kept him sequestered in the keep, mostly against his will because he was recovering from a terrible illness he'd caught last winter. Now, he felt like a prisoner, finally free of his jailor, as he made his way to the gatehouse.

But soldiers saw him moving and the call went up, alerting the gatehouse that the Earl of Canterbury was on his way. David de Lohr, Earl of Canterbury, was within twenty feet of the enormous gatehouse when a knight suddenly emerged from the guardroom that was located just inside the gatehouse. Quickly, the knight ran to him, splashing through muddy puddles as he went.

"My lord," Gerid du Reims, currently in command of Canterbury's troops with Maddoc du Bois away on an assignment, was quick to meet his liege. "May I be of service?"

David eyed the man; a powerful knight with uncanny intelligence and piercing black eyes, he was a younger son of the Earl of East Anglia, a local and strong ally to Canterbury. David had known the knight and his family for a very long time and could, therefore, be brutally honest with him.

"I was told there was a royal messenger here," he said. "Why have you not sent for me? Why did I have to hear it from my valet?"

Gerid cleared his throat softly, trying not to appear too guilty. "I did send for you, my lord."

"You did not."

Gerid stood his ground. "Lady Emilie insists that all messages for you must go through her," he said. "I sent your wife word that a royal messenger has arrived. If she has not yet told you, then you must discuss that with her."

David's eyebrows flew up, outraged, but it was the same old story. He really shouldn't have been upset by it. In his seventieth decade, he was still a fine figure of a man, still powerful and still handsome with his graying blond hair, even if his health had been questionable as of late. The chest infection he'd contracted during the winter still hadn't gone away completely and his energy had suffered. Even walking out to the gatehouse had him breathing heavily and struggling not to cough, although he pretended he was fine.

"I am in command here," he said firmly. "Not my wife. She means well but she does not run Canterbury. Am I making myself clear?"

Gerid could see how the man was struggling to breathe. "Aye, my lord."

David sensed that Gerid didn't mean a word of it and he scowled at the man before continuing his course of conversation. "Where is the messenger?" he asked. "What news does he bring?"

Gerid sighed heavily. "He brought a missive, my lord," he said. "I sent it to Lady Emilie so that she could present it to you."

David rolled his eyes and turned away from Gerid. "Then let us go hear what the king has to tell my wife," he said. "Come along, du Reims. I want you in the room when I tell my wife that she is no longer in command of Canterbury. If a message comes for me, it will be sent directly to me. She must understand this."

Gerid took up pace behind the earl. "Aye, my lord."

"And if she tries to force me into submission, then I expect you to defend me."

"Aye, my lord."

David didn't say anything more, mostly because it was difficult to walk and talk at the same time, given his poor breathing these days. He labored up the stairs to the block-shaped keep and passed through the entry just as his wife was coming out.

Elegant blond Lady Emilie yelped and stumbled back as David reached out to grab her so she wouldn't fall. Dressed in heavy robes herself, and a heavy woolen scarf wrapped around her head, she looked at her husband accusingly.

"Where have you been?" she asked. "You know that you are not supposed to go outside in this weather. It is too damp for you."

David's expression was impatient. "I heard there was a message for me," he said. "Since you seem to want to keep everything of importance from me, I sought to find it myself."

Emilie frowned at her stubborn husband. The man had nearly died a few months ago from illness and was only now starting to get better. But he had a long way to go. Lifting her hand out of her robes, she produced the elusive missive.

"I was just bringing it to you," she said. "If you would have a little patience, it would have come to you directly."

David pursed his lips irritably and held out his hand. "May I have my missive?"

Emilie put it in his palm. "I have read it," she said. "I am prepared to ride to Henry at this moment and slap the man across the face."

David lifted his eyebrows at his normally-docile wife. "Why would you say that?"

Emilie snorted, pointing to the missive. "You shall see," she said. "Read it."

Standing in the keep entry, David did. He read it twice. Then, he turned calmly to Gerid. "Go and saddle my horse and my wife's horse," he told him. "We are riding to Winchester to slap Henry."

Gerid fought off a grin. "If you insist, my lord."

He started to move but Emilie held out a hand. "No need, Gerid," she said. "Come inside; I think you should be involved in this, too. Let us go into David's solar and discuss this."

David was still reading parts of the missive but he began to walk, heading into his lavish solar with the furs on the floor and the great plate on the hearth, displaying the wealth of the de Lohr family. He meandered to his favorite chair, next to the hearth, and sat heavily, his gaze still on the pale yellow missive. When he spoke, there was confusion and disbelief in his tone.

"Henry states that a relative says that Daniel has usurped a local lord and taken over the man's fortress," he said. "He says that not only has Daniel taken over the fortress, but that he has also threatened the life of Henry's relative and has also taken the man's betrothed. The king therefore demands we do something about our aggressive and outrageous son or he will send crown troops to Shadowmoor Castle in West Yorkshire and clap Daniel in irons."

Gerid, who had known Daniel for many years, listened to the contents of the missive with mounting disbelief. When David was finished, Gerid's expression was wrought with confusion. The Daniel he knew would do no such thing.

"Daniel, my lord?" he said. "Daniel de Lohr?"

David held up the missive to the man. "Read it for yourself," he said as Gerid took the missive. "It would seem that my son has turned into a despot and is ravaging all of West Yorkshire."

Gerid eyed the man. "Do you believe that, my lord."

"Not even a little."

"Then what shall you do, my lord?"

David scratched his chin and turned to his desk where another missive sat, one from his brother that he'd received the previous week. "I am sure this all has to do with what Daniel told my brother," he said. "Chris' missive said that Daniel had run into trouble with a local lord who claimed to be Henry's nephew. Apparently, the man is terrorizing the countryside and it was bad enough that Daniel asked for Chris to send military reinforcements, which he did. They are already heading north. Chris said that he also sent Maddoc with the troops to get to the bottom of what was happening, so whatever is going on, it has reached the ears of Henry."

"And we know that Henry's will shall prevail above all," Emilie put in, grossly unhappy with what was happening. "If this relative of Henry's pleads his case against Daniel and the king agrees, then it sounds as if my son will be in a good deal of trouble."

David struggled against a sense of foreboding; the de Lohrs had always been strong supporters of the crown but Henry's reign, much as his father's reign, had been contentious at best. There had been times when Christopher as well as David had been on the opposing side of Henry. Therefore, David hoped this wasn't Henry's attempt to get back at them for what he considered to be the lack of de Lohr support, but something told him not to rule that out.

"That is possible," he said quietly.

Emilie wasn't thrilled with that answer. "I will not allow my son to live out the rest of his life in Henry's vault, David," she said pointedly. "If Henry is sending you a missive about Daniel, then it is clear he wants something to be done about it."

David looked at her. "What would you have me do?"

Emilie frowned. "Send a missive to Daniel and tell him to leave this Shadowmoor," she said. "He has gotten himself mixed up in something terrible and now Henry is involved. That will only bring Daniel trouble."

David shook his head. "It will bring *Henry* trouble," he clarified. "If you think for one moment I am going to sit back and allow the king to bully and slander my son, then you are mistaken. Chris and I will stand against Henry in support of Daniel and Henry will be the one to back down. The man is poking a sleeping lion and the lion is about to rise up and slash him, especially if it involves my only son."

Emilie felt marginally better with David's declaration but she was still upset. "Then someone must ride for West Yorkshire to tell Daniel that Henry has contacted you about the situation," she said. "Your brother may be sending men up to assist Daniel, but they cannot know that Henry has been made aware of the situation. They must know."

David couldn't disagree with her. "You are correct," he said. Then, he looked at Gerid. "How would you like to ride to West Yorkshire to see what in the hell my son has gotten himself in to?"

Gerid nodded. "With pleasure, my lord."

"And take six hundred men with you," he said. "Leave one of the lesser knights in charge here and send me word once you have spoken to my son and discovered the truth about what is happening at this Shadowmoor. Daniel would no sooner usurp a lord and steal a woman than I would, so something is amiss here. I want to get to the bottom of it."

Gerid nodded smartly. "Aye, my lord," he said. "With your permission, I will go about my duties."

David waved the man off and Gerid handed him back the missive, quitting the solar in a hurry. There was a sense of urgency in the air. When the knight was gone, David looked at the missive again. He was quiet and pensive for a moment while his wife stewed nervously about the situation. When David spoke again, his voice was soft.

"Chris must be sent word also," he said. "He must know that Henry is involved now. That changes things a bit."

Emilie sat down in the chair opposite her husband, her dark eyes studying his face. "I am worried," she murmured. "Daniel has never been foolish but to attract the king's attention on something, against a relative of Henry's no less, frightens me. Whatever could he have done?"

David sighed as he stood up, laboriously, and coughed as he moved to the table that held all of the things he needed to administer his earldom and more besides. His brother's missive lay carelessly on the tabletop alongside quill and ink, phials of sand, and several rolled maps. David set Henry's missive down.

"Daniel is altruistic in all he does," he said. "He is a true and noble man. I can only imagine he saw a situation where people needed help and sought to give it. I have confidence that Maddoc and Gerid can handle the situation."

Emilie stood up. "But we are speaking of Henry, David," she said softly. "You or your brother should see to this situation personally, at the very least. Or, go to Winchester and assure Henry that the situation with Daniel will be resolved. What happens if Henry grows impatient and sends his army north? Would Henry actually kill my son?"

David looked at her, seeing the worry on her face. "He will not kill him," he assured her softly, although he wasn't sure he believed it. "He has asked me to do something about it so I do not think he will act before I have had a chance to resolve the situation."

Emilie stared at him a moment longer before turning away. But David saw the tears in her eyes as she did; she hadn't been fast enough to conceal them. He left his table and went to her, putting his arms around her to assure her that all would be well with their only son. She nodded her head, as if agreeing with him, but he knew in his heart that she didn't agree with him at all. He knew she was terrified.

It was that terror that spurred him into action. David wasn't entirely sure Henry wouldn't move on Daniel before he'd had a chance to settle the situation, either, and if some kind of skirmish claimed Daniel's life, at Henry's doing, then the blood would spill all over England as the House of de Lohr declared war against the crown. The consequences, should Henry harm Daniel, would be nothing less than catastrophic. David knew that, on some level, Henry knew that as well, but he wasn't willing to let Daniel suffer this situation alone.

His only son needed him.

Lady Emilie was under the impression that her husband had written a missive to send to his brother about the situation in West Yorkshire, informing the man of Henry's involvement. What she didn't know is that David sent the missive to his brother by way of swift messenger while David, and Gerid, and eight hundred Canterbury troops headed north the very next day, before dawn, while Emilie was still asleep. When she awoke, it was to a note in her husband's handwriting, placed upon his pillow, that declaring that he had to see to his son's issues personally and promising he would return to her.

In truth, Emilie wasn't surprised at the note. For her husband, the sun rose and set on Daniel. He was the man's pride and joy, his shining star, and she knew that David couldn't sit back and worry over the man, not while there was still breath left in his body. It was true that he was still not fully recovered from his sickness but Emilie also knew that trying to keep him at Canterbury, while Daniel was in danger, would have been an impossible task.

David had to go to his son.

And all Emilie could do was wait, praying her husband and son were still alive when all was said and done. With Henry involved, she couldn't be sure of anything.

CHAPTER FIFTEEN

Shadowmoor, ten days later

THE BANNERS THAT the seamstress in Siglesdene had made for Daniel were absolutely spectacular. He'd selected dark blue and gold silk, the de Lohr colors, and the woman had made some beautiful pieces – simple sleeves for the joust poles that would encase them in color, but also three goodly sized banners to hang from the poles as well as a banner that could be flown from a post, announcing Daniel's arrival to one and all. He was incredibly pleased with the work and paid the woman handsomely for it.

Meanwhile, he'd struck up a bargain with Liselotte – he agreed to pay her very well if she would sew two blue and gold tunics for him, and she did using fabric he had purchased from the seamstress. In fact, her skill at sewing was nearly as good as the seamstress, and Daniel was exceptionally satisfied with it. There had been the added bonus of having her fit him in various stages of completing the garment, and he'd even stolen a kiss or two from her during the process. It had all been great fun.

In fact, the days following the fiasco with Bramley at Siglesdene had been days of peace and happiness. Brynner had been returned to Shadowmoor and buried next to his father in the yard beyond the stable, but neither Liselotte nor Gunnar had grieved for him. The truth was that Gunnar didn't even really know his own brother and Liselotte had stopped caring about him the moment he confessed to killing their father, so he was buried and forgotten while life at Shadowmoor improved by the day. With Brynner gone and Liselotte effectively in charge, the days were brighter altogether.

More supplies from Netherghyll and from Daniel meant that everyone had enough food to eat. The tiny huts inside the fortress walls that people were living in had been cleaned up and repaired. The smithy and tanner were both earning their keep again and the inhabitants of Shadowmoor began resuming productive lives. There were men who would go out and cut peat from the moors, returning to sell it for cooking fires for a small sack of grain or the promise of a meal. Although there was still hardly any coinage exchange, people were trading, making sure everyone had what they needed, ensuring that they would continue to survive.

They were living again.

But survival wasn't the only thing going on at Shadowmoor these days; there was some excitement, too. The inhabitants of Shadowmoor all knew about the coming tournament and Daniel had invited everyone to travel to Skipton to watch him compete on behalf of Shadowmoor. It was all rather thrilling for people who hadn't had any enjoyment for years and as the tournament grew closer, it was all anyone could talk about. Not only was hope filling Shadowmoor these days, but the thrill of competition was, too.

It was especially thrilling for Gunnar. He was the heir of Shadowmoor now, the next generation to oversee the fortress, the last in a long line of Saxon lords, but he didn't really know it. His sister and Daniel were overseeing the fortress and he was content being a boy with two goats and four puppies, all of whom he loved dearly. He wouldn't sleep without the goats, or the dogs, and Liselotte had given up trying to keep the animals out of his chamber, so these days, he slept with all six animals on his small bed. Sometimes the animals would crowd him and he would sleep in odd positions, much to Daniel's amusement. He thought it was about the funniest, and sweetest, thing he'd ever seen.

But the thrill of the animals aside, Daniel told Gunnar that he could help squire for the coming tournament so Gunnar trained with Daniel on a daily basis. The ward of Shadowmoor was so vast that Daniel set up a training area near the stables, and he and Ares would train daily along the makeshift guides that Daniel and Caston and several soldiers had set up. Caston was at Shadowmoor quite often and he would train with Daniel when he was able. Gunnar watched it all through the eyes of a child who had never seen such a thing, with awe and great wonder. He made an eager if not somewhat clumsy squire, but that was part of his charm.

With the tournament only three days away, Daniel and Caston had begun their training early on this day. They were making practice runs against each other and the entire fortress had turned out to watch. It had been a very long time since knights had been the center of attention at the fortress, so it was quite a spectacle. The smithy had admirably repaired Brighton's old joust poles and Daniel was impressed with the man's craftsmanship, thinking that he more than likely had some of the best-crafted joust poles around until he saw Caston's gleaming steel-tipped poles.

That brought on a fit of jealousy and Daniel tried to mix the poles up so he could more easily steal Caston's. But Caston was on to him and took fiendish glee in knowing how much Daniel admired his poles. The practice, and the clashing, went on well into the morning.

Liselotte could hear it from her chamber high in the keep. Her window happened to face south, which meant it faced over the kitchen yard and the stables, and she had been listening to Daniel and Caston yell at each other, good-naturedly, all morning. It made her smile to hear Daniel's voice, the voice of the man she had fallen so deeply in love with. The fears of him breaking her heart were long over. In fact, she couldn't even remember what there was to fear about Daniel any longer.

He had become such a part of Shadowmoor and their lives that she was sure he would never leave them. He had worked so hard to bring hope back to them all. *To her.* She couldn't imagine that he would ever want to leave people he'd given such hope to. Perhaps it was a fool's hope, but it was her hope nonetheless.

On this bright morning, she was just finishing the embroidery on Daniel's tournament tunic. He'd purchased the gold thread in Siglesdene when he's purchased the fabric and she had embroidered a lion on the front of the gold de Lohr shield. It wasn't a very big lion because she'd had to move quickly, but it was exquisitely done. She knew he would be pleased.

Excited to show him the finished product, she left her small chamber and headed down the narrow spiral stairs, down to the entry level of the keep. In the room that used to be her father's solar, two female servants were cleaning it out and sweeping the floor, preparing it for the fine lady's room that Daniel had promised her. Liselotte paused in the doorway, watching the work in progress, thinking of her father and hoping that, wherever he was, he was happy to see the changes going on at Shadowmoor. She knew, in her heart, that he must have been thrilled, even with the fact that she was taking over his solar.

It was sunny outside, a brilliant sky the result of a storm that had blown through the night before. The ground was muddy but some of the men were now starting to grade the ground a little, making it easier to walk on and filling in the holes so someone wouldn't break a leg. Daniel was paying them a pence a day to do it, and they did it happily. The bailey, in general, was starting to look much better than she had ever seen it. It didn't even look like the same place anymore.

Daniel's touch had seen to that.

Rounding the side of the keep, she headed to the area where Daniel and Caston were practicing. They were off their horses at this point and Liselotte could see the smithy bending over the right front leg of Caston's horse, inspecting the iron horseshoe. Gunnar was running around nearby, playing with his goats and puppies, and she grinned at her younger brother who was so very happy these days. He'd even put on some weight with the good food, looking like an entirely different boy with his little rounded belly. The transformation was astonishing.

"My lady!"

Daniel called to her, pulling her attention away from Gunnar. She smiled at the man as she came near.

"Is everything well, my lord?" she asked, gesturing to Caston's horse. "Is the horse injured?"

Daniel looked at the horse. "Nay," he said. "He lost a nail. The smithy will fix it."

Liselotte nodded. "That is good to hear," she said. Then, she held up the tunic in her hand. "I have finished the lion. I thought you would want to see it."

Daniel's face lit up and he reached for it. "Indeed, I do," he said, then quickly drew his hands back. "I do not want to touch the tunic, for my hands are dirty. Hold it up so that I may see."

She did. Daniel lavished praise upon her and even Caston complimented her embroidery skills, but his issue with his horse was more pressing so he and the smithy took the horse over to the smithy stall, leaving Daniel and Liselotte still standing on the edge of the practice field. Daniel finally gave up trying to keep his hands off the tunic and took it from Liselotte, holding it up in front of him to see how it would look when he wore it.

"Magnificent, my lady," he said. "I am very impressed with your sewing skills. You will be handsomely rewarded."

Liselotte blushed at his praise. "You have already paid me for the tunic," she said. "It is reward enough that you shall wear it. I… I have never had a knight wear my handiwork, much less wear it in a tournament."

He grinned, still visually inspecting the details of the lion. "Not only will I wear your tunic, but you shall be my favored lady that day," he said. "I will carry your favor with me and it shall bring me luck."

Liselotte was rather surprised to hear that. "Truly?" she said. "What shall I give you? I have never given anyone a favor before."

He shrugged. "A silk kerchief," he said. "A glove, a scarf. Some women even make favors especially for their knights, embroidered with their name on it. It does not matter what you give me; I will carry it and I will win."

She smiled. "You sound confident."

"I am. With your support, I could be nothing less."

Her smile faded. "You will always have my support, Daniel," she said quietly. "You have done so much for us that I could do nothing less. You shall have my support until I die."

He lifted his eyebrows, still looking at his tunic and unaware that she was watching him very closely, perhaps looking for something of hope for their future in his expression. That was why she had said what she did; she was hoping he would respond to it. But he was oblivious to what she was suggesting.

"I am greatly appreciative," he said. "And I shall win the purse for you. The money that I win will become yours to help Shadowmoor survive."

It was the first time he'd told her of his intentions with the prize money and she was understandably surprised. Then, she was deeply grateful. "Are you sure?"

Daniel looked at her, seeing her shock. He'd purposely not told her of his intention to donate the prize money to Shadowmoor because he knew she would have argued with him about it. But now, so close to the event, there wasn't much she could do. He smiled.

"I am," he said. "So is Caston. He will donate whatever he wins to Shadowmoor as well, but I do not expect him to win anything because I will triumph in every event, so you can expect all of the donations to come from me."

He said it rather pompously, humorous, but Liselotte could barely smile for all of the astonishment she was feeling. That both Daniel and Caston would willingly donate their winnings was beyond her comprehension. Once again, Daniel was doing so much for them that she was having trouble expressing her gratitude to him. It seemed as if the man's generosity had no end.

"Your kindness is limitless, Daniel," she said sincerely. "And Caston's, too. But the two of you have done so much for us already."

He looked up from the tunic, smiling into her grateful face. "I have only just begun," he said. "Shadowmoor will be restored to her former glory, I promise you. Already, she is emerging from her hell. Can you not see it?"

Liselotte nodded firmly. "Indeed, I do," she said. "But… but I am still not certain why you have done all of this. I have said from the beginning that we are not your responsibility. That you would be so generous to us is still unbelievable to me. Every day I am astonished anew."

His smile softened. "I told you why," he said quietly. "I am doing it for you."

Liselotte took it as an opening to probe him about his intentions. She had been wanting to ask questions of him for some time now but it had never seemed like the right time. Weeks of gentle flirtation and exquisite thrill had never been the right time because she hadn't wanted to ruin whatever was developing between them. She wanted to enjoy it. But now, he had opened the door. She was going to take the opportunity.

She needed to know.

"But why?" she asked, her voice soft. "My father offered you my hand in marriage but you refused. Why should you do this for a woman you do not intend to marry?"

Daniel's smile faded. He knew this moment would come and he had been dreading it. He was suddenly uncertain, feeling cornered, without one of his practiced and polished answers. He knew it was a perfectly legitimate question. He simply didn't know how to answer her. Or perhaps he did but he was afraid to.

He knew he loved her. There was no question in his mind. But he was terrified to admit it, even to himself. He had been perfectly happy all of these weeks, going along as they were going, with stolen kisses and sweet glances. Aye, he'd been perfectly happy because there had been no serious talk of commitment. But now she was asking him a question that scared him. She was looking for answers. Clearing his throat softly, he lowered his gaze.

"Is it not enough that Shadowmoor is on the road to recovery and we are happy?" he asked. "Is it not enough that you know of my affections for you? I told you that I was not the marrying kind."

Liselotte's warm expression vanished. She felt as if he had hit her in the gut with his answer and she took a step back, reeling. Feeling so very hurt and ashamed.

"So you have been toying with me?" she asked. "Is that what all of the kisses and gentle touches have been? Nothing more than you toying with my feelings without any intention of being honorable about them?"

Daniel looked at her and sighed faintly. "That was not what I meant."

"Then, exactly, what did you mean?"

He could see that she was very quickly growing upset and he hastened to soothe her without wading into that dangerous whirlpool of giving her the answers she sought. He would be sucked right down into saying something he didn't want to say or was afraid to say.

"I simply meant that you know I am fond of you," he said. "I told you before that I would speak of my feelings when I was ready to."

He was being evasive; she could see it. It only served to fuel the hurt she was feeling. She pulled the tunic out of his hands and stepped away from him.

"Then until you are ready to speak of such things, I will reserve the right not to make a fool of myself any further by allowing you to kiss me whenever you please," she said crisply. "I thought I meant something to you, Daniel, but I can see that I was wrong. Mayhap I am simply another project for you; you seem intent on rebuilding Shadowmoor so mayhap you are intent to rebuild me as well. So you toy with me and buy me pretty clothing and tell me I am beautiful, thinking it will build me up when, in fact, everything you are doing will be torn down the moment you leave me. Is this how you have been your whole life? Shallow and insincere, using women to flatter you and feed your pride before disposing of them? If that is the case, then you can leave Shadowmoor now. You have done a great deal for us and I am truly grateful to you, but I will not let you treat us as if we are simply projects to satisfy your ego."

Daniel was feeling a great deal of disappointment as she backed away from him, but he was also feeling ashamed. Everything she said made perfect sense, as if she could read him like an open book. He'd wanted to build up Shadowmoor and, in truth, he'd wanted to build her up as well. *A purpose in life.* He'd seen Shadowmoor as a purpose in life. But he saw Liselotte as more than a purpose. Perhaps she was *his* purpose.

Perhaps she had been his purpose all along.

God, why can't I tell her that?

"Leese, please," he said, moving after her as she tried to walk away. "Please do not go. I did not mean to hurt or offend you. I… oh, hell, I do not know what to say to all of this. You are not a project. You mean far more to me than that. You mean everything."

Liselotte came to a halt, turning to look at him. "I mean everything to you but marriage," she said. "Isn't that what you mean? If that is the case, Daniel de Lohr, I want you to leave Shadowmoor. I will not be your toy or your mistress or your… your concubine. As much as I adore you, and I adore you very much, I will not let you do that to me. I will not let you show such disrespect to me."

Daniel was torn, struggling to find the right words, knowing what he wanted to say but unable to bring the words forth. He'd never in his life told a woman he loved her, at least not a woman who meant something to him. But something in what she said had his attention.

"Do you love me, Leese?" he asked softly.

She held his gaze a moment longer, trying to be strong, before turning away. There were tears in her eyes. "I do."

"Say it. Let me hear it."

She broke down into soft tears "Nay," she whispered. "I will not."

"Tell me."

"I won't!"

He sighed heavily. "I did not know you felt that way," he murmured. "Say it… let me hear it. Nothing in this world will ever mean so much to me."

Liselotte broke into soft sobs and fled before he could stop her. With a hugely heavy heart, Daniel went to follow but a Netherghyll soldier caught his attention. The man was running for him, running past Liselotte as she ran for the keep. Then he put himself between Daniel and Liselotte, and Daniel had no choice but to stop. Heartbroken, he growled at the soldier.

"What do you want?" he demanded.

The soldier was polite. "My lord, we have sighted an incoming army," he said. "I have already notified Sir Caston. He says you must come immediately."

An incoming army. Concerned, and confused, Daniel struggled to forget about Liselotte as he followed the soldier across the massive ward, heading to the great gates and the wall that had a wooden wall walk built on it, a projection out from the stone that had been seriously repaired over the past few weeks. He mounted the nearest ladder and headed to where the soldiers were gathering, pointing to the west. Daniel leaned over the wall, peering down the moor and seeing a distant gathering, like an army of ants, approaching up the hillside. He heard Caston behind him.

"Mayhap it is Bramley," he said, somewhat ironically. "Mayhap the man has been telling the truth all along and that is Henry coming to lay siege."

Daniel gave him a half-grin. "That would just be our luck," he said. "With that in mind, however, mayhap you should prepare your men. Let us lock up the gates and make sure everyone is prepared. Leave nothing to chance."

Caston fled, shouting to his men on the wall walk and also to those down below in the bailey. Something was brewing and although they weren't sure what, exactly, it was, it was better to be safe.

Shadowmoor hadn't faced a real siege in decades. Bramley's harassment was one thing but a full-blown siege was something completely different. A sense of genuine fear spread through the inhabitants of Shadowmoor as Caston and his men began to mobilize and people began to scatter. Daniel could hear the commotion behind him as he stood on the wall, watching the human tide roll up the hill. Truth be told, he wasn't particularly worried, but he was curious.

And then he saw it.

The sunlight caught the flash of a banner and, instantly, Daniel was flying off the wall, shouting at the men to open the gates. Startled, the Netherghyll men began to pull on the old iron chains, working alongside Shadowmoor men, heaving and sweating to roll open the heavy gates. When the gap was wide enough, Daniel burst through. Caston, puzzled at his behavior, ran out after him.

"What is it?" Caston demanded. "Why are the gates open?"

Daniel was beaming. "That is not Henry," he said frankly. "It is my Uncle Christopher. That is the de Lohr army I sent for."

Surprised, but in a good way, Caston turned his attention to the army that was now coming closer, lumbering up the hill with horses and wagons, becoming more distinct as they drew closer. He, too, could see the de Lohr banners flying, the dark blue and gold, and he could also see the heavily-armed men, well dressed and well supplied. This was a professional army. There were two big knights in the lead, bellowing orders to the men. With a smirk, Caston turned to Daniel.

"So you really are who you say you are," he said. "Any man can boast that he is a de Lohr but this army proves it."

Daniel laughed softly. "Nay, my friend, I did not lie about it," he said, his gaze lingering on the knights. Suddenly, his smile vanished. "In fact… God's Bones, is that *Maddoc*?"

His eyes widened as he stood there, mouth open, as a knight suddenly broke off from the pack and charged at him astride a big roan warhorse. Daniel stood his ground as the knight ran at him, the horse's massive hooves tearing at the earth. Dirt and ripped foliage flew. But as Daniel watched the man come towards him, he suddenly broke away from Caston and went to meet him. Something, in that moment, had occurred to him and it was imperative that he speak with Maddoc before introductions could take place to Caston.

To Brighton de Royans' twin.

The horror last year that Brighton had created had been directed at Maddoc. He had challenged the man for the woman who was now Maddoc's wife and, in the process, had badly wounded Maddoc. Maddoc had dragged himself from his death bed to rescue the woman he loved, the result of which had been Brighton's death. After a brutal fight, Maddoc had drown the man in a horse trough. Not a dignified way to die for a knight of Brighton's standing, but Maddoc had been too weak, and too furious, to care at that moment. He'd knocked the man senseless and drowned him.

Therefore, Daniel knew that Maddoc was going to have much the same reaction to Caston's appearance as Daniel had. But given that Daniel had come to know the de Royans family, and their generosity, he didn't want Maddoc to give any indication as to the death of their brother. Daniel still wasn't sure he should ever say anything, knowing how it would hurt Caston and Easton, and knowing how it would damage his friendship with them. Better to let things lie, he told himself yet again. He just didn't see the point.

"Maddoc!" he bellowed, holding up his arms as the knight brought the big horse to a stop. Daniel crowed when Maddoc flipped his visor up so his face could be viewed. "Oh, my giddy young man! It *is* you!"

Maddoc grinned, dismounting his horse and heading for Daniel. When the two finally came together, it was in an enormous embrace, each man squeezing the life from the other. They were such dear friends that no other greeting was possible. They were brothers to the core and moments like this between them were rare. Daniel wandered so much that, at times, they had gone years without seeing each other.

Therefore, this moment was precious to them both.

"Of course it is me," Maddoc replied, releasing Daniel long enough to look in the man's face as if to reassure himself that Daniel, his dearest friend, was well and whole. "I was at Lioncross when your missive to your uncle came, so your uncle asked me to bring the army north. He also asked me to find out what in the hell was going on. What have you gotten yourself into this time, Danny?"

Daniel's expression didn't falter. He was still thrilled to see Maddoc, still caught up in that excitement. "What did my uncle tell you?" he asked.

Maddoc's gaze moved from Daniel's face to the beastly image of a fortress that was absolutely massive. He could see that repairs were going on but, on the whole, the place looked terrible. He pointed at it. "*This* is Shadowmoor?"

Daniel turned to glance at the structure he'd become so familiar with. "It is," he said. "How did you find it?"

Maddoc's brilliant blue eyes fixed on the place. "We knew it was north of Bradford from what you said in your missive," he said. "I stopped at the cathedral in Bradford and asked the priest. He told me exactly where to find it."

Daniel clapped the man on the shoulder. "Well and good that he did," he said. "I am very glad you are here."

Maddoc looked at him, then. "Are you?" he said. "Then take me inside, feed me, and tell me why I am here. Your uncle wants to know what is going on."

Daniel's smile faded then. "It is quite a story."

Maddoc shook his head, slowly, but with agreement. "With you involved, it could be nothing else."

Daniel snorted but put out a hand to stop Maddoc as the man took a step towards the fortress. "Wait," he said, lowering his voice. "There is something you must know before we discuss anything. There is no easy way to say this, so I will come out with it. I am afraid I must take you back to that terrible time in your life when Brighton de Royans nearly killed you and abducted your wife. I will not even ask you if you remember that time for I know that you do. That being said, you must be aware of something – Brighton de Royans' family is an ally of Shadowmoor."

Maddoc's serious young face remained steady but something changed in the brilliant eyes; they began to smolder, the surprise at the mention of the name of the man who had nearly killed him. Whom *he* had finally killed. As the news sank in, he began to show more reaction.

"De Royans?" he repeated, his voice like ice. "His family is here?"

Daniel nodded. "Maddoc, there is no time to ease you into this situation so I will be blunt," he said. "You must listen very carefully to me. Are you listening?"

"I am."

Daniel squeezed his shoulder in a gesture of comfort. "The home of Brighton's birth is about ten miles to the north," he said. "I met them quite by accident and, understandably, was surprised as well as wary. I hated the mention of the name de Royans almost as much as you did. But these people, Maddoc… they are nothing like Brighton was. They are generous and kind. They are quite likable. In fact, Brighton's brother, Sir Caston, and I have become good friends."

At that point, Maddoc hissed and tried to turn away, unable to stomach what he was being told, but Daniel grabbed him, preventing him from leaving.

"Nay, my friend, *listen* to me," he implored. "I believe you will like Caston if you will only give him an opportunity. But know that they are unaware of the fate of Brighton and I do not have the heart to tell them. For now, keep silent on the matter. They have been tremendous allies to Shadowmoor, more than you know. I do not want to ruin that relationship and, frankly, I see no need to tell them what has become of Brighton. For Shadowmoor's sake, do not tell them what happened. I know this will be harder on you than it ever was for me, but I am asking you, as my dear friend, not to say a word. Can you do this, Maddoc?"

Maddoc's expression was full of angst, the bright blue eyes flickering unsteadily. There was great emotion there, deeper than he could express. But Daniel had made a request of him, in the name of friendship, and he would not disappoint the man. It all narrowed down to that one little request. For Daniel, Maddoc would try to overcome his inherent hatred of anything that had to do with the de Royans name. After a moment, he nodded his head.

"Aye," he said. "If you ask this of me, I will do it."

Daniel had to admit that he wasn't certain what Maddoc's reaction would be, considering Brighton had been his mortal enemy. But he was pleased that the man complied without much of a fight. He also knew he had agreed strictly because of his friendship with Daniel. He trusted Daniel completely, even with something that had such a bitter taste to him. Daniel breathed a sigh of relief.

"Thank you," he said sincerely. "Know that Caston and his father, Easton, are good men. I do not know how or why Brighton went so terribly wrong, but his brother and father do not have the same evil streak in them that Brighton had. Give them that consideration."

Maddoc drew in a deep steadying breath at the unexpected turn the situation had taken. Had he not been so surprised by it, he might have even laughed at the irony. "I will try," he said.

"Good."

"But of all the homes in all of England, *you* had to find the house of the man who tried to kill me? Who tried to steal away my wife?"

Daniel snorted wryly. "I thought the same thing, believe me," he said. Then, he sobered. "But there is something more."

"God, what now?"

"Caston de Royans is Brighton's twin. They look exactly alike."

Now, Maddoc could not help the deluge of emotion that filled him. He rolled his eyes and hung his head. "Are you serious?"

"I am."

Maddoc snorted unpleasantly. "What is this devilry?" he hissed. "Am I to be punished for defending what was mine? For protecting my life? Am I to look into the face of a dead man as a reminder of the worst time in my life?"

Daniel could see that he was becoming agitated. "Steady, lad, steady," he said softly. "Caston is a good man. Remember what I said. After a while, you will not see Brighton when you look at him. Trust me on this matter."

Maddoc simply shook his head. "Danny, I do not know if I can do this," he said. "After everything that happened…."

Daniel cut him off. "You can and you will," he said. "You will do this because I ask it of you, because we love one another, as brothers. I would not steer you wrong. I know this is difficult for you, but you will remember that Caston and his father had nothing to do with it. They have no idea what Brighton did and, given what I have come to know of them, I am sure they would strongly condemn his actions. But keep a level head, man. It is important to what I am trying to accomplish here."

Maddoc lifted his head, looking at him. "What *are* you trying to accomplish?"

Daniel grinned and tugged on his arm, pulling him towards the fortress. "Come and see."

ଓ

THE GREAT HALL of Shadowmoor was much different than it had been the first time Daniel had ever seen it.

Back then, it had been old mutton and pea stew because it was all they had, but in honor of the arrival of the de Lohr army, it was stuffed to the rafters with soldiers and knights, all of them eating from a big cow that the de Lohr army had slaughtered the day before. The carcass was roasting over a massive fire in the kitchen yard and everyone was enjoying the succulent beef. The smells of food and the light from the fires spread throughout out the bailey of Shadowmoor and filled the night air.

It was a festive mood, too. A few of the Netherghyll soldiers had brought along their instruments and the sounds of the drums and citole could be heard in the hall. One soldier, who'd had a bit too much to drink early on, was singing a song called *Tilly Nodden* that had everyone joining in at the appropriate chorus. It was loud and irreverent at times, but it was also joyful.

It was good to hear the life again within the old walls, Liselotte thought, as she moved through the hall with the female servants, overseeing the meal and insuring that the men were satisfied. It was the Netherghyll army inside the hall, mostly, while the men from Lioncross Abbey had massive bonfires throughout the bailey and were enjoying themselves beneath the cold, dark sky.

But even as she moved through the hall and the men, she was on the lookout for Daniel. After fleeing him earlier in the day, she had retreated in shame to her chamber where she'd locked herself in, fearful that Daniel might come after her and try to use manipulation and sweet words to convince her that marriage wasn't necessary. She didn't want to hear him.

But she soon became angry at herself because the heartbreak she had feared, the pain she had convinced herself didn't matter in the long run, began to matter a great deal. She was hurting, badly, as if her heart had been ripped from her chest by a man who had told her, from the beginning, that he wasn't the marrying kind. God, she'd so hoped to change his mind. He was such a part of Shadowmoor that she knew they would all be shattered when he left. And he would leave; she knew that now. There was nothing left for her to do but face that reality.

So she had calmed herself, wiped her tears, and left her chamber to see to the evening meal as she always did. But she made very certain to stay clear of anywhere she thought Daniel might be. He didn't usually come to the kitchens so once she was there, she was safe, and she went ahead with her duties.

One of the sheep had been slaughtered a couple of days before and she had the cook boil the mutton in a peppercorn gravy, something that was quite delicious. Bread was made from rye and wheat, and butter was made from the cow's milk. There was more cheese as well because they'd started making sheep's milk cheese as well, so there was an abundance of dairy products to feast upon.

The cook, who had always been very talented at stretching any stores Shadowmoor had, now had a plethora of ingredients to choose from and she began to make some rather tasty dishes like she had in the days before Shadowmoor was starving. Daniel had sent men into town a few days before to gather more supplies and they had returned with bushels of cabbages, onions, beans, turnips, leeks, carrots, and small sacks of spices like rosemary, mint, cardamom, and dill. There were also bags of peppercorns and expensive salt.

It had been a great deal of food and the cook had made a cabbage pottage three days in a row that was delicious. Even now, she was making it again, with cabbage and leeks and carrots and a hint of cardamom, and the entire castle smelled of cooking cabbage, enough to lure in Gunnar and his gang of animals, who were hungry and looking for something to eat. The cook sat him down with a bowl of pottage for him, old cabbage leaves for the goats, and scraps of fat from the mutton for the dogs. Everyone was happy.

So the pottage had been headed for the feasting table, along with the mutton, but those plans were changed when a soldier came to tell Liselotte that an army had been sighted. Fearful, and thinking that it was Bramley again, she and the cook had waited fearfully in the kitchen for word and were subsequently told that it was the de Lohr army that had arrived. Liselotte's relief was great but so was her worry that they now had to feed hundreds of men. But the fear was short lived when Caston came to tell her that the de Lohr army had brought their own beef. A spit was set up in the kitchen yard and soon the smells of cooking beef mingled with those of cabbage.

Liselotte had never seen so many men at Shadowmoor nor had she ever seen so much food. It was a bit overwhelming but she enjoyed the noise, and the revelry, quite a bit. She'd never seen anything like it. Gunnar was thrilled, of course, excited to see the de Lohr knights as well as the soldiers, as he and his pets sat in a warm corner of the hall and watched the activity. It was a great deal of excitement for the young boy.

But all the while that the food was cooking and the army was settling in, Liselotte couldn't help but think of Daniel. He was never far from her thoughts and as much as she had wanted to stay away from him, that resolve began to buckle and by nightfall, she was eager for the sight of him. She thought that perhaps she should apologize for pushing him towards marriage when he had told her from the onset he was not the marrying kind. Liselotte had always hoped to marry but if she couldn't marry Daniel, she didn't see much need. It wouldn't be fair to marry one man when her heart belonged to another.

But she never saw Daniel as she went about her duties and she eventually became very busy with the kitchen and food output for the guests they had. Then, he finally appeared; she saw Daniel enter the hall in the company of two unfamiliar knights as well as Caston, the four of them making their way to the feasting table.

Through the smoke and noise, Liselotte saw them claim their seats. She knew that she should go and introduce herself, as the Lady of Shadowmoor, and it took considerable effort to swallow her nerves and approach Daniel and his guests. She knew she had humiliated herself earlier in the day with him and she hoped he wouldn't hold it against her.

She hoped he was the forgiving kind.

"Greetings, my lords," she said as she came to the table with a pitcher of ale that had been made from some of the grain Daniel had purchased. Mostly, she was focused on the two knights she didn't recognize. "I am Lady Liselotte l'Audacieux. Shadowmoor is my home. I bid you welcome."

A bold move for the lady to introduce, without a man giving her a proper introduction to other men, herself but no one seemed to mind. The two unfamiliar knights stood up to formally greet her and a very big knight with the brightest blue eyes Liselotte had ever seen responded to her address.

"Thank you for your hospitality, my lady," he said. "I am Sir Maddoc du Bois and my companion is Sir Marc de Russe. We brought the de Lohr army to Daniel's summons."

Liselotte forced a smile, not looking at Daniel because she was too embarrassed to do so. "You are most welcome, my lords," she said, her attention moving to the knight introduced as Marc de Russe. He was very tall, with broad shoulders and dark, messy hair. "Have your accommodations been settled yet? I was unaware that you were here. Forgive me if you have not been shown to your sleeping quarters."

Maddoc waved her off. "Daniel has taken charge of that, my lady," he said. "We are well settled. In fact, Daniel has been telling us of your trouble with Lord Bramley. May I ask you some questions about the situation?"

So she would be forced to sit with the men. *With Daniel.* So much for fleeing. Trembling, and increasingly nervous, Liselotte set her ale pitcher down and sat at the end of the table. Daniel was to her right but she had yet to look at him. She could feel his eyes upon her.

"I would be happy to answer your questions, my lord," she said. "But before you ask, allow me to say this – whatever Daniel has told you, the reality is worse by tenfold. Four years ago, Shadowmoor was a self-sufficient fortress. We were even moderately prosperous. Then the event of Lord Bramley happened; when the man made an offer for my hand and my father refused, he did all he could to make our lives miserable. He killed our livestock and blocked all attempts to leave the fortress for food and supplies. He even burned the crops we had sewn outside of our walls. When Daniel came upon us, we were starving to death. Had it not been for him, we would all be dead. I am as sure of that as I am sure of the sun rising in the morning. Daniel has given us our life back and for that, I shall always be eternally grateful."

Maddoc picked up the pitcher she had set down and moved to fill his cup. "That is essentially what Daniel told us," he said, pouring the drink. "Looking at the fortress now, it is clear that it is under repair but it hardly looks destitute."

"That is because Daniel has spent a good deal of time and money returning Shadowmoor to what it should be. All you see is the result of his generosity."

Maddoc glanced at Daniel, who only had eyes for the lady. It took Maddoc a moment to realize that Daniel was staring at her quite intently. *Deeply.* It was curious to see Daniel so focused on a woman but then he recalled what Christopher had said about the situation; *Daniel is doing this because of a woman.* From the expression on Daniel's face, Maddoc could easily see that it was the truth. But surely it was infatuation and nothing more. The Daniel he knew wasn't capable of anything more. But he wondered just how far gone Daniel was with his fascination for the tall, slender, and very lovely Lady Lisclotte.

"You must understand, my lady, that I am here on a fact-finding mission," Maddoc said. "Daniel's uncle, Christopher de Lohr, has sent me with reinforcements but he wants to know the truth behind Daniel's request. Am I to understand that all of this started because of a rejected suit?"

Liselotte shrugged. "That was part of it, my lord," she answered, "but I truly believe there is far more to his greed. Daniel knows this to be true, also. Bramley wants Shadowmoor and her lands, and her contracts, because we have the legal right to collect tariffs on the roads leading into Bradford. We are also entitled to taxes from Ilkley, Keighley, and several other small villages, and for many years we collected those taxes peacefully. When Bramley arrived, he used armed men to chase us off when we tried to collect our taxes and he took the money for himself. He steals from our villagers and from us."

"Then he is a thief, but that is hardly reason to summon a massive army," Maddoc said as neutrally as he could. "Why have you not brought your grievances to the Sheriff of the West Yorkshire?"

"That would be my father," Caston interjected, looking between Liselotte and Maddoc. "I think I can answer that question – Shadowmoor has always kept to themselves. They are an old and proud fortress, purely Saxon for the most part, and everyone in West

Yorkshire has largely steered clear of them, always. It is my sense that they never brought this to my father's attention purely out of fear that they would be ignored. Is that not so, my lady?"

Liselotte nodded, looking somewhat ashamed. "I think it was a matter of pride on my father's part as well," she said. "He thought that we could deal with it ourselves. There was something shameful in seeking help."

"Yet you accepted Daniel's help," Maddoc pointed out, not unkindly. "Why take his help?"

Liselotte still wouldn't look at Daniel, feeling his gaze upon her like a weight, pulling at her, demanding her attention. But she couldn't bring herself to face him.

"Because he was a stranger," she said. "He did not know us. He did not know that our forefathers entered into a treaty with the Normans so that we could keep our lands. But that treaty made us traitors to our allies. It is a dishonor that has never left us, but it was one Daniel did not know of. He did not have that prejudice towards us that others did."

Maddoc digested the information and everything he had been told since he'd arrived at Shadowmoor. He seemed indecisive, enough so that Liselotte leaned forward, her gaze upon him intense.

"My lord," she said. "I realize this looks like a local problem. It looks to be silly and insipid. But I assure you that there is nothing insipid about Bramley's harassment. Not long ago, he abducted my younger brother in an attempt to force my father to surrender both me and Shadowmoor. My brother miraculously escaped and it was then that Daniel entered our lives. He saved my brother and was thoughtful and kind enough to remain at Shadowmoor to help us with Bramley. But, somehow, Bramley got to my older brother and convinced him to kill my father. Did Daniel tell you that? My older brother killed my father and it was only two weeks ago that my brother was killed in a skirmish, siding with Bramley against Daniel and Netherghyll. You may not wish to help but I will tell you what will happen if you do not;

Netherghyll and Daniel have already committed themselves to aiding Shadowmoor. Bramley told Daniel that he has sent word to Henry to summon crown troops. If you do not stay and help, all that Daniel and those at Netherghyll have worked for will be destroyed once Henry sends his army. Please, my lord… please, help us. This may be a foolish situation to you, but to me, it is my life. Shadowmoor is all that I have. Please help me to keep it."

She was verging on tears by the time she was finished and Maddoc, who was truly soft-hearted beneath that stiff exterior, could feel himself relenting. His manner eased.

"My lady," he said. "You need not worry. I will not leave Daniel here alone to face Lord Bramley and whatever the man can throw at him. But you do understand that it was Daniel who killed your brother."

Liselotte nodded, wiping daintily at her eyes. "He told me what happened," she said. "You must understand that my brother was a foul drunkard, my lord. He would do anything for drink, including siding with our enemy if the man promised him more ale for his allegiance. Daniel told me everything that happened in that skirmish and I believe him implicitly."

Maddoc believed Daniel, too, for the man was not a liar. Still, he wanted to understand the lady's point of view on everything. He could see how badly she was affected. "I believe him as well," he said. "That is not the issue. I am simply trying to understand the situation clearly."

Liselotte sniffled, ashamed at her outburst that was very close to begging. "The situation is that Lord Bramley is trying to erase us from this earth," she said. "My father once said that he believed Daniel was sent by God to help us. When I look at you, I would like to think that God has sent more of His avenging angels to aid us in our fight. For whatever you can do for us, please know that I am eternally grateful."

Maddoc gazed at the woman that Daniel couldn't keep his eyes off of. "I will do my best to ensure that Bramley is turned away from Shadowmoor once and for all."

Liselotte closed her eyes, deeply relieved. She was also quite emotional. Fearing another outburst, she simply forced a smile and stood up.

"Thank you, my lord," she said. "If you will excuse me now, I have duties to attend to."

Quickly, she fled, disappearing into the smoke of the crowded room before Maddoc could ask her anymore questions. Maddoc and Marc turned to quiet conversation as Daniel watched Liselotte fade away. He couldn't help but notice that she'd had no interest in looking at him the entire time she sat at the table, which made his heart quite heavy. He knew she was hurting; he was hurting, too. Spending the afternoon with Maddoc and Marc and Caston, discussing strategy against Bramley, had only served to distract him. The ache from his earlier confrontation with Liselotte was still there, weighing upon him more strongly than ever.

He knew he wouldn't be able to think or concentrate until he spoke with her and cleared the air between them but the problem was that he still couldn't bring himself to say what needed to be said, what was in his heart. It was such a slippery slope because he knew once he opened that gate, there would be no turning back. He couldn't take back what he said. He would be committed, forever. He wasn't sure if it was in his nature to be committed forever.

But he was equally sure that he couldn't stand the thought of spending the rest of his life without her. Frustrated, he stood up.

"I will return, good men," he said. "Do not talk about me when I am gone, please."

Maddoc reached for his ale cup. "No promises."

Snorting, Daniel headed off in the same direction Liselotte had gone although he was trying to make it appear as if he weren't following her. The knights at the table knew differently, however. They knew exactly where he was going.

"He is trying to fool us," Caston said, cup in hand. "He wants us to think he is not going after her."

Maddoc glanced over his shoulder, seeing Daniel disappear into the darkness of the hall. He sighed faintly; he didn't want to be here because of Daniel's infatuation for a woman but it was clear after speaking to her that there was a genuine need. He felt rather sorry for the woman. Daniel had told him the entire sordid tale that afternoon, including the deaths of her father and brother, so it was clear that she had been through a lot as of late. It was equally clear that there was something going on between her and Daniel.

Maddoc turned to say something to Caston but he held his tongue, just for a moment. He was still having a difficult time speaking to a man who looked exactly like the man he had killed last year. In fact, it had been so disturbing that he'd hardly looked at the man all afternoon, even when Caston had enthusiastically greeted him. He felt as if he were looking at a ghost and that was wholly unnerving.

It had taken all of his control not to show his confusion as well as his angst over what had easily been the most difficult situation in his life. But, much as Daniel had told him, Caston wasn't like Brighton at all. He might have looked and sounded like him, but their personalities were markedly different. That was the only reason, hours later, that Maddoc was now able to at least look at Caston. Still, the entire happenstance had him rattled.

"How long has this been going on?" he asked.

Caston took a long drink of his ale. "Since I have known them," he said. "Daniel told me that they are betrothed."

Maddoc, who had been drinking his own ale, suddenly sprayed it out all over the table at Caston's declaration. Astonished, he stared at the man as he wiped his lips. "*Betrothed?*" he repeated. "Daniel?"

Caston chuckled at Maddoc's surprised reaction. "So he told me," he said. "He said that Lady Liselotte's father offered him her hand in marriage."

Maddoc was beside himself, much more animated than was usual. "*Him?*" he said. "Are we speaking of the same Daniel de Lohr?"

Caston's eyes narrowed, good-naturedly. "I take it that you are shocked by this."

Maddoc's eyebrows lifted, genuinely speechless for a moment. "Shocked is not an adequate term," he said. "I have known Daniel since we were lads. He will never marry anyone. Ever."

Caston grinned. "I could be wrong, but I have seen men in love before and Daniel has all the signs," he said. "See if you do not agree. You have only been here a short while, but mark my words. Daniel is in love with her."

Maddoc just stared at him. Then, he picked up the ale pitcher and drank directly from it. "Good God," he hissed, fortifying himself for what was to come. "Caston, I think you'd better tell me everything."

As Caston relayed what he'd seen over the past several weeks, Daniel was heading out of the hall, following the path he thought Liselotte might have taken. The hall was warm from the bodies crammed inside, and smoky from the fire pit in the center of the room, so when Daniel emerged into the cold night, it was brisk and refreshing. He headed straight for the kitchen, seeing the spit with the cow roasting upon it, and he could see people moving around in the kitchen structure back behind it.

As he came near, he could see Liselotte helping one of the servants with the ale that was being served. She was ladling it out of a bucket and into pitchers. She had her back turned to him as he came up behind her.

"Leese," he said quietly. "I have a need to speak with you."

Startled by the sound of his voice, the ale in the ladle spilled out onto the ground before Liselotte was able to get it back into the bucket. Wiping her hands on her apron, she faced him nervously.

"Of course," she said. "What about?"

Daniel didn't say anything for a moment. Looking into her face, he could see how jittery she was. His appearance had her nervous. Gently, he took her elbow.

"Come with me," he said quietly.

Liselotte refused to go. She firmly pulled her elbow out of his grip.

"I will not," she said. "Anything you have to say to me, you can say it here."

Daniel tried not to become frustrated. He scratched his head. "I do not wish for others to hear what I have to say to you," he said. "Will you please come with me now?"

Liselotte backed away. "Nay, Daniel," she said quietly. "I will not go away with you where you can steal kisses and ply me with sweet words. If you have something to say to me, please say it now."

He sighed heavily, looking into features that were creased with a wary, yet stubborn, expression. He could read the hurt all over her. She wasn't going to go with him and he didn't want to create a scene, so he simply lowered his voice and spoke quietly.

"I am sorry if I hurt you today," he said softly. "Liselotte, you know I would not knowingly hurt you for the world."

He could see her eyes as they began to water. She fought off the tears. "It does not matter," she said. "You told me that you were not the marrying kind and I should have listened. But I had hoped you would have changed your mind. I thought you might have. I was a fool to think such things."

He sighed heavily. "Nay, you were not a fool," he said, "because you were not far from the truth. When I came to Shadowmoor, you were right when you said that it was a project to serve my pride. I wanted to make it great and strong again. I wanted to impress you. And then, I had every intention of moving on, leaving great and wonderful stories of Daniel de Lohr who had brought Shadowmoor back to greatness. So, in that aspect, you were correct. But in my haste to make myself a great and powerful restorer of men's souls, something happened. A beautiful and tragic young woman somehow managed to sneak her way into my heart, which is strange considering my heart is protected by walls stronger and greater than Shadowmoor's enormous walls. My heart is a fortress unto itself. But, somehow, you managed to breach that fortress. Does that make sense?"

Liselotte was looking at him with wide, dubious eyes. When he asked his question, she looked rather confused. "I… I do not know," she said. "I suppose I understand. But what does it all mean?"

He rubbed a hand over his face, wearily. This entire situation was draining everything within him. He was trying to maintain control over something that could not be controlled. He was trying to control emotions that would not be contained.

"It means that I cannot leave you," he said. He looked at her, sorrow and confusion on his face. "I may not be the marrying kind but I will not let someone else marry you. I could never live with myself if I did."

Liselotte didn't want to hold out any hope that what he said was true but it was difficult. She could feel hope building within her.

"What are you saying?" she whispered.

He shook his head, refusing to look at her. Then, he reached out and pulled her into his arms, holding her so tightly that he heard her grunt from the force of his embrace. Face buried in the side of her head, he inhaled deeply, experiencing her scent and knowing that he could never be without it. Suddenly, he felt weak and powerful all at the same time.

Is that what love does to a man?

"I do not know if you will have me," he murmured against her head. "I have done things I am not very proud of, Leese. I have toyed with women, robbed them of their virtue and then congratulated myself because I was not punished for it. My father has paid off fathers of young women who were compromised by me. I had little respect for women in general, other than those in my family, until I met you. And now… now I have met a woman of such strength and virtue, and I feel utterly unworthy of her. Mayhap that is why I told you I am not the marrying kind. Who would have someone like me?"

Liselotte held him tightly. "I would," she said quietly. "I would have you without question. It does not matter what you have done in the past, Daniel. All that matters is what you have done since I have known you, and, in that time, you have proven yourself to be a man of great bravery and feeling and generosity. I cannot help but love you."

He pulled back to look at her, his hands on her face. "Then you do love me?"

She sighed, feeling his warm palms against her cheeks, melting into him. "Of course I do."

He kissed her forehead, her lips. "I have never been in love before but I suspect that is what I am feeling in my heart," he said. "Be patient with me, Leese. Be patient as I explore what I am feeling for you, for this is all quite new. I am not as brave as you are in expressing my feelings. But know that I will never leave you, ever, and I will be the man you will marry."

It was everything she wanted to hear. The joy in her heart was indescribable. "And I will love you until the end of time and beyond that, still," she whispered. "I will be a good and true wife, Daniel. I swear that you shall want for nothing."

He kissed her again, pulling her into a crushing embrace right there in the kitchen yard as servants worked around them, looking at the pair and giggling. But Daniel didn't care; he knew he loved the woman and he didn't care if the entire world knew that. Everything he was feeling for her was coming full circle, making itself plain to him. At that moment, he felt stronger than he ever had.

He felt joy beyond compare.

"Come back to the hall," he said against her lips. "I want you by my side tonight. Will you do this?"

Dazed, Liselotte nodded. "As you wish, my love."

My love. Daniel had heard those words before where they pertained to him but they had never meant anything to him until now. Now, those two little words meant everything.

With a grin, Daniel led Liselotte back into the hall.

CHAPTER SIXTEEN

DANIEL DE LOHR was in for a surprise.

Astride his expensive horse and dressed in robes of leather and fur, Bramley could only smile smugly to himself, knowing what news he was bringing to de Lohr and Shadowmoor. It was everything he'd hoped for from Henry and more besides.

With him, he carried a missive from the king that was directed at de Lohr. It was in response to the missive Bramley had sent to Henry those weeks ago, telling him that de Lohr had usurped Brynner l'Audacieux's rightful place at Shadowmoor. It had come only two days ago, well after the fight that had taken Brynner's life. Consequently, what Henry didn't know was that Daniel had killed Brynner in that skirmish, but that didn't matter at this point. Bramley finally had what he wanted.

He had Shadowmoor.

Heading north from Bramley Castle under fair skies and strong winds, Bramley had most of his one hundred-man army with him. He didn't think he would need them but he wanted to have a show of force in case de Lohr wasn't willing to surrender the fortress. That would be foolish, of course, unless de Lohr wasn't afraid of the king or his army, because if he didn't surrender Shadowmoor, then military might was the next step. The very thought made Bramley smile.

All of the harassment over the past four years couldn't accomplish what one small piece of vellum could. Bramley was coming to think that he should have gotten Henry involved long ago, but he supposed it really didn't matter. Now he had what he wanted but once he claimed Shadowmoor, he was going to write to Henry and tell him that Netherghyll was allied with de Lohr and must therefore be punished. He wasn't going to let Baron Cononley get away from this situation unscathed. He would suggest to Henry, of course, that Cononley was untrustworthy and therefore unfit to continue as High Sheriff of West Yorkshire. Bramley thought that title had a rather nice ring to it and would graciously suggest himself as Cononley's successor.

All was going as it should, in his favor, and as he and his men began the trek up Rombald's Moor, to Shadowmoor at the top of the peak, he thought the day was rather beautiful. The sun was shining and there was no rain in sight. Not even a cloud. It would be a fine day for a wedding, which was what he intended to do with Lady Liselotte. According to Henry's missive, she belonged to him now and he would marry her this very day and take his pleasure with her as he'd so wanted to do. It was difficult to lust over a woman for four years and never even have a taste of her. Tonight, he would not only taste, he would gorge himself. Aye, he should have involved Henry in this situation long ago.

Finally, it was coming to an end.

As they mounted the hill, he knew that the Shadowmoor sentries could see him. He didn't care. They were a bunch of weak fools, anyway. Bramley had stayed away from Shadowmoor over the past couple of weeks, ever since the beating he'd been dealt in Siglesdene, but his men had still gone out on regular patrols and it was la Londe and de Witt who told him that Netherghyll had stationed some troops at Shadowmoor. They hadn't seen many men but they'd seen enough to know that Netherghyll was involving itself in a situation they had no business being a part of. It was all part of that punishing Bramley had been considering towards them and he decided, as he drew closer to the fortress, that he would, indeed, seek Henry's wrath against them. Everyone involved must be punished, including the House of de Lohr.

But that would be a bit trickier to achieve. Even Bramley knew how powerful the House of de Lohr was and how important they were to Henry. Bramley didn't really think Henry would punish the de Lohr brothers but Bramley was going to see to it that the de Lohr who held Shadowmoor was punished. The man had usurped the command of the fortress and taken what did not belong to him. That was grounds for punishment, indeed.

They were all fantasy scenarios that Bramley worked up in his mind as they approached Shadowmoor, a world where he could take what he wanted and punish whom he pleased. He was a bit of a madman that way and all of his men knew it, for it was all about revenge for Bramley. After the beating de Lohr had dealt him in Siglesdene those weeks ago, resulting in Brynner l'Audacieux's death, vengeance was all he could speak of, only this time, he had Henry's blessing.

No one, not even a de Lohr, would refuse the king.

So he rode up to the gates of Shadowmoor like a conquering hero, yelling at the men at the gate to produce de Lohr immediately. There was a good deal of hissing and scattering, men running about now that Bramley had made an appearance. He knew they were rattled, which pleased him greatly. This moment was about to be a tremendous triumph for him and he was eager to savor every second of it.

But the men at the gates didn't seem to be producing de Lohr fast enough and Bramley continued to shout at them. La Londe and de Witt even began to shout at them, with la Londe dismounting his horse and going right up to the gate to shout at the men inside. But the moment he went up to the gate and got a good look at the interior of Shadowmoor, he suddenly backed off. Eyes wide, he looked again and it was that second look that sent him rushing to Bramley's side.

"My lord," he hissed. "We may have a problem."

Bramley frowned. "What problem?" he demanded. "There is no problem. Where is de Lohr?"

La Londe wouldn't be brushed off so easily. "My lord," he said again, more firmly. "The entire bailey is full of fighting me. It looks as if an army has come to Shadowmoor and is lodged within her bosom."

Confusion rippled across Bramley's features. "An army?" he repeated. "What do you mean?"

"Precisely that, my lord. There is a big army housed within Shadowmoor. I suggest we leave immediately."

Bramley's confusion turned to shock. "But… how can that be?" he asked. "You have been patrolling Shadowmoor and the surrounding areas. How could an army slip by you and into Shadowmoor?"

La Londe was very, very nervous. "We have only had a few patrols out," he said, running his hand through his dirty hair. "Because we know de Lohr has gone to Siglesdene, we have only been concentrating on the east side of the moor. We've not run a patrol along the west side in a week at the very least. It is very possible that they came from that direction and we simply didn't see them."

Bramley looked at the man, dumbfounded. "What do you mean you have only run a few patrols?" he asked. "That was not my order."

It wasn't. It had been la Londe who had ordered fewer patrols and now he was forced to explain himself. "We took a very bad beating in Siglesdene two weeks ago," he said defensively. "If a patrol ran into de Lohr and his men, what then? Do we take another beating and lose more men? I ran fewer patrols simply to keep an eye on the activity at Shadowmoor whilst you sat in your solar and drank. Running more patrols would not have prevented an army from reaching Shadowmoor; it would simply have gotten us all captured, or worse."

Bramley was beginning to grow angry. "I have been waiting for Henry's reply these past weeks," he said, defending himself for the fact that he had gotten drunk every day since the events at Siglesdene, ashamed of the beating he had taken and certain that he was back to the beginning as far as trying to gain control of Shadowmoor. "I did not give you permission to run fewer patrols."

La Londe looked at him in disgust. He was only serving the man because he was a mercenary and Bramley paid him well. He didn't have to like him. "Be that as it may, my lord, there is an army inside of

Shadowmoor," he said. "I suggest we leave very quickly."

Bramley nearly refused. It was on the tip of his tongue. But then he looked around at the men he'd brought with him and there weren't nearly enough to stand up to an army. Torn, and growing nervous because la Londe was nervous, he was about to give an order to retreat when he heard commotion at Shadowmoor's old iron gate. He turned just in time to see de Lohr standing there, on the other side of the gate. And there were heavily-armed men with him.

"I am surprised to see you here, Bramley," he said, "or Roland. Or Fitzroy. Or whatever you want me to call you. What do you want?"

Daniel always had a knack for greeting Bramley in the most humiliating way possible. Embarrassed, Bramley's anger returned.

"You will not be so smug when I tell you why I have come," he said. "You would be wise to vacate Shadowmoor now, de Lohr. Make it easy on yourself."

Daniel simply looked at the man through the iron grate. "*What* do you want?"

It was that question again. Inflamed, Bramley bailed off his horse and stumbled, looking like an idiot when he fell to one knee. Standing up, he brushed off his knee and stomped over to his saddlebag, untying the sack and pulling forth a large, yellowed roll of vellum. Holding it tightly, he stomped over to the gate, remaining out of arm's reach. La Londe and de Witt were close behind him as he held up the missive.

"Get a good look at this, de Lohr," he said. "This will change your life today. This is a message from Henry. In it, he declares that Shadowmoor belongs to me, as does Lady Liselotte. By royal decree, she is now my betrothed. Unless you want royal troops here to lay siege to Shadowmoor, I suggest you vacate the fortress immediately."

Daniel didn't change expression but his hand came out from the iron bars. "Let me see it."

Bramley took a step towards him, unrolling it. "Look at it," he said, holding it up for Daniel to see. "Read his words and note his royal seal. Ah, you were so very smug with your thievery of Shadowmoor, but no longer. It now officially belongs to me and I want you out. And where is my bride? If you have compromised her, I will have you brought up on charges of thievery!"

Daniel could see the words on the vellum and he could, indeed, see the royal seal. After the events of the previous night, after declaring his love for Liselotte, it had been a glorious evening and an even more glorious morning. He'd awoken early in spite of the fact that he'd had too much to drink the night before, dressing quickly and heading to the kitchen where he knew Liselotte would be. She had been helping the cook with the bread dough but she had spared Daniel a few moments of her time and a sweet good morning kiss.

It had been one of the best mornings of his life as he'd watched her work in the kitchen, thinking all the while that she now belonged to him. Finally, a woman he could love.

Someone that belonged utterly to him, and he to her.

But now, it seemed that glorious morning might be in jeopardy, at least somewhat. As he looked at the vellum, several things came to mind, not the least of which was killing Bramley and all of his men and disposing of the bodies as if they had never existed. Bramley was threatening his happiness and he didn't consider the measures to prevent that too drastic. He struggled not to appear shocked or off-balance by the missive that very much looked like the real thing.

He refused to believe it.

"You could have easily forged that, Bramley Roland Fitzroy," he said. "You have had enough time since the last time I saw you to forge a document of this type. Do you really expect me to believe you?"

Bramley scowled. "You must believe me, for this is real," he insisted, taking another step closer to the grate while still holding up the vellum. "Look at it! That is Henry's stamp!"

"Another forgery."

"Are you so much the fool?"

He had gotten too close and Daniel reached out, as fast as lightning, and snatched the missive from him. As Bramley yelped with surprise,

Daniel yanked the vellum inside the iron bars where he and Caston and Maddoc inspected it closely. They moved away from the grate so Bramley couldn't hear them as they looked over the official document, dissecting every inch of it.

"That is Henry's seal," Maddoc said quietly. "I have seen it many times."

Daniel nodded. "As have I," he murmured, his heart sinking. "Damn Bramley! Is it possible that the man really does have some connection to Henry? I had been hoping all along that he had been lying."

Caston was reading the contents of the missive over Daniel's shoulder. "You are ordered by royal command to surrender Shadowmoor and Lady Liselotte to Roland Fitzroy, Lord Bramley," he read aloud. "The lands, property, and lady rightfully belong to him and you are ordered to comply."

Daniel drew in a deep pensive breath as he drank in the words; suddenly, the morning had turned very bad, indeed. He knew, as he lived and breathed, that this had been sent from Henry and a royal missive was not meant to be disobeyed. It was a terrible turn of events in the battle for Shadowmoor and even as he read the words that had been carefully drawn by a royal scribe, he knew that he would not comply.

There was no doubt in his mind.

"Well," he said thoughtfully as he passed the missive over to Maddoc. "Let us discuss our options. I have no intention of complying so we can do one of two things; either kill Bramley and all of his men and declare we never saw the missive, or we can simply refuse to believe this is from Henry."

Maddoc's gaze lingered on the vellum. "I am in favor killing the man and everyone connected with him," he said. "If you refuse to believe this is from Henry, he will simply send the king another missive to that effect and Henry will send an army up here to lay siege. However, if Henry receives nothing from Bramley, ever again, he will assume that the situation has resolved itself. Truthfully, Danny – this is a very tiny battle in a reign that has been full of them. I cannot imagine Henry will give this situation any more consideration than this missive."

Daniel pondered that. "If we eliminate Bramley, then we are not directly disobeying a royal decree."

"Nay, we are not."

"We are simply eliminating the source of friction."

"Amazing how your mind works."

Daniel smiled humorlessly at Maddoc before turning to Caston. "If we do this, you will not be involved," he said. "You will take your Netherghyll troops and go home. I do not want you implicated in anything."

Caston looked surprised. "I am not going anywhere," he said stubbornly. "I am part of this whether or not you like it."

"I do *not* like it. You and your father have been far too good to Shadowmoor for you to be pulled into any murder plot. This is something I must do and I cannot let you assume any blame. Please, Caston; go home."

Caston shook his head. "I will not," he said firmly. "Until I met you and became involved with Shadowmoor, I had been leading a fairly useless life. I was helping my father manage his lands, delivering missives for him, and other worthless things. I am at Netherghyll because my brother is not; I have no choice. Brighton left to find fame and fortune, leaving me behind to tend lands that will become his upon my father's death. I have been working all of these years for something that will not even be mine. It is a desolate feeling, I assure you. But when I met you and became involved in Shadowmoor, I felt like I was doing something good, as if I had found a sense of purpose. In a sense, Shadowmoor is mine just as much as it is yours. I will not leave something I have worked hard to rebuild, much the same as you feel. So do not ask me again to leave because I will not. I will fight for Shadowmoor until the very end."

"You would fight for a fortress that does not belong to you?"

"I would fight for my friends."

Daniel was touched by his speech, glancing over at Maddoc to see how he was reacting. Caston had brought up Brighton and that was always a great source of uneasiness, especially to Maddoc. He tried to read the man's expression.

Daniel hadn't had the chance to speak to Maddoc since his arrival yesterday with regards to Caston, or his feelings on the man, but Daniel had seen Maddoc's interaction with him the night before and it seemed that he harbored no aversion or ill-will towards Caston in spite of Maddoc's relationship to the man's brother. But he expected nothing less of Maddoc, for the man was more honorable than most. He'd done what Daniel had asked; he'd kept his mouth shut about Brighton, at least so far, and hadn't judged Caston by his brother's actions. Therefore, Daniel was interested to see how Maddoc would react to Caston's declaration.

Of a declaration of undying friendship from the brother of the man he killed. It was as touching in nature as it was complicated.

And, truthfully, sad.

"Caston," Daniel finally said. "Your motives are altruistic and true, but you do understand that by participating here, you could possibly bring Henry's wrath upon you."

"I understand."

"And that does not concern you? Mayhap you should discuss it with your father."

"My father would say the same thing."

Daniel looked at Maddoc for support, but Maddoc was looking at Caston. Daniel wondered if, deep down, he was still seeing that man he'd killed when he looked at that man's twin. It was hard to know what Maddoc was seeing, for his thoughts ran very still and very deep.

"Maddoc?" Daniel asked quietly. "What say you?"

Maddoc's gaze lingered on Caston for a few moments. Truthfully, Daniel's question was an interesting one, at least from his perspective.

He still wasn't over the shock of seeing a man who looked exactly like the man who had nearly taken his life last year, but in spending the previous evening with Caston and coming to know him slightly, he could already see that Caston was nothing like his brother had been.

Caston seemed thoughtful and honorable, as evidenced by his willingness to involve himself in a situation that could quite possibly get him into trouble with the king. Only a selfless man would say such a thing. Maddoc was starting to think that between Brighton and Caston, Caston was the only one who had inherited any good qualities.

Perhaps all of the de Royans weren't as wicked as Brighton had been, but that would truly take time to determine.

At least, he was willing to try.

"He understands what he getting himself in to," he said, looking at Daniel. "This is his area and his family is the law here. I say he has just as much right to subdue Bramley as any of us do."

Daniel lifted his eyebrows. "That is a good point," he said. "As the High Sheriff of West Yorkshire, your father has every right to administer justice."

Caston nodded, considering that very thing. "Agreed," he said. "We spoke of this last night, knowing that pride kept Lord Etzel from asking for help. Daniel, since you speak for Shadowmoor these days, will you now ask my father for help?"

Daniel nodded fervently. "All that he can provide."

"Then it shall be done. And I am staying to fulfill my father's obligations as sheriff."

It was settled, then. No one was leaving so long as Bramley was at the gates, demanding Shadowmoor.

"So what do we do?" Maddoc asked the obvious. "What help will Netherghyll and the House of de Lohr give? Do we erase Bramley from this earth?"

Daniel thought a moment. For him, it was a very serious moment in his life, something that, once acted upon, would change the rest of his life forever. He knew that and did not take the decision lightly. Quietly, he cleared his throat.

"As I said, I have no intention with complying with this order, and most especially not in turning Liselotte over to Bramley," he muttered. "She and I will be married at some point and I will not hand the man my future wife. Therefore, I am fighting for her. I will fight until the death, even against Henry."

Maddoc stared at him. It was the admission he'd been waiting for since Caston had told him of Daniel's intentions towards the lady last night. In fact, he looked a little dumbfounded.

"Caston told me you had intentions towards the lady but I doubted him until this very moment," he said, fighting off a grin. "So that is what this is all about. You *are* doing it for a woman."

Daniel nodded, trying not to look too embarrassed. "Not just any woman," he said. "My future wife."

"Are you serious, Danny?"

"I have never been more serious in my life."

Maddoc couldn't help the grin now. He actually started laughing, which was rare for him. He put a big hand to Daniel's cheek in an affectionate gesture. "You fool," he said. "You silly besotted fool. I cannot believe my ears."

Daniel was trying to keep a straight face, for this was serious business. Usually, it was him mercilessly teasing his friends or making jokes. Now, the situation had turned on him and he was trying very hard not to give in to Maddoc's teasing. It was a somewhat humiliating experience for him.

"Believe it," he said. "You love your wife and would do anything for her. I would do the same for Liselotte. There is no great mystery to that."

Maddoc could see that he was growing insulted by the teasing and he stopped laughing, trying to straighten up. "It is just that I am very happy for you, Danny," he said. "My wife has brought me more joy than I ever knew to exist. I am so very glad that you have found a woman you can love. Your parents will be utterly thrilled to hear this, you know. Your father might even cry."

Daniel did smile, then. "It is not as bad as all that," he said. "They knew I would marry, eventually."

Maddoc snorted. "Eventually?" he said in disbelief. "For you, eventually could be when you are old and gray and have no one to wipe the drool off your chin or feed you mushed foods. Your father was hoping for a grandson from you, an heir, before he died, so this will be tremendous news to him. I am incredibly happy for you, Danny, truly. Liselotte must be a woman among women."

Daniel nodded. "She is," he said. "I am mad about the woman and that fat bastard beyond the gate will never get his hands on her. He has caused her, and Shadowmoor, enough trouble. He is responsible for the death of Etzel l'Audacieux at the very least. Caston, is that enough to arrest the man?"

Caston lifted his eyebrows. "Unless you have proof that he is responsible for Lord Etzel's death, it is not enough," he said. "The only person who could testify to that is dead. But for the harassment he has dealt the denizens of Shadowmoor, he should be punished at the very least."

Maddoc was nodding his head in agreement as Caston spoke. "Thrown in the vault and then set fire to the vault," he said, looking at Daniel. "If you do not end this now, he will haunt you the rest of your days. You will never know peace. I seem to remember someone giving me the same advice about…."

He froze, suddenly realizing who he was speaking in front of. He was about to mention Brighton de Royans by name, for when Brighton tried to kill him and Maddoc had the opportunity to fight back, Daniel had advised him to kill the man because if he did not, he would never know peace. He would be looking over his shoulder every day for the rest of his life, waiting for Brighton to pop up and try to steal his wife from him again. It had been Daniel's advice that had contributed to Brighton's demise.

Daniel, too, was looking at Maddoc, trying to conceal his horror at what he knew Maddoc was about to say. Very quickly, he sought to finish the man's sentence before Caston asked any questions about it.

"I gave you advice about an enemy, Maddoc," he said, trying to cover. "An enemy much the same as Bramley. If I allow Bramley to live, then I will only know turmoil. The man has committed so many atrocities against Shadowmoor that it is justice we will be dealing out. Think of your oath as a knight, Maddoc. What does it say?"

Maddoc recollected the words easily. "I do swear by the Eternal Power of the Trinity, to be both a true and chivalric Knight, to obey my Commanders and to aid my brethren," he recited quietly. "I also swear by all that is holy and dear unto me, to aid those less fortunate than I, to relieve the distress of the world and to fulfill my knightly obligations. This oath do I give of my own free and independent will, so help me God."

Daniel smiled at the recitation of the chivalric oath. "To aid those less fortunate," he repeated softly. "To relieve the distress of the world. Is that not what we will be doing? It is right there in the oath."

Maddoc nodded firmly, looking to Caston. "It *is* in our oath."

Caston nodded as well. It seemed that there was no question as to what they needed to do. The weak must be protected and Daniel must fight for his lady at all costs.

It might be very costly, indeed.

"Now what, Danny?" Maddoc asked, turning to eye Bramley, still standing at the gate. "Do we open the gates and bring him in?"

Daniel turned to look at Bramley. "Would it really be that easy?" he muttered. "Inviting the man in under the pretense of surrendering Shadowmoor and then cutting his throat when his guard is down?"

Maddoc crossed his big arms, eyeing Daniel and Caston. "It may or may not be that easy," he said. "Let us prepare for the worst. I will go and find de Russe, and we will gather the men and prepare them for the ambush. Danny, I suggest you tell Bramley that we are preparing to turn the fortress over to him. Give me ten minutes to spread the word amongst my men and put them into position. Caston, you had better let your men know as well."

"Bramley may be too smart to simply walk in," Caston said pointedly. "What do we do if he refuses to enter?"

"Then we hunt him down like an animal," Daniel said. "Whether he dies in the bailey of Shadowmoor or we are forced to chase him down, out there on the moors, either way he dies."

It was settled. Now, they had to put their plan into motion, the plan that would once and for all rid them of Bramley and his poison. Up until this moment, until the missive from Henry, Daniel was simply hoping the man would fade away and leave them in peace, but it was clear that he would never leave them in peace. By bringing them the missive from Henry, Bramley had signed his own death warrant because they were all banded together to rid their shire of the man once and for all. Today Shadowmoor, tomorrow Netherghyll. After that, there was no knowing where his greed would stop. Therefore, they had to stop it while they still could.

Now, the time was right. They would wipe Bramley from the earth along with his men, and they would pretend they'd never seen the missive declaring that Shadowmoor, and Liselotte, belonged to Bramley. At this moment, Daniel finally knew what it meant to do anything for the love of a woman. The wanderer with the bachelor's soul had transformed into something more than a man, more than a knight. He was now a warrior driven by love, the most powerful force in the world.

Now, he understood.

And that brought him great peace and confidence in what needed to be done. As Maddoc and Caston went to collect the men for the coming battle, Daniel made his way over to the gate. Bramley was still there, his angry face evident in the open slats between the iron bars. Daniel still had the missive in his hand as he approached.

"Well?" Bramley demanded. "Are you satisfied that it is real?"

Daniel nodded. "It is real."

Bramley's expression turned triumphant. "Then you have until sunset to get out of my fortress," he said. "Get out and take all of your men with you."

Daniel cocked an eyebrow. "For a man who is outnumbered ten to one, you speak boldly, Bramley Roland Fitzroy."

"Stop calling me that!"

"Aren't those your names?"

Bramley scowled. "Nay," he said through clenched teeth. "You may call me the Lord of Shadowmoor now."

Daniel didn't say anything to that statement, but inside, it was the spark that lit the fire, and that fire burned hot. He silently indicated for the men at the gate to open it, and they dutifully complied, rolling back the old iron chains as they creaked and groaned, slowly opening the ancient gates that had stood for so very long.

Daniel stood at the apex of the opening gates, right in the center, so as they rolled open, it was just him standing there, alone. Bramley, now able to step inside the fortress, did so even though la Londe and de Witt were pulling at him, advising him not to do so. He ignored his hired henchmen, charging into Shadowmoor as if he owned the place.

Finally, it was everything he had been waiting for.

"Get out of my fortress, de Lohr," Bramley commanded.

Daniel folded his big arms around his chest. "Make me."

Bramley's eyebrows shot up, gravely insulted. "You would deny me?" he said. "Even with Henry's missive in your hand, you would deny me? I told you to get out. I meant it."

Daniel simply stood there. "I will when I am ready."

Bramley, infuriated, marched up on Daniel as la Londe and de Witt followed him nervously. Their liege had stepped into the lion's den and didn't seem to care, but they cared a great deal. They were heavily outmanned and they knew, instinctively, that this was a trap.

Something bad was about to happen.

Something bad, indeed. As Bramley drew close, Daniel could see that the man was balling a fist to strike him. Therefore, he was prepared. When Bramley came close enough and lifted his hand, Daniel lashed out a massive fist and caught Bramley right in the face.

The man fell to the ground and from that point, the fight was on.

CHAPTER SEVENTEEN

EVEN AS OUTMANNED as Bramley and his men were, the fight wasn't as simple as one would have expected. Bramley had hired mercenaries as his men-at-arms, and his knights, so these were seasoned fighters who fought dirty when the situation called for it.

This situation called for it.

They went after the knights first, the head of the command structure, which was actually very astute. They may have been mercenaries, but they knew battle. They knew how to destroy a command structure and cripple an army. As Bramley scrambled to get off of the ground where Daniel's blow had sent him, la Londe and a few of Bramley's men-at-arms went after Daniel while de Witt and several more men went after Caston. Seeing this, Maddoc and Marc de Russe unsheathed their broadswords and began swinging, killing men that got in their way and tossing aside the injured.

De Lohr men and Netherghyll troops closed in as well but there was a problem with that; the two armies didn't know each other very well and it was difficult to know precisely who the enemy was. It turned into a bit of a mess with three armies all struggling with each other in the center of Shadowmoor's bailey. With Daniel and Caston in the midst of a multi-man attack, Maddoc and Marc began to see how the armies were clashing. Some de Lohr men were accidentally beating up on Netherghyll men.

As Maddoc plowed forward to help Daniel and Caston, Marc backed off of the fight and went to settle the confusion among the men. Pulling some of his senior sergeants out of the fray, he pointed out the difference between the Netherghyll men, who were uniformly equipped, and the Bramley men, who were not. The senior sergeants then had the duty of moving forward to explain to the de Lohr and Netherghyll men what they were looking for. Because the brawl had happened so fast, there hadn't been time for Maddoc and Caston to explain the situation to all of the men. Now, word was spreading slowly and the focus of the battle was shifting.

After that, many of Bramley's men were subdued or killed right away. The de Lohr and Netherghyll armies, working in a team, were a fearsome thing. Meanwhile, Maddoc had managed to make it to Daniel's side. Daniel had a bloodied lip, and he'd taken a few blows, but he was whole for the most part. He'd been set upon by at least ten men, including la Londe, but in the years to come, that amount would increase to twenty or thirty men. And Maddoc would insist that he had single-handedly saved Daniel from death. But all of that aside, the real goal was to get to Bramley.

Leaving Maddoc to trade vicious blows with la Londe, Daniel went on the hunt for his target. The last he'd seen of Bramley, the man had been on the ground, sent there by one of Daniel's heavy hits. But now Bramley wasn't where Daniel had left him and as he emerged from the tumultuous gathering of men, looking like the roiling sea during a storm, he caught sight of Bramley between the area of battle and the keep.

And he had the missive in his hand.

Daniel was seized with fear when he saw that Bramley was closer to the keep, and kitchens and hall, than he was. Liselotte was over there, somewhere. The last he had seen of her was near the kitchens. He hadn't had the time to seek her out when Bramley had been sighted so he could only pray she'd gone into the keep and locked herself in, but he couldn't be sure. Wherever she was, he had to make sure he got to her before Bramley did. He broke into a run, heading for Bramley, but Bramley saw him coming. He had his sword in hand, holding it defensively.

"Stop where you are, de Lohr!" he shouted. "Come no further. This is my fortress now and you are commanded to leave. If you leave now, I will not tell Henry how you defied his command. Take your men and go!"

Daniel wasn't in any mood for the man's buffoonery. "I am not leaving," he said. "And I have told you this before. Do you think you are the only one who had Henry's ear? My uncle and father have far more influence with the man than you could ever hope to have. Right now, my men are killing every one of your men. Their bodies will be in a burning pyre outside of the walls by nightfall and you will join them. I am at an end tolerating you and your foolery. This will end today."

Bramley seemed to be pondering what Daniel was saying; no more jesting, no more flippant attitude. The man was deadly serious, in every way, and Bramley struggled not to let fear get the better of him.

"You have no right," he hissed. "You killed Brynner and for all I know, it was you who killed Etzel. It is you who have caused terrible tragedy to Shadowmoor, more than I ever could."

"Lies."

"I may have taken their food, but you took their lives!"

Daniel raised his sword. "I will not debate this with a madman," he said. "I hope you are right with God, Bramley Roland Fitzroy, because you shall soon be meeting Him personally. You can explain to Him why you did what you did and how your deeds justified the end, how you bribed Brynner with drink to kill his own father and how you starved the people of Shadowmoor to the brink of destruction simply because you wanted what they had. Is that what you have always done? Persecuted those who have denied you? Your mother was not only a whore, she was an evil bitch as well to raise a son like you."

He was saying it to deliberately provoke Bramley, to try to coerce the man to make a stupid move. But Bramley didn't move; he stood there with a red face, his mouth working angrily.

"You know nothing of me," he hissed. "You will not slander my mother, you bastard."

Daniel raised an eyebrow. "It is not I who is the bastard," he said. "I believe that title falls to your sister. Quite a family, Bramley Roland Fitzroy – a bitch for a mother and a bastard for a sister. And now a fool for a brother."

Bramley, for all of his foolishness, seemed to sense what Daniel was doing. He was still red in the face, and still quite upset, but he held his ground. He didn't move. After a moment, he held up the missive.

"That may be," he said. "But I have been legally granted what you so badly want. What does that make you?"

Daniel smiled thinly; he could see they weren't getting anywhere and it was time to end this. He was ready to be finished, with all of it.

"Your worst nightmare."

With that, he charged Bramley, who tried to hold him off, but Daniel was stronger than Bramley was. Two crushing thrusts on Bramley's sword and Bramley stumbled back, nearly falling. But Daniel didn't let him rest; he continued to charge madly, beating Bramley down, hardly giving the man time to recover before he was dealing out several more blows that sent Bramley to the ground.

Now, it was getting serious as Bramley rolled away from Daniel's thrust just in time to avoid being gored in the neck. Bramley grabbed a handful of dirt and threw it up into Daniel's face, trying to blind him, but Daniel had been far enough way that the dirt didn't make it into his eyes. He grabbed for Bramley, catching the man on the shoulder, but Bramley brought his sword around and narrowly missed cutting off Daniel's left hand.

On and on it went as the two of them rolled through the bailey near the keep, viciously fighting. Bramley was a surprisingly strong opponent, much to Daniel's displeasure, because he'd hoped to make short work of him. Somewhere, somehow, Bramley had been given decent training because he knew how to handle himself in a fight. As far as

Daniel was concerned, it wouldn't save his life – it would only prolong it.

The death watch began.

Most of the fighting in the bailey with the armies had come to a conclusion. La Londe lay dead of a sword strike to the neck, courtesy of Maddoc, while de Witt had come to a gruesome end when Caston gutted him. Nearly all of Bramley's men had been subdued or killed, and those who were still attempting to fight were being cornered and forced to surrender. Dead and wounded littered the dirt of the bailey.

Maddoc, Caston, and Marc de Russe had made their way over to the battle between Daniel and Bramley, watching Daniel deal blow after heavy blow and watching Bramley grow progressively weaker. They wouldn't interfere, of course, but it was rather astonishing to watch Daniel's ferocity when dealing with Bramley. Daniel had always been a strong fighter, but this was different. It was more than fury behind his fight.

It was the love of a good woman.

As they watched the battle continue, they didn't notice a slender woman with bronze-colored hair standing in the kitchen yard. Liselotte had been in the kitchen when the fight had started and she had remained there, terrified, until one of the servants told her that Sir Daniel was doing battle with Bramley over by the keep. Then, she could no longer stay away.

She had to see for herself what was happening and now she stood, watching Daniel deal Bramley a nasty beating. But as she watched, she found herself wishing he would simply end it with Bramley. She thought maybe Daniel was toying with him somehow, drawing out his death to satisfy his own sense of vengeance, and she didn't like watching it one bit. What if Bramley got the upper hand? The mere thought terrified her.

But as she witnessed the beating, something more occurred to her. Daniel was intent to punish the man for everything he'd done, for the pain he caused. But the truth was that Liselotte had been dealing with that pain daily for the past four years. She'd always felt so guilty because of what Bramley had done to the people of Shadowmoor, as she'd once told Daniel, and as she watched Daniel fight on her behalf, there was something in her that felt the need to do her own fighting. As strange as it seemed, and probably as foolish as it seemed, she felt the need to settle this once and for all by herself.

She'd never had that chance. The chance to defender herself from a man who had done all he could to destroy her. He had never really wanted her; she knew that. He'd only wanted Shadowmoor and saw her as a simple way to achieve his end. But the truth was that she had only been his excuse, never his goal.

She'd been the victim of a petty vicious fool.

As she stood there and continued to observe the battle, she caught movement out of the corner of her eye and turned to see Gunnar standing there. He had two puppies in his arms, two following him, and then two goats that seemed to want to nibble on his pants. He kept pushing them away. But he, too, was watching the fight.

"Will Daniel win?" he asked.

She could hear the fear in his voice. "Aye," she replied. "He will soon."

Gunnar was mostly looking at Bramley as the man struggled against Daniel's strength. "I wanted to kill him, too," he said. "I would have killed him for you, Leese, if I was bigger."

Liselotte put her hand on her brother's head, comfortingly. "You are a very brave boy, Gunnar," she said. "I know you would have helped if you could."

Gunnar reached into his tunic, the one that Daniel had bought for him, and pulled something out of the pocket. It took Liselotte a moment to realize that it was her father's dagger, the same one Brynner had used to kill him. Because it had been Etzel's, Liselotte had given it to her younger brother as a keepsake. It had turned into Gunnar's most valued possession.

"I was going to use this on him, someday," Gunnar said. "When I got big enough, I was going to do it with Papa's knife because it would be as if Papa killed him, too."

Liselotte stared at the dagger, very sharp, and a thought occurred to her. Gunnar wasn't far wrong; using the knife that had had belonged to Etzel, that Brynner had used against his own father at Bramley's direction, would be sweet justice if the weapon were used to kill Bramley. It was a very old dagger, passed down through generations of the Lords of Shadowmoor, and as Liselotte stared at it, she knew what she needed to do. As clear as day, she knew. Generations of l'Audacieuxs were calling to her through that blade, telling her what needed to be done. For peace, for family pride, for everything, she needed to end this with her own hand. With Etzel's blade.

She needed to reclaim their honor.

Taking the blade from Gunnar, she ordered the boy to stay behind as she began to move forward, towards the fighting. She could see the three big knights standing off to the left, watching the battle, but she couldn't see Daniel from her position. The big keep was in the way. Therefore, she made her way around the keep, cautiously, to the other side where, suddenly, she had the men in her line of sight.

Daniel was dealing the man a fairly serious beating. When the sword wasn't swinging at him, the feet and fists were kicking and punching Bramley all over the place. It was clear that Bramley was exhausted and terrified, and at this point he wasn't doing much to fight back. He was simply defending himself. He was trying to get away from Daniel, stumbling away, holding up his sword to ward off Daniel's powerful blows, but little more than that. It was clear that the battle was waning.

Liselotte knew she had to act quickly if she was going to make a difference in this battle, to exact vengeance again this man who had tormented her for four years. Quickly, she moved up to the corner of the keep, peering around the side to see that Daniel and Bramley were making their way in her direction. She watched their battle stall out several feet away as Bramley tried to crawl away and Daniel simply kicked him in the gut. She was eager for them to get on with it, to come in her direction so that she could deliver the death blow to Bramley. She was afraid that if she tried to make her move now that Daniel would prevent her from doing it. Therefore, she had to wait until they were very close so Daniel couldn't stop her.

It was something she had to do.

More fighting, more kicking, and more crawling by Bramley, but the man had staggered to his feet and lurched in her direction, towards the keep. Liselotte ducked back, pressing herself right at the corner of the keep, just out of sight, but she could hear that the men were very close. She held the dagger tightly, praying for strength to do as she must, to seek vengeance for all that Bramley had done to her.

Then, the moment was upon her.

Bramley fell right by the corner of the keep, his upper torso exposed. Liselotte didn't even think about what Daniel was doing at this moment; she had seen him kick and punch so much, especially when Bramley was down, that she expected more of the same. She lifted the dagger and threw herself forward, falling atop Bramley and plunging Etzel's dagger straight into the man's neck. Blood spurted as Bramley stiffened in what was the first of his death throes.

But what she couldn't have known was that Daniel had been preparing to deliver the death blow, too. He had his sword lifted, preparing to strike, as Liselotte suddenly appeared from out of his line of sight, right at the corner of the building, and launching herself onto Bramley.

Horror filled him and he tried to stop his momentum as he brought the sword down; God help him, he tried as hard as he had ever tried for anything in his entire life. But he was moving too swiftly, and Liselotte was too close, and as she rammed the dagger into Bramley's neck, he caught her on the right side of her torso with his broadsword.

Daniel would have cut her in half had he not been trying to stop his momentum, but it wasn't enough to stop the blow completely. He cut her deeply, her screams mingling with his own, as Liselotte lay atop of the dying Bramley, bleeding heavily as Daniel realized what he had done.

After that, chaos reigned.

CHAPTER EIGHTEEN

Three Days Later

"WE SAW YOUR army approaching, my lord," Maddoc said, astonished, as he found himself speaking to his liege. "Forgive me my surprise, but what are you doing here?"

David was beyond exhausted. Pale and hacking up blood, he was in no mood for chatter or lighthearted greetings. Standing at the open gates of Shadowmoor on a cold and misty morning, he looked around at the burned bodies outside of the walls, the smell of burnt flesh heavy in the air. It was a macabre and sickening greeting.

"What in the hell is going on here?" he demanded of Maddoc. "Who *is* this?"

He was pointing to the funeral pyres, still smoldering as the smoke was trapped by the mist. Maddoc glance at them but didn't look any more than that; he had been seeing them, and smelling them, for three days.

"We have seen some action here, my lord," he said, stating the obvious. "Forgive me, but… how did you know to come here? And Lady Emilie permitted you to come with the sickness you have been suffering?"

David looked at him. "She could not stop me," he said, hacking a nasty cough. "I had to come. Daniel is involved in something serious and I would not stay away. Answer my question, Maddoc; what is going on? Where is my son?"

Maddoc could see that David was irritated, and weary, and still ill. He was drawn and very pale, especially on this cold morning. But his appearance was a great shock. "How much do you know about the situation?" he asked. "You must have received the missive from Lord Christopher. I was there when he sent it. Did he tell you to come? If he did, I was not aware."

David shook his head. "Nay," he said flatly, turning away from the gruesome sight to face his captain. "He did not tell me to come. Henry sent me here."

Maddoc's eyebrows lifted in surprise. "*Henry*, my lord?"

David nodded. "In addition to my brother's missive about this situation, I received a missive from the king telling me that my son had usurped a castle in West Yorkshire called Shadowmoor," he said, his gaze moving to the big walls of the fortress. "Henry told me that my son had stolen the property, and the heiress, from a relative named Bramley. Henry demanded I do something about it so here I am. I have ridden for several very long days to get here and I am in no mood for foolery, Maddoc. Where is my son? What is going on here?"

Maddoc understood a lot in that brief and irritated statement. "I see," he said. Then, he pointed to the smoldering bodies. "That is Bramley's army."

Shocked, David looked at the smoking piles again. He simply stared at it for a moment, wondering how he was going to tell Henry that his son had burned the king's relative's army like last night's meat. More confused than ever, and fed by his exhaustion, his frustration was evident.

"I think you had better tell me what is happening, Maddoc," he said, coughing yet again. "All of it. Why is my son making a Viking funeral out of Bramley's army?"

Maddoc could see that David wanted all of the information as quickly as he could deliver it. That was the way David's mind worked. Maddoc had been with David for many years and knew how the man operated. Therefore, he indicated for him to follow him inside the fortress.

As David went with Maddoc, Gerid, the knight who had accompanied him north, hung back to take charge of the army. The men from Canterbury were a bit on edge by the grisly sight of the burning dead, so Gerid got them moving, following their liege into the great rundown fortress that was evidently their destination. The gates opened before them like the gates to Purgatory.

Inside the fortress, things weren't much better. It was clear there had been a battle and David found himself looking around in concern. Maddoc, however, was immune to the sight. He spoke.

"I am not sure where to start, my lord, so I will simply start from the beginning," he said. "First of all, let me assure you that Daniel did not usurp or steal Shadowmoor from anyone. Quite the opposite, actually. Lord Bramley had been harassing Shadowmoor for years, burning crops and killing livestock, so much so that by the time Daniel happened across the fortress, they were starving to death because of Bramley. It is Daniel who took up the defense of Shadowmoor, reached out to a neighbor to establish an alliance, and generally try to help these people as Bramley continued to threaten and lie and harass. Bramley even managed to coerce the heir of Shadowmoor into killing his father by promising the man lands in France in exchange for Shadowmoor upon his father's death. It has been hellish for these people, my lord. Daniel was simply trying to do something good."

David wasn't surprised by the story. In fact, that was the son he knew, the man he adored. Daniel had a heart of gold and, to be truthful, David was greatly relieved. It made the long and arduous ride north worth it to hear the reality of what Daniel had involved himself in. But there was more to the story that he needed to know.

"Then why is Bramley's army burning outside of the gates?" he asked.

Maddoc sighed heavily. "This is where the tale grows unhappy, my lord," he said. "Three days ago, Bramley brought a missive from Henry awarding him Shadowmoor and the heiress."

David's brow furrowed. "You saw this missive?"

"I did, my lord."

"Was it genuine?"

"It was, my lord."

David had a sinking feeling. Not only had Henry sent a missive to him, but evidently he had sent one to Daniel as well. He wasn't sure he wanted to hear the rest but he forced himself. "Where is it?"

"Burning with the men outside of the fortress walls."

David grunted softly, briefly closing his eyes in distress. "You destroyed it?"

Maddoc nodded. "We did," he said. "It is now in ashes, as is anyone who knew about it. If Henry ever inquires, we will know nothing about it."

It seemed that they had done everything possible to ensure the message and contents and anything related to it were erased and David struggled not to become increasingly distressed over it.

"Do you think Henry will simply forget about this?" he asked. "He is not a fool, you know. He is aware of this situation and you simply seek to destroy the evidence?"

Maddoc nodded. "That would be a fair statement, my lord."

David could hardly believe what he was hearing. "Are you truly so arrogant, Maddoc?" he demanded. "You think that by burning all of the evidence, this will all simply go away? Is that really why you did it?"

Maddoc paused, facing David in the heavy mist. The weather was as gloomy as his mood. "We did it because Bramley demanded that Daniel turn the fortress and the heiress over to him but Daniel would not comply," he said, lowering his voice. "My lord, Daniel is in love with the heiress and she loves him. They plan to be married. He was not about to turn over the woman he loved to the likes of Bramley. Not even for a royal decree."

That brought David's building rage to a blinding halt. David looked at his captain, shocked by what he was hearing, for many reasons.

When he should have been gravely concerned that his son had not only disobeyed a direct order from the king but burned the evidence, he found that he was focused on something that was far more important to him, personally.

"Daniel is in *love* with her?" he repeated, astonished. "Maddoc... are we speaking of the same Daniel?"

"We are, my lord."

"My son?"

"Aye, my lord."

"The wanderer who swore I would be dead before he provided me with a grandson?"

Maddoc sighed. "Aye, my lord."

David was beside himself. A hand flew to his face in shock. "Is it true?"

"It is, my lord," Maddoc said. "But that joyful news has taken a tragic turn. When Daniel and Lord Bramley were battling to the death, right here in this very bailey, the woman that Daniel is in love with, Lady Liselotte, was badly wounded. We think she was trying to kill Bramley herself, which she accomplished, but she got in Daniel's way. He accidentally cut her, quite badly. Even now, she lies unconscious in the keep and Daniel is inconsolable. He wounded her, my lord, and he cannot forgive himself."

David was pale by the time Maddoc was finished. Hand still on his face, he turned his gaze to the big square keep looming through the fog. He was trying to take it all in, this great and terrible news, and he was having difficulty. It was all so astonishing.

"Jesus," he finally hissed. "Where is he?"

Maddoc indicated the keep. "This way, my lord."

David hacked and coughed as he followed Maddoc to the keep, entering the heavily-fortified doorway into a room that had a second room adjoining it. The second room had a fire in the hearth and as David glanced at it, he noticed a boy sitting near the fire with four puppies and two small goats. When the boy saw him, he jumped up.

"Are you another knight?" the boy asked eagerly.

David smiled faintly. "I am."

"Gunnar," Maddoc said quietly. "This is Daniel's father, the Earl of Canterbury. You must show him all due respect. My lord, this is Gunnar l'Audacieux, who is now the Lord of Shadowmoor at the deaths of his father and older brother."

David looked at Gunnar as the boy came towards him, holding a puppy. "It is an honor to meet you, young Gunnar," he said. He gestured to the dog. "That is a fine animal."

Gunnar was inspecting David with big curious eyes. He finally managed to look at the puppy because David stuck out a finger to pet the animal's head. "His name is Mark," he said. Then, he turned to point to the rest of the pack. "The other dogs are Luke, Matthew, and John. The goats are Joseph and Mary. They are my friends."

David nodded at the charming little boy. "Fine names," he said.

"Even the female dogs have male names," Maddoc leaned over to David and muttered. "And both goats are male."

David lifted his eyebrows, thinking that to be a rather funny quirk. The child had obviously had the Bible drilled into him, so much so that he was naming his animal after holy characters regardless of their sex. Reaching out, he patted the lad on the head.

"Fine animals," he repeated, but his attention was turning to the stairs that led up to the upper floors. "Again, it was a pleasure to meet you, Gunnar. I am sure I will see you soon."

Gunnar stood there, holding his puppy, as David continued to follow Maddoc and the two men proceeded up the stairs. But before they could disappear from view, Gunnar ran after them.

"Are you here to help my sister?" he asked.

David and Maddoc paused on the stairs, glancing at the boy. "Does she not have a physic?" David asked Maddoc.

Maddoc nodded. "She does, my lord."

David returned his attention to Gunnar. "All is being done to help her, boy," he said. "I am here to see my son. Do you know Daniel?"

Gunnar nodded. "He is my friend, too."

David smiled. "I am glad to hear that," he said. "He is a good friend to have."

Gunnar didn't say anything more but it was clear the wheels of his mind were working. He was a bright lad, curious as to the earl's appearance. He thought it might have something to do with his sister, as everything did these days. They were keeping Gunnar away from her so she could rest and recover, and that was difficult for Gunnar. His father was gone and now his sister was injured. He felt very alone these days. Silently, he turned and went back into the solar to keep company with his animals.

As the boy went back down the stairs, Maddoc and David continued up to the next level where there were two chambers, one adjoining another. In the far chamber, they could see firelight and hear voices. People were moving around in there and the heavy scent of cloves wafted from the door. It was the smell of the physic and his medicaments, as strong scents were thought to ward off infection.

Maddoc approached the entry, pushing the panel open slightly. David was behind him, blocked from view by the door, as Maddoc's gaze sought out Daniel. He found the man sitting on the other side of the bed, sporting a growth of stubble and appearing generally exhausted and distressed. But Daniel had been like that for three days, ever since the tragedy happened. Maddoc called softly to him.

"Danny," he said quietly. "I have need of you."

Daniel heard his name but didn't react right away. He had been staring at Liselotte, who was sleeping heavily on the bed. His blade had carved into the right side of her torso, cutting deep, and she had lost a massive amount of blood as the knights had desperately tried to stop the bleeding. It had been the most horrific moment of his life as they'd struggled to staunch the flow of bright red blood that had spilled out onto Bramley, lying dead beneath her. Daniel was certain that he'd killed her, too.

But the physic from Skipton didn't seem to think any vital organs had been cut, fortunately. He was, however, concerned about her blood loss and any poison that might set in, so he had been watching the woman diligently for two and a half days, ever since Easton de Royans had come to fetch him. He'd cleansed the wound and stitched it, and even now continued to take the bandages off and douse it with wine every so often to try and keep the poison out. Something in the wine, he said, helped kill any poisons.

It had been Daniel's world for three days. He had spent the days sitting with Glennie, and at times Easton and Maddoc and Caston when they came to visit for a while. Easton and Glennie had come when Caston had sent them word on what had happened. Easton had ridden to Skipton himself for the physic, bringing both the physic and his daughter to tend the lady. Even now, they were all in the room, helping the physic with whatever he needed.

Daniel had been very grateful for the help. With the physic in charge of Liselotte's health, Daniel had been reduced to sitting and waiting. He was certain his buttocks had grown to the stool he had been perched on and when Maddoc called quietly to him, he pretended not to hear him but Maddoc hissed again and Daniel could no longer ignore the man.

Therefore, he wearily rose, stretching his big body as he made his way to the door. Passing by Liselotte's bed, he reached out to touch her foot as if to silently beg her pardon while he left her side. It was a bittersweet gesture to the unconscious woman, one not missed by Maddoc or anyone else in the room. Everyone felt a great deal of pity for Daniel. The man had barely reached the panel when Maddoc reached out and pulled him through.

It was dark in the chamber beyond the doorway but the first thing Daniel saw was his father's weary face. It took him a moment to realize what he was looking at and furthermore realize that he wasn't dreaming. Then, his eyes bulged and he threw himself at his father, hugging him tightly. His eyes filled with tears.

"Papa," he breathed. "In God's name, why are you here? How did you… for Christ's sake, how did you know to come?"

David embraced his son, more relief than he could express filling him. To have his son whole and healthy in his arms was worth every worry, every difficulty he'd had to endure on this trip north. He simply held the man for a moment before speaking, emotion tightening his throat.

"You sent word to your Uncle Chris for help," he said. "Why did you not send word to me? I should beat you senseless for excluding me like that."

Tears on his face, Daniel grinned, released his father, and promptly put his hands on the man's face and kissed his forehead. Then he laughed.

"The veins on your temples are throbbing again," he said, touching the one on the right side of David's head. "I call them the Daniel veins. They always twitch when I do something to displease you."

David cocked an eyebrow at his facetious son. "My whole face twitches when you do something to displease me," he said, coughing into his hand before speaking again. "Daniel, I received word about your missive to your uncle but I also received a missive from Henry himself. He said that you had usurped Shadowmoor from someone named Bramley. *That* is why I am here – to see the situation with my own eyes. I was not going to leave this to chance and hope it resolved itself."

Daniel still had his hands on his father; they were resting on his broad shoulders. Daniel was about a head taller than his father, easily as tall as his Uncle Christopher, who was a tall man, indeed. He found himself looking down at his father, re-memorizing the sound of the man's voice, drinking in the very sight of his features. He hadn't seen him in almost a year. But in looking at him, he could also see that he was very tired and, from the sound of his cough, evidently ill. His eyes narrowed in concern.

"Are you well, Papa?" he asked. "You do not sound well."

David waved him off. "I am well enough," he said. "Do not change the subject."

"He is *not* particularly well," Maddoc interjected, much to David's displeasure. "He contracted a lung ailment during the winter and we nearly lost him. He is not well at all and should not have made this trip. I think his very presence is a testament to the fact that your safety, and your well-being, surmount your father's health."

Now, Daniel's eyebrows lifted in outrage and concern. "You risked your life to come here?" he demanded. "How could you do something like that?"

David scowled at Maddoc, very unhappy with the man for saying such things about him. "Maddoc, still your tongue before I am forced to do something drastic," he told him. Then, he looked at Daniel. "I will again say that I am fine. And you will not change the subject. What is going on that I had to come all the way from Canterbury, Daniel? What did you do?"

Daniel sighed softly and dropped his hands from his father's shoulders. "The right thing," he said quietly. "I did the right and chivalrous thing. And it very well may cost me everything."

David could see the emotion in the man's expression, remembering what Maddoc had told him about the lady. *He is in love with the heiress.* His manner softened.

"Maddoc told me mostly everything," he said, his eyes growing moist. "He told me what happened to the lady. Daniel, is it true? Have you really fallen in love?"

Daniel nodded, averting his gaze. Then, he snorted ironically. "Life is strange sometimes," he said. "I have had my share of women, as you know. You paid for some of those ill-advised affairs and I would laugh about them, about the women I hurt, and congratulate myself on my cleverness for escaping their clutches. But now… now, it seems, the fates have caught up with me and they are not kind. They are punishing me for being so careless with the feelings of others."

David had never heard his son speak so. Daniel was usually so glib about romance, never taking women seriously. He hardly took anything seriously, which was part of his charm. It was as if he wouldn't let himself feel what he should have. Now, that lack of feeling was catching up to him. He was very serious now.

"The fates do not work that way," David says. "Nor does God. He would not bring you to a woman you could love and then cruelly take her away. Mayhap… mayhap He simply wants to be sure that you really do love her."

Daniel's brow furrowed. "What do you mean?"

David tried to explain. "Maddoc says that he thinks the lady was trying to kill the man you were fighting and got in your way."

Daniel nodded. "That is what we think. I have not asked her yet. She has not been awake very much."

David put his hand on the man. "Does she love you, Danny?"

Daniel softened. "She has told me so."

David squeezed his arm. "Then mayhap she was trying to kill the man to protect you," he said, eyeing Maddoc. "I remember seeing my granddaughter try to do such a thing for Maddoc last year when he was fighting de Royans. Do you remember? She came at Brighton with a dagger and that is when he gored Maddoc. She was trying to save him but ended up nearly getting him killed. What I am saying is, mayhap, that is what your lady was doing for you as well. She was willing to sacrifice herself so that you could survive. That is what love does, Danny. Mayhap God was trying to show you that through the actions of your lady so I cannot imagine He would let her perish. He is doing this to teach you a lesson."

Daniel smiled faintly at his father, who always made so much sense. "What lesson is that?"

David patted the man on the cheek. "That you are destined for great love, just as I had always hoped for you," he said softly. "Mayhap He is forcing you to truly face your feelings about her with the thought of losing her. How do you feel about her still?"

Daniel had a lump in his throat now. "I love her with all of my heart."

David moved in to hug his son again, so very sorry for the man to be facing such a crisis. But as he did, he noticed a body standing in the doorway. Easton was in the doorway, looking between David and Daniel and Maddoc. He had been just inside the door when David had arrived and he'd heard every word spoken, including his son's name mentioned. It had been a shock, at first, but as the words began to sink in, his confusion and concern grew. Now, as he looked at the three men, the expression on his face rife with concern.

"I heard my son's name mentioned," he said, mostly to Daniel. Then, he looked at David. "You *did* mention Brighton de Royans, my lord, did you not? That is my son."

Daniel and Maddoc stood there with shock when they realized that Easton had heard David speak of Brighton. They, themselves, had been so very careful not to mention his name and not to get onto any subject that might lead to talk of the events from last summer, but David didn't know anything about their care or anything about the situation involving the House of de Royans.

Now, it was going to be a mad scramble to try and right the situation, to throw Easton off the scent, but as Daniel looked at Maddoc, he realized there was no way out of this. They couldn't lie their way through it, or be evasive about it, with David standing there. He would think they'd gone mad.

Sickened with the awareness of the news he had to divulge, Daniel struggled to speak but David was faster; he had no idea of the delicate nature of the situation so he addressed Easton directly.

"Brighton de Royans was your son?" he asked, studying Easton from head to toe. His eyes narrowed. "Who *are* you?"

Easton had some idea who David was based on the fact that Daniel had called him Papa, so he knew he was addressing one of the great de Lohr brothers. "I am Easton de Royans, Baron Cononley," he said. "My seat, Netherghyll Castle, is to the north of Shadowmoor. We have become great friends with our allies to the south because of Sir Daniel. We have all been helping in the fight against Lord Bramley, which mercifully ended three days ago."

"He and his son, Caston, have been great allies, Papa," Daniel said, very quickly trying to smooth over the situation. But he feared it was a lost battle already. "Sir Easton has provided Shadowmoor with food and men, and he has incredibly generous. His son, Caston, has become a good friend. They told me that their son and brother, Brighton, serves Norfolk but they've not seen or heard from him in over two years. Papa, they do not know anything about him. Not a thing."

He said it in front of Easton, who was greatly confused by Daniel's words, but David picked up on it right away. He was a sharp man and from what Daniel was saying, and the strained manner in which he was saying it, he came to understand that the father of Brighton de Royans knew nothing of his son's fate or actions. Quickly, he realized that the situation had the potential for going very badly at this point, at least as far as Easton was concerned. The man, from what he could gather, knew nothing of his son's death yet he had heard David speak of him. David could not deny that he'd spoken of him, which would mean that he knew Brighton. David wasn't quite sure what to say to all of that but Easton, whose confusion was deepening, spoke.

"Daniel, I thought you said that you did not know Brighton," he said. "I recall that Caston asked you if you had heard of him and you said you had not."

Daniel looked at his father, closing his eyes briefly, painfully, as he realized he was going to have to deal with a very painful subject now. He couldn't lie or jest his way out of this one. Easton and Caston now had to be told of the fate of Brighton. They could not refuse to tell him, not now.

Daniel put his hand on Easton's arm.

"Where is Caston?" he asked quietly.

Easton was starting to think that something was very, very wrong from the expression on Daniel's face. "I believe he is in the hall, eating," he said. "That was the last I saw of the man. Why, Daniel? What is wrong?"

Daniel squeezed his arm. "Then let us go find him," he said softly, with great reluctance. "I have something to tell you that you both must hear."

He started to move but Easton balked. He put a hand over Daniel's, stopping him from moving forward. "Daniel, you are frightening me," he said. "What has happened? Why did you lie about knowing Brighton?"

David stepped in; he had to. It had been his mistake to speak of Brighton so he would take the burden for explaining the situation. It was best, anyway. A father should know when he has lost a son. From one father to another, David tried to be gentle.

"I will tell you," he said quietly. "My lord, I am David de Lohr. The earldom of Canterbury is mine. My granddaughter was the object of affection for Brighton about a year ago. He was very persistent. The problem was that she was already betrothed to Maddoc."

He pointed to Maddoc, whom Easton had only met a few days ago. Easton eyed the big dark-haired knight before returning his attention to David. "I see," he said. "And you told Brighton this, of course?"

David nodded patiently. "Many, many times," he said. "I told him, Maddoc told him, and my granddaughter told him. He would not be dissuaded. He decided to challenge Maddoc for her hand. It was a brutal battle, my lord, and when my granddaughter tried to help Maddoc by making an attempt to kill Brighton, Maddoc was distracted and Brighton managed to gore him. But it did not end there. He abducted my granddaughter and held me off at knifepoint when I tried to intervene. He rode off with her, screaming, leaving me to deal with the aftermath."

By this time, Easton's features were pale with horror. "Oh, God…," he breathed. "Please say that he did not do this. Please tell me this was a terrible mistake."

David shook his head. "It was no mistake, I assure you," he said. "I called upon my brother and fellow allies to help me track my granddaughter and get her back. Meanwhile, Brighton tried to marry her but she turned into a wild animal and would not let him. A priest refused to marry them and he threatened the man. He then took my granddaughter to Arundel and tried to hold her there, but his liege, d'Aubigney, would not have it. He told Brighton to return the lady and restore his honor, but Brighton would not listen, not even to his liege. Meanwhile, Daniel tracked them to a town not far from Arundel where he and Brighton fought a nasty battle and Brighton was wounded. But my granddaughter asked Daniel not to kill Brighton, so he did not. But Maddoc, who had been close to death for weeks due to the injury Brighton inflicted on him, dragged himself from his deathbed to find Brighton and avenge himself. It was a matter of honor, my lord, as well as a matter of safety. We knew that Brighton would not give up in his pursuit of my granddaughter. He said that he would not. For the sake of my granddaughter's safety, and for his own sense of vengeance, Maddoc found Brighton and did battle against him. Your son lost."

Easton was overcome by the horror of the situation. He stumbled back, smacking into the wall, even as Daniel and David reached out to steady him. Easton was having a difficult time standing on his own feet. He was woozy and distraught. Gripping David, he looked imploringly at the man.

"Tell me he did not do all of this," he said, his voice cracking. "Why would he do this? He was always a selfish, stubborn lad, but I did not believe him to be wicked. He truly abducted your granddaughter?"

David nodded sadly at the man. "He did," he said softly. "If you do not believe me, ask his liege. D'Aubigney chased him away because of it."

Easton was at a loss. He absorbed the information, struggling to steady himself. He finally pushed himself away from the wall and politely waved off both Daniel and David as they continued to try and hold him steady. He didn't need or want their help. He was horrified. His gaze moved to Maddoc.

"And you," he rasped. "He did this to you?"

Maddoc nodded solemnly, lifting up his mail and tunic so Easton could see the huge scar on his torso. "He did this," he said. "My lord, you must not be angry at Daniel for not telling you what he knew about Brighton. It was a horrible time in all of our lives and the more he came to know you and your son, the more he did not want to hurt you, for it is a hurtful and terrible thing to hear that your son behaved most dishonorably. It was a terrible secret he held because he did not wish to upset you. He withheld it for no other reason than that."

Easton looked at the scar for a moment before returning his gaze to Maddoc's face. "Did you kill him?"

"I did, my lord. But he was trying to kill me. I had no choice."

Tears rolled from Easton's eyes and he dropped his head, digesting what he'd been told. A sense of sadness settled with all of them, seeing a man who had just been told his son had been killed. No one was particularly sure how Easton was going to react after this; he'd just learned that people he had come to know, and trust, had essentially lied to him. No one would blame him if he stormed from the castle and took back everything he'd donated to Shadowmoor. In fact, that was what Daniel fully expected. But as he watched, Easton did something very surprising.

The man suddenly came off the wall, heading for Maddoc. Maddoc tensed, preparing for some weapon or fist to come flying out at him, but Easton abruptly threw his arms around Maddoc and began to weep loudly. Stunned, Maddoc had no idea how to respond. He looked at David and Daniel, his eyes wide, and David simply shook his head sadly. In that moment, Maddoc could see that perhaps all Easton needed was a bit of compassion, which did not come easily to him. Gingerly, he put his arms around the man and hugged him.

"I am sorry," Easton wept. "I am so sorry he did that to you. Brighton was an aggressive boy, a spoiled boy, but I did not know he had such evil in him. I am so sorry he took your betrothed and tried to kill you. Please… please do not hate him. Please forgive him. For my sake, I must know that you forgive him."

Maddoc was genuinely torn. Hating Brighton de Royans came as naturally as breathing, so it was difficult for him to think otherwise. He had no idea what to say to the grieving man, struggling to bring the words forth.

"I do not blame you, my lord," he said. "But Brighton made his choice. He chose dishonor in a situation where a true and good man would have taken a different path. He caused a lot of pain and sorrow."

Easton released Maddoc, wiping at his eyes and laboring to control himself. "I know," he said. "I know my son. I can easily see how he would have not given up against something he very much wanted. But… but in time, if you could forgive him, I would be grateful."

Maddoc felt a good deal of pity for Easton, the grieving father whose son had died doing something ignoble. But his hate was still very fresh for the man's son; it would take time to get over that. His inclination towards pity upon Easton did not overcome his sense of hatred towards Brighton. He sighed heavily.

"I will try," he said. "I can only promise you that I will try."

Easton nodded as he continued to struggle for his composure. "And I am content with that," he said. Then, he looked at Daniel. "I do understand why you did not tell me. I am sorry my son brought so much shame to the House of de Royans by violating the House of de Lohr as he did. I pray you understand that we do not condone Brighton's behavior. Although I am shattered over the loss of my son, I am very ashamed for what he has done. I pray in time you will forgive him his stubborn shortcomings."

Daniel put a hand on Easton's shoulder. "His shortcomings are not your own," he said softly, insistently. "That is why I was reluctant to tell you the truth. You and Caston have become good friends and allies. I shall always be grateful for the generosity you have shown. You are great and honorable men, and your friendship will always be treasured."

Easton forced a smile, patting Daniel's hand. "You are most gracious," he said, taking a deep breath. "Now, if you will excuse me, I must find Caston. He must know what has happened."

"Would you have me go with you?" Daniel asked.

Easton shook his head. "Nay," he said. "I will tell him alone."

With that, he stood tall with as much dignity as he could muster and walked away, heading down the stairwell that led to the entry level. They could hear his footfalls moving away but there was a heavy sense of sorrow that he had left behind. They all felt a good deal of pity for him. When the footsteps faded, Daniel looked at his father.

"I know we did the right thing by telling him, but I am still sorry that we had to," he said. "It makes me hate Brighton all the more that he has hurt his father so. Easton is a truly good man."

David lifted his eyebrows, pondering the situation. "It had to be done," he said simply. "A man has a right to know of the death of his son."

Daniel nodded reluctantly. "I suppose."

He started to say more but movement in the chamber abruptly caught his attention. Daniel could see the legs on the mattress moving, which meant Liselotte was moving. Surprised, he bolted into the bedchamber with David and Maddoc close behind him.

As soon as the men entered the warm smelly chamber, they could see that the Liselotte was awake and speaking. She was holding Glennie's hand and Glennie was hovering over her, smiling and whispering. But when Glennie saw Daniel enter the room, she pointed to him.

"Look!" she said to Liselotte. "Here he is. Wonder no more about him."

Daniel rushed up to the side of the bed, falling to his knees and taking Liselotte's hand from Glennie. Daniel gazed at Liselotte as if there were no one else in the room; he drank in her pale complexion, her tired eyes, but to him, she had never looked more beautiful. He put a big hand to her forehead.

"You are awake," he whispered, kissing her hand. "How do you feel?"

Liselotte smiled weakly at him. "Tired," she said. "As if someone tried to cut me in half. My body is sore."

Daniel snorted at her attempt at humor, kissing her hand again. "I was fighting a battle and suddenly, some mad woman was throwing herself on the man I was trying to kill," he said. "Was that you, perchance?"

Liselotte's smile faded. "It was."

Daniel's humor faded, as well. He kissed her fingers again. "Why, Leese?" he asked softly. "Why would you do such a thing?"

Liselotte fought off the cobwebs in her mind, struggling to think back to that moment in time when she gored Bramley with her father's dagger. She felt incredibly weak and nauseous, but the same strong sense of determination swept her. She remembered everything that happened, exactly as it happened. She would have done the same thing again if given the chance.

"Is he dead?"

"He is."

She breathed a sigh of relief. "I am glad," she said, tears coming to her eyes. "I am so very glad."

Daniel tried to soothe her. "But why did you kill him?" he asked. "I had the situation under control."

Liselotte gripped his big hand with both of hers, an intense and desperate gesture. "I did it because the man had done so much to try to destroy me," she explained. "My father is dead because of him, my brother is dead, and all of Shadowmoor suffered. I had no control over that… there was nothing I could do to stop him. But as I saw you battling him, I suddenly felt like the moment to take back my life was upon me. For everything he'd done, he deserved to be killed. I needed to do it; not you. It was not your right to exact vengeance against him. It was mine."

Daniel understood a great deal in that softly uttered sentence. "So you sought to punish him?"

"Aye."

He nodded his head, comprehending her need for justice. "I can understand why. I suppose it was your right more than anyone's."

Liselotte nodded in agreement. "I think so," she muttered. "I am sorry if got in your way. I supposed I was only seeking the opportunity and not thinking on the consequences. You were so brave and strong in battle, Daniel. Papa once said he thought you were sent from God as our avenging angel, and I still believe that. After seeing you fight Bramley, I believe it all the more."

He smiled at her, kissing her hand again, reverently. "It is over now," he said. "Bramley is dead and it is over. You and I shall be married as soon as you are strong enough and the rebuilding of Shadowmoor will continue in earnest. I will have the best fortress in West Yorkshire by the time we are finished."

Liselotte's smile returned as well. She could hardly believe that after everything they'd been through, the trials and tribulations, that their marriage would be a reality, something she'd dreamed about since nearly the first moment she had met him. But it was more than the marriage; it was the love she had for him, the respect and adoration for this man who had risked everything to save her and her people. It was this man who had fought, and won, for love.

This man, her savior.

"Then I shall will myself to recover very soon," she said. "I do not want you to change your mind."

"I will not let him," David said from the foot of the bed. When Liselotte looked at him, puzzled by the sight of a stranger in her room, David smiled. "I am Daniel's father, my lady. You cannot know what a pleasure it is to meet you. I heard Daniel say he intends to marry you and I will hold him to it, at the tip of a broadsword if necessary."

Daniel grinned at his father. "It will not be necessary, Papa," he said. "I will go willingly."

David lifted a dubious eyebrow. "Swear it?"

"I do. My wandering days are over."

With that, he leaned in to Liselotte, kissing her more sweetly than he had ever kissed her before. As David stood at the foot of the bed and grinned, Glennie fixed on Maddoc and inched her way over to him, wanting to stand next to the handsome husband of her dear friend.

Maddoc saw her coming and simply winked at her, having come to know a rather silly and sweet woman over the past several days. He could see why his wife had liked the woman so.

"Do not believe what he says," he whispered to Glennie. "We must go find the broadswords so he will not go back on his word."

Glennie giggled. "Can I help?"

"Indeed, you can."

"Good!"

But broadswords were not necessary when the wedding eventually came. Daniel never made it to the tournament at Skipton later that day, choosing instead to remain by Liselotte's side as she recovered from her battle injury.

Caston, however, did compete. Even after learning of his brother's death and the circumstances surrounding it, he did not hold a grudge. He understood Brighton better than most and he knew what the man was capable of. He chose to compete in the tournament and donate any winnings to Shadowmoor, just as he had agreed to. Five days after Liselotte's brush with death, Caston returned to Shadowmoor on a dark and stormy night and delivered into her hands a fairly valuable purse.

It was an impressive and thrilling gift, one that would help bring Shadowmoor back to its glory. It wasn't really necessary any longer with the addition of Daniel's personal fortune to the l'Audacieux family, but it was more the value of the gesture; much as his father had, Caston hoped that Daniel and the de Lohrs would someday forgive Brighton his actions, but Daniel assured him that Brighton had long since been forgiven. Easton and Caston's generosity towards Shadowmoor, since the beginning of their association, had seen to that.

Now, Shadowmoor, and the House of de Lohr, had strong new allies in the House of de Royans and it would be a bond that continued on for generations to come.

The wedding finally came. Nearly three weeks after Liselotte's injury, she was strong enough to stand in the doorway to the cathedral in Bradford and recite her vows before the priest. David, Maddoc, Caston, Easton, Glennie, Gunnar, Marc de Russe, and even Ares the horse were in attendance to witness the vows. Liselotte and Daniel only had eyes for each other or they would have noticed Glennie sidling her way over to Marc de Russe, who was seemingly quite interested in the lovely blond. Love bloomed again on that sunny breezy day as Daniel de Lohr took a bride.

And Daniel never saw the hint of a broadsword at his back through any of it because it was never needed, not once. He was exactly where he wanted to be, gazing into the face of the woman he had sworn to love forever and beyond.

Finally, the wanderer had come home.

☙ THE END ❧

The de Lohr Dynasty:

While Angels Slept (Lords of East Anglia)

Rise of the Defender

Steelheart

Spectre of the Sword

Archangel

Unending Love

Shadowmoor

Silversword

About Kathryn Le Veque

Medieval Just Got Real.

KATHRYN LE VEQUE is a USA TODAY Bestselling author, an Amazon All-Star author, and a #1 bestselling, award-winning, multi-published author in Medieval Historical Romance and Historical Fiction. She has been featured in the NEW YORK TIMES and on USA TODAY's HEA blog. In March 2015, Kathryn was the featured cover story for the March issue of InD'Tale Magazine, the premier Indie author magazine. She was also a quadruple nominee (a record!) for the prestigious RONE awards for 2015.

Kathryn's Medieval Romance novels have been called 'detailed', 'highly romantic', and 'character-rich'. She crafts great adventures of love, battles, passion, and romance in the High Middle Ages. More than that, she writes for both women AND men – an unusual crossover for a romance author – and Kathryn has many male readers who enjoy her stories because of the male perspective, the action, and the adventure.

On October 29, 2015, Amazon launched Kathryn's Kindle Worlds Fan Fiction site WORLD OF DE WOLFE PACK. Please visit Kindle Worlds for Kathryn Le Veque's World of de Wolfe Pack and find many action-packed adventures written by some of the top authors in their genre using Kathryn's characters from the de Wolfe Pack series. As Kindle World's FIRST Historical Romance fan fiction world, Kathryn Le Veque's World of de Wolfe Pack will contain all of the great story-telling you have come to expect.

Kathryn loves to hear from her readers. Please find Kathryn on Facebook at Kathryn Le Veque, Author, or join her on Twitter @kathrynleveque, and don't forget to visit her website at www.kathrynleveque.com.

Made in the USA
San Bernardino, CA
26 September 2016